PERIPHERAL VISION

OTHER PRESS

NEW YORK

A NOVEL

PATRICIA
FERGUSON

PERIPHERAL
VISION

Production Editor: Yvonne E. Cárdenas

Text design: Simon M. Sullivan

This book was set in 11.25 pt Filosofia by Alpha Design
& Composition of Pittsfield, NH.

10 9 8 7 6 5 4 3 2 1

LIBRARY OF CONGRESS CATALOGING-IN-PUBLICATION DATA
Ferguson, Patricia.
Peripheral vision / Patricia Ferguson.
p. cm.
ISBN-13: 978-1-59051-287-6 (acid-free paper)
1. Women—Fiction.   I. Title.
PR6056.E6193P47 2008
823'.914—dc22   2007046608

For Richard, Tom, and Roly

PERIPHERAL VISION

SYLVIA'S BABY, 1995

ON MARITAL LOVE, on love when the baby is sleeping lightly in the very next room, Sylvia had views, more to the point feelings, but didn't in the least know them, however, having adopted, well before gestation, a firm habit of not examining too closely anything her own body told her.

"Are you terribly tired tonight?" Adam might ask her, mock-roguishly, for this had quickly become code.

"Yes," uttered flatly, of course meant No, whereas "No," even spoken consideringly or wryly or doubtfully, meant Yes.

Yes to Adam's request, first, that she sit naked astride him, yes to his second, that she give him what he invariably called a little encouragement, and yes also to listening to him telling her once more that she was a thunderingly good fuck.

Tell him to fuck off, Sylvia's body these days smartly told Sylvia, when Adam got to first request, or even beforehand, when he was still being roguish. But Sylvia wasn't taking any notice.

She was too tired for one thing. And she was also in the awkward position of having everything she had ever wanted. Ever since she was fifteen, when she had broken her right leg falling off the wall behind the cricket pitch, she had wanted to be a doctor; as soon as she started medical school she knew she wanted to be a specialist, a consultant; all through her twenties she had increasingly wanted a husband and children, and done various quite difficult and discouraging things in order to get them. Now she had everything on the list.

1

She was so highly successful that she had long ceased even to consider herself unusual, had long ago lost the sensation of lone perilous hand-to-hand climbing, of narrow toeholds, and dizzying near-misses, and avalanches just avoided, that had caused her so many nights of neurotic insomnia during her major exam-taking years.

So she wasn't taking any crap from her body, which so incontinently wanted out.

"No, not really. Are you tired, Adam?"

Adam was quite a bit older than Sylvia, at fifty-three. He had lived in the far grander house near her own for several years, as half of a perfectly nice couple, with both of whom Sylvia had been on lightly amicable terms, until the wife had run off with a much younger man, a friend of a friend of her own grown-up son's.

Adam had been beside himself with grief and despair. He had had several loud drunken arguments with his estranged wife, he in the street, she leaning out of the upstairs window of her lover's little house in a backstreet of the neighboring town, until policemen had arrived, and threatened him with charges of disturbing the peace. Adam, disturbing the peace! Adam, who until those terrible nights had not so much as a parking fine on his civic conscience!

After several months of anguish and poor work performance Adam had gone on holiday by himself, bicycling ferociously around Northern France, pedaling uphill all day until, after eating a huge meal at whatever place he had reached by nightfall, he fell exhausted into whatever hotel bed. His wife had detested bicycles. She also hated strenuous exercise, going anywhere without booking first, and garlic. Adam's deserted-husband holiday was a combination of everything his wife had not let him do for nearly twenty-five years.

On the fifth morning Adam was aware, as he shot out into the sunshine, and began toiling away toward the heat haze already ahead in the middle of the smooth black road, that he was happy. That he wasn't missing her; not even defiantly thinking to himself, Look, I'm not missing her! But really, actively thinking about other, nicer things for large stretches of sweet French hilly pedaling time.

On the long ride toward home and reality he had stopped at a pleasant little market town and bought presents. This too had been something of a first. His wife had often told him he was rubbish at present-buying. For years he had left it all to her. Even her own, even her birthday. Perhaps that had been a mistake, thought Adam now, carefully locking his faithful bicycle to a lamppost outside the covered market. Within he bought cheese.

He tried and bought fourteen presents of beautiful French cheeses. Some were wrapped in waxed paper, some packed in stout little wooden boxes. One was studded with peppercorns, another veined in delicate blue. He bought the firmly resilient, the softly deliquescent, some with hardened calloused rinds, some cloaked in damp mushroomy velvet. He chose cheeses aromatic, milky, honking with garlic, sending out violent messages of complex and tempered decay: smells moldy, fruity, acidic, and downright fecal.

His wife would have hated them all.

He had packed them all singing to high heaven in his one roomy rucksack, and set off for home with a light heart.

He took a selection to the offices of the law firm where he worked, and was gratified by the squealing consternation of the secretarial staff. More than one he took with him to the dinner parties he was now being invited to, as that desirable social entity, the unattached male. And one, a nice pure goat's cheese, unpasteurized, enticingly wrapped in red-and-white-checked waxed paper within its neat snug wooden box, he on a sudden whim one hot summer evening took to his closest neighbor, that nice Miss Thing.

Sylvia, opening the door in clean white shirt and small white shorts, saw a familiar face wearing an unfamiliar tan. Adam too was in shorts. Dark soft curly hair peeped out at Sylvia from the neck of his light summery blue shirt. He looked what he was and at that moment felt, a healthy, virile, fit, and powerful man.

True, he was old enough to be Sylvia's father. But Sylvia's own father had happened to be a great deal older than fathers generally are, old enough, almost, to be her grandfather; if the touch of white over Adam's ears put her in mind of fatherliness it was the potent delightful father of her early childhood who strode whistling across her unconscious: that hero.

"Sylvia!" smiled Adam on the doorstep, for it was only her surname he had had trouble remembering, "d'you like cheese?"

"Love it!" said Sylvia, gratefully. She had had an abysmal afternoon.

She was involved with fundraising for the hospital she worked for. Somehow, without in the least volunteering it, she had become the focus of the campaign to raise enough money for a new and even more precise ophthalmic laser. Photographs of her smilingly being presented with outsize checks made of cardboard appeared almost weekly in the local press, for the Friends of the Hospital were many and energetic. They organized things they liked to do, did them, and summoned Sylvia. Already that summer she had attended a donkey gymkhana, presented prizes at a flower and produce show, made two after-dinner speeches about lasers at two separate dinner-dances, and repeated the gist of these speeches all one afternoon during an interminable river boating party.

All these occasions had ended with the smiling presentation of the outsize cardboard check, furious applause, and the local press photograph. Sometimes, to her intense embarrassment, Sylvia was also given a bouquet, again commonly of outsize proportions, and sometimes a big smacking kiss on the cheek, should the hander-over of the outsize cardboard check be male.

This afternoon's jaunt had been the Friends' Summer Picnic. It had been held in the garden of one of the Friends, a stately home-style creation of artfully cascading waterfalls faked so long ago that they looked almost like the naturally occurring real thing, a famous avenue of pleached limes (Sylvia was more than once informed), an enormous lake full of water lilies, and a plaintive silver band, hired for the occasion.

All afternoon Sylvia had eaten scones, drunk tea, listened to the plaintive band, and traipsed up and down the avenue of pleached limes. All afternoon she had had exactly the same conversation with a series of gentle elderly faces. Talk, talk, talk, laser, laser, laser.

And all the time she was conscious of their attitude toward her. Sometimes she could almost hear them thinking it.

4

Look at her! Just look! So young! Just a girl, and a doctor, a consultant! Isn't she wonderful! Isn't she lovely!

It was largely this unspoken commentary that made the presentations, the bouquets, the applause, so excruciating. Sylvia did not think of herself as young, wonderful, or lovely. What woman would, aged thirty-three? Sylvia looked in mirrors and saw a professional, intelligent, and immensely competent grown-up. She knew she was all these things. And yet somehow she had been sold to the Friends, these generous worthy old folk—or was being sold by them, it was quite hard to tell, really—as a dear little thing, the ingénue, to smile for the cameras. It was not her professionalism they wanted her for, she had realized almost immediately; it was her pretty face.

Doctor Sylvia, the local paper always called her. Not Sylvia Henshaw, or Dr. Henshaw, certainly not Miss Henshaw, which would actually have been correct, since she was a surgeon; but always the infantilizing, the telly-fied, the tabloid comic-strip Doctor Sylvia.

Sylvia had no actressy impulses. To be admired for being small, for being delicately put together, for having curly hair and a neat freckled little face, was all very well, of course, in private, but to be publicly admired and cosseted for them was very hard to bear. It went against all her deepest instincts. She felt, too, a fraud. They thought she was a dear little thing; she knew she was not one; therefore she was a fake.

And at the same time she did not in the least want to baffle or disappoint anyone by insisting on being herself, being significantly professional, intelligent, and competent. And the hospital needed the laser; patients needed it.

She had come home from the Garden Party headachy and exhausted with politeness and pretending, pulled off her neat little blue silk suit, and showered off Doctor Sylvia before stepping still damp—it was a humid evening—into the clean white shirt and small white shorts. Barefoot on the cold stone floor of her kitchen she had opened a bottle of red wine and just swallowed her first big swig when the doorbell rang. She gulped another before she went to the door. So she opened it a little flushed, her hair still damp, and there was Adam, brown and healthy and proffering gifts.

"Sylvia! D'you like cheese?"

"Love it!" she replied, and on an impulse added, "Why don't you come in?"

And that had been that, really.

From thinking of her vaguely as that rather nice-looking young woman round the corner, pleasant enough, Adam had within minutes found himself unable to breathe properly, with desire; small movements beneath the not-quite opaque white shirt tremulously promised little brown-nippled breasts, and the freckles he could see on Sylvia's slender arms and legs tormented him with wondering how far up they went, and whether there was any part of her that did not have a tender sprinkling of them, and how he was to settle the question.

While she, freighted with five cups of tea, three scones, and an equally indigestible overload of collective sentimentality, thrilled to the diverting spectacle of a decent-looking man half-choked with honest lust.

And even more piquant, he was that nice Adam, a person she had been exchanging neighborly pleasantries with for several years! It was strange, she thought, how his being someone else's husband had made him almost invisible. As she exclaimed over the red-and-white-checked waxed paper and the delicate goaty creaminess within she could feel his awareness of her every move.

With her back to him as she got him a glass she could feel his gaze, and was aware herself of the long lines of his body, his great muscled calves, his tanned splendid forearm resting on the kitchen table. His square hairy hand delicately hesitating over one of her glistening garlicky olives.

For a little while they had talked of neighborly things, of hosepipe bans, of the pub across the road which was being refurbished, of the heat, of Adam's French holiday.

"Must be off," he had said abruptly, standing. She stood up as well. The top of her head just reached his shoulder.

"Oh, must you?"

"Well, unless . . . would you . . . would you like to have dinner with me?" For it was the electrifying thought, as he sat helplessly staring at his neighbor, that he could simply ask her out if he felt like it that had propelled him to his feet.

He was a free man! It was freedom that had made him see Sylvia's nipples through her shirt, it was freedom that, when she turned round, clamped his eyes to her little white shorts, and made him need so sweatily to know whether or not she was wearing any knickers underneath them, it was freedom that, for a long and rather agonizing moment while she prattled about hosepipes, had made him so thickly tumescent that he had been as afraid as any helplessly erectile adolescent that he was actually going to have an orgasm in public, behind the kitchen table; freedom had brought all these Lord of Misrule things about.

Time to step up, time to act on freedom, to stop it acting on him.

"Spinners'? At eight?"

"Oh, lovely," said Sylvia, "Yes. Yes, please."

Part of her own excitement at the time had come from the fact that for the first time in ages Sylvia felt lucky. She felt able to manage Adam. As if she had an Adam-instinct, just this moment discovered.

Adam-instinct told her that while his serendipitous arrival just as she was ousting dear little Doctor Sylvia with knickerless barefoot wine-swigging had served her gloriously well, he would now be even more beside himself if for the evening she took the opposite course and went for demure. Appeared as neighbor, neat friendly Miss Henshaw. It would be reassuring, yet at the same time deliberately teasing. He would be floored.

And so it proved. For several months the ease with which she could floor Adam had enchanted Sylvia. And their combined age of eighty-five years gave them plenty to talk about.

Of course there were a great many adjustments to be made. Sylvia's mother, Adam's estranged wife; his children, her friends; even his mother (who really was eighty-five), all these people needed to be protected from the truth, then allowed to guess about it, and finally confronted with it; they needed to be soothed, consoled, reassured, convincingly lied to if absolutely necessary and to some extent introduced to one another. All this took many more months, at the end of which

7

Sylvia let her own house and moved into Adam's far more extensive double-fronted Georgian splendor, and stopped using any contraception.

Sylvia had studied obstetrics as a medical student. She had delivered twelve babies herself, and as a Junior House Officer had completed a six-month gynecological rotation. She knew considerably more than most educated middle-class women about the hormonal changes of the human reproductive cycle. She was enjoying a great deal of sexual activity, and she was not using contraception.

Yet how did she react, when she discovered her pregnancy?

She was stunned.

All that day, when the line had so clearly gone blue, she had trembled, and felt her heart beating fast all the time as if she had been running.

What, me?

It did not seem possible to Sylvia now that she could have behaved so thoughtlessly. Literally thoughtless: no thought had gone into her decision to ditch the diaphragm or not bother about getting any more spermicidal foam when the little can was empty.

Oh, forgot again, but never mind, this tiny smear of the stuff will do. . . . Diaphragm's got a bit past it actually, I need a new one, no point using that one . . . It's my safe time of the month . . . Oh, let's not bother, it'll be all right . . .

She thought she had decided only not to decide. It had not occurred to her consciously, somehow, that this might be the same as deciding to try to get pregnant. At no point in all the long months of gestation was Sylvia able to recognize the fact that she had been trying to get pregnant, and had merely succeeded in doing so.

No, it was all a mistake.

For a few agonized days she even thought about abortion. She stopped doing so when she realized where the agony came from. She had not intended, of course, to get pregnant, she told herself and Adam and her mother and her friends, but now that it had happened (somehow!) she was quite happy about it, really.

Quite happy about it! That she could say such things aloud, and not slap her own face for shame! But then Sylvia had no idea how tremendously she was lying. Of course she knew all about the idea of the unconscious mind; she was perfectly ready to admit to owning one, but vaguely she supposed it must occupy, what? a third, say, of available space? Less, perhaps, since she was after all a competent, educated, professional grown-up. A third of your mind couldn't be in charge, obviously. For the idea of inner democracy was also part of Sylvia's unexamined belief. So two-thirds evidently had more weight than one. You might unconsciously want to get pregnant, but if more of you consciously didn't want to, it was an accident if you did, right?

Right, Sylvia told herself, those first few agonizing days, when she tried to get back into the driver's seat of her own life by considering ending what she had begun. But Sylvia's unconscious, that ruthless particularity, came up with tenderly unfocused notions of smallness, of roundedness, of nestling; and like the perfectly hidden fifth columnist it was prompted the rest of her into more articulate thought: argued that time was running out, what was she waiting for? Reminded her that childbearing was a bus anyone could miss, if they dawdled. Reminded her that, since Adam was delicious, so too would be his child; whispered that Adam loved her, loved his children, would be a good father: knew how.

All this constant mental effort to win herself round to something she already wanted was very tiring. Sylvia put the tiredness down to pregnancy, and anyway soon had more pressing concerns. It was very difficult to work when she was so constantly sick. She tried all the remedies, and none of them had the slightest effect. Wearing pressure bands on both wrists, munching ginger, sipping peppermint water, looking on the bright side (at least the Friends had stopped calling), eating little and often, she still needed to carry a bowl around all day in case of accidents. In the clinic she vomited swiftly between patients; whilst operating was several times forced to leave an anesthetized patient on the table, the eyeball actually opened, while she shakily re-scrubbed; in short, she became someone else, someone who really belonged in a Victorian novel, weepy, prone to fainting fits, easily exhausted, and so feeble that the mere sight of a glossy new pile of dog shit, or a splat of phlegm on the pavement, caused instant gagging nausea.

Sylvia remembered with remorse the women she had cheerily told, when she was a House Officer, that their sickness was a normal and minor complication of pregnancy. She remembered that she had told them that it would stop, like magic! at the end of the third month. She remembered, as she winced her way in and out of the bathroom, that she had also once thought hemorrhoids rather a joke. They were a minor complication of pregnancy too, like stretch marks and thrush. Christ knew, thought Sylvia, what the major ones felt like, in that case.

Soon Sylvia did, too. It was evident, at a twenty-eight-week assessment, that the baby was not growing as it should. The placenta was not functioning as it should.

"Sorry, Sylvie," said the senior registrar, an old friend. "We're going to have to keep an eye on you."

Having an eye kept on her meant Sylvia interrupting her already interrupted and hectic working schedules by visiting the obstetrical department twice a week for long monitoring sessions. She peed in big jars for twenty-four-hour urine collections, she provided daily blood samples, she lay hooked up to machines which demonstrated her inadequate placental perfusion in different colored inks, she recorded fetal movement and took her own blood pressure every four hours.

She was no longer Sylvia Henshaw, consultant surgeon, FRCS Opth. She was a set of observations which together added up into a syndrome. Abruptly she was admitted.

"Not that bed rest actually works," said the registrar, mistakenly under the impression that as a doctor Sylvia was capable of detached professional interest in her own disease. "I mean, nothing actually works but delivering the baby, and we won't want to do that at this stage. Not until it's safer out than in."

Sylvia had never been a patient before. Without asking her they had put her in a single room, because, she supposed, she was a consultant.

"I'm only an eye doctor," she told the midwives, "I don't know anything about babies." She wanted them to sit on the bed and carefully explain things to her, she wanted them to pat her hand and tell her everything was going to be all right. But her notes of course told them that she was Miss Henshaw, FRCS, and no one wanted to risk patting that expert professional hand. At the same time no one wanted to be too deferential either. So Sylvia was generally treated with polite circumspection, and no one explained anything at all, not even where the bathroom was.

One evening, when Adam had just arrived on the ward with two new paperbacks, a fresh bouquet and a chilled bottle of Aqua Libra, the young student midwife, whose name was Susan, put Sylvia on the ordinary monitor for her routine evening trace. For a moment Adam, Sylvia and Susan all listened with satisfaction to the fast galloping triple rhythm of the baby's heartbeat, shown in constantly changing bright yellow electronic numbers per minute, 140, 148, 144.

There was talk of allowing Sylvia home for the weekend, as if she were a parole prisoner behaving well. Adam opened the bottle and had just passed Sylvia a cool fizzy glassful when something happened.

"Oh, I'm getting a contraction!" said Sylvia excitedly, her eyes on the monitor. Adam looked, and sure enough the monitor paper, slowly spooling out in concertina'd folds, showed the straight line that usually just reflected Sylvia's breathing sloping upwards, higher and higher.

"What does that mean?" said Adam, whose previous children had been born in a different generation, one that kept fathers at a distance.

"Does it hurt?" asked Susan.

"I can hardly feel it at all," said Sylvia wonderingly, for the monitor certainly could, the slope was still rising. No, it had peaked; the needle now was slowly falling again.

"Braxton Hicks," said Susan, expecting Sylvia to know what she meant.

"What's that?" asked Adam. But Susan had gone very quiet. She was staring at the monitor. She was entirely still, fixed.

"What is it?" he said again, but no one replied. The baby's heartbeat seemed to be slowing down, he realized.

Strange. Slower and slower. Was that bad?

He looked at the monitor, where the little brightly lit figures blinked back at him: 84, 88, 84, 82.

"Back in a minute," said Susan abruptly, and left.

"What does it mean, Sylvie? Is something wrong?"

Sylvia made no reply. All her attention was focused on the electronic figures at her side. The baby's heartbeat was still slowing. 76, 73, 62.

The door opened and Susan came back in, with a senior midwife, a much older woman. Neither of them spoke.

63, 61, 59.

"Call Bill," said the older midwife. "Turn onto your left side, please," she said briskly to Sylvia, and she crossed round the bed, pulled the oxygen mask off the wall, and gave it to Sylvia, who put it on.

"What's happening?" said Adam again. Though by now he knew.

Sylvia could frame no words at all. The baby was dying inside her, and all she could do was listen to its death, helplessly witness the moment when the failing little heart just stopped.

52, 54, 48, 44.

She was a car crash happening, in rigid incredulous silence. Instantly she had remembered all sorts of obstetrical information: that what her baby was demonstrating was the terminal cardiac decline known as a late deceleration, following the minimal extra insult of the Braxton Hicks practice contraction; she knew the oxygen would have no effect; she knew that they had given it to her because there was nothing else they could do.

A man in a suit came in, stared briefly, wordlessly, at the monitor, flipped quickly through the rest of the trace, and strode out again. Through the door he left open came noises of hospitalized alarm, running feet, squealing trolley wheels, muffled yells.

48, 46, 44.

The room was crammed, two more urgent figures ramming a trolley alongside the bed. Sylvia groaned aloud. Unconsciously she lay writhing on the bed, her hands twisting at the coverlet.

40, 42, 40.

Then, as if a sudden switch had been thrown, 64, 78, 88.

And suddenly the fast galloping triple rhythm of life was cheerily back, 142, 144, 148, as if nothing had happened. Adam, overlooked in a corner and trembling violently all over, remembered a line from a poem he had not read since he was at school. It jumped straight into his head:

everyone suddenly burst out singing

for he was witnessing the brief instant, the barest half of an instant, when everyone in the room had made a tiny collective sound as of relief, though without a moment's letup in the stern intensity with which they were furiously having at Sylvia, whom he could barely see for the crowd of people all doing things to her.

Someone said his name and pulled him away, and then he was in the corridor, half-running along beside the careering trolley, on which lay Sylvia festooned with tubing and wires, and the anguish in her small face struck him so painfully that for a moment he could hardly breathe for guilt, knowing that he had done all this to her, him and his goat's cheese all the way from France.

"I love you," he managed, just as the trolley swung round the corner and vanished, with a great doom-crashing of heavy operating-theatre doors, and then he was alone on the clean shiny linoleum. Not quite twenty minutes had passed since his breezy arrival on the ward with roses and Aqua Libra, a concoction he was never to bring himself to drink again.

Presently someone led him somewhere else, and gave him a cup of tea, which he sat and looked at. There were little pools of oiliness floating on its surface. He blew gently on these, sending them from one side of the chipped blue cup to the other. He felt as if he had committed a murder, accidentally, perhaps, but murder all the same, for which no expiation or excuse was possible. To and fro went the oily milky bubbles.

In the operating theatre Sylvia suffered one of those jolts in reality common to those experiencing life-changing trauma. She was at home in operating theatres. Her body felt at home. It mentioned this to her conscious mind, which dazedly worried about scrubbing up. How could she wash her hands properly if she was lying down? How did they expect her to operate in these conditions, anyway? But then suddenly, for the first time in months, she felt wonderfully comfortable. Not in the least bit sick, not in the least bit frightened. The operating table was as soft as a cloud; she floated on it, swinging, lighter and lighter with happiness and peace.

13

"Oh Christ," said the anesthetist, as Sylvia's blood pressure became unrecordable, and he noticed that he had failed, in all the panic, to shut off the hydralazine. "Oh, Christ!"

Goodbye, said Sylvia, or thought she said. I'm going now.

Amid a flurry of expletives and wild rummagings through drug trays, hectic blood loss as the surgeon tore into Sylvia while the fetal heart rate crashed once more below forty beats a minute, while Sylvia's own heart came close to stopping altogether, so stupefied was it by the contradictory orders of several sets of opposing medication, amid this panic-strewn bloodbath, the baby, scrawny cause of all this private and professional terror, was yanked limp and grayish into the world.

There is perhaps no silence as terrible as the silence made by a newborn baby that does not cry.

This is a thick and heavy silence, measured in the painful heartbeats of those who hear it and know what it means. They work over it, second by second, carrying on doing what they would be doing if all was well, but their voices are hushed, self-conscious, and every sound they make echoes over that terrible prolonging silence.

A whole minute is passing.

At the resusitaire the pediatric registrar and the junior are vividly, intently alive, the junior trembling in her borrowed theatre shoes, her stethoscope half-covering the baby's little-bird chest, and tapping the fingers of her other hand together to signify the heart rate. They have suctioned the liquor and mucus from the baby's larynx, and patted the skinny little body dry, and puffed several good firm squeezes of oxygen into its weedy lungs via the miniature face mask, thus bouncing its heart rate back to normal; it looks slightly less gray, but it is still not breathing.

At Sylvia's body the surgeons, the midwives, carry on mopping and stitching, all of them suffering beneath the terrible heaviness of the baby's silence.

None of their heart rates are anything like normal.

The minute draws to a close. The baby lies flaccid, frogwise, splayed beneath the warming lights of the resusitaire.

It is still not breathing. Time to intervene. The senior pediatrician picks up the intubation tube, removes the mask, tips the tiny head back and opens the mouth, scanning the larynx to intubate, but as the cold metal touches the baby's lips its squashed little face twitches, as if registering discomfort. The skinny little hands clench, and suddenly the whole body tenses beneath the pediatrician's gloved fingers as it hauls in air, for that first, deep, painful? tearing? breath. It gives a tiny piping mew like a kitten, drags in another wobbling gulp of air, utters a series of high-pitched spluttering noises and then at last the decisive full-throated agonized-baby screech.

And everyone suddenly bursts out smiling, laughing, talking at once. It's a party, a celebration, while for a shared blissful instant a crying baby makes the most wonderful sound in the world.

Though bliss soon fades; survival is, after all, the norm here.

Sylvia herself is still dangerously ill, but she is one person again, and no longer two, with conflicting requirements. The anesthetist, still trembling from the near-miss, deepens her anesthesia; the obstetrician can take his time now, repairing the mess.

The pediatric registrar discovers he needs a sit-down; while the child lay unresponsive a certain small part of his brain insisted on reminding him that its parents included not only a consultant at this very hospital, but a senior barrister as well. Even now this combination, with its truly horrifying implications for career- and life-destroying litigation, makes him feel almost giddy with unease.

He puts out a hand, and curves it over the baby's head, shielding its eyes from the light. Immediately it stops crying. Its eyelids are swollen; it can barely force the lids apart.

"Hello," he says, smiling, forgetting his theatre mask.

The baby, with the mysterious composure of the newborn, looks back at him. Its face, he thinks, with the usual catch at the heart this still gives him, even now, seems full of a calm celestial wonder.

"What have we got?" says the surgeon, finishing his inspection of Sylvia's large intestine, some of which has unluckily looped itself out of her gaping abdomen. He starts the tricky business of squashing it all back in again.

For a moment the junior pediatrician doesn't understand what he means. Clutching her notes she stands aside to let the midwives fix identity name-bands on the baby's miniature ankles. Apgar score at birth, she reflects, would have been one, out of ten; we had a heartbeat then of less than a hundred, we had no respiratory effort, no muscle tone, no reflex irritability, and we were the color of old putty. We were dead. Or as good as.

But at sixty seconds, at the full joyous official minute, we scored eight. We were pink and flexed and screaming. So what have we got? A miracle? A close thing? A good day's work? An ordinary day's work?

"Oh," says the junior pediatrician, understanding at last. She smiles. "Oh. A girl," she answers.

"A girl," repeated Adam, standing up in the waiting room.

"Would you like to come and see her? We had to take her straight to the Special Care Baby Unit, she's going to need a bit of looking after, but not much. She's fine. Screaming the place down."

Adam, trying to smile, was obliged to cover his eyes with one hand until he could control himself again. Following the midwife down the corridor he tried to take in what she was saying, but although he heard every word none stayed in his mind, just floated straight out again.

The sight of his fourth child and second daughter was, then, yet another fearful shock.

A being closely resembling the rabbit he had been forced to skin and dissect many years ago at school lay displayed inside some sort of clear plastic case. Wires flowed from it, from chest and wrist and foot; a plastic tube had been stuck down one nostril and taped in several places to the thin sticky hair of its tennis-ball-sized head, and a miniature version of Sylvia's drip had been inserted not into its wrist but with nauseating precision into one of the tiny blue veins in its forehead.

There was really not much of it to see at all, under all the tubing. But it was still far too much for Adam. His overwhelming impression was of unseemliness. That one should be able to see this small raw thing, its spectral limbs, elongated with such un-babylike, such fetal slenderness! Its terrifying frailty! Its translucent skin! It was not finished. It was not proper.

"Say hello," prompted the nurse, encouragingly. "You can touch her. Come over here and wash your hands, then you can touch her."

Adam did not want to touch this thing in the least. He wanted to go somewhere and moan in private, but he had been taught so ferociously and for so long not to give way to such longings that instead he followed the nurse without a word of protest and washed his hands as instructed with every appearance of paternal solicitude.

"There!" said the nurse, and she opened a little porthole in the side of the cabinet and indicated that here Adam was to insert his scrubbed Brobdingnagian hand. "Touch her hand, go on!"

Surely he would crush, bruise, tear this fragile half-formed thing just by looking at it, let alone assaulting it with his monstrous person? He held his breath and lowered his immensity of trembling little finger toward the baby's perfect miniature left hand, which lay palm up upon the mattress. The finger was, of course, by reflex immediately and tightly grasped. The spectral bluish fingers could barely close round his, but for an instant Adam and his new baby daughter held hands.

Adam gasped and shuddered as if the baby's touch burnt him, as if it were he who was too fragile to make contact. Then the little fingers relaxed, and fell away, and the baby tensed all over and uttered a tiny convulsive sound: a sneeze, Adam realized, and felt something tickling his chin, and put up his other hand to discover that his face was running with tears.

"Well, hello," he whispered to the miracle, the unlooked-for daughter of his old age, who along with his little finger had instantly taken hold of his heart, and who would never let go of it again. "Hello, my little darling, my little beautiful, hello."

He had a head start on Sylvia, who, groggy with much anesthesia and the mind-altering drugs which lower dangerously high maternal blood pressure, and further dizzied by a nice big shot of postoperative diamorphine, was later rolled into the Special Care Baby Unit on her trolley, a drip in either arm, a catheter tube in her bladder connected to a urine bag hooked onto the rails, an electronic blood pressure machine attached to one arm, and a wound drain sutured to her abdomen and leading to a glass bottle which nestled between her thighs.

She did not, unsurprisingly, feel up to any introductions, especially to someone as important as her own first child. But it was hospital policy that such introduction be made as soon as possible.

"Right," said Sylvia faintly, on being drawn up alongside the plastic box. "Very good," she added vaguely. It wasn't that she felt anything like Adam's shock or revulsion; she had seen far more premature and sickly children; she just couldn't get up much interest either way, what with one thing and another.

"Thank you so much," she said to the midwives manning the trolley, and hoping that she would now be allowed to lapse into unconsciousness, which was all that she desired. "Lovely," she added, politely, for Sylvia had been brought up to be polite.

The midwives, however, failed to take the hint, and were besides further constrained by hospital policy to encourage new mothers to enjoy immediate postbirth skin-to-skin contact with their newborn, in order to facilitate mother–child bonding; there was a box which had to be ticked, and explanations had to be given, should such skin-to-skin bonding not take place.

Sylvia was therefore untucked, and curtained off, and someone unclasped the plastic box, and very carefully taking into account all the trailing tubes and wires, gently lifted the sleeping baby from her mattress, and placed her on the trolley at Sylvia's side.

Never had a more alien creature touched Sylvia in so intimate a place. The baby's limp delicacy, clammy against her own small frightened breast, felt more like a washed-up sea creature than a baby. Or a damp flannel. Sylvia hurt all over, and had been afraid to move anyway; now she was almost afraid to breathe.

"Please," she called feebly through the curtain at the midwife, who had withdrawn to allow a private moment for mother and child, "please . . ." but she had not the wit to say she felt sick, or dizzy, or merely dreadfully ill, even though all these things were true. She just lay there for what felt like a very long time, while the baby made not a move, just looked unbearably fragile, terrifyingly fragile, and overwhelmingly *there*.

I'm not ready, was Sylvia's only conscious thought. It's not fair: I'm not ready.

And she didn't feel any more ready through all the immensely uncomfortable days that followed. The wound drain came unstitched and fell out, and had to be put back elsewhere; Sylvia's bowels, discomfited at being handled—for intestines are very temperamental items, and hate to be touched so much that the merest stroke of the surgeon's sterile glove can make them down tools and go on strike for days on end—refused to move at all, and lay coiled inside her sulkily allowing themselves to fill up with various gases, and simply not doing a thing about it.

Distension further pained the abdominal wound, and pulled at the hidden rows of stitches within; the catheter irritated Sylvia's bladder, and made her feel that she wanted to pee all the time, even though, as the midwives kept on reassuring her, there was a tube taking it all away already.

Every now and then a terrific wave of pain would grip Sylvia inside, and make her groan aloud.

"It's your womb contracting," said the midwife. "I'm afraid I can't give you anything for it just yet." For hospital policy decreed that patients only needed pain relief at set intervals.

"Oh, leave the door open, please," begged Sylvia when night fell, when the midwives had finished attending to all of her attachments and left her in peace for a sleep. For it was true: suddenly she was afraid of the dark. She was afraid to be alone. Sylvia Henshaw, FRSC, so grown-up and competent and intelligent!

"No, leave the light on, please!"

And sometimes she slept, and sometimes pain kept her awake, and all the time desperate fears assailed her. She was not ready. She really wasn't ready. What was she going to do? How could anyone, let alone a doctor, a consultant, a bold clever woman in her thirties, admit to being frightened of her own baby?

Every so often the midwives trundled Sylvia in her bed, or later in a wheelchair, along the corridor to visit SCBU. Sylvia like Adam washed her hands and inserted them into the baby's display case, and stroked the thing within. But unlike Adam she felt not a shred of emotion. Not love, not possession, not even connectedness.

Didn't people sometimes refer to a newborn baby, cozily, as a little stranger? The phrase jumped stridently into Sylvia's mind over and over again. The maddening soppiness of it, as if the littleness was supposed to make up for the strangeness! She was surprised every day by how unlike the baby was to anyone she knew or cared about. She had, she realized, expected the baby to look like Adam. Hadn't even thought about it; just assumed it. Absurd to feel so disappointed!

Not that it looked much like a baby anyway, set about as it was with so much electronic equipment. It looked like vivisection, she thought once, as the midwife parked the wheelchair alongside the plastic observation-box in which the creature lay pinioned; and then for a while she couldn't stop herself remembering a certain snippet of medical research to do with newborn kittens, which had so sickened her when she had first heard it that it had haunted her in weak moments ever since.

As the various tubes and drips one by one were discarded, and the baby could wrinkle its face, and purse its little lips, and frown, it became clearer and clearer that the child was the perfect image of Adam's elder sister, who was indeed pretty elderly, recently retired from the civil service, intellectual, big-boned, and charmless: this was Geraldine's baby, a miniature version of hairy guffawing Geraldine!

Sylvia felt shocked and cheated, as if she had unwrapped what she thought was going to be a wonderful surprise present, to find, say, a set of plastic measuring spoons or a hot water bottle.

Often those midwives prepared to overlook the fact that Sylvia was Miss Henshaw FRSC spoke kindly to her about the baby's chances, how well she was doing, and that soon she would be able to leave the unit and stay all the time with Sylvia in her room on the ward, not long now, honestly! And Sylvia would force herself to dry her eyes and nod, lest the evil truth be suspected.

It did not occur to her that her feelings were informed by shock and illness. But then very little occurred to her at all. Her breasts swelled and prickled, as milk forced its burrowing way through as-yet unused unopened channels. The baby, brought down at last in a different plastic box, one without a lid now, and covered in a cozy blanket as if it were a real baby, was removed at intervals from its wrappings and folded in beside Sylvia, so that it could learn how to suck.

But as soon as the midwives picked it up it cried, and placed beside Sylvia in her bed it actually turned its head as if trying to squirm away from her. Her voice, her hand, did not comfort it; it wanted her to leave it alone, thought Sylvia, it wanted her to keep her distance.

It knew.

"There!" said the midwife triumphantly, as the baby suddenly cottoned on to the business of feeding, and at last began relentlessly to suckle. "What did I tell you? She was just that bit premature, see? Sucking reflex doesn't really kick in before thirty-seven weeks. Doing beautiful now, though, aren't you, my lovely?" she said crooningly, to the baby.

Not, of course, to me, thought Sylvia, with the profound irritation of the invalid. For she also suffered a great deal from the feeling that she had lost her Self.

She was an abdominal wound, a set of protesting bowels, a possible urethritis, a hypertensive, a stalled drip, a blocked wound drain, a pair of sore hard breasts. There was no room left amongst this busy array of discomforts for the real Sylvia Henshaw.

I feel I've been exploded apart, thought Sylvia. Ka-blam. Was that what everyone else felt? Perhaps it was.

But if everyone else felt exploded, why had they kept it such a secret? Friends had of course complained of tiredness, of the relentless pull of a twenty-four-hour responsibility, but they hadn't let slip that they had personally disappeared.

Had anyone else felt like this, as if they were being saddled with total care of some distant family member, some doubly incontinent stranger? No, it *was* being saddled with some doubly incontinent stranger! The little stranger. The little Geraldine, champing her bony jaws on Sylvia's sore engorging nipple.

But slowly the days went past and presently Sylvia's insides recovered their usual equanimity, and went back to work. Her blood pressure slowly fell back to normal, her wound began healing, pain receded. And Adam, her friends, her family, her colleagues, her patients, began bombarding her with flowers and cards and bottles of this and that, and tiny suits of petal-soft velour, and cuddly toys, and helium balloons bearing absurd messages of congratulation and hope.

At first Sylvia found these offerings almost painfully touching. She felt she had been to the very jaws of death, as indeed she had, though the anesthetist, popping round as if casually to visit one morning, was relieved to discover, from her answers to his careful questions, that she had no notion of exactly how close, or of his own part in that near-miss.

Above all she was terribly shaken: all her life she had assumed child-birth to be a natural process, essentially commonplace. And it had not been like that. It had been a trip to chaos. She had been shown the wait-ing possibilities of pain, and fear, and death itself.

And what did humanity do, in the face of these terrors?

It brandished pink velour teddy bears. It waggled silver helium balloons, and gladioli wrapped in cellophane. The gallantry of this puny defiance, this pathetically determined frivolity, brought tears to Sylvia's eyes.

But everyone knows new mothers cry a lot, so no one was too dismayed.

Presently, further along in her series of constant mental adjustments as to what was normal, what was real, Sylvia remembered that the flow-ers and other presents were intended to signify celebration. The world considered her to have done something delightful, achieved something good. The meter-high bouquets signified not defiance, not even pro-pitiation, but merely pleasure.

Sylvia breathed in their perfume, and found it soothing. The midwives strung her cards all around the walls like pretty Christmas decorations, and soon the bearers of more flowers, and of boxes of chocolates and opulent baskets of fruit and small wooden toys, began to troop shyly into Sylvia's room. With what eager awe they peeped into the plastic cot!

"Oh, isn't she beautiful!"

Until every day took on the appearance of a party, and Sylvia herself was almost convinced, especially when the room was full of happy con-gratulatory people, that everything really was all right, that she was sim-ply a lucky woman who had just had a baby, and obviously that always took a bit of getting used to, no one simply sailed into motherhood care-free, did they? Did they?

Alone with the little stranger, the little Geraldine, she was still coldly aghast.

She grew better and better at hiding this though, until at last she was able to hide it, for most of the time, even from herself. And then it was time to go home.

The glorious relief, two months later, of going back to work!

How Sylvia has ever since impressed her colleagues, by being just as efficient and competent and hardworking as she was before! Just as many clinics and operating lists, just as many overseas research students and teaching commitments and GP lectures. Of course she doesn't bother with private practice, but she hasn't even tried to get out of any of her share of time-consuming NHS committee work. And alone among her peers she can be trusted not to weary them with baby chat, or photographs, or toddler-care crises. Well done, Sylvia!

Occasionally, waking before dawn, Sylvia briefly allows herself to examine a truth, to turn it over in her hands.

It would be better if I had died. Better for Clio to have a loving father and no mother at all than to grow up with a mother who is only pretending. How soon will she suspect the lack? How will it distort her? She will grow up mad and sad and bitter.

Why don't I feel the way everyone else does? Why can't I? What's wrong with her? What's wrong with me?

I am not natural, thinks Sylvia bleakly, in answer.

And punishment, just and terrible, would run concurrently with this crime. She was to live for twenty years in the closest possible service of someone she did not love.

WILL'S MOTHER, AUGUST 1995

—————————

OF COURSE YOU DIDN'T SMOKE in front of her. You nipped out into the garden, sat down on the wooden seat your old mum had painted herself with teak oil just a few months ago, when everything was normal, and you quietly smoked your cigarette where she couldn't see you or smell the smoke.

And if it was dark enough you could cry a bit, stealthily, quietly, because the garden wasn't that big and neighbors would have their windows open, and things were bad enough for soulful glances from neighbors already, thank you very much.

On the one side, Gerry, elderly, fat and be-dogged. Dog fat also, always a bad sign, Will thought. Gerry apparently unattached to any human creature, and possibly just what Will himself was going to swell up into in twenty years' time.

On the other side a fairly new one, a tiny shriveled old lady, Ida, or perhaps it was Rita, or Ada: one of them. Shriveled old Ida talking *refainement* with an occasional touching twang of antique Cockney.

"And arz yer mum today?"

"Not so bad, thanks."

"Iss lovely, what you're doin'," and more than once as she had said this, Ida's little old milky eyes had filled with tears, sincere, or luxuriantly sentimental, or possibly both, who could tell? Not Will. He felt his stomach turn anyway with embarrassment and shame. Nor could he come up with a decent answer, he found.

A shrug, and *Someone's got to do it.*

Noble, *It's my duty.*

Tearful, *I want to do it.*

Reasonable, *What else can I do?*

Chilling (that'd sort Ida out), *Well, it's not going to be for long, is it?*

Straightforward, *I couldn't bear not to do it.*

Also straightforward, *I can't bear doing it either.*

All of these replies were usually true. Sometimes though he felt so trapped and frantic with misery that packing a bag and getting on the next flight to anywhere seemed the only endurable option.

This evening the wooden seat was warm to the touch, still holding some of the day's sunshine. The cigarette made Will feel pleasantly dizzy. Oh smoke, so delicious. Hadn't Oscar Wilde said something about smoking, that it was a perfect pleasure, since desire was never really satisfied? What you on about, Oscar? Another deep sweet whole-body drag.

Today, officially over, had worked well enough. Tomorrow should follow a similar pleasant outline. He would set the alarm for six, make sure he was awake before her. She could have tea with the first set of pills and a rest before breakfast: porridge. After a tidy-up he would read her some more *Mapp and Lucia* before Sue came, and then he would make everyone some coffee while Sue did her stuff. Quick shop and home in time to do lunch: whatever she wanted. And in the evening she had episode three of *Pride and Prejudice* to look forward to; rather painful for him at first of course—Colin Firth being just his own age—but wearing off now. And he was definitely going to have another go at grandma's mythical steak and kidney pudding.

(Not about taste, about smell, he had e-mailed Sylvia the week before. Am trying to recreate washday pudding aroma circa 1938. Resultant rubber stodge offered to fat dog next door. Dog willing.)

It was the afternoons which were harder to fill. There was washing, of course. Load and unload. There was Judy, his mother's own dog, a small fox terrier–like mongrel. Nervous Judy, offered the misshapen rubbery pudding, had run away and hidden behind the sofa. Even now she often reacted to the sight of Will coming into the kitchen by racing out of it, claws skittering on the lino. Still, she needed frequent airings.

"Just taking the dog out, Mum!" And myself.

There was cleaning. Vacuuming (Judy behind the sofa again). There was stuff to squirt the bath clean, there was Mr. Muscle to do the work so he didn't have to. And there was gardening: he could sit pulling further curtains of algae out of the pond. That was useful. He could trim the hedge again. He could go and stare at the plums again, presumably the bastards would have to get ripe sometime, they couldn't hold off forever.

Carefully he put out the stub beneath his heel, pocketed it, and went back into his mother's house.

Was she awake?

Silently he crept to the door of her room, always ajar now. The inflating mattress ticked, stealthily breathing in; he had to concentrate to decipher his mother's own softer breaths. She seemed asleep, but she was good at doing that. He slid furtively inside, and crouched beside the bed, jug in hand.

The dog, Judy, curled neatly against his mother's legs, raised her small narrow head, then laid her graying muzzle down again with a little sigh.

Still no sign from Mum. He opened the catheter's spigot, holding it so that the stream emptied itself silently against the side of the jug, and presently, again by stages, soundlessly withdrew.

There. Another triumph, thought Will, for the piss-thief. Piss-artistry: the art of emptying the urine bag without his mother trying to apologize for having thus to fill it. Unless, of course, she had only been pretending to be asleep, in order to skip the apologizing on her own account. This was a painful thought. It was perfectly all right for him to spare her feelings, but if she were too tired to go on trying to spare his that could only mean a further deterioration, a further slippage from the whole real person into the dying stranger, the woman he most feared, the one who only looked like his mother.

"Billy?"

In the bathroom, rinsing the jug, he heard her puzzled voice.

"What you doing, love?"

"Just running a bath, Mum." He crossed the landing. "Sorry, did I wake you?"

She was smiling now. "I had such a funny dream!" Her fingers found the bed's remote control, and as she spoke the bedhead made its deep electronic exhalation, and slowly arose beneath her, raising her head and her shoulders, as usual bringing irresistibly to mind Dracula, arising in his coffin.

"We were waiting in the queue in Littlewoods, we were having a cup of tea. Me and your dad."

Will felt a tiny familiar sliver of irritation. Even in dreams she was so diffident. Queuing at Littlewoods, for Pete's sake. You'd think she could afford to splash out a little in her own dreams.

"And your dad says to me, Shall we dance? And we were dancing a fox trot, and all the queue was watching so impressed. I didn't see his face properly, but I knew it was him."

"Nice dream," said Will.

"It *was* nice. What time is it, lovey?"

"Nearly ten. At night," he added smoothly, just in case. Sometimes, getting in first meant she didn't fully notice her own confusion. And that was the next best thing to no confusion at all. "Want some tea?"

"You have your bath, love. Perhaps later."

He gave the bed-table a quick once over. Everything was to hand, the radio, the spouted plastic beaker of water fresh that afternoon, the little brass bell from the mantelpiece, to summon him if need be, the TV remote, the bed remote still alongside her good hand on the duvet.

"OK then." He turned and went off whistling, a carefree boy, the sort his mother so loved to hear about the house. Strange, this constant sensation of being, in oneself, a profound treat. He was a walking cause of satisfaction. He was a source of comfort and joy, a living Christmas carol, just being there, just sitting on the sofa.

Well, in truth he knew that she would probably have preferred him to sit idly on the sofa: the shopping and cooking and nursing duties were all out of shape as far as his mother was concerned. So a further extension of his role was constantly stressing how easy it all was. What was a bit of shopping, for heaven's sake! He just nipped out to Sainsbury's, didn't he? Actually I quite enjoy cooking, it's soothing, I quite often cook for friends, you know, it's nothing special, anyway I've got to eat too, haven't I?

In the bath he was aware of her aware of him. She would be lying there awake listening to the faint splashes with, he knew, the liveliest pleasure.

In his teens the depths of this love had expressed itself in unendurably boring strictures and constant rows. She had been so maddeningly frightened all the time of what she called "something happening." Not without cause, really, when he thought about it. Hadn't he climbed happily into cars beside youthful drivers he knew to be as drunk as himself? Hadn't he eagerly tried the several kinds of illegal this and that fashionable at the time, and stepped off dance floors with girls he hardly knew? Plenty of scope for something to have happened there.

For a long time now though she had been less frightened, he thought. He was clearly a man, and she had been brought up to defer to men, to assume them capable and wise.

And now she was dying; soon she would be able to relax the last tiny rootlets of the mighty nerve of anxiety within her, sprung to vigorous life the moment he was born, in the final certain knowledge that for as long as she lived none of the somethings she had once so dreaded, had so unceasingly enumerated in darkness whilst waiting for him to come teenagedly home in the small hours, or heard and seen exemplified in the terrible things that so constantly happened to other people's grown-up wandering children, that none of these arbitrary or unforeseeable or even common everyday horrors had visited themselves upon her child.

Yes, she had almost stopped worrying about him, and was left mainly now with her delighted love, of similar growth and complexity, so that the very sound of him splashing in the bath across the little landing made her warm with happiness. There will be no aloneness more complete than the aloneness I will feel when my mother's rapt attention is at last entirely withdrawn.

Sometimes when this thought occurred Will felt simple panic, as if he were a small child whose mother was dying. Sometimes it merely gave him further patience, so that he could stand her apologizing for filling the urine bag, or needing help to turn over, or fresh bedclothes.

"No, Mum, I want to help out."

Not look after you, or nurse you, those words would imply that she was actually ill; and both Will and his mother had begun pretending almost as soon as Will arrived to stay that this was far from the truth. Helping out: it sounded temporary, lighthearted, masculine, something a neighbor might do.

In the T-shirt and shorts he wore in bed he took another peep through the open door.

"Mum?"

No reply. Asleep again. The ripple mattress made one of its long implosions, stealthily deflating; out-stared as usual by the small red eye of its On switch Will passed barefoot to his mother's dining room, where he had laboriously set up his computer. Ha! The outside world. It was still really there. Probably. Anyone calling me?

Maybe not Sylvia yet. Well, she was busy busy busy. She was busy in ways you couldn't touch her for.

What d'you mean, you were sewing back into place the tear-ducts of a little girl attacked by her grandmother's Alsatian, or expertly salvaging the punctured right eyeball of some gink too dopey to spot the essential connection between hand-drilling through steel plate and a pair of plastic goggles, what about me?

No, Sylvie inviolable. What with the baby as well, obviously needing every second of quality time she could squeeze from the rest of the day when she wasn't out curing the blind.

At last the blank screen cleared itself, and informed him he had e-mail. Ah. There's my girl.

Hi, suppose M&S s&k pud won't do? Mum said good. She's
sending me Jane Grigson recipe from 'English Food', will send on.
Also said that Mrs. Beeton v. vague as to quantity, uses batter,
could that be right? Will send Mrs. Beeton also. Is Mapp and Lucia
any good, let me know if not, have others, give your Mum my love
please, thinking of you love S

I need a recipe of smells for my mother, Will thought. Would a book of smells work? The Illustrated Book of Smells. Manufacture the smells you need whenever you need them. Steamed steak and kidney, c. 1930. Fish and chip shop on the front at Morecambe, East End pie shop. Soot. Cut grass. Hay. All of them comfortable everyday smells.

Tell your Mum thanks, he wrote. May try new bread, smell allegedly easy. M&L perfect, thanks.

Mum regretted Sylvia, of course.

"Oh, she's such a nice girl!"

Too nice for me. How could I ever live with someone that nice? She's at least eight times nicer than me, Mum. Honestly, anyone's limit is four or five times.

"Billy!" From across the landing he heard the tinkling bell as well.

"Hello?"

"I couldn't reach the light, I'm sorry . . ."

She sounded frightened.

"There you go." He sat down in the armchair beside the bed. His own heart fluttered. Was this it? Her breathing sounded different, she was gasping a little, as if she'd been running.

"Mum?"

Was this it?

"I had this awful thought . . ."

He took her good hand in his own. She was calming down, her voice now clearly tearful. His own throat ached in sympathy.

"What?"

"So silly—it was that dream."

"The dancing one?"

"Yeah. I thought—suppose there is a heaven. And he's there. I thought . . ."

"Don't cry, Mum. What?"

"He wouldn't recognize me."

"Oh, Mum, what a terrible idea, honestly, of course he would."

"I look so old."

Christ, what was he supposed to say? Rummaging wildly in the mental ragbag to which he had long consigned all items of religiosity he came up with Jesus being asked a question on similar lines, and how had He got out of it? No marrying or giving in marriage. Even as the angels. Yes. Adroit politician, that Jesus. Perfect answer-avoidance.

He smiled at his mother. "Can't see Dad as an angel, sorry."

There were two fast mental pictures of his father: an ancient one, from earliest childhood, of the broad-shouldered enormity, in a wide-brimmed hat like Humphrey Bogart, and the later version, half a head shorter than his son, in zippered cardigan and slippers.

"I'm so changed." She had been ten years younger than her husband. But now she had caught up with him.

This time Will came up with vague memories from a novel read years before.

"I reckon we're all thirty in heaven."

"Do you really?"

Yes: caught her attention. It was like diverting a child, he thought. But then she wanted so much to be diverted. Perhaps almost anything would do.

"Most people's best age, don't you think?"

"I don't know," she said seriously, as if the matter required proper attention.

"Reckon it was mine," he said, putting himself in the same camp: those past their peak. Too late he remembered that she wouldn't like that. Not for her precious baby.

"Don't be daft," she said, in something like her own voice. She had developed the older person's vagueness as to the youth of the young, he thought. Everyone looked similarly fresh and dewy now, he supposed: everyone under fifty. Whereas the young have the opposite illusion about everyone over thirty. I'm in the gap in the middle, he thought. Young to the old, old to the young.

"Want a cup of tea?" It was the idea of tea she liked, he thought, rather than actually drinking the stuff. Like the smell of cooking. She

31

was leaving all earthly desires behind, just hanging on for now to their more ethereal attributes. The notion of tea, the perfume, the warmth. Above all, he knew, the idea of himself in the kitchen, making it for her.

"Yes please, lovey."

Left alone Annie considered being thirty in heaven. 1960. What had she been wearing in 1960? They had still been in America then. That last year in Virginia. A dark cotton sundress, with a full bias-cut skirt and tight well-fitting bodice, and a little bolero jacket. And peep-toe high heeled shoes. Red lipstick and the powder compact Joe had given her for their first anniversary.

Thirty. Strange it was the only way you could really remember what you looked like, she thought. Thinking back to clothes, to your reflection in a long-ago mirror. She had looked in mirrors with satisfaction then. Turning round to check the fall of the skirt at the back. Catching her own eye over her shoulder, smiling back.

"Billy," she said, when he came back in with the tea, "that box on top of the wardrobe, yes, that one, could you get it down for me, please? You'll need a chair . . ." and forgot, for a second, that she could no longer nip up and fetch the chair herself. Her good hand entirely forgot, and pushed aside the duvet, leaving her looking down for a moment's perplexity at the hopeless side of her own self, that no longer obeyed direction.

"No . . . it's OK, I can reach," he was saying, of course, he was so tall, taller than his Dad at fourteen years old, and after all that time she'd spent worrying about him being smallest in the class. She pulled the covers back over herself before he turned round and noticed.

"Oh. Photographs?"

"Don't worry, I won't get upset. Oh dear, this is a bit of a mess . . ."

"What you after?"

"Me at thirty. Want to check."

Photographs spilled over the bed, a confusion of decades. Her honeymoon, that was intact; she must have used better glue.

"Weren't you gorgeous!" He had opened the little album in the middle: their trip to New York. Her own New York, the city of 1950. She wore a utility dress she had made herself, very plain, with three strings of white beads and no hat.

"I was just twenty."

"How did you walk in those shoes?"

"It was easy. Couldn't walk in flats in those days. Your calf muscles shorten."

"Yuk."

"Ah, look, that's the dress. Remember that one?"

Mum, of course I don't, he would have replied, furiously aged fifteen, patiently aged twenty five. But he was thirty-five now, and she was dying.

"Let's see . . . when was this?"

"I'm not sure. England anyway. So some time after 1962."

Full skirt, neat little high heels. It was, Will recognized, his earliest deepest idea of what a mother should look like. Short curly hair like the Queen. Handbag in the crook of the elbow.

"Those shoes were lined with kid. You can't get shoes like that nowadays."

"No," he said, regretfully, as if he agreed with her, as if he regretted the same old days, instead of feeling all his insides tighten with a shriveling sense of boredom so intense as to be almost indistinguishable from dread.

Be me one day anyway, he thought. "You can't . . . nowadays." Fill in the dots how you pleased, and watch your younger listeners writhe with longing to escape your presence any way they can!

"And here's your dad on the *Queen Mary*, we had the *Queen Mary* going out, and the *Queen Elizabeth* when we came back."

He looked with more interest at this one, the young man lying back smiling, not just on a deckchair, but actually on a deck. It was black and white, and he could make out the beginning of a funnel at his father's shoulder, and definite floorboards; a deckchair on a *wooden* deck!

"There was an onboard photographer," said Annie, "like they used to have at the seaside, don't suppose you remember them, anyway, this chap used to stroll about taking snaps, every day he'd stick the proofs up on this notice board and if you liked the photograph you'd get it properly, you know, printed up."

Will did not answer. How, he was wondering, could he himself be so closely related to someone who had thought wooden decks in ships perfectly normal? Who had, for Christ's sake, emigrated to America on a boat?

They had sailed from Liverpool, his father had once told him, and as was usual then a pipe band had assembled on the dock with the families of those setting sail for the New World (his dad! His mum! Nineteenth-century parents!) and as the ship slowly parted from the harbor wall the band had played the lament *Will Ye No' Come Back Again?*

And all the people waving on the ship, all the people waving on the shore, had joined in with the chorus through their tears,

> *Better loved ye canna be,*
> *Will ye no' come back again?*

their voices lost at last in the churning water and the deepening rhythm of the engines.

"I ought to put these in order," said Annie, frowning through her glasses at a battered envelope full of tiny prewar snaps.

Will considered. Putting photographs in order was one of the things his mother often told herself she ought to do. But what better time could there ever have been for her to do so? I could help her put them in an album, he thought, and I could write on the back who everyone is.

He was aware of a further thought, that soon, when he came upon some stray old photograph, there would be no one to ask about it; that his own family would soon be like those sad portraits you came across in junk shops and market stalls, pictures in cellophane packets of faces all ages and varieties, and the only thing you knew about them was that they were all as dead as dodos. You wouldn't want your own family disappearing into that sort of lost world. You should take better care of them than that.

He let this thought circle the outside of his mind, then booted it out before it got too close, before it got to its logical conclusion and showed him his mother in cellophane packets, anonymous and up for sale; showed him, perhaps, himself.

"I could get you one of those albums," he said cheerily, aloud, "you just slide the photographs in. So you could do it one-handed."

34

"I'll pay for it, mind," said Annie, instantly brisk. "You get the money out of my purse."

This was her latest worry, amounting sometimes almost to mania: that he was spending all his money on her, when of course being (as she put it) *looking for work* he should really be saving every penny, perhaps to save himself from a spell in the Fleet debtors' prison: it was hard to know sometimes quite how her mind worked, given that she was essentially a Victorian person in modern masquerade.

There was an edge to it, too. Letting him know what she thought of his career path so far. A hint of Told You So concealed within the Victorian ethic of paying her own way.

Look, I'm not fucking hand-to-mouth, you know, I'm not on the fucking dole!

Will did not fully think this ferocity, but felt it appear on his face for his mother to see. He turned away fast, but was still impelled to his feet by the force of his rage, finding himself beside the window, where he pretended to adjust the curtain until his heart slowed down.

He thought: the photograph album was such a good idea that for a moment it actually made her forget how ill she is: so she talked to you as she would have done if she'd been well. She needled you.

That's Mum there, dying. You *going* to be needled? No. You are not. You are never going to be pissed off with her again.

Not just for her sake. For your own. So when it happens, when it's all over, there's nowhere, no time you're going to sit down and pull your hair out about the things you said to her and can't unsay.

This is what you're *doing*. It's a *task*. This is what you're doing *now*.

"I'll go to Boots," he said gently, turning round. "I think they do the sort you want."

THE NEXT MORNING it was Susan. She was Will's favorite, a large comforting presence, rosy-cheeked, slow-moving, with a strong cozy Welsh accent and a bosom so immense, so impersonally friendly somehow, that he had more than once been tempted to pat it affectionately in greeting.

Hello, Sue; hello *you*!

When had he realized, how old had he been, when he had finally accepted that you couldn't look at a woman's breasts without her noticing? In his twenties, probably. Hadn't it been Sylvie who told him?

"Stop *doing* that!"

"Doing what?"

How had he been supposed to notice women noticing, if he hadn't actually noticed what he was doing himself?

"Anyway it wasn't my fault," he had told Sylvie. "I wasn't looking at your bust, it was looking at me. I was just looking back. I was just answering."

"Hello, Sue," said Will now, smiling at her and not at her bosom, though as usual he was struck afresh by how jolly nice a bosom it undoubtedly must be.

"Hello, my love. How's things going? She have a good night?"

"Pretty good, I think. She was getting some pain around five. I gave her the dose early, the six o'clock."

"Did you now."

"Well, I thought . . ."

"Don't get me wrong, lovey, you did the right thing, 'course you did. I'm thinking perhaps we should be changing the dose. That's all. Maybe try something else if it's not getting her through. I'll make a note, get the doctor to drop by later, OK? How about you? Looking peaky. If you don't mind my saying so."

"Well. You know."

She gave him the look all the nurses had given him sooner or later. It was a look full of complicated feeling. Most of it so soft and warm that depending on his mood he had either wanted to break down in tears or stamp about the kitchen smashing his mother's china.

Look at you, a man, looking after his mother on her deathbed!

Isn't that lovely!

She must have been a lovely mother.

You must be a lovely son.

You're doing the right thing. So few of us ever get the chance to do a thing so clearly right! And here you are, doing it!

It was as if he was doing the right thing not only for his mother and himself but for everyone else, for the world.

As well as somewhere—or was he imagining it?—a faint chilly notion that there must be something just a little bit strange about him, spending all this time, two months so far, just living in his mother's house, where was his family then, was he all alone but for his mother, was that right, wasn't that just a little bit sad and strange?

Out of work too, wasn't he? Resting, wasn't that what actors called it?

Sometimes Will thought, Christ yes, out of work and thirty-five and all alone, how did it happen, what's wrong with me? And sometimes, just as often, he thought, Of course not, I'm only thirty-five, had my little taste of fame, thank you very much, and who knows what the future holds; had lots of happy relationships, just haven't quite got there yet, so?

It was, he recognized, the sort of thing you couldn't get away from when your one remaining parent was dying. It was part of the package. You were part of the package. Parent-child-parent, that was the regular way, and how had you managed? Parent-child-fullstop.

As yet. Because it was a bright sunny morning, and Sue's friendly breasts had reminded him how nice breasts were, today Will was only thirty-five, and where was the hurry? After all plenty of his friends were on their own. Admittedly most had some sort of family by now, however raggedly held together, or actually divorced. But he wasn't the only childless one. Tim, for instance. And Brig. And Mimi, and of course Sylvie, until so recently.

Annie's bedroom door was closed. It was the only time now that they had this privacy. Since the nurses had arranged for the hoist, and the special bed with its handgrips and clever rails, washing Annie had become a one-attendant task again.

"That's the beauty of a bungalow!" Sue had said, the day the hoist arrived. Will agreed with her there; indeed, he had always considered bungalows in general, and more particularly his parents' own, situated as it was in the heart of a suburban downmarket postwar housing estate, and all now ruthlessly ringed about with later motorways and even newer shopping centers, the quintessential, the acme, of suitable places in which to wait for death.

Of course you could manipulate your hoist. Of course your wheelchair could roll you easily from room to gimcrack poky room as your final days wound by. That was the beauty of a bungalow.

"Back in ten minutes, OK?" he called through the door, and escaped out into the warm quiet air, Judy cringing along beside him, looking up at him every now and then with little flinching old-lady glances, as if constantly unable to believe in the hulking male horror at the other end of her extending lead: making up Judy's thought processes often occupied Will's small outings with her.

Secretly he was a little discomfited by her refusal to get used to him after all this time. It seemed like a comment on his own charm. On his Thirty-five and All Alone and What's Wrong with Me days Judy's unassuagable fears were a confirmation of his own.

"Good dog," he told her softly, when her bulbous brown glance met his eyes. But her response was to hang her head, a condemned dog being led out to die.

Round the first circle, cross the empty road, and onto the second. The housing estate, he had lately decided, was not after all a mere figure of eight within an oval; it was a slightly different figure, a particularly elongated figure of eight, something some ancient Greek or another had called an alamma, the road leading nowhere but back into itself: infinity, no less.

The housing estate alamma lay sideways on a hill, signifying bungaloid infinity in semi or fully detached versions, and featuring front room windows so uncompromisingly enormous that no one tried for long to do without net curtains. For nearly fifty years a mostly transient population had tinkered with front door styles, erected lean-tos, committed crazy paving, and planted quick-grow conifers and flowering cherry trees.

It was a desert of spiritual and cultural emptiness, draining the life-blood of anyone fool enough to live in it, or it was a peaceful haven, a safe and gentle place to raise a child; it depended on your mood like everything else, thought Will, reaching the next curve.

As usual he found himself glancing at each set of secretive windows as he passed. Curtain-twitching was a lie, he thought, made up by those who have never lived behind them. Nylon nets don't need twitching, you can stand at the other end of the room and see out just as well. The point was that no one could see in.

He remembered, as he so often did on this particular circuit, the miniature village which had so enchanted him as a child, where was it, somewhere outside Canterbury? Aged five or six he had begged to be taken again and again, to walk like a giant through those hushed tidy streets, to peer with care at the occasional tiny model people waiting for a train, or having their little photographs taken outside the church after the wedding, hoping that if he was quick and clever enough he would catch one of the tiny people out: moving: being alive.

Had he noticed the likeness even then?

Down the steepest hill, useful challenge to the novice roller skater, round the second elongated circle of curtained dwarfish housing. At the last curve Judy stepped with a sigh into the gutter, and carefully deposited a little turd there. Standing holding one end of a dog's lead while it crapped at the other was one of the smaller but still vicious embarrassments of his present life, Will thought.

Still it was a good job well done, he informed Judy, who gave him another tremulous glance in reply before they set off for home.

"Hello!" he called in the kitchen, checking in. It was code, for Need a Hand? While he was putting the lead away Sue appeared in the doorway, and raised her eyebrows: Yes please. He followed her into Annie's room.

"Hey Mum," mild, casual, as if it was a perfectly ordinary thing to come across your helpless mother wrapped in damp towels and dangling sideways out of a sort of domestic forklift truck in her own bedroom. As if his mother's eyes were not full of effortful good humor.

"Damn thing's stuck again," she said brightly.

"It *don't* like the carpet," said Sue calmly, almost complacently, granting the hoist its little ways. "I was thinking, if you could like steady your mum, Will, while I gives it a bit of a *shove*, OK?"

The only way he could hold the seat was to clamber across the bed, to kneel on the edge.

"Hang on. OK, Mum?" He put one arm round her shoulders, the other beneath her knees. She smelt of soap, and Johnson's baby powder, and of something else less pleasant, some sour emanation of her breath. She smelt unfamiliar.

Sue crouched, squeezing her largeness egg-shaped, her striped blouse tautening across her shoulders.

"Caught on the pile." Her voice was muffled by her own folds as she pushed with both hands on the pedestal. Presently it came free with a sudden little jerk, which would perhaps have translated into the merest swing further up, had Will not been holding on tight, but the merest swing would have been far too much for Annie. Even so half of her still stiffened in his arms. The other half, cause of so much anguish and dread, could express neither. Will took his arms away, and kissed his mother's cheek.

"OK, Mum?"

Frightened smile in reply.

"I'll make us all some coffee, shall I?"

"That'd be nice," said Sue, straightening up, flushed and ineluctably buxom. Her breasts looked for a moment back at Will, signaling straightforward friendliness.

When he came back Annie was in bed again, looking almost normal. Her curly hair neatened, her yellow face smoothly relaxed against the clean flowery pillowcase. He put her plastic beaker down on the bed table. In the armchair beside her Sue was writing up her notes. She had big round handwriting. Sometimes Will read these daily updates.

Annie slept well and appears cheerful with no complaints of pain. Pressure areas checked and appear normal. Catheter care given, urinanalysis: nothing abnormal discovered. Diet tolerated well.

Just by looking at such words Will could turn his mother into someone else, he felt: a textbook person. The patient. The *patient*, to whom routine care was given. It felt very strange to think of her so.

It reminded him of the times he had lain awake at night as a little boy, still afraid of the dark and of being alone in it, and tried to comfort himself by pretending that instead of lying here in his own bed at home he was out walking in the woods, in gathering nighttime darkness; he would take some time imagining it all, how he would be telling himself he knew the path, and mustn't panic, that he was just out in the dark, nothing to be afraid of, and then, while his heart was quickening with these imagined terrors, he would suddenly switch off the engine of pretense, and luxuriate in reality, in safety. Not there at all! Here!

There was a similar game of solace to be played, Will thought, with his mother's nursing notes. *The patient* whose routine care was recorded in them offered after all a version of reality. Reading the notes while his mother slept he could enter into this reality and find a refuge there. Everything was routine. There were boxes to tick or fill. There was an entrancing vision of orderliness in those structured timesheets. It was a cozy other-world, like something out of a children's story.

If only, holding the notes like a magic key, he could escape into the world of cozily ordered textbook nursing care! The patient. The nurse. The doctor. Textbook people.

Reading Mum's notes is like being able to pretend for a moment that you're really safe in bed at home, when really you're alone in the woods in the dark.

"Coffee, Sue."

"Oh, thank you, my lovely," she said absently, still drawing her huge round screed. Writing to match her self, he thought.

"Be Judith tomorrow," said Sue, sliding the finished sheet into the envelope with the rest. "Doctor should be looking in later, do a bit of fine-tuning."

"Right."

"Any problems you've got the bleep."

"Right. Biscuit?"

"Get thee behind me, Satan, oh all right then. Just one. Ta. Ooh, haven't seen this before, have I? Who's this, Annie, your husband?"

The photograph had been loose at the bottom of the box on top of the wardrobe. Will had been a little outraged by such carelessness. There were so few pictures of his younger father. One of the baby in complicated white laciness, looking almost as stolidly lifeless as the stuffed donkey on which he sat; one of a tense round-faced schoolboy with flattened hair, his tight stiff jacket, shorts and long thick socks turned over at the knee clearly demonstrating the origin and meaning, Will thought, of the phrase buttoned up.

And this one, clearly a snapshot, unposed, outdoor, a slender ado-lescent in uniform. Someone had caught him relaxed, smiling directly into the camera, the tin helmet tipped back, one hand holding a ciga-rette. The face was extraordinarily touching, so young and tender and cheeky, so clearly someone's child, not the man and father Will had known.

He had been standing beneath a tree, Will had thought, interpreting the shadows across his father's chest. He could not remember ever hav-ing seen the photograph before. You could use it in a history book, he thought. It had that universal application. The pose, the cigarette, dat-ing it precisely: The Nineteen Forties.

"Joe, was it?"

Annie turned with an effort to look. She was fighting to stay awake, Will saw. The bath had exhausted her.

"A long time ago," she said, with her own sweet smile. You had to smile back at a smile like that, Will thought.

"He was at Dunkirk," he said, because everyone had heard of Dunkirk, though in fact Joe had been evacuated from Cherbourg, where, to stop the Germans getting it, he had been ordered to throw his army motor-bike off the harbor wall into the sea.

Will had crossed the channel to Cherbourg on his own aged nineteen, in 1979, at the start of a summer's relentless traveling, but the quiet harbor there had been unexpectedly memorable, the clean gray stone, the small friendly café where he had ordered his first grown-up café au lait in real French, the ordinary neon signs for pharmacies or hairdressers: all of it the place where, not so long ago, the only other person in his family who'd ever been there had been shot at from dive-bombing airplanes!

Joe had been nineteen too, on his only visit to Cherbourg. And from a home so wretchedly city-poor that he had had to catch a bus to the town baths once a week if he wanted a proper wash. The ship across the chan-nel with the Expeditionary force had been his first trip abroad. He had never so much as ridden in a car in his whole life, and yet in the course of a few months the army had taught him how to drive, given him a motorbike, let him ride it, and then made him fling it finished with into the ocean, like some extravagant military Toad of Toad Hall.

Hearing this story, one of the very few his father had ever told about the war, Will as a child had often thought longingly of the motorbike, imagining it still deep underwater in the unknown harbor of Cherbourg, covered in barnacles, waiting for rescue.

In 1979 he had thought of it again. Preposterous, surely, the idea of Germans shooting at Dad. Traffic lights, zebra crossings, Boulangerie, Coiffure, Pizza. Dad then was the small balding cardiganed version, volubly irritated when Will couldn't be bothered to empty the kitchen rubbish bin or rewind the garden hose tidily onto its reel. Had this old nag been dive-bombed by Stukkas?

And at the same time he was the wartime hero, who had dashingly flung a motorbike into the sea; also, for the first time, a fellow teenager, someone who must have loved the motorbike as Will himself would have loved it. And he had thrown it away without a moment's thought, because that was what being shot at felt like. Presumably.

Not Dunkirk. Cherbourg.

"Lovely looking fella," said Sue, picking it up for a closer look. Her eyes flickered over to Will. He could almost hear the nice flirtatious things she wanted to say to him, the things she would have enjoyed saying but for the fact of the dying mother. As it was she would say none of them. And every woman he met treated him with the same delicacy, he thought. All the nurses. The two women GPs in the practice. Sandra from two doors down. Holly. Sylvie. Every woman who knew. He had become the sexual equivalent of untouchable, and not because he was beneath notice, but because he was above it. Tender glances directed at him were all qualified, rendered quite different, by the heavy freight of maternal or sisterly approval they carried. For he was doing such a Right Thing.

Sometimes it was pleasant enough to bask in this diffuse asexual glow. Because he'd never felt less like sex anyway. Not since he was twelve years old. And sometimes he feared it was a door closing for good.

Suppose he never got his cock back? Suppose looking after your old mum just killed things off for ever? Suppose that was why men in the old days just steered clear of this sort of thing, leaving it to the women, who were hardier, or designed for it in some way? Suppose the old ways had after all been suffused with unknowing wisdom?

Suppose you cut the crap, thought Will clearly, catching himself out again in this not unfamiliar loop. Suppose you think about what's really important here for a change, OK?

"Who will it be this afternoon, d'you know?" he asked, in the tiny hallway.

Sue paused, her hand on the front door.

"Taylor, I think. Or Whitby. One of the two. Have you thought any more about the hospice?"

"She really wants to stay at home."

"I know. I don't mean permanent. I mean just a weekend. Give you a break."

"It's too much upheaval. And she's afraid of hospitals. It doesn't matter how nice they are to her, she'd just be lying there, in a state. She'd pretend everything was all right. But I'd know. I wouldn't get any rest anyway, you see."

"You haven't asked her, have you?"

"I can't."

"Why not?"

"Because she'd say yes."

"To please you, you mean?"

"Yes. To spare me."

"And you won't let her? D'you think that's fair?"

"It's like this: I don't think she should sacrifice herself any more, for me. I know she would. It would make her, what, a quarter happy. Well, not happy, but you know what I mean. A quarter okay. Three-quarters lost, and away from the only place she wants to be when she's dying. But a quarter okay. If I don't let her do it, she's three-quarters okay. More, mostly, if people like you, sorry, but people like you don't so much as mention the word *respite*; I don't need respite from my mother. Pretty

44

soon I'll have all the respite from her I can ever have, and I'll have it for ever and ever, so where's the rush?"

She'd been nodding and making little agreement noises through most of this, but he had found himself getting more and more heated, as if she were arguing with him. Now she just looked at him, her hands palm-up toward him, as if warding him off.

"Sorry," he said, after a short pause.

"I just want to say, look, you don't have to stick to this, all right? I'm not trying to talk you into anything. But, if things change, or you change your mind, well, you can, all right? Any time, that's all I'm saying, OK?"

He nodded. She had made this last speech in a voice so gentle, so coaxing, that for a moment he found himself completely diverted by suddenly wondering what on earth it could be like to be her child, ac- tually mothered by so vastly, so dizzyingly maternal a presence, Christ they'd never get over it, would they, her kids? A nurse as well! What sort of world would *they* grow up expecting?

"'Cos you look whacked, if you don't mind me saying so. Are you eat- ing all right?"

"Me? I'm fine."

"I'm sorry. I'll probably look in again this afternoon," she said in a brisker voice, as she opened the door. Her bust gave him a sideways glance. Remember Me? it said, pertly, for a bosom so large. He ignored it. He was only twelve years old anyway.

"Thanks," he said.

GEORGE'S ACCIDENT, SEPTEMBER 9, 1953

Present in Theatre Two:
Consultant: Mr. Barr
Senior Registrar: Dr. Beaconsfield
Anesthetist: Dr. Pym
Sister Holt (scrubbed in)
Staff Nurse Stoddard (runner)
Mr. T. James-Harper (medical student)
Mr. R. Wilding (medical student),

writes Helen Stoddard in the theatre book, in the laborious longhand Sister Holt requires, once the operation is well under way.

The patient, the only person not named as present, indeed lies almost entirely hidden from view, deeply unconscious beneath large squares of sterile drapery. A small hemmed window in one of them exposes the reason for this particular theatrical gathering, which proceeds in silence, apart from the rhythmical utterances of the anesthetics machine.

Not a calm silence.

"Pick it *up*, man!" hisses Mr. Barr at last through the thin cotton of his theatre mask. He thoroughly dislikes his current registrar.

"Superficially clever, pleased with himself, and oily," is his private verbal judgment, which of course carries a great deal more weight than the more equivocal written reference he will supply when Beaconsfield tries for promotion. "A slacker," adds Mr. Barr. And challenged to supply examples of this slackness he would do so; he is honorable; he is unaware that he would have coolly overlooked similar levels of slackness in subordinates who were not so clearly Jewish. Or merely not so plain as burly flat-footed Beaconsfield.

"What are you playing at?" he whispers menacingly over the patient's motionless shroud.

"Can't quite . . ."

"Can't quite what?" says Mr. Barr, now brutally loud. He catches the eye of Norma Holt, theatre sister, who looks quickly away, lest he suspect her of daring to agree, or (unimaginably worse) disagree with the cause or degree of his anger. Mr. Barr makes her heart beat faster. His presence makes her feel more alive. She is terribly afraid of him, and addicted to the polite disdain with which he rewards her submissive devotion.

"Can't quite see what I'm doing, actually," says Mr. Beaconsfield easily, throwing in the towel. Within he is molten with distress. In the ferocious operating lights his forehead glitters with the effort of doing his best whilst simultaneously swallowing rage and humiliation. Sounding tranquil is his only recourse: "Would you care to take over, sir?"

"Gloves," says Mr. Barr coldly to Norma, who of course has his size ready on her tray.

It is the high point, the meaning, of his life, this extraordinary skill. His fingers are delicate, and wise with the experience of nearly forty years. Through the immense heavy magnification of his lenses he peers down more closely at the fragmented muddle.

Beaconsfield has not done so badly. He has fully opened the conjunctiva, and removed some obvious bits of lens and other material which might or might not be retinal. Repair all that you can see: that's the idea. Mr. Barr notes salvageable iris. Delving delicately with his forceps he dredges up another fragment from the chaos. Yes; there may well be enough. He will try to draw these floating bits of wreckage into something resembling a circle. He will use silken thread fine enough to float upon the air, to stir like a strand of cobweb on one's own filtered breath.

Holding it, noting the natural tremor of his fingers magnified by the lenses into a vast erratic shaking, Mr. Barr wills himself into an almost superhuman steadiness.

"Like this," he says, now immensely affable. His sudden warmth of tone is all the apology he is capable of.

He is an artist, a virtuoso in performance.

"Little bite here, d'you see?" He stands back, so that Beaconsfield may note his perfection of technique, learn, admire, and suffer; Beaconsfield does so.

"And a little bite there. What do you think, Sister?"

"Very nice, Mr. Barr."

"Thank you, Sister." And in the glory of his happiness, his virtuosity, Mr. Barr's own eyes smile down at Norma until she feels dizzy with unfocused longing. "Come along you pair of duffers, bear up!" cries Mr. Barr, turning now to the medical students. "Can't see anything over there. Crowd in, crowd in!"

One of them, the fat one as it happens, turns from his first close view and rushes from the room, his hands pressed to his mouth. The other, willowy Rob Wilding, much more Mr. Barr's type, is better able to control himself.

"We may be wasting our time here, Mr. Wilding," says Mr. Barr. "I should like you to tell us all why."

"Urm," says Rob huskily. His color fluctuates, wan to scarlet and back again. "Possibility of sympathetic reaction, sir," he mutters at last. His voice has an engagingly adolescent timbre.

"Mr. Wilding is correct," says Mr. Barr to Norma, "if telegraphic. Pray continue, Mr. Wilding, if you would be so kind. You may wish to include articles in your answer; I refer to the definite and indefinite variety. Another suture, Sister. Proceed, Mr. Wilding."

By now completely at a loss, Rob looks wildly all round the room for help, and since Mr. Barr is once again bent over his patient, Beaconsfield winks at him, and gives the barest possible, almost imperceptible, nod.

"A sympathetic reaction," says Rob, his eyes fixed on Beaconsfield,

48

"occurs when one eye is injured or infected. Inflammation may arise in the uninjured eye, and all vision be lost as a result."

"So why aren't we taking this eye out right now, then?" demands Mr. Barr.

A dreadful pause. Rob has no idea. The eye looked such a mess that the right answer doesn't occur to him.

"I don't know, sir."

"Surely enucleation would be the safer option?"

"I can't tell, sir."

Mr. Barr sighs theatrically, bemused yet again by the incompetence of all around him. "We are cobbling these poor fragments together, Mr. Wilding, because there is a chance, surprising perhaps, that there may eventually be some vision in this eye. We have no idea whether the object that caused all this damage reached the retina. There's simply too much damage to tell, d'you see?"

"Yes, sir."

"So. While there is such a chance, we do not simply whip out eyes willy-nilly, do we, Mr. Beaconsfield, you see, Wilding? Even Mr. Beaconsfield agrees with me that whipping eyes out willy-nilly is hardly our best plan."

He's so nice when he's in one of his good moods, thinks Norma, and lovingly she admires the long crescent-shaped wrinkles that curve elegantly upwards from the outer edges of his eyes. They're such classy wrinkles, she thinks. She fully believes that he is made of superior clay to herself.

"We will give this eye a chance, Mr. Wilding. Corneal suture, please, Sister."

Slowly the delicate membranes are drawn together in their separate layers.

It's like building work, thinks Rob, struggling to understand his own sensations. He feels the same sense of frustrated mystification as he did at school, when first presented with the idea that chemicals had, so to speak, private lives, versions of themselves occurring naturally, formlessly, in the world. That, say, his mother's copper kettle was not only a well-polished

49

totemic item signifying domestic comfort, but had a sort of family background, its own place reserved at the periodic table; had close or difficult relationships with other substances; had an eerie metallic reality of its own.

So too with the human eye, the mirror of the soul. Essentially it was, of course, an object. It had components. It worked by machinery. It could be taken apart and, up to a point of course, put back together again. Here was Mr. Barr, expertly doing just that, as if he were mending a watch or a bicycle.

And yet it was an eye, which not only saw, which not only gazed, or glanced, or missed things that were important or got things all wrong: it worked both ways, it expressed, it shiningly conveyed emotion, understanding, humanity itself. How could this personal instrument of the spirit have working parts, like a bicycle? Be mended like one? It was very disturbing, this feeling that what Mr. Barr was doing was inherently unlikely.

How could something that both saw and expressed the most delicate heartfelt intangibles be itself so tangible, so mechanical, so . . . bloody?

"Nurse Stoddard," says Mr. Barr cheerily, as he takes another cobweb suture from Norma's ready hand, "kindly look after Mr. Wilding, will you? I believe he needs to sit down."

Helen Stoddard fetches the extra stool from the scrub room, its wheels squeaking on the marble floor, and positions it just in time, as Rob's legs suddenly weaken beneath him.

"Head right down," she says, kindly enough. Though she's not feeling any too well herself. Just a bit sickish. Again. Remembering how sick she was yesterday too a little tremor of fear runs all over her, as she stands looking down at Rob's slim childish neck. Surely everything's all right? She's been late before. Much later than this. And they'd been careful. Of course they had. No, it was absurd to worry, just because you felt a bit sick. Her thoughts go round and round.

Rob looks at the pattern hidden in the floor, the greenish crystalline streaks and angles, and then at various heavyweight fixtures now at eye level, the clamped wheels of the operating table and the theatre trolley, and Sister Holt's thick ankles and hard black shoes.

"Remove the clamp now."

Above him Beaconsfield unscrews the scissorlike apparatus that has stretched the patient's eyelids wide open, and slides it free. The eye will be blind, he is sure. Blind, and painful, and dangerous. He himself would have removed it, got it over with.

"Thank you, Sister."

Rob rises groggily to his feet as the doors swing shut behind Mr. Barr. Beaconsfield and Norma between them begin to pull away the sterile drapes, while Mr. Pym is taking a final blood pressure.

But Barr must have his moments of glory, thinks Beaconsfield bitterly, closing the swollen eyelids with his fingers. And suddenly the patient, until then so terribly wounded, looks almost whole again. His curling golden hair falls back, a little damply. His face has the extreme delicacy of blond infancy, the skin palely transparent, the closed eyes set in circles of brownish bruise. He lies upon the operating table, a wan and beautiful child, as if he had just fallen asleep.

Rob gives a gulp, for now he sees that the patient, up until then a mere potential as far as he was concerned, is really a very little boy.

So does Beaconsfield, hesitating with the sterile eye pad in his hand; so, piercingly, does Helen Stoddard, as she goes to stuff the used drapes into the linen basket; so does Norma, clasping her hands together, Norma Holt, who so longs for a child of her own that sometimes, half aware, half in secret even from herself, she sits in her armchair at home holding a cushion to her lap, so powerful is the need to hold and cherish; so too, with a dreadful lurch at the heart for his own three darlings, does Mr. Pym, family man.

For a brief silent unacknowledged moment everyone in the room sees the same child, with the same sighing clutch of pain.

The moment ends, and the workaday world returns without comment. Mr. Pym and Helen Stoddard gently wheel the child into Recovery, Rob goes to find Tim, and a cup of tea if he possibly can, Norma Holt has one of her private little fits of tears as she washes the used instruments, Beaconsfield writes up the notes and hurries away to do his ward round.

The dramatis personae depart.

POSSESSED OF AN unearthly inner calm and enjoyment of all things, courtesy of Dr. Pym, anesthetist and family man, he simply lay quiet for a long time after he awoke, looking at Student Nurse da Silva, Iris to her friends, who was sitting beside his bed sewing in the lamplight.

Iris was very pleasant to look at. She was nineteen years old, and had a slender velvety face with a small brown mole to the right of her mouth and very dark blue eyes, cast down for the moment over the white linen in her lap. Her hair was black and curly, tied into a fat hard knot at the nape of her neck, but trying to escape all round her face, by means of preliminary tendrils and wispy corkscrews, from the complicated stiffly frilled white cap she wore primly central over her parting. The skirt of her faded blue striped cotton dress, soft with much boiling, fell gracefully, as she sat, almost to the floor; her bibbed apron was brilliantly white and pinned very tightly round her slim waist; her stockings were black.

Iris was, in short, something of an iconic object, a fact of which she herself was pleasantly aware.

Presently she got up to adjust the light over his bed; then she saw his open eye.

"Hello there!" said Iris. Her voice was low, warm, and cockney. "You're awake!"

He thought for a moment of agreeing, but realized that this would involve effort, and decided against.

"Anything hurt anywhere?"

This was a puzzling thing to say, he felt. He considered. Presently it came to him that there was in fact a certain amount of ache about him somewhere. Though it didn't move it was somehow hard to place. It was like the sounds grasshoppers made in the grass, always seeming to come from somewhere else. He had recently spent much of an entire afternoon trying to catch grasshoppers. But he didn't want to catch the ache. He preferred it to stay hidden in the long grass.

"Want a drink?"

He noticed now that he was very thirsty, and that his throat was extraordinarily dry, and sore. He tried to speak, to say Yes, please, but it hurt a little when he tried to clear his throat. The ache hiding in the long grass rustled menacingly.

"Here you go, gorgeous," said Iris. She came closer, and a straw gently poked itself against his parched leathery lips. He could smell her now, Camay mingled with a faint personal smokiness, that worked somehow on his insides, making them flutter with delight. He drew on the straw, and a delicious rush of cool water flooded his wrinkled tongue. He swallowed luxuriously.

"Not too much. More in a minute," said Iris. "Better?"

He nodded. Or rather, he tried to nod. But to his vague surprise his head seemed not to move. Something seemed to be holding him firmly into place. That was very odd, wasn't it? And wasn't the ache a little clearer now, moving in on him, circling a little closer?

"Who are you?" he said. His voice was such a strange croak he had to say it again before she understood. She gave a quick glance round before replying. She leaned forwards, and whispered.

"I'm Iris."

He whispered back.

"What are you doing here?"

"I work here," said Iris.

There was a pause. This, he now understood, was a nurse. Since when had a nurse worked at his house? His heart began at first sluggishly to beat faster, he felt hotter, then discomfort suddenly flamed all over his body, making him twitch and moan.

"Now now!" said Iris, warningly.

But terror was suddenly stronger than heroin.

This wasn't his house! He was in a strange place! Alone! Where was . . . the thought could not be finished. At the barest notion of his mother the ache leapt free, and landed like the tiger it was full on his face, gouging at his eye with its claws.

Reassure the patient and firmly explain why he must remain immobile, says Iris's textbook, without troubling itself to go into details. How firmly, for instance? Jumping up in a panic Iris considers placing her hand pretty firmly over the child's mouth, for she is terribly afraid of the Eye Ward sister, a fearsome old trout called Norris, who insists on her nurses kneeling for prayers at the beginning of each shift, and whose inviolate office, from which she ferociously emerges only at moments of gravest crisis, is just three doors down the corridor from this room, where the patient, poor little sod, lies struggling against the network of straps and bandages that hold his head still to protect Mr. Barr's elegant stitchwork, and shrieking for Mummy at the top of his voice.

Iris gives up thought and opts to reassure the patient by embracing him. Quickly she squeezes her arms under and around him and squashes him tight against the starched bib of her apron, beneath which lie her small girlish breasts and her beating heart.

To her surprise he goes quiet almost straight away. For Mummy, though loving, is not a demonstrative woman, and cuddles are rare delights. Iris's perfume surges all around him, a tendril of her hair tickles his cheek. The child sobs and shudders still, but stays quiet.

Iris feels better too. His cries tore at her, she could hardly bear them. She trembles still, holding him. After a little while she recognizes that she cannot stay a moment longer bent over him like this and breaks several more strict hospital rules by shifting herself sideways until she can lie down beside him on the bed, one arm holding him close. Norris would go berserk, of course. Iris trusts to luck.

Reassure the patient, and firmly explain why he must remain immobile.

Like all her generation Iris has not noticed that all her textbooks refer to male patients, as if women never need nursing. She has not even noticed that there is anything there to notice. She starts firmly explaining, her voice warm and sweet.

"You got to stay still, lovey. 'Til your poor eye gets better. You hurt your eye, remember? You got to stay still, like a little limpet. Like a little limpet stuck to a rock, see?" She strokes his hair, and murmurs into his ear. "There, there, oh you're being such a brave boy, you're a real little soldier, you know that? Your mum's gonna be so proud of you when I tell her how brave you are, yes she is, and she'll be here tomorrow yes she will, lovey, don't you cry, there there . . ."

Rose-tinted fluid is seeping from beneath the bandage covering the right eye.

"That's it, really still, like a little limpet, have you ever seen a limpet?" she goes on wildly. The textbook does not mention the possibility of postoperative tears.

"Limpets look like little umbrellas, see, tiny little pointy seashell umbrellas stuck on the rocks at the seaside, have you ever seen them? Have you ever been to the seaside?"

The boy makes no reply.

"Have you?"

At last he mutters back, into her bosom: "Yes."

"I thought you had. Was it a sandy beach? Or was it pebbles?"

A further pause. "Pebbles." He sniffs. "And sand."

Iris goes on patting his back, caressing his head with her cheek. "I like the sound of the sea, don't you? The waves breaking. D'you like that noise, lovey?"

Very faintly: "Yes."

"And the smell of the sea, and it's so bright! The sky's so blue, and the sea's so blue, nearly the same but not the same, you can just see where they meet, far away, and if you're lucky you can see a sail, a tiny little white sail on the horizon, where there's a boat far out on the water," says Iris, and she can feel him loosening in the circle of her arms, every word seems to soften him. She can feel him listening. His eye is closed.

Iris closes her own eyes, and goes on softly whispering, slower and slower: "And the sun glitters on the water, and you hear the waves breaking . . . And you can hear that noise people make walking on the pebbles, crunch crunch crunch . . . And there are children calling and laughing . . . and dogs barking . . . and the seagulls calling . . ."

Winchelsea the month before: he is putting the little paper Union Jack on the topmost sandy tower of his castle.

Iris herself is in Southend in 1938, which was the last time her parents and brother and sister all went to the seaside together. She is six years old, and her mother smiles at her from beneath the brim of her shady straw hat, which has a blue stripe and a dark blue ribbon round the crown.

". . . and when the tide's right out you go down to the sea, to the water, and you dip your fingers into the foam. And it's all cold, and you taste it, and it's all salty, and it's nice and it's nasty both at once, and you dig your toes into the sand, gritty, and soft, and wet . . . and your footprints walk after you, wherever you go . . ."

Someone walks noisily down the corridor outside and Iris gasps and startles. But the child is fast asleep. Cautiously Iris rises, climbs very carefully off the bed and brushes her skirts down.

She feels very strange, upset and yearning and at the same time peaceful inside. She remembers the hat with wonder; it's a real memory, she is sure, as vivid as if she had seen her mother in it yesterday. She feels as if she's really just seen her mother, visited her in the past, as in time-traveling, which is painful as well as wonderful, for Iris's mother did not survive the war.

We both want our mothers, thinks Iris as she looks at the bed. She dries her eyes against her short sleeve, and stoops to pick up her sewing from beneath the bed. As she rises someone turns the door handle from the other side, and the door creaks open. Norris, lumme, that was lucky! If she'd been two shakes earlier . . .

But it is not Norris. It's a boy. A medical student.

"Hello," says Rob Wilding, huskily.

"Hello."

Awkwardly they stare at each other. Neither has yet developed a professional manner. For a moment, feeling lost, they fall into other earlier patterns of behavior, and become teenagers helplessly eyeing one another; the bus stops of Iris's schooldays gave her much experience of this, while Rob, whose adolescence was spent immured in the countryside with several hundred other boys, can only come up with the occasional embarrassments of being forced to attempt conversation with his mother's friends' various schoolgirl daughters.

Iris is thus first to recover. She whispers: "You with Mr. Barr?"

Rob nods. He turns his eyes to the bed. All afternoon the sudden revelation of the injured child, the piercing surprise beneath the sterile drapes, has recurred to him, making him feel so miserably upset that he has begun to wonder once more whether he is really cut out to be a doctor at all. Only when he was putting on his coat to go home had it occurred to him that as a member of the hospital, albeit of the humblest variety, he could simply turn up on the Eye Ward and see how the kid was; he recognized that this might make him feel better in some way, or on the other hand usefully, decisively, worse.

56

"How is he?"

"Not too bad," says Iris.

"Good. Good." Rob turns, as if to leave.

"I was in Theatres," he says, "so I thought I'd come and see how he was." His fingers discover a loosely dangling button on his short white coat, and twiddle with it. Iris sits down. The soft worn skirt falls into its graceful womanly folds. There is, Rob notices, another chair on the other side of the bed. For a moment, still turned toward the door, still twiddling his button, he hesitates. Then he crosses the floor and sits down too.

Poor kid, he thinks, but he is aware already that whatever it was that so unmanned him in Theatre Two hardly hurts at all anymore. Swiftly he forgets that it ever had. He is here from professional curiosity, he decides. He is, after all, a keen and successful student, one of the brightest of his year.

"Are you staying in here with him?" he asks, keenly.

"Yeah. Specialing him. Just for tonight."

Rob looks down at the sepia-stained bandages.

"Still asleep."

"Nah, he woke up. Poor mite. Didn't half carry on."

Rob raises his eyes to look across at her. His first clear sight of the little mole beside her lips gives him a sudden explosive sensation within. The mole is somehow a shock. He can't cope with it at all. He turns quickly back at the patient again. But the mole seems to have a magnetic power. He wants another look at it. Just a quick look. Somehow he doesn't quite dare.

"He looks very peaceful now," he says. Timidly he raises his eyes. Emotion then seems almost to roar inside him, impossible to assimilate: for the beautiful dark eyes that meet his are full of tears. As he watches one sparkling diamond drop gathers on the thick lower lashes, trembles there for an instant, and falls onto the petal-like skin of her cheek.

"Sorry," says Iris. She doesn't want him thinking her soppily unprofessional. Firmly she pushes away her mother's blue-striped hat, the shaded smile.

"I got a little brother his age," she says, and Rob, all sympathy, nods, his heart beating fast with the early pangs of love.

Of this first real meeting, this first exchange of helpless glances, both will have vivid and tender memories; to come are first kisses, first declarations, first passionate wildly exciting acts of physical love, but already, within two minutes, Iris, of all the many lies she will tell Rob in the future, has recklessly ventured on the first.

"Just his age," she says, and reaching out she touches the child's pale cheek.

HE WAS STILL so very drowsy. He knew something very bad had happened, but could not for the moment remember what it had been.

"Mummy . . ."

"I'm here, dear."

But there was something disturbing about her, something wrong with her face, with her eyes. He struggled to rise, and then remembered that he was not allowed to move any more, since the bad thing had happened.

"Mummy!"

"Don't try to move, old chap," said a funny croaky voice from the other side of his bed.

"Daddy?"

"The doctor says you need to keep quite still, still as you can," the croaky voice went on.

"Is it hurting much, lovey?" Mummy's voice, also croaky.

He saw then that her face was rendered unfamiliar by her anguish. He recognized that the very bad thing had been done to her, and that he himself had done it. His body flushed all over with guilt.

"Mummy. I'm really, really sorry."

For, despite its gory unlikeliness, it was an accident his mother had foreseen. She had foreseen so many, though. Looking on the black side was practically her hobby.

HER NAME WAS Ruby. She was a thin dark pretty woman, posthumous only child of a handsome young second-generation refugee from some obscure and poverty-stricken tract of northern Latvia. In marrying him Ruby's mother had infuriated her own family, while his, in a welter of savage and theatrical Slavonic curses, had vowed never to speak to him again, a vow all the same undertaken in the heat of various moments; not meant.

But Ruby's father had suddenly developed appendicitis and septicemia after the operation, and died two days later, still unspoken to, four months before Ruby was born.

Ruby's mother was married again, scarcely a year later, to a red-haired genial Irishman, a Catholic who liked a drink. Ruby, dark-haired and aquiline in a growing family of snub-nosed Irish half-siblings, knew all the outsider's aloof and fragile pride, longing to be part of the whole, and at the same time doing all she could to distance herself, for her difference was all she had.

Cleverness at school didn't count, for her mother was of the opinion that all such cleverness was really a form of showing off. Ruby's resemblance to her first husband did not please Ruby's mother. She regretted the whole thing, one way and another, and refused Ruby leave to so much as walk down the street where her yearning Latvian grandmother still lived.

Ruby complied. Only once had she disobeyed an express command of her mother's. Sent to the corner shop aged eight to buy margarine, she had bought butter, for the price, for some reason, had been less. She had expected her mother to be mildly pleased with her business acumen.

Ruby's mother was a small but powerfully built woman, much beset by money worries, too many children, and a fondness for drink she had quickly learned from her second husband. Buying butter when you were sent for margarine summed up Ruby's character all too well, she felt. It was all one with giving yourself airs, and being teacher's pet, and sitting about reading when you could be helping out with the little ones. Ruby's mother saw red; she took the pat of butter, tore open the neat waxed paper, and after pursuing Ruby, bellowing with rage, up the stairs, held her eldest child down with one hand whilst rubbing the butter hard into her hair with the other.

"That'll learn you to do as you're told!" she had roared, over Ruby's screams. And indeed it had.

Leaving school without fuss at fourteen Ruby meekly began work with her stepfather, who was helping to run a furniture business in White-chapel. This involved learning the rudiments of French-polishing as well as certain secret though unsubtle furniture-bashing techniques designed to produce the appearance of antiquity.

Luckily Ruby was so useless at these tasks that she was soon allowed to work in a factory instead, where she remained, crouched over a sew-ing machine in a sweatshop full of other girls crouched over sewing machines, until Hitler invaded Poland.

By then Ruby had been handing over her pay packet to her mother for thirteen years. As well as paying rent she did housework, childcare, shopping, cooking, and cleaning, for the pub called more forcefully to Ruby's mother with every succeeding year. In her heart, well-hidden especially from herself, Ruby resented nearly every aspect of all these essentially feminine tasks. At the same time, in order to demonstrate to the rest of her family how different and superior she was, she had trained herself over the years to be an efficient housekeeper, an authoritative nanny, a thrifty shopper, a reliable cook, an assiduous cleaner. She was, in short, the family nag.

Sometimes Ruby lay awake at night gripped by despair. The books she read and the films she saw showed her women in high heels rearrang-ing flowers in polished hallways; Mrs. Miniver, for example, though tired from her afternoon shopping, still took the time to appreciate the glowing autumnal beauty of the chrysanthemums she had bought on the way home from the library, before ringing for tea.

Ruby longed to be able to come home and ring for tea, though she knew her place in the world decreed that she would always be the one in the kitchen, being rung at. But was it still too much to ask that com-ing home worn out from a day spent machining quilted silk onto the lapels of gentlemen's dressing gowns destined for the cheaper end of the department store market, she might make and drink her own tea in peace, without, for example, any of her younger brothers publicly, audibly, squeezing their spots before the mirror over the fireplace?

Nor would Mrs. Miniver's younger sisters, had she been cursed with any, have swanned off to work leaving a batch of blood-stained drawers soaking in the kitchen washing-up bowl, all set about with dirty crockery. Mrs. Miniver, confronted with such a sight after a particularly exhausting spell at the library or out choosing bouquets would probably have fainted dead away on the lino, silly bag, thought Ruby, grimly peeling potatoes round the vile bowlful on the evening in question.

For Ruby partly admired her sisters' insouciance. All of them had boyfriends, all of the time. They shrieked and laughed and argued, they slammed the front door behind them and recklessly went down to the pub, or out dancing, leaving teacups smudged with sticky lipstick all over the kitchen table.

"Come with us, Rube!"

But Ruby did not like pubs. She didn't like being looked at. She was afraid of being looked over. And overlooked. She went on doing the washing up, resentfully, enviously, and drugged herself to sleep every night with Edgar Wallace, Hugh Walpole, and Mary Webb.

Hitler's invasion of Poland caused much talk amid the sewing machines. The girl who sat next to Ruby, whose name was Hilda, announced that when Hitler arrived in London she, Hilda, planned to prise open the sweatshop window, lug over her heavyweight sewing machine, and chuck it out onto the heads of the invading soldiery as they passed by below.

Everyone was very impressed with this show of purpose and several other girls tried their strength on their Singers, promising to join her at the window when the time came. Ruby did not. She felt pretty sure German soldiers weren't going to stand about letting girls throw sewing machines at their heads. It sounded like a waste of sewing machines to Ruby. And they would shoot back; with tank guns.

"I'm not gonna do that," said Ruby. "I'm not gonna sit about waiting for 'em."

"What you gonna do then, Rube, join the army?" jeered Hilda.

"Yes," said Ruby. Who until that very moment had not so much as briefly entertained the idea. However as soon as Hilda spoke the words

Ruby realized that Hitler had given her the perfect reason to escape from her mother, from her entire family in fact, as well as the perfect place to escape to.

True it would be another form of bondage, but it would be different, and it would, in its way, be safe and organized. It seemed like a good bet to Ruby, who had learned long ago not to take chances, or rely on initiative, especially her own. So without telling anyone she slipped away to the recruitment office after work one day, and signed up to join, not the army, but the WAAF, fearful but rejoicing all the way home, because she knew that there was nothing her mother could do to get her out of it.

For a year or so Ruby was shuffled to and fro between various uncomfortable and often extremely remote training camps. But then someone noticed that she had brains. She was swiftly taught to type, and given office work.

Office work, that transcendent goal of her adolescence! Work requiring and resulting in clean fingers had seemed the ultimate luxury, from the oily depths of her stepfather's French-polishing shed, the sewing machine merely an unkindly ironic answer to such longings; but in an actual office, carpeted! inhabited by toffs! who thanked her politely when she brought in their letters! she was extravagantly happy, for the first time in her life.

Ruby worked as hard as she could, and soon she was promoted. She nipped about smartly, carrying a briefcase. She wrote reports, summarizing those of others, and in that style most difficult to achieve, that giving the effect of spoken English. Her own speech altered swiftly; she was a gifted mimic, and without consciously trying to easily acquired the argot of her fellow workers, their squashed vowels, their murmured greetings, their expressions.

"Oh, top hole, sir! Good show!"

It was more protective coloring than social climbing; Ruby had disliked feeling conspicuous. Speaking nicely, she blended in more. Soon she was promoted again. Never in her life before had Ruby been able to look down on other people; now it was officially required. Underlings jumped guiltily when she came in unexpectedly, and hid their cigarettes; they saluted her, and addressed her with careful circumspection.

Ruby began going to parties, and dances, and shows.

She was no longer dumb with shyness, but she was still virginal and prudish, narrow-minded and easily shocked. She thought homosexuality a crime passing belief. She disapproved of sex before marriage, and thought that the best contraception was No, though in fact she found the idea of sex even after marriage pretty disgusting, and frightening, and so had no trouble herself with contraception of any kind.

These were widespread attitudes at the time, especially for women of the respectable working classes, to which (though her mother had risked even this precarious status by getting drunk in Irish bars) Ruby belonged. But the war had mixed up a great many of the usual signals between the classes, between the sexes.

Girls who had been to public schools now saluted Ruby and called her Ma'am. She went dutch with girls called Fiona who knew how to play tennis. She had drinks with men whose fathers were in the professions, who had been to university, who had had piano lessons and their own bicycles. Every week she sent money home to her mother, who very occasionally wrote back, in her Board school print, on postcards Ruby quickly burnt.

Rube thanks for yr. last mrs s got bombed out her boys in africa yr affect. Mum

All sorts of people now accepted her for what she seemed to be, middle class, educated, a cut above themselves. But at the time all sorts of people were in constant danger; they were far from home, or homeless, or displaced. To such people Ruby's timid prudishness seemed like sensitivity, her cool manner proud reserve, her narrow-mindedness purity, her prejudices the commonsense values of a vanishing and better world.

One of them married her.

On Ruby's part, it was a failure of nerve. She had for some time suspected herself to be one of nature's spinsters. Sexual instinct in her was not so strong that she could not happily subdue it, placating it perfectly well with Hollywood, or Ethel M. Dell. But the end of the war meant the end of Ruby's official superiority. With hundreds of thousands of men awaiting demobbing Ruby knew herself to be on shaky ground as an office worker at all.

The sewing machine, even the mucky French-polishing shed, beckoned. Besides, her younger half-sisters were all married by then, one of them even on a second husband, courtesy of the Luftwaffe; her mother was pleased with them all and pleased by her grandchildren, and deep within her Ruby still hoped that one day she too would be able to please her mother.

She sent in her papers, and married Ted. For a while, renting three pleasant rooms in a house in Stoke Newington, Ruby played at being Mrs. Miniver. True, she had no one to whom she could ring for tea. But her floors were polished, her kitchen immaculate, and her curtains, thanks to her old skills on a sewing machine, fashionably ruffled and pleated. There was always a floral arrangement of some kind, set on a hand-crocheted doily, in the very middle of the dining table, which Ruby kept well polished with spit and cigarette ash.

It was here, after three years, that the extensive system of headaches and mysterious stomach pains Ruby employed to keep her husband's grosser requirements more or less at bay finally failed her, and she got pregnant. Everyone was very pleased with her, even, at last, her mother. Resignedly she put the doilies aside and began crocheting bootees instead.

But privately Ruby rather hoped she would die in childbirth, so long as it didn't hurt too much. She knew about babies. They screamed all day and all night, they wore stinking wet nappies you had to scrape out and leave to soak in malodorous buckets under the kitchen table, they spewed curdled messes all down your front and got sticky eyes and ulcerated bottoms.

Ruby knew she hated babies. It was all the more of a surprise, therefore, when the midwife first handed her her own son, nicely washed and cozily wrapped in a clean white hospital blanket, and Ruby looked into his little face, and saw, not her husband's likeness, but her own. Her own infant face, familiar from mirrors of long, long ago: an old friend; impish, intelligent, and yet more beautiful than an autumn chrysanthemum, purer and cleaner than the purest cleanest kitchen on this earth. And she, Ruby, was simply being given this extraordinary piece of perfection, was being allowed to take it home, and keep it, forever!

Presently, Ted was promoted to a management job in his firm's latest venture, a zip factory newly built in the countryside just outside London, and he and Ruby put down a deposit on a house, in one of the estates then springing up in the area. Ruby could not resist queening it a bit over her sisters then. Not just a husband in management, not just a fine sturdy little boy, but a whole new house in the country! With garage! "Of course we really don't need a car just yet," Ruby wrote to her sisters.

With what was left of her wartime social daring she joined the Women's Institute, sitting for the most part shyly wordless at the back, while other women, or ladies, and sometimes even Ladies, demonstrated various posh Miniverish mysteries such as tapestry or fruit bottling.

Within months Ruby owned her own vacuum cleaner, a weighty cylinder of solid electrical modernity, with facings of bright steel and an enormous length of heavy but flexible green and gray tubing, while her sisters had to make do with dented old carpet sweepers at best; and within the year, oh masterstroke! Ruby's husband had bought her a washing machine. Ruby's sisters wheeled their wash in battered old prams to local laundries full of the sweaty stink of other people's intimate grime, and dirty swimming floors, and steam, and raucous talk, and coarse laughter; Ruby thought about them with the most complete satisfaction she was capable of every time she set herself to dragging her very own clean new washing machine out of the cupboard under the stairs where it was normally housed and into the kitchen.

No easy task: like the vacuum cleaner Ruby's washing machine was a particularly solid item, built to last, as perhaps befitted such a significant symbol of domestic progress. Its outer casing of thick cream colored enamel stood almost chest high, and if you lifted off the heavy circular lid, you could watch its mighty single upright blade swinging to and fro in majestic slow motion, sloshing your clothes clean with a heavyweight turn of suds and water and a deep sonorous electrical hum.

Its fully electric detachable mangle got your sheets so smooth, Ruby wrote with not entirely unconscious malice to each of her sisters in turn, that once you'd hung them up to dry, outside, on your own back garden washing line in the fresh country air, you barely had to iron them at all.

Early every morning Ted walked out of the housing estate and across the open field beside it to a deep wooded lane, at the end of which, despite his managerial suit and tie, he caught the works' bus. It was a lovely walk in summer, with the dew, and the birds singing, and little pink flowers everywhere. Looking back at it he would one day realize that this peaceful start to the day had been one of the reasons that first year in the new house had been the happiest of his life.

"I'M REALLY, REALLY sorry, Mummy," says Ruby's child George, and a tear trickles out of his uninjured eye.

"There, there," says Ruby, and wipes it away gently enough. But in her heart she knows he has spoilt himself. He is no longer the perfect beautiful thing that he was, that she had made. Wherever they go now strangers will stare not at his beauty but at his disfigurement. Strangers will know at a glance that she has failed to protect him. He is a badge of failure pinned to her breast. Strangers will know, and as for her sisters—oh, how they will sympathize, how kind they will be to her! Their children, plain dullards all, are still whole. Only her own perfect child has messed himself up. She cannot forgive him. She cannot forgive herself.

"There there," says Ruby, and the false tenderness in her voice is so immediately apparent to him, and so painful, that he makes frantic and soon effective efforts to pretend to himself that he has noticed nothing. He pretends also to be soothed, in order to soothe her. The long process of his deeper injury has begun.

SYLVIA AND THE BEAR TOO FAR, 1995

ON THEIR WAY BACK from a rather difficult weekend trip to stay with Adam's mother, on the occasion of her eighty-seventh birthday, Adam, Sylvia, and baby Clio were forced to stop at a motorway service station.

For while Adam, he claimed, could and, for reasons of parental strategy, *should* completely ignore Clio's violent shrieks and plunges, Sylvia could not. It had taken several more miles, and a certain amount of shrieking on her own part, in truth only partly down to the difficulty of making herself heard over Clio, to persuade Adam to pull over into the slow lane at the next service sign.

"It's all right for him: he's as deaf as his old mum," thought Sylvia unkindly, maddened not only by Adam's as-usual good-humored imperturbability, but by the earlier lengthy provocation of two whole days spent shouting everything twice, when mysteriously enough the old lady had seemed to have no trouble taking in anything said by Adam or by Clio's big-boned doppelganger the endlessly garrulous and moustachioed Aunt Geraldine.

Deaf as his sodding old mum, thought Sylvia, as best she could over Clio's fulminating roars.

"Please, Adam! Turn off! Please!"

And then, quieted immediately by the bright lights and colors of the service station, Clio had fought her way out of Sylvia's arms on the way to the Ladies and made one of her novel and still-precarious runs right into the shop, stopping short, apparently thunderstruck, at the toddler-high profusion of soft toy animals near the cash desk, all lurid nylon fur and flat plastic eyes. She had gently taken the nearest bear-shaped object, bright mauve and cheaply shaggy, into her hands, and bent her whole upper body forwards and sideways in a beautiful curving movement, as if in a dance, and stood there with her head on one side and the toy pressed to her cheek, her eyes closed in pleasure.

But of course she can't be acting, can she, thought Sylvia watching all this in perplexity. She's not demonstrating something; she's just feeling it. It's not her fault it looked so, well, so obvious: like someone miming babyish delight. It *was* babyish delight. And here am I feeling the same exasperated boredom I'd feel at a grown-up doing it. I just automatically think ill of her, that's what it is.

At the same time her heart almost hurt with pity: poor little baby, loving such dross!

"You've got much nicer ones at home," she had said aloud.

Adam caught up, with the pushchair and the big soft bagful of baby requisites, and instantly made the small crooning noise adults make on being touched by babyish antics: "Ts-aw. Look at her. Shall we get it for her?"

Sylvia hesitated. "She's got so many already, all sorts of fluffy stuff."

"Another one won't hurt, then, will it?" And in the queue he had said, "They're all alive, to her, d'you remember that feeling? The whole shelf-full, furry animals all alive."

And all waiting and all fearful, Sylvia thought, with the baby's own fears. The little purple bear had looked at Clio, and spoken to her, asking for her love. It had loved her first, Sylvia saw.

"No, it's all right," she had said as they reached the counter. "It's all right, I'll get it."

To the self-service café, Sylvia carrying the baby, the baby carrying the bear.

It was an emergency, Sylvia imagined herself saying, defensively, as if to someone mercilessly quizzing her about this bear-too-far. Yes cheap import, yes sweat-shopped. Vile. Purple. Yes. I know. But it was an emergency . . . and then realized what she was doing. Honestly, who the hell was going to chastise her for buying her own baby a present? Whose business was it anyway but her own?

68

It was as if, when she was doing anything with and for Clio, there was always an audience present somehow. A huge critical audience of better mothers, a faceless stadiumful of them, all in harsh judgment of every single move. They knew best. They knew how. And they knew you were crap. Sometimes you did something they liked, say, you fed the baby something carefully nourishing perhaps, and the baby liked it and ate at least some of it, and then they let you feel a slight lessening of their otherwise implacable disapproval. But usually the baby spat it out, or screamed until you gave in and let her have the cake icing, and then you could feel the monstrous weight of their nagging thousand-fold contempt.

After all they knew. Your failings. Your secrets. Your secret secret secret . . . but here Sylvia's thought shied away. It had been a long time since she had directly acknowledged a lack of love. For a slightly dizzy moment, holding Clio in the queue for Hot Beverages, she felt the shying away as a strange dip in her awareness, as a rushing feeling of emptiness within.

Then she remembered Clio needed a high chair, and that one would need antiseptic wipes to properly scour its table, and doubted there were any left in the baby bag, and unzipped it to see, and so was able to move herself away from danger with hardly any effort at all.

WILL AND THE FOUNDLING, 1995

THERE WERE OTHER BOXES, of course. Two albums of America, the lost world. His mother on the long smart white front porch of the house in Virginia, his father caressing the sleek aeronautic flank of a 1955 Studebaker. Coming back to Britain in 1960 they had actually shipped this very car home with them. It had not fitted into the bungalow's garage; for years Joe had had to leave the doors propped open, wedged into place with bricks.

"Why did you do it anyway? Must have cost a fortune."

Annie smiled. So far it was one of her good days. "Things were so different then. You forget how different. There weren't that many cars around at all. Let alone ones we could afford. People didn't have cars the way they do now, it was cheaper to bring the Studie back. Anyway we loved it."

"Yeah . . ." Will could remember the Studebaker. "That long front seat, like a sofa," he said. And he remembered the little silver airplane, like a figurehead, in superb constant flight on the long broad green bonnet, the special deep majestic note of the engine, the immense solidity of door and window and glossy wooden dash.

And people everywhere turning their heads for another look as they sailed by, people waving; even then, he thought, he had understood that the Studebaker was a great deal more than just a car.

If you had sat as a child between your mum and dad, cozy and proud on the front seat of a 1955 Studebaker, he thought, you were marked for life. You had known heedless luxury. You had inhabited grandeur. You could practically claim American citizenship. "I cried when we sold it," he said, remembering.

"So did I," said Annie. "It was like having your dog put down. All those years we kept it. Eaten up with rust, it was. And no spare parts, of course. I think your dad shed a tear or two as well. I mean, driving away from the scrapyard leaving it there! Felt awful. Especially for him. He hadn't wanted to come back at all, not really."

From your own wooden porch-fronted house set in acres of open space, and your great sleek beast of an American car, to a gimcrack housing estate bungalow, and a Morris Traveller; you could see his point, thought Will.

"But you were homesick," he said.

"Well, yes . . ." Annie turned the page of the album. Black and white, deckle-edged, she sat on a beach in South Carolina, her dark painted lips smiling. Crying the next minute, she remembered.

"Oh Joe, I'm so hot!" Lying on their bed in the motel, crying with discomfort. And dread, of course. The first few dark spots in her knickers. Not red. Rusty brown. Old blood. She hadn't told him yet.

Temperature in the high nineties. Her fingers so swollen. Joe going to the great tall fridge in the motel reception, filling the icebucket to soak her hand in, so they could get her rings off in time.

Peeing, that was worst. Every time you hardly dared look. Sometimes there was nothing. And you thought, perhaps this time it will be all right after all. But then the time after, was that a tinge, there? And you'd be awake all night, scared to get up, scared to turn over in bed.

All those children, she thought, as she had thought so many times over the years. Four of them. All my boy's brothers and sisters. Though perhaps if they had lived Will himself would never have been born, so how could she wish for that?

Just 'cos his wife's homesick, Will was thinking. He gives up everything he wants, everything he's achieved, and goes back to the country that's done nothing for him, where his spirit, expanding perhaps in the great exhilarating openness of America, must contract again to fit into Home Counties lower management, the housing estate, and the Morris Minor van.

71

How could she have let him do it? It hadn't just been the material things they had said goodbye to. It was enterprise, it was zest, it was youth itself, he thought, turning the pages between America and Home. There they were young and free, roaring off into the black and white sunset in that totemic automobile; and here they were Mum and Dad, in slippers, in the faded early colors of the late Sixties, wan beiges and anemic blues, middle-aged, bungaloid.

"Had to come home," said Annie. Her voice had a certain strain to it. Something was hurting her, Will thought, looking at her. And she wasn't due any more dope for nearly an hour.

"You ok, Mum?"

"I said to him, You stay here, Joe, but I've got to go home, if I lose another baby I'll just die. And I was right, see? Soon as we got home everything was all right." Her eyes flickered strangely; and then she was gone.

Mum?

Will stood up. He held his breath. He reached out, and touched her shoulder.

"Mum?"

She made no reply, but breathed out suddenly, strongly. Was she asleep?

Or was this it?

Unconsciously Will gave a little whimper of distress. He should what, phone the doctor? Or Susan? He reached his hand out and touched her warm cheek. She opened her eyes and smiled at him.

"All right?" she said.

He could not reply. But she was beyond noticing, he thought. "So sleepy," she said, and closed her eyes again. Her breathing sounded completely normal.

Shakily Will sat back down again, and rubbed his face hard all over in his hands. He felt like something washed up on shore after a storm at sea, he thought, all limp and battered. Then he remembered today's small miracle: he had heard from his agent. A possible Possible. Another wildlife voice-over thing. Something to do with wallabies, he had gathered. Still. It was work. And he could be there and back in a day; he would ask Mrs. Allbright, or that other one from two doors down. To Mum-sit. Death-sit.

So get off your arse, he told himself sternly, and get something done.

She still looked peaceful, surrounded by her little scattered pictures of the past. Gently he began to gather up the photographs, scooping them back in the box for another time. Should there be one. As he picked up the album on Annie's lap a folded piece of paper fell out of it. He picked it up, to slide it back in where it belonged, but it slipped from his fingers and fell onto the carpet.

Kneeling to retrieve it he was struck by its ancient-document feel. He opened it, and saw with surprise that it was his father's birth certificate. Should put that in the drawer with the others, he thought, and then suddenly held his breath. He read the thing again, exclaimed aloud.

"What the . . . ?"

It wasn't a birth certificate at all. It just looked like one. This certified that William Joseph Keane, and his wife Isobel Maria Keane, née Rivers —Grandpa, Nanna—were officially adopting a male infant, aged approximately six weeks, from St. Thomas's Church of England Children's Home, Streatham, on October 12, 1921, witness this my hand.

"Jesus!"

A nameless baby; in brackets where the child's original surname should have been was the word *foundling*. Will felt suddenly very cold, and shiftingly sick within. He sat back on his heels, and moving bars of black and yellow arose before his puzzled eyes, and then, from some distance, as if his brain had somehow disconnected itself and floated away all by itself, he seemed to hear his own thought, implying without urgency that this was dizziness, and that he was falling, gently, softly.

After this, there was a short comfortable sleep, perfectly warm and cozy, until the floor began abruptly to harden beneath cheek and hip-bone, turned unfriendly again.

Fainted!

Well, that was odd. Wasn't it? Or perhaps not. Watching your mum die, perhaps people often fainted when they were doing that, all by themselves. Ugh, sweaty, sickish now. Slowly, on hands and knees, Will gathered himself together. Washed ashore. Take a few breaths, he told himself. Steady. There: better already.

Sitting back in the chair for a few moments more he remembered the adoption certificate. It lay looking up at him from the carpet, inscrutable. Will left it there while he made his way cautiously to the kitchen, made himself a cup of sugary tea, and sat slumped over it trying to think.

Nanna and Grandpa. He could hardly remember them. Grandpa was a collarless shirt with a vest showing through at the top, he was thick webbing braces holding up his trousers, he was carrots pulled from the soil by their feathery tops. Grandpa had rinsed them off beneath the allotment tap, and given them back to Will to crunch up then and there. Nanna crouched to hold a sheet of newspaper against the fireplace to get the fire going, and the fire behind it sucked at the paper angrily, until a great yellow flower of flame abruptly opened in the middle, and Nanna jumped back with a little squawk of laughter.

He had been fond, he realized, of these small memories. And all the time they hadn't been Grandpa and Nanna at all; not really. They had given his father Joe their name. And Joe had, it seemed, merely shrugged, and passed it on. William Joseph Keane: three names, in fact. And had said not a word.

Did Annie know? And if she had, why hadn't she said anything either, didn't he have some sort of right to know?

It was, he thought, somehow typical of himself, to find out that he was a foundling's child. Not for him the shapely and recognizable drama of discovering that he had been adopted; trust me, he thought vaguely, to come up with finding out *Dad* had! Sort of secondhand. And hopelessly old news, of course. No chance to question the old man now. What were you supposed to feel about it, anyway?

I don't even know if it actually feels important, Will thought. People in books and films always knew what they were feeling. Other people knew. Someone like Sylvia, she always knew what she was feeling. She only felt sensible feelings and she knew what they were. That was one of the reasons she was such a successful person.

He remembered the wallaby script, and that he could maybe take a quick look at it while his mother slept. So he finished his tea, and went to his computer, and began.

ROB AND IRIS ON THE TRAIN, 1954

Before announcing their engagement Rob and Iris journeyed down to the West Country, to the coastal village where Rob's parents lived. They went by train. Most of the time they had a compartment to themselves. Once at Bath someone opened the sliding door and made to enter, but Rob and Iris began at once to exchange a long kiss, and the door was quickly closed again; they broke off laughing, though not for long.

Iris wore: a navy blue pencil skirt and matching jacket of fine soft wool, made by (and for) her elder sister, who worked in the fabric department of a large store in Oxford Street; a hat of exactly matching shade, with a brief frill of black lace, which could be drawn down over her eyes; stockings with seams, held up by suspender belt; three inch heels, black, which made her perilously close to Rob's own height; and a set of prewar underwear of embroidered honey-colored crepe de chine, procured illegally, and of a petal-smoothness and glossy sheen very like that of Iris's own white skin.

Rob wore: his suit. He had no other. He had grown since it was bought for him, in his first year at university, and the sleeves were too short. It was a dark blue pinstripe. He wore also a broad-brimmed hat, and carried a raincoat, which, like his shoes, black Oxfords once the property of his father, and his heavy cotton underwear, and his ex-Army shirt, were all, like Iris's crepe de chine lingerie, older than he was himself.

Within these venerable clothes Rob and Iris glowed with youthful fresh desires. Once they had seen off the would-be fellow traveler at Bath they went on kissing anyway. Sometimes Iris thought that kissing

Rob was like some extra food and drink to her. It was refreshment, of the deepest kind. The curves of his mouth entranced her.

They were not lovers, technically. Fear kept them back. Iris, Rob knew, was a virgin, as he was himself. Whilst he felt often that if he did not instantly make love to Iris he might actually drop dead or burst from sheer thwartedness he was unable, for the moment, to imagine how he could possibly subject them both to contraception.

He knew about condoms, of course, and that you were only supposed to put them on once you were ready. But when, even in imagination, he reached this stage of readiness, he was aware that any further stimulation—Iris, say, undoing one further button on her blouse— would cause him to climax immediately. And then what? He'd be standing there—for some reason he never pictured this scene actually happening in a bedroom, but only in some non-specific imaginary sitting room, with armchairs—standing there in front of Iris, the adored, the unbelievably beautiful, clutching himself all wilted and hung about with what would essentially be a small slimy bagful of jism, and she would see this. Iris, who had almost certainly never seen an erection before, let alone a drooping one encased in wrinkled rubber!

No. No, it couldn't be done. Obviously there were other ways. You could pull yourself out, apparently. You'd be lying there (again, for reasons Rob could not clarify, particularly as he was not fully conscious of what he was imagining anyway, lying there on the carpet between the armchairs of your imaginary sitting-room of love), having what the newspapers of the time always referred to as Intimacy with Iris, actually doing it, and yet at the same time you were somehow supposed to be able to judge when you were about to come—as if you wouldn't have come immediately anyway, when she undid that first button—and abruptly fling yourself away sideways and backwards, as if she suddenly had live electricity down there, as if she'd stung you, and how could you do that without grunting and gasping, without ferocious effort of body and mind, without wrenching? Coitus interruptus: wrenching yourself out.

And if I've never done it before, how am I going to know when I'm going to come anyway?

He was constrained, too, by a sense of what was proper. It would be wrong to make love to Iris, unless they were officially engaged. Morally wrong. They would both, he knew, feel ashamed afterwards. Loving Iris also meant respecting her. Rob had been taught such notions all his life, and saw no reason to doubt them; they explained, perhaps, the uncomfortable and relentlessly inappropriate furnishings of his erotic imagination.

But above all, he was afraid of hurting her, of involuntarily carrying out grievous vaginal harm. He had read up one or two completely horrifying cases. When puncturing the hymen (and you did that with your prick! Wouldn't it hurt you as well? It sounded awful! The slow stretching first, and then the sudden tearing of hidden inner tissues!) had at the same time punctured blood vessels of such consequence, and so hard to get at for compressing-the-wound purposes (Oh, God!) that the poor girls involved had practically bled to death! Had gushed pints, straight out of their . . .

Here Rob's imagination, for once allowing him to picture a bed, had shown him also his own panicking hand, thrust wrist-deep into Iris and holding back torrents of blood, a picture so vile that he had shut his mind to it as hard as he could, and consequently cracked the tea cup he happened to be holding at the time.

The pain had also occurred to Iris.

"Dunnit hurt?" she had asked her sister Jo. Jo was seven years the elder, and lived a rackety if entirely discreet life in a flat in Camden Town.

"Not if you've got any sense," said Jo.

"How d'you mean?"

"It hurts if you don't really want to. If you want to, it won't hurt."

"But how do you know beforehand?"

Jo had to light a cigarette, thinking out how to answer that one. Privately she did not in the least want her baby sister getting up to this sort of lark. But the kid was nearly twenty after all.

"D'you think we ought to wait until we're married?"

"Do you?"

"I don't know," said Iris. "I don't want him to think I'm easy. Suppose he goes off me once we've done it?"

"Better he went off you before you married him than after," said Jo. "What's the point marrying someone who might go off you?"

"He won't," said Iris.

"May as well wait then."

"But I sort of . . . don't want to. You know."

It was hard for Jo, who had passed this particular barrier so long ago, and so many times since, to summon up any real interest in the question. Her own deflowering had not been particularly painful. It hadn't been much fun, either. At least Iris would be doing it with a nice-looking boy her own age.

"Honestly," she said at last, "it just isn't that important. It's men think it's so terrific. Most girls'd rather have tea at the Ritz quite frankly. Or even just tea."

Which had worried Iris a little. When she thought of undressing in front of Rob, or of touching his naked chest, or stroking the silky skin of his back, she felt such a dizzying dropping feeling in her stomach that she couldn't breathe properly. Whenever they touched she had a lovely but rather frightening thrilling and throbbing feeling, right down there where It was all supposed to happen, as well as the dizzy dropping feeling. If she felt like that just standing in his arms fully clad outside the cinema, how was she going to equate the real overwhelming naked melting connection with a nice cup of tea, no matter how ritzy?

So perhaps there was something a bit wrong with her. Something a bit not nice. A bit animal and dirty, when Rob obviously loved her because she was so fresh and pure-looking, he just didn't know what she was really like, better to keep all that well hidden, pretend you didn't really want to do anything at all.

"Better not," she had thus whispered in his ear, when they had both got rather carried away one afternoon in Epping Forest, when the trees could have shielded them easily, and Rob had for the moment forgotten all his usual anxieties. "Best not . . ."

And he had sat up straight away, apologizing, not made any fuss.

"Oh, I do love him, Jo!"

"You watch your step," said Jo.

79

Watching her step had brought her here, to this train, meeting Rob's parents.

"Oh, they will like me, won't they?"

"Course they will," said Rob easily, as the train pulled into the familiar little station at last. How could anyone, he thought, not love Iris?

For while Rob had many virtues, common sense was not always one of them.

GEORGE, AFTER THE ACCIDENT, 1954

———————

AFTERWARDS IT SEEMED to the boy's father that the accident had happened more to his wife than to his child. She was never the same afterwards, thought Ted, and presently his pity and regret became tinged with impatience.

How could she persist in thinking it had been her own fault? And she seemed to imagine that having one fantastically unlucky accident had somehow upped the poor kid's chances of having another one.

"Hold my hand," was Ruby's mantra, hissed or shrill, at the beach, on the prom, walking to the shops, queuing in the fish and chip shop.

"Hold my hand!" Not allowed out of her sight, not allowed to cross the street. Never allowed a chance to forget what had happened to him, poor kid.

"For heaven's sake, Ruby, can't you . . ."

"Can't I what?" Full-face venom. Unanswerable.

"We were lucky," Ted said to her once, early on, when he still had some courage in the matter, when he still thought they were all in this together. "He could have died. Didn't they say that? A bit further in, and it would've reached his brain. We'd've lost him, Ruby. We were lucky, can't you see it like that?"

No, Ruby cannot see it like that. In her deepest heart she would rather the child had died than lived spoilt. This is the truth she cannot look at. She does not for one moment acknowledge it. It is there, though, tainting everything she does. It makes her husband's caresses, once merely something to put up with, simply unendurable. It spurs her on to feats of housewifery, to ferocious levels of domestic neatness. Chaos has broken her child, so chaos must be watched out for. Any sign of approaching chaos such as toast crumbs, or a dirty sock left beneath a bed must be fiercely beaten back, must be obliterated with all weapons to hand.

Biscuits must be eaten over a plate held just under the chin, and in the kitchen; no item of clothing may be left for any reason on any surface whatsoever; shoes, removed on stepping onto the doormat, obviously, must be neatly placed on the shoe rack in the hall.

Rugs are banned: they slip. Dust-collecting items disappear one by one from shelf and mantelpiece: the wedding present brass ashtray in the shape of Manhattan, complete with minuscule Statue of Liberty, and all the little china jugs each helpfully painted with reminders that they are presents, and where from, vanish bit by bit into shoeboxes stowed in the attic, whilst Ruby's own small and cherished collection of glass animals, gathered slowly over many years of thoughtful summer holiday purchase, the turquoise peacock, the playful yellow dog, the breathtakingly delicate tiny pink pig, are ruthlessly massacred overnight, are tipped with barely a tinkle of breaking glass into the kitchen bin, punished for existing in perfection, and for being loved by Ruby, who has through carelessness broken a living child.

"Don't slouch. Hold your head up. Stare back," instructs Ruby, as if to make sure that the child realizes how much he is stared at.

He is, of course, stared at a good deal. Ruby feels these stares like arrows in her side. Before the accident they stared at his prettiness. Now . . .

Some neighbors are kind. "Poor mite," they say, "what bad luck." Others cross the road rather than speak.

"They're embarrassed," says Ted. "They don't know what to say. They're scared of saying the wrong thing."

Ruby sniffs scornfully. She read no fear in those carefully, brightly averted faces. She saw judgment. She saw disgust. She doesn't blame them. She wouldn't talk to herself either, if she could manage it. She tries to manage it. She avoids mirrors. She stops curling her hair. She buys new clothes, when she must, without trying them on. She stops using makeup, perfume, high heels. She's past all that silly stuff, she tells herself. She's grown out of it.

"How did it happen?" ask some of her neighbors, and when Ruby tells them they lower their eyes, their two perfect seeing eyes, so that Ruby can only guess at the levels of distaste they must feel for her. She guesses wrong almost every time, but there is no telling that to Ruby. She alone knows the extent of the injury that has befallen her.

"It didn't happen to you, did it!" shouts her husband in anguish, on the night that the child was first re-admitted to hospital, the broken eye seeping pus, "it didn't happen to you, it happened to him!"

Ruby, shouted at, remains calm. Dry-eyed, while he sobs. It is lost content he weeps for, but Ruby is hardly in a position to appreciate that.

"I know it happened to him," she says, almost gently. "But I did it, don't you see? I did it to him. You know what I wish most? I wish it had been the other way round. I wish it was me in there having my eye out. They could take them both. I'd tear them out of my head myself if it would make him back the way he was . . . No!" she adds sharply, suddenly, as he makes a move toward her, "No, don't you touch me. No. You leave me alone."

He does so.

IRIS MEETS MAY WILDING, 1954

Rob's mother smiled prettily at Iris, and held out her hand. In her heart she had rent apart her own garments, and dropped to the floor writhing and screaming curses; but Rob's mother was generally quite a stranger to her own heart's desires, and so assumed herself to be merely noting the vulgar tarty suit, the unfortunate hat, and (heavens!) the accent.

"How lovely to meet you!" she said to the woman who had come to steal her most precious possession, her reason for living, her deepest joy. "Rob's told us so much about you!"

"Oh dear!" returned Iris, smiling weakly. She didn't like the sound of that, of course. But then, she hadn't been meant to.

"Darling, we've put Miss da Silva into the Blue Room. Will you run up and show her, while I see about tea?"

Mrs. Wilding was a nice-looking woman, slim and even elegant in her ancient tweed skirt and her well-pressed blouse. Of the agonizing tumult of rage and hatred beneath there was no sign at all. She came from a world that did not give in to emotion. It was a world of visiting cards, of formal charity work, of moral certainties on all sorts of matters; a world, in short, as least as old as Iris's underwear, and similarly insubstantial, decorative, and fragile.

Mrs. Wilding sped away to the kitchen, where Meadows would be waiting. Meadows must be faced. Meadows, at first sight of Iris, would know straight away that this was a *young person*. The important thing for now was to be herself blithely unaware of Iris's personhood.

"Tea in ten minutes, please," said Mrs. Wilding, putting her head round the kitchen door. Meadows was, of course, a person herself. Though possibly she had never been young at all.

"Very good, madam." Meadows, acme of parlor maids, had the trolley standing ready. The delicate Coalport teapot was warming on the back of the Aga. So was the pot for the extra hot water, originally a Georgian silver coffeepot of particularly beautiful make; Mrs. Wilding had a very good eye for the antique. Slowly over the years she had trained her husband to accept the inferiority of his aesthetic sense.

Just because a teacup was a practical thing did not mean it need not be beautiful, she had briskly informed him years before, when he had queried the necessity of pink lusterware decorated with tiny and irresistible curlicues of gold. Yes, certainly she was fully aware of Presbyterian views on luxury; let him not disregard hers, on personal meanness; let him not forget the social importance, for a working GP at the beginning of his career, of the appearance, at least, of some degree of gentility. Or perhaps he wished only to treat the poor? Of course he was at perfect liberty thus to sacrifice himself; he must perforce sacrifice also his wife and only child; perhaps he might, having made such a choice, be man enough to say so; let no one be under any illusions that he had ever intended to put his family first; and so on, and so more.

Dr. Wilding had certainly not been man enough to stand up to this sort of thing for long. He had been pained at first, watching his tea being poured from Georgian silver; he did not describe such acquisitions to his mother, who lived so piously, but presently he began to enjoy the complicated pleasure of feeling anxiously proud of these fine and high-class belongings whilst at the same time scorning his wife for seeking them out in the first place.

"I prefer the simple things," said Dr. Wilding, complacently stirring his coffee with a dog-nose silver spoon. Mrs. Wilding, if she was in a bad mood, heard *Ah prefair thuh sumple thungs*, and felt quite murderous.

Over the years she had made it her task to fill her husband's home life with treasures. Often she quite forgot that she had done so for herself as well. Most of the time she felt vaguely that it was her husband who had the life anyway; she herself was an accessory, granted certain privileges, but of very much less importance in the general scheme of things. Thus it was primarily her husband's home she had made beautiful. Indeed it was entirely his in law. Mrs. Wilding had never seen the deeds; she would not have been in the least surprised to discover that she lived in her husband's house, and that everything in it belonged to him. It was a point of view with which she would have instantly concurred.

Ah prefair thuh sumple thungs, said Dr. Wilding, forgetting that until his marriage he had hardly so much as guessed at the existence of thungs made otherwise.

"Is the lassie here?" asked Dr. Wilding now, entering the drawing room where his wife sat beside the fire with a copy of *The Listener* open on her lap. Mrs. Wilding was listening out indeed, for sound of the raucous giggling female squawks she felt grimly certain Iris would squealingly emit at every turn. Thus far, though the Blue Room was only one floor above, she had heard nothing.

"Eh?" said Dr. Wilding, standing in front of the fire and lifting the hem of his jacket to warm his bottom, in a way Mrs. Wilding had begged him many times not to do. Standing thus he had his back to the eighteenth century mirror Mrs. Wilding had spotted in a junk shop in Dartford, and to the delicate Staffordshire figures she had bought for a song from a secondhand dealer in Tewksbury, who had assumed they came from Woolworth's.

The walnut grandfather clock to Dr. Wilding's right told the seasons as well as the time, in tiny enameled pictures of merry Georgian laborers in nicely matching outfits barely bothering with labor, but consecutively eating strawberries, lying about in haystacks, ice-skating, and pelting one another with flowers. The little piecrust table beside Mrs. Wilding's winged velvet armchair was Hepplewhite; her bureau the simplest glossy satinwood Sheraton.

Everything else in the room, carpet, curtains, the sofa, was modern, comfortable, and artfully muted, showing off these lovely pieces without making too much of them, thus avoiding any hint of the museum: Mrs. Wilding's drawing room, in fact, was a triumph. It was therefore her chosen arena: lucky it was teatime. She sat in her velvet chair, with her worn elegant shoes side by side, her pose relaxed, her hair neat, her heart pounding.

"If you mean Miss da Silva," she said, without looking up from *The Listener*, even turning a page as she spoke, as if idly, "Yes of course she is. She and Robert are just coming down. She seems . . ." here Mrs. Wilding paused, so that her meaning would be clear even to Dr. Wilding, whose ability to ignore nuance was so endlessly baffling, "she seems . . . very nice. Do try to be kind to her, darling."

Mrs. Wilding was thus addressing her own deepest heart, whilst naturally assuming that she spoke to her husband; he was known to be somewhat gruff outside the sickroom.

The door opened. Robert, and that woman.

"Ah, do come in, both of you," said Mrs. Wilding archly. "And I shall ring for tea."

RUBY'S LETTER, 1954

Ruby had an anonymous letter. She got so few letters that the bare sight of the envelope filled her with immediate dread. Her sisters occasionally wrote, but this was no hand she recognized. The postmark was too blurred for her to read. She hid the letter beneath the doormat until her husband had left for work. Even then she left it there while she did her usual washing and dusting round. She went upstairs, and made the bed. She looked in the child's room, which was of course very tidy and clean, since he was back in hospital; this soothed her a little.

Finally she could stand her suspense no longer and went downstairs and ripped the envelope open standing in the little hall. There was one sheet of paper. In the same biro'd handwriting as the address, the note read: *You should of looked after him better. You cow.*

The extraordinary thought came to her: that she had in fact written this letter herself, and sent it to herself, and somehow forgotten that she had done so. But it's not my handwriting, she thought, and there was a twinge of comfort in that, that she hadn't actually gone really mad after all.

Then she realized that she felt a bit sick. She got down onto her knees on the hall floor, and crouched there for a while until the nausea retreated and her heart slowed down. There were some crumbs, she noticed, on the lower level of the small wheeled tin tea trolley she kept there. She would have to take care of them. In a minute.

She felt the letter still concertina'd into one hand. Sitting on the floor now, she opened it flat and read it again, in case there had been some mistake, but it still said what she thought it had said.

Well. It was true, after all. Was it still a poison pen letter if it was true? Anyone could have sent it, and anyone would have been telling no lie. Any of those averted faces. Any of those accusing ones. Anyone who knew her. Anyone who didn't; the story had reached the local press. When next she went out, when next she walked up to the village for her shopping, she wouldn't know which of the faces on the street thought this of her strongly enough to write it down and let her know.

For several minutes Ruby sat rocking herself to and fro on the hall floor, thinking about how that would feel, and how it felt now, just imagining it. She had no words to describe her feelings. Asked, she would not have been able to name her desolation, though she was engulfed in it. Then she got up, brushed down her skirt, and briskly went to fetch the vacuum cleaner.

THE ACME OF PARLOR MAIDS, 1954

MEADOWS WAS PRIVATELY sixty-three years old, an orphan, brought up in a loveless children's home which had schooled her in the various techniques of domestic drudgery. At twelve Meadows had been rising at four in the morning, scrubbing floors by rush light; at sixteen, promoted to general servant in the house of the village greengrocer, she had worked a constant one-hundred-and-twelve-hour week; at nineteen, lower housemaid to Miss Inchmore, of Inchmore House, and proper gentry, she had learned more subtle techniques of servility, carefully spreading sacking over the carpets before opening up her well-stocked housemaid's boxful of black-lead brushes to make the fireplaces bright, wiping out chamber pots with turpentine and scalding water, buttoning on her specially voluminous and spotless upstairs apron before setting about making the beds, spreading used tea-leaves on the parlor carpet before sweeping it, to flatten the dust, and impart a pleasant fragrance.

Meadows knew how to remove ink stains, how to keep oil lamps bright, how to freshen velvet, and how to use a crimping iron. She could wait at table and build fires that lit with one hasty match. Not one of the people she had worked for throughout her life had ever had cause to complain. They had appreciated her efficiency, and largely failed to notice that she was human. This was hardly surprising, when Meadows herself seemed unaware of it too. Meadows treated herself like the machine her life had made her. She serviced herself regularly with nourishing food. She rested at appropriate times. She wore flannel next to the skin, and kept her fingernails neatly pared.

Things Meadows had never done: she had never visited London, or any other great city. She had never worn a new dress. She had never had her photograph taken. She had never been addressed by her Christian name. No one had ever sent Meadows a postcard, no one had ever bought her a drink, or asked her to dance, or looked with affection into her eyes. No one, asked, could have said what color her eyes were; Meadows herself, perhaps, would have needed to check.

Mrs. Wilding, on marrying Dr. Wilding and setting up home, had engaged Meadows in 1930 and become immediately aware that Meadows was a Treasure. That Meadows must be guarded, lest other unscrupulous local ladies try to snatch her for themselves, suborn her with higher wages, and separate flatlets, and fewer hours. Meadows was that prized and by then mythical figure, the devoted servant, zealous in pursuit of her mistress's comfort, and in the daily attainment of utter household dustlessness.

So, one afternoon in February, 1931, despite her morning sickness, young Mrs. Wilding herself had taken charge of the large cardboard box brought by the baker's boy, equipped the cake she had ordered with little candles, and rung for tea.

"Ah, thank you," she had said with an anxious little smile, as the tray was lowered into place. "Ah—I wanted to wish you a happy birthday, Meadows. I've got you a little present. Um. There."

In fact Mrs. Wilding had intended just the cake. But the evening before her husband had annoyed her by coming home from a trip to Scotland with a surprise present. This was a pair of gloves, of almost gauntlet design, made of stout brown leather, and thickly lined with fur.

"What on earth are they?" Mrs. Wilding had asked, taking them out of their box, stiff as kippers.

"I thought they'd keep you warm," replied her husband, already defensive. He pronounced the last word in two syllables, with a rolled r; *wurr-urm*. In her present sickly state this unrestrained Scottishness made his wife positively palpitate with irritation.

In fact the gloves had dimly reminded Dr. Wilding of a story that had delighted him as a child, that of the Snow Queen. Had not the Robber's

Daughter given faithful Gerda just such a pair of sturdy warm gloves, as a token of her love, so strong, so practical?

"Darling, they are simply hideous," Mrs. Wilding had exclaimed pettishly, and put them on to show him how they fell off her little delicate hands, which of course she usually shielded in fine Italian leather, lined with silk. Not that such fripperies kept out the cold, of course.

Dr. Wilding had been hurt. He had sought to please his wife with a token from one of his most private stores of ancient happiness, and she had told him his gift was hideous; while he had no idea of why her rejection of a pair of gloves she had never asked for in the first place upset him so much, the ensuing fierce row was clearly if very suddenly about their next-door neighbor's willful chicken-keeping, which they commonly quarreled about, and then even more suddenly about Dr. Wilding's mother, who was also high on the list of usual grievances.

The gloves clearly had to go. Obviously, thought Mrs. Wilding looking at them the following morning, they were in fact more suitable for a servant, built to last forever, and warm, and so very plain. Then she remembered that of course it was Meadows's birthday. She had already ordered the cake. That really was treat enough. She was quite sure none of Meadows's previous employers had bought a birthday cake. Perhaps adding the gloves would be rather a dangerous precedent. Perhaps Meadows would start expecting such presents every birthday, given such munificence first off. On the other hand, of course, she *was* Meadows, possibly the most perfect parlor maid in the country. Wouldn't a little kind notice be all to the good, when others attempted to bribe or entice her?

"A little present, Meadows. Um, there."

Meadows had known about the cake. The baker's assistant, with whom she sometimes took tea, had already passed on its every detail. Meadows, austerely, had been pleased. It was a decent fruitcake, decoratively iced with a design of edible silver baubles on its pink and yellow top. Meadows approved of the cake. She had been aware for some years of the shift in the workforce, that where once she had been merest dross, she was turned lately to gold. A cake was proper tribute.

But the gloves were a complete surprise. Their arrival was too recent for her to have come across them, clearly despised, in one of Mrs. Wilding's cupboards or drawers. She had heard nothing of the row, for she slept on the top floor of the house, and was in any case a little deaf.

The gloves, as she drew them from their wrapping of tissue, were obviously new. They had the succulent smell of new leather. They were exactly the right color to match her good coat. She drew one hand within the stout warmth, the soft clean fur, and saw that the gloves were a perfect fit. They had been bought for her, she surmised. Mrs. Wilding had looked at her hands, and noted their size. She had looked at Meadows's good coat, and remembered the shade. This was not tribute. This was a personal present. Bought just for her.

A terrible sensation began to burn and tear inside Meadows's breast. It felt like a fire all round her heart. Over it she retained complete composure. Her stony face did not change. She took off the glove she had tried on, and stood smoothing the two together. Then she spoke:

"Shall I pour you a cup, madam?"

"No, thank you, Meadows, I can manage," said Mrs. Wilding rather coolly.

Meadows heard the coolness.

"Thank you for the gloves, madam," she said. She spoke without an atom of audible excitement or pleasure.

"That's quite all right, Meadows. Don't forget your cake."

"No, madam," and Meadows had escaped, holding the cake balanced on its little china stand, on top of the glove box, her whole heart aflame.

SYLVIA AT WORK, 1995

THE CLINIC WAS A MESS. No one knew whose fault it was, and no one had time to begin to find out, but Sylvia's senior registrar was on study leave, and the other registrar, as well as the houseman, was new and junior and anxious; there should have been a maximum of fourteen new patients, and yet along with all the follow-ups there were twenty; impossible to get through them all without making some of them wait longer than the amount of time prescribed by government edict.

Sylvia, aware that she would be interrupted every few minutes by the telephone, or by the anxious houseman, by the new and inexperienced registrar or by one of the little troop of medical students currently assigned to her care, had quickly worked out that even without the interruptions she could see each patient for a maximum of five minutes if she was to get through the clinic in time for her operating list that afternoon. Five minutes was not enough, of course. Five minutes for people who had traveled miles to see her, after a wait of months! It was an outrage, but what else could she do?

"Apologize," she quickly told the medical students, as she opened the door to call in the first patient. "All that patient charter stuff means they think they've got a right to complain. Complaining takes time and it makes you feel cross; it's hardly your fault, is it? So stymie them straight away: I'm so sorry you've been kept waiting. Admits nothing, saves you time in the long run, and makes them feel better. And that's what we're in the business of, remember. Agnes Perks!"

Agnes Perks, jaws working ominously beneath a round knitted brownish hat like an upturned bird's nest, is wheeled in by her stout perfumed attendant: her daughter, by the deliberate and slightly menacing way she sits down beside the wheelchair and looks about her with the air of someone about to start taking notes.

"Good morning, Mrs. Perks, my name's Sylvia Henshaw, please say if you mind the medical students being here, what seems to be the problem?"

"She can't hear you," says the daughter. She turns sideways and yells, with sudden surprising vehemence, right into the old lady's ear: "Can you, Mum?" Mrs. Perks smiles the wide chinless smile of a woman who has left her teeth on the bathroom windowsill.

"Eh?" she says.

"The GP said she had a cataract," says the daughter, and they begin the tricky and time-consuming business of inducing Mrs. Perks to sit at the slit lamp, to lay her whiskery chin on the chinrest, to open her eyes without simultaneously opening her mouth and thus moving her eyes out of range; to keep her eyes open even and particularly while Sylvia shines a very bright light into each of them, to shut her mouth again; to keep looking right at the bright light, sorry; to shut her mouth again.

By the time Sylvia has finished with Mrs. Perks eight precious minutes have flown by. The telephone has rung twice. The houseman has popped his head round the door, asking her to see his patient. And she has not even begun to explain that, while Mrs. Perks certainly has cataracts, her macular degeneration will almost certainly mean that her vision will not improve very much; that her current near-blindness is after all irreversible, despite what all her neighbors and friends have so encouragingly said.

I cannot hurry this, thinks Sylvia. I must not. As clearly as possible, as slowly, she explains to Mrs. Perks's daughter that there is nothing to be done.

"I'm so sorry." The telephone rings again.

Eventually Mrs. Perks's daughter, tight-faced, thanks everyone, and wheels her mother away. Mrs. Perks's bird's nest hat is no longer comical; her toothless and uncomprehending grin of farewell makes all the medical students look away in pity and fear. They have seen a future, and wonder if it could ever be their own. The telephone rings.

Sylvia calls in the next patient, and the next, and the next. One by one the medical students slip away, for a pee, for a quick coffee, for a breath of air, since the room, necessarily kept darkened, is also airless. Only Sylvia stays where she is. The next patient is operable, four minutes; the telephone rings, the houseman pops his head round the door and asks her to see his patient; the one after that is not, nine. The telephone rings, the registrar asks her to see his patient. The next one is younger, barely forty, and expecting reassurance, but the funny little sore on his eyelid, he hardly knows it's there, doctor, to be honest, is certainly a rodent ulcer, six minutes; the telephone rings; and the next one, rare horror, has a malignant melanoma already penetrating her eyelid, poor woman; the operation will be disfiguring, and there is every possibility that she has left it too late anyway, and that the thing has fatally spread itself about her body. Twelve minutes, during which the telephone rings.

Once a woman from the WRVS brought the consultants coffee and buns on a trolley at eleven, but those days are long gone, before Sylvia's time. Seven patients, eight. Two more operable cataracts, a uveitis, and a child with a droopy left eyelid. Five more telephone calls, two visits from the Houseman.

Outside the crowd grows restive. Eyes follow Sylvia when she gets up and goes swiftly to the toilet, resentful glances mark her return. How much longer are they to be kept waiting? They are old, they are sick, they are frightened, they are sitting here in agonies of anxiety, their appointment time was hours ago, they've been waiting here so long, nurse, have they been forgotten, surely that woman came here after me, are those notes in the right order, nurse, why haven't I been seen?

"No, close your mouth, please. And open your eyes."

Another macular degeneration. Another cataract. Three minutes flat, that one. The telephone rings.

"Hello, Sylvia Henshaw," says Sylvia, for the thirteenth time that morning.

"Sylvia. Hello. It's me. Will."

"What, sorry?"

"Will Keane. I was wondering . . . sorry, is this a busy time for you?"

Sylvia laughs.

"Sorry, um, can you call me back?"

"Not till later, sorry," says Sylvia. "Is it your mum?"

"No. She's, well, she's the same. Call me when you can, yeah?"

"All right," says Sylvia, hanging up, perplexed, anxious, for a second; Will has never tried to call her at work before. There is no time to think about this, however, as the telephone immediately rings again.

"Call the next one in, will you," says Sylvia, her hand over the earpiece. "Hello, Sylvia Henshaw."

Sylvia's stomach rumbles. She finishes the call and scans the notes.

"I'm sorry you've been kept waiting so long, please say if you mind the medical students being here, what seems to be the problem?"

By the time she's sorted him out—a dangerously acute on chronic glaucoma: admit and refer, it is two-forty-five. Luckily there is no one else in the lift going up to theatres so she can open her briefcase and swallow as much of her sandwich as she can get down before the doors open and it is time to be late for her operating list.

Of course because she is in a hurry the scrubs are all mixed up, the top she takes from the Small shelf turns out to be Extra Large, the trousers are the right size but their elastic has gone, and there aren't any others, she has to rush over to Theatre One and pinch a pair. She bursts into the anesthetic room still panting, and snatches up the notes.

"Good afternoon everyone, sorry I'm late . . ." she meets the eyes of all three of them, the same anxious junior houseman, oh dear . . .

"Hello, Miss Henshaw," says the houseman, and even his voice trembles. At least the nurse, thank heaven, is dear Rosie, who meets her eye and winks; and there's the first patient, so patient on the trolley.

Oh yes. Basal cell carcinoma, left lower eyelid. Mrs. Battersby, Gina, aged fifty-three. White with terror.

"Soon have you sorted out, Mrs. Battersby," says Sylvia gently, and the list begins.

Swiftly, gracefully, Sylvia sorts out the basal cell carcinoma. Medical students, possibly the same ones as this morning, file in as she does so, shuffling their feet in their blue plastic overshoes. Bearing in mind Mrs. Battersby's terror, she instructs them, calmly, naming names, muscles, instruments, in orderly process; how run-of-the-mill, she implies, is this minor surgical procedure! How simply accomplished! A nice job, Mrs. Battersby. Yes. See you later.

Then the ptosis, a tricky one. Mild; a barely detectable drop of the child's left eyelid.

"But even the slightest difference in the appearance of your eyes will register. With other people, I mean," Sylvia tells the houseman. "You'll get called names at school. Tormented and bullied. Or worse; all those legends of the evil eye; people just don't trust people with funny eyes. It's one of those rules we all unconsciously live by, like personal space. You may not see exactly what's wrong, you just notice they're looking at you with their funny eyes. And you don't like it."

"Instinctive," says Rosie, holding out the next stitch.

Sylvia allows the houseman to imagine that she trusts him to go it alone with a suture. "Very good," she murmurs, as his shaking forceps at last catch the thread, "Oh well done!"

All the while she is entirely absorbed. Her heartbeat is slow. All the processes of her body are calmed. Within she feels the great lively peace of creativity.

Tying the last knot she slides her needle through the lower lid, draws it up to cover the exposed cornea, takes the piece of tape Rosie has ready and sticks the thread to the child's forehead.

"Why am I doing this? Anybody?"

A consensus on this one; yes, if you've just carved up someone's upper eyelid, you need to make their lower one stand in for it overnight. No, overnight is fine. All you need.

"Just distraction," she says, answering a question. "They hardly notice usually. You say, Look over there! And snip, it's out." A useful first for the nervous houseman though. "Make sure you're there," she tells him, as they scrub for the next case.

A squint: simple. This child, a little girl, is just four. Patching over her straight eye has not encouraged the other diverging one to mend its ways. They have taken her glasses, and elastoplasted over the good left eye's lens, but still her right eye wanders.

"What will happen to the squinting eye, if we just leave it?" she asks the medical students.

She doesn't look at them, but she can feel them looking at one another.

"Well," one of them ventures at last, "it won't get better on its own."

"No," says Sylvia. What else? asks her tone. "Any of you? No? Go on," she prompts the houseman, who will, of course, be happy to look knowledgeable in front of someone, even if it is only medical students.

"The deviating eye goes blind," he says solemnly.

"Why's that, then?"

"Um . . ." But he knows, really. "Your brain will only stand for one image," he says. "See two and your brain will automatically turn one eye off. Sort of thing," he adds, rather unprofessionally.

"And we don't know how the brain does it," says Sylvia. Beneath her the velvet-brown eye, held widely open in the speculum's metal grasp, looks blindly to the left. Placidly, intently, Sylvia cuts delicately through the lateral rectus muscle. "And we can't turn it back on. A neglected squint means a blinded eye."

We know this because of kittens, she remembers.

She tries to get them to talk for a while about the various disadvantages of being one-eyed, but all of them, she sees, are too riveted and nauseated by what she is doing on the operating table. They are new, she remembers.

Later she has a few bad moments with the final ptosis, a re-do. She is tired, and for a while, perhaps a whole minute, she cannot find the muscle she is looking for. Someone else, several years ago, was a little too cavalier with the scissors. Sylvia, conscious that everyone in the room except the patient is aware that something is going wrong, and that the patient is awake, and listening out desperately for just this sort of slow thick rising tension, measured in the timbre of her voice, or the length of a silence, must at one point wrenchingly force herself not to sound at all abrupt or urgent, or even crisper than usual.

Nor, a little later, exultant, or thankful, or even cheerful.

"Tricky," murmurs the houseman, when at last she has caught the sliding peekaboo edge and coaxed it slowly into position.

"Hmm," says Sylvia, as one who leisurely agrees to, say, an awkward putting shot, or stands chalking a cue beside a snooker table. "Hmm. Yes. Bit of a challenge . . . you all right there, Mr. Barraclough?"

Mr. Barraclough bleats a quavery tenor assent from beneath his shroud of sterile green.

After the list Sylvia and Rosie sit in the coffee room, with a mug of tea each.

"How's things?" asks Sylvia.

Things, it seems, are looking up.

Sylvia has closely followed Rosie's problems, for more than three years now, and sometimes feels a certain guilt that Rosie knows nothing of her own. But publicly of course Sylvia now has none anyway. Besides, how could she begin to complain, when she so clearly has everything poor Rosie wants already?

Still, this time Rosie has a new and promising man, met by chance a month or two back, whilst she was rattling a collecting tin for the Hospital Friends; he is apparently unattached and heterosexual and keen without being off-puttingly desperate. Sylvia is encouraging, but gently, for Rosie has said all this of others, and turned out to be thoroughly mistaken, sometimes on all four counts at once.

Rosie, who knows this perfectly well herself, is half-resigned, half-hopeful.

"He's an artist," she says, which Sylvia understands means that he is unemployed: also par for the course.

"Oh, how interesting," says Sylvia kindly, and then she sees that Rosie wants to say more, is clearly building herself up for some complex and lengthy unburdening, so she heads her off by pretending not to notice, tipping the rest of her tea down the sink and busily rinsing the mug out, since she is already nearly twenty-five minutes late for the six o'clock Audit Steering Committee meeting, which she is chairing.

As she had hoped, however, everyone else is late for it too, and by the time they have reached the last item on the agenda, it is well past seven-thirty. The anxious new registrar clearly ought to be taken out for a drink and bolstered up, but Sylvia has run out of time, her midnight has struck.

It is surely her duty to go out with the anxious new registrar, and bolster him up, but she cannot do it. She can only tell him she will see him tomorrow, to which he glumly assents, poor thing, and then she begins her long drive home. Which is not long enough.

Too soon, she has to turn off the ignition and the chatty legal affairs program she was half-listening to on Radio Four and gather up the arm-ful of notes she needs to go through this evening and climb the stairs to her own front door and face the music. All day Sylvia has been pa-tient, calm, and gentle. She has been grown-up, competent, and effi-cient. All day there is nothing she has set out to do which she has not done, with energy and grace and kindness.

But now she is home.

IRIS AND THE HOLIDAY CAMP, 1954

SHE'D BEEN FINE right up until the moment Rob's mother had opened the door and smiled that cold and terrifying smile.

Obviously Rob came from money. He was going to be a doctor one day. You could tell anyway from the way he spoke. Obviously he was a bit posh. But he couldn't help that, could he? And he hadn't seemed so very different from anyone else she knew. He liked going to the pictures, and dancing, he hadn't batted an eyelid when she took him back to the flat or to Lyons for tea, he was a bit scruffy to look at as well; how was she supposed to have known that he'd come from a house like that down a long gravel drive, and much much worse, oh worst of all, unimaginably worse, from a *mother* like that?

Iris had been looking forward to meeting Rob's mother. She had pictured, not her own mother exactly, but someone with the same atmosphere. Of course she and Rob had talked about their parents; they were at an age when parents loomed large.

"Always there when we got home from school. When she made drop scones she used to pour the batter into anything you asked for, your initial, or a daisy, or . . ." Iris sketched in the air that familiar triform silhouette "or Mickey Mouse. She always wore these aprons, flowered cotton, she used to run 'em up herself. She knew about material."

"Feel that, that's best worsted, last forever!"

Before her marriage, Iris told Rob, her mother had worked in a drapery in the market town in Sussex where she had been born.

"Crepe, see? Fine as you like. Drape lovely, that will."

"Helping fine ladies choose the right silk for an evening gown, or a whole season's afternoon frocks!"

Those would have been her glory days, when she had been young and pretty, unrolling a brilliant glistening yard of yarn-dyed taffeta, and giving it a little shake the better to demonstrate the shivery rustling sound it would make as a ball gown.

Iris could see her so clearly, standing in the light beside a nice curved bay window, the warm shop fragrant with the cleanly sweet smell of new material, surrounded by a glorious infinity of potential new dresses and suits and slips and coats and lustrous silk blouses: a figure of the utmost feminine romance, helping the picturebook ladies choose their finery.

Iris loved this picture. It came to her, vividly, every time she stepped over the threshold of Lewis's in Oxford Street, or snuffed the air in Liberty's. Of course there were other more recent pictures, ones Iris could really remember, her mother clicking her teeth over the terse mystifications of a knitting pattern, or standing behind Mike, her arms round him, her hands over his on the frying pan, helping him toss his pancake. And sitting on the beach, of course, smiling beneath the shady hat with the blue ribbon trim.

But it was mainly her mother's atmosphere that Iris remembered, the feelings she seemed to bring with her wherever she went. How safe you felt, when she tucked your sheets and blanket in tightly at night! Safe, lying in front of the fire reading while she darned or knitted, safe, listening at night for Dad coming back late from the foundry, safe, hearing the lowered conversational voices and the clink of cutlery while the two of them ate a bit of late supper together.

It was this sensation of safety that Iris associated with motherliness. She had hoped to bask, just a little, in the glow from Rob's mother; it would be nice, she had vaguely assumed, to note that sensation once again.

"How lovely to meet you!" Rob's mother had said on the doorstep, holding out her narrow manicured hand and smiling prettily, and Iris's heart had knocked with terror inside her borrowed blouse, and her knees had trembled violently, so that the high heels were even harder to manage, and she had actually tripped on the enormous sisal doormat in the hall, and would have fallen heavily over if Rob hadn't grabbed her elbow and pulled her up again, saying, "Whoa!" and laughing.

For Rob's mother was a lady. Everything about her said so, her height, her straight back, her slim hips and long elegant feet, her cold blue eyes and delicate skin. She did not seem young to Iris, because no one over twenty-five could, but she seemed beautiful, and implacable, and indescribably not like someone's mother. There was no contest, no battle of wills; Rob's mother spoke, and Iris, within at any rate, crumbled away to nothing at the sound.

Nothing, scarlet with embarrassment, had slunk along the hallway gulping at the smell of furniture wax and roses, feebly trying to pretend she passed down such mirrored loveliness every day; *nothing* had given up the attempt not to stare about her at the height of the ceiling, the immense luster of the oaken staircase wide enough to drive a car up; *nothing* had made a little helpless gasp when being shown a downstairs cloakroom where she might wash her hands, and which was hung about with coats of all varieties, and lined with Wellington boots: they had a whole room, just to stick coats in! A room the size of home, just to line with Wellington boots!

"We're taking tea in the drawing room," Rob's mother had said, and disappeared, thank God; but there was no escape from her, no matter how carefully Iris washed her hands and dried each finger she was going to be ready eventually, and there was Rob, hanging about outside the coat-place with his hands in his pockets.

"Oh Gawd, Rob!"

"Don't be scared. You look gorgeous. You are gorgeous."

Pushing him away, hissing at him: "Why didn't you tell me?"

"Tell you what?"

"Well, she's so, she's so . . ."

"She's so what? She's only my mum. You weren't scared of my dad, were you? Calm down. She's all right."

"She hates me!"

"She what? What are you talking about? Come and have a cup of tea. Everything's all right. It is, Iris." He kisses her, and for a moment everything is fine. He is himself, deliciously, with, even, a further added spiciness now, that of being That Woman's possession: stolen goods. Iris helps herself to another long kiss, just to make sure whose side Rob is on.

Clearly her own, for the moment. Still she quivers as they open the drawing room door and sidle in.

"Oh, this is Meadows, Miss da Silva."

"How d'you do," says Iris, remembering that this is what posh people say on being introduced, and holds out her hand, at which Rob unforgivably sniggers, and takes her hand himself, while the woman with the tea-cloth, stone-faced, simply takes herself off, without a word, so what was going on there, then? Trembling anew with discomposure Iris sits where she is bidden, not noticing until too late how low the chair is. Her knees stick up, rudely, she feels. Her skirt rides up. She wriggles forward; her every move seems clownish to her, even her breathing is clumsily stertorous.

There is a low padded thing like a table in front of the fireplace, where more roses give off a clean powerful scent. On the padded thing, the world's most frightening tea tray sits loaded with precious breakables; there are little silver sugar tongs for picking up lump sugar with, obviously fraught with dangers; there are weird shallow cups with small curly unholdable-looking handles, all matching; there's a shiny presumably solid silver rounded thing like a washing up bowl turned upside down; beneath it, Iris understands, there will be hot things dripping butter, to spot chairs and carpets and of course one's own sister's (oh, Jo! If only I were home with you and not here, not here!) precious fine wool skirt, and similarly perilous there is jam, jam not of course in an ordinary sturdy jam jar but spooned out into another break-if-you-look-too-hard and doubtless easily tip-upable little china thing with spindly bow legs.

"Milk, Miss da Silva?"

Why aren't they sitting at a table? Because they are posh. Why is having tea whilst sitting in armchairs posh? Because it is difficult.

This is not tea, feels Iris, so much as it is a test: only a lady can handle this frightful collection of potential disasters and still go on resolutely chatting. Only a non-lady would spot the dangers in the first place.

"Sugar?"

"No, thank you."

Rob, perhaps regretting the snigger, does not obey his immediate cheerful impulse to point out that Iris usually takes two or even three spoons if she can; he has no idea why she has turned down something she is usually so endearingly greedy about. Best not to ask, he decides. And isn't his mother's manner just a little, well, *grander* than usual? Dimly he perceives that there is tension somewhere in the room.

"Oh, not for me, thanks" says Iris, offered the salverful of teacakes. "I'm not hungry, thanks."

A lie, Rob knows. Iris is always hungry. "I'm starving," she had said, stretching luxuriously, just as the train pulled into the station. He watches her. The tea cakes must be a torment, their golden toasty smell faintly laced with nutmeg, another of Meadows's little triumphs. She is afraid to eat, he realizes.

"D'you know this part of the country at all, Miss da Silva?"

"A bit," says Iris.

"On holidays," says Rob, casually. "Iris used to go to Coogan's, Mum; didn't you, Iris."

"Oh really," says Rob's mother, also casually, putting down the teapot.

Metaphorically Rob, from his white charger, has speared his dragon mother in the vitals, pinned her with his ruthless lance right into her saddleback armchair.

I love a girl who has stayed at a holiday camp. I am on Iris's side. I am in the holiday camp camp, mother: take care.

For the local holiday camp has, as it happens, a certain mythic place in Rob's own past. As a very little boy, when the place was quite new, he had very much longed to go to the camp now so conveniently—so he had argued—close to their own village, where there would be so many other children to play with, and where he and Mummy and Daddy would live for a whole week in one of those nice little wooden houses!

Coogan's Holiday Camp, built so disastrously (if you were of Mrs. Wilding's opinion) or so delightfully (if you were a Coogan's-camper) close to the sea, yet boasted a large swimming pool, a sprung-floor dance hall with a proper stage at one end for nightly live entertainments, a huge refectory full of small round tables, discreet lavatory blocks on every other corner, and rows and rows of (even in Mrs. Wilding's grudging opinion) rather pretty wooden chalets, with windows on either side of the door, each cheerfully painted blue and white, and each with its own tiny square of roofed and balustraded front porch, where the temporary occupants might shelter together on deckchairs. The chalets were merely for sleeping in, or board games; meals were all-in, served in the refectory, whence the Coogans-campers were summoned by three short blasts of a factory-style hooter.

Mrs. Wilding, cutting roses in her garden, could sometimes hear the hooter quite plainly on a still summer's morning, and shuddered even when she was alone. The only good thing about it, from her point of view, was that the Coogan's-campers rarely ventured outside the pink-washed concrete render walls of their compound. They were, presumably, allowed out if they chose; occasionally a little group of them might reconnoiter the sandy beach over the road from Coogan's front gate; and the coaches that met them every Saturday in season at the railway station chugged their road-hogging way along the cliff-top lanes, on regular midweek excursions; but in general the campers stayed put.

Whilst no one Mrs. Wilding knew had, of course, ever stayed in a holiday camp (how the words sounded in her mouth, each syllable dripping with hauteur and disdain! Had Mrs. Wilding ever been in a position to play Lady Bracknell, she would have known exactly how to pronounce that famous *handbag*) the details of life inside those high pink-washed walls were soon current in every well-to-do household in the area:

The campers were served three large cooked meals a day; there was a separate dining room for the children; there were tennis courts, as well as crazy golf (another handbag moment there, for Mrs. Wilding) and putting greens. Nightly residents danced to a series of visiting dance bands, and daily they were encouraged by the resident uniformed Coogan Captains to run races, play team games, attempt otherwise to Keep Fit with organized physical jerks, and enter Talent Contests, while their children were similarly but again separately employed, under the jolly but watchful eye of their own Coogan Cadets, each of them proud club-members of the Coogan's Scamperers, singing their own special Coogan's Camping Song, "We are Coogan's Scamperers, Scamp'ring everywhere . . ."

For every working family in the area soon had a relative employed in producing the three large cooked meals, or Captaining, or Cadeting, or looking after what the brochure called the well-tended gardens and beautifully kept lawns. So local children, even those as sequestered as the small Robert Wilding, knew of the swimming pool and the diving board, and the playground with the swings and the big roundabout, and the ping pong, and the cinema where, it was said, films showed all day long.

Coogan's Holiday Camp, the Mecca of Rob's early childhood, that fantasy of longing, of which he had had occasional piercing colorful glimpses, from the upper deck of one of the open-topped buses that ran to and fro along the front in summer; Rob's own longed-for lighthouse, so near, so ever-present, and yet so unreachable, and which he was never to visit.

For after the long wartime closure, the camp reopened unutterably changed during his adolescence, looking simply tawdry and uninteresting, no land of lost content but merely a drab series of tatty sheds strung along cracked concrete paths, providing cheap weeks away for people who couldn't afford to go anywhere better.

It had been a tremendous giddying surprise to find out, when they were swapping childhood stories, that Iris had actually visited the place herself, aged eight, when it had been Rob's idea of heaven. Suppose after all he had gone there, when he had most wanted to! He would have met Iris! She would have been the world's prettiest little girl! In the blue bathing suit knitted by her mother! They would have met, and loved; circumstances had merely delayed them.

It was strangely sweet to picture that childhood meeting. In Rob's eyes it assumed the quality of a very near near-miss. How many times had he skirted those pink-washed walls hoping for a free way in! If only he had after all dared simply to swagger nonchalantly up to the man at the gate, and pretend to be a lost Coogan's Scamperer at last scamp'ring back to the fold! If only he had known Iris was waiting in that forbidden paradise!

"Oh, Iris, what was it like?"

And at her reply he had felt a great wave of regret crash over him, as if he had missed a wonderful chance forever, as if he had never mooched sullenly along those cracked postwar paths with his hands in his pockets, as if he were eight years old again, feverish with longing.

"Oh, it was grand!"

Iris had loved Coogan's Holiday Camp. Her time there, she told Rob, had been one of the most lovely memories of her childhood:

No, they weren't that small, though it was hard to remember, she'd been so small herself after all; but there had been room for Mum and Dad's double bed; she and Jo had shared the bunk, Jo on top because she was eldest, while Bobby had a further little bed that slid under the lower bunk by day. It was nice sleeping in the same room as your mum and dad: it was safe.

You could just hear the music, lying in bed, and Cadets patrolled the paths, listening at doors for any crying children, so that their mothers could be fetched from the dancehall; the best bit was lying waiting for your parents to come back from dancing, because all the time, when it got really late, you could hear other grown-ups walking slowly along your path, dawdling, chatting in lowered voices, laughing softly with each other, and there was nothing in the world, said Iris, that was so cozy as that softened peaceful sound, the sound of adults who have had a good time sauntering along in the summer dark.

And in the morning you went to get Dad's hot water for him to shave in, and there was an enamel jug, you queued at the hot water tap, it had a special hot clean metallic smell, and you carried it carefully back to the chalet without spilling a single drop, and your daddy taught you a dance—there was a photograph snapped by the camp photographer —and also you sat all five of you on an immense family-sized tricycle, pedaling away, and laughing when you bounced over a bump in the path.

"Oh, Iris, Coogan's, I can't believe it!" And strangely almost as he spoke he could feel this last memory entering his own consciousness, he could easily fit his own small self into the family-sized tricycle beside Iris, his sandshoe-shod feet taking it in turns with hers, in her plimsolls and ankle socks, to push at the pedals, all of them swinging along down a clean sandy pine-scented woodland path, laughing as they bounced over roots and hillocks, the trees rolling by on either side with their upper branches meeting high above into a green tunnel, a light arching roof overhead, flecked with bright sky and shifting bars of gold.

So Coogan's had really been paradise, after all. How extraordinary, and how fitting, that it should be Iris who showed him, after all this time, the way inside! It just went to show how much Iris and he were meant for one another.

"OH REALLY," says Rob's mother as she puts down the teapot. Her voice is light, interested, despite the sharpened lance her son has thrust into her side. "What a coincidence!"

"Isn't it," says Rob cheerfully, and he meets his mother's eyes, to let her know that he knows about the lance, that he drove it in on purpose, and that, unless she behaves, he is perfectly willing to twist it. Meanwhile he has taken a plate and blobbed jam onto a teacake; now he cuts it neatly into four, and passes it to Iris.

"Tuck in, old girl," says Rob.

WILL AND THE DOCTORS, 1995

Will lay on his side on the hard trolley and thought about poetry. For years the same fragments had come handily to mind just before take-off, when the engines roared, and then again just before landing, and in the dentist's chair.

At the moment, though, every word seemed to have deserted him.
Now sleeps the crimson petal, now the white,
Nor Christ, something about goldfish . . .
Then something something *waken thou to me . . .*

"OK?" said the registrar. She was a really good-looking young woman, very slim and with a particularly elegant aquiline nose and thick dark hair, which kept falling forward over her high white forehead.

At first sight of her Will had felt his resolve weaken a little. He had envisaged being able to change his mind and beg for the Valium after all. But he wasn't going to bottle out in front of call-me-Julia. Long legs too, and a very nice bum indeed.

"I'm not really very happy about this, Mr. Keane," she had said straight off.

"Will, please. I know. I'm very grateful."

"I'm not sure you know quite what you're letting yourself in for."

"I know it's not going to be fun."

"No; not for either of us," she had said, and he'd realized then—how could he not have realized it before—that it was going to be hard for her, making her do it like this. Making her torture him.

"Sorry."

"Well. Let's get on with it, shall we?"

So here he was, hunting round in his mind more and more desperately for something to hang on to while she had at him again. It was bad not being able to see quite what she was doing under that blue sterile paper thing. Or perhaps it would be worse to be able to see it.

"I'm going to insert the introducer again, now, OK? Try to keep absolutely still."

Will closes his eyes. The pressure on his hip increases, becomes a point, becomes—he holds his breath to keep in the groan—a sudden overwhelmingly agonizing wound; a knife, a body of steel is being driven against his bones, harder, harder; all words desert him; numbers—

One two three four. Five. Six seven. Eight—

"Sorry."

The agony resolves instantly into pain. Sweating, Will lets out the breath. He is trembling violently all over, he realizes. He hopes she will not notice this. For she is a good-looking woman. He could reach out his free hand and stroke her bottom right now. He can tell from her face that again it hasn't worked. Poor girl. Looks a bit sick. Can't blame her.

"You're not in, are you."

"No. Sorry. I'm going to give it one more try. The trouble is, you're not a little old lady."

He hears his own snuffle of laughter.

"I generally do this on little old ladies," she goes on. "Their hip bones are generally a whole lot, well . . ."

"Crumblier?" suggests Will, when she trails off.

"Completely crumbly. Absolutely. Lace curtains. No trouble at all. You're an athlete, aren't you?"

Will smiles at her, her lovely clear ivory skin, which gleams a little over the bridge of the fine aquiline nose.

"I've *acted* athletes. If that's any help."

She smiles back. "I meant, well, the reason I'm having so much trouble getting in is because your bones are so strong. Active, you see."

"Is that good?"

"Well, usually. Of course it is. Just not right now. When I'm trying to poke you in one of them. Crumbly would actually be better for you at the moment."

Her voice has an absent quality about it; she is concentrating, he realizes. She's going to stab him again, and he must lie here still, letting her do it.

"Ready?"

For had he accepted the Valium she usually uses he would have needed to sleep it off all afternoon. In Recovery here, all afternoon. And groggy all night as well. No driving home. And he might have got Whatshername across the road to Mum-sit for an hour or so, but not that long. Not without having to explain. And he isn't going to explain why to anyone. Because that would mean it all being true, and at the moment, even here now lying on the trolley waiting for nice-bum-call-me-Julia to stab him again, he isn't going to admit to any of it being true.

It was nice Welsh Sue's fault, she'd started it. Making all that fuss. He'd just stood up too quickly, that was all. Obviously, stood up too quickly and felt faint. His real mistake was telling her it had happened before. When he'd found the adoption certificate. And he'd been upset, too, he'd thought his mother's time had come; anyone would've passed out, wouldn't they?

Well, no, apparently. They wouldn't have. And yes, well, come to think of it, yes, it *had* happened before. Once before that, too: he'd had to lie down on the grass one time. In the garden. He'd lit a cigarette and felt a bit funny. Because he wasn't smoking much now, anyway. So that first one in several days had made him feel a bit faint. No, he'd just felt like lying down. On the grass. He just felt tired. It was tiring, what he was doing. That was all.

"Hmm. Take a deep breath, please," said the GP, not the soppy woman but one of the blokes, the heavy-faced bald one, when he came round later to check up on Annie. Will had tried to head him off but somehow the man was unstoppable; two minutes after he'd shut Mum's bedroom door he'd got Will flat on his back on the living room carpet, the better to paddle his big heavy hands about in Will's stomach.

"Deep breath!"

Sod off, thought Will feebly, but he had done as he was told, and let bald git have his own way.

"Definite spleen edge," the bald git had said, rising from his knees and brushing down his trousers. Will lay where he was on the carpet.

"What, sorry?"

"I can palpate your spleen."

Was that a boast? Will did not speak. He had not been fully aware that he had a spleen, let alone one that all comers could palpate if they insisted hard enough and knew where to look.

Splenetic. That meant angry, didn't it? Spleen. Wasn't it a medieval humor, choleric, splenetic? A palpable spleen. It sounded medieval. Something carthorses might have trouble with, something vets in tweed jackets shook their heads over.

"Is that bad?" he said at last, but the GP did not reply. He was writing something on a yellow block of paper, which he tore off and handed over as Will rose to his knees.

"Should be able to get you in this afternoon," he said. Will looked at the form, and saw it was an X-ray request.

"What do I need an X-ray for?"

"It's for an ultrasound," said the bald git, shutting his great black bag. He had circled Ultrasound, Will saw. And Abdomen. And Urgent.

Though after the ultrasound it seemed they'd changed their minds, because they'd x-rayed him as well, all over, while he lay inside a thing like an enormous washing machine.

What did he need a CT scan for?

He would have to ask his doctor that, sorry.

Blood test? Why?

I don't actually know, dear, sorry, I just take the samples. You'll need to ask your doctor.

Luck of the draw it had been the soppy woman one showing him the shadowy films two days later.

"No, nothing's definite. But here, d'you see? There. And there."

"They shouldn't be there?"

"No. Diffuse areas of infiltration."

"Infiltration of what?"

"Well. That's what we don't quite know, you see. I'm very sorry, Will. But it's clearly indicative. We can't ignore it. It means something."

Still not heart-pounding. Couldn't believe it, of course. This wasn't happening, not really. He wasn't sitting here in the doctor's surgery talking about himself. It was Mum who was ill: not himself.

"What then?"

"Well, I'm afraid it's possibly lymphoma. It's a sort of cancer. We can treat it. But we need to know what stage it's at."

"Possibly?"

Just beginning to tremble now. Cancer. Just a light tremor.

"Or leukemia. It might be a leukemia. I'm sorry. We won't know until we've had a look at your spleen."

Look at it? Hadn't they just had a look at it, and found it full of holes like a cartoon chunk of Gorgonzola sitting inside him?

"I mean a closer look," she went on, as if he had spoken, "at the cells."

"You mean, like a biopsy?"

"No, not exactly. I'm afraid we can't take biopsies from the spleen, it's too vascular; damage it and it just goes on bleeding, it's er, a bit like your liver, you see. It won't mend."

A few seconds more, to consider this, to make out what the soppy woman was actually saying. Heart thundering now.

"You mean, you're going to have to cut me open to have a look at my spleen?"

"We, or rather, I mean they. The surgeons. They won't have to cut you open, no. It will probably be done through a keyhole incision. Ah, several keyhole incisions."

"Oh." Surgeons, in masks of course and horrible wet rubber gloves like washing up Marigolds, knelt squinting over Will supine, splayed beneath the powerful lights, taking keyhole looks at his Gorgonzola spleen.

"They make keyhole incisions, and insert a probe; there's a sort of little suction-thing attached . . ."

"What? Attached to what?" Back in theatres Annie's elderly long-necked vacuum cleaner roared into life, and the dog Judy peered out from behind the sofa with her bulbous velvet eyes.

"They just sort of suck your spleen out. It's not exactly minor surgery. But it's getting there."

Will was silent, considering. It seemed to be taking him a very long time, he thought, to hear her words as she said them. They seemed to float all by themselves in the air for a while, like e-mail messages when you'd switched off your computer. There, but not processed. Spoken, but not received.

"So," he said, after what seemed a very long time, and into a type of thumping silence consisting of a tremendously magnified heartbeat—his own, he realized shortly—"they've got to take my spleen out, in order to have a look at it."

"Yes."

"And they're going to suck it out, through tubes."

"Yes."

"So, doesn't it get all sort of minced up, then?"

"Yes. Yes it does."

"Oh. Can't put it back then."

"No."

"Don't I, you know, need it, then?"

"Well. Yes. But we can do without it. And you're definitely going to be better off without yours."

"Because it's got holes in it."

"Areas of diffuse infiltration, yes."

"Holes."

"Yes."

"When?"

"What, the splenectomy? Ah, pretty soon, actually. As soon as possible after we've done a few more tests."

"Right."

"Any questions?"

Are you serious?

That was a question. There were so many more, too many to work out which one to ask first. What was a spleen anyway? What did it look like? Where was it, how big was it, what on earth did it do, it had to do something, didn't it, you didn't have entire organs just sitting there inside you just taking up space, did you? And if you didn't really need it, why wouldn't taking it out, mashed or liquidized or sodding well pureed into a fine spleen coulis, simply solve the problem? Why my spleen anyway? Why me? Isn't this all a mistake? You mixed me up with someone else, haven't you? You do realize this is me, right? Is all this supposed to be real?

"A bone marrow biopsy first. In fact there's been a cancellation . . ." a death, thought Will instantly; thought processes up to speed sometimes, then, evidently; "so I've made a few telephone calls and we can actually get that part done this afternoon, if that's OK."

That was when he first remembered. Annie, his mother, and the Task. Oh Christ: Mum! She mustn't find out; she was peaceful, letting go of him, consigning him to the world she was leaving; what would she feel, how she would suffer, if she knew that her child was probably going with her!

Or indeed: going first. There. That was a notion. No. Surely whatever dreadful L-thing he had, leukemia or the other one like a loofer, whatever it was, surely he had longer than his mother, on her deathbed three months since? Surely. Surely?

"How long?"

A pause. Wants me not to be asking this, he thought, watching her haggard face across the desk. How old was she? Older than himself, in her late forties probably, teenage kids, a bit worn out. How many times has she said this to people? Wonder if she ever wants to laugh. He remembered Sylvia telling him how she had once had to tell someone their younger daughter had just died in a motorbike crash, and that a frightful misgiving had seized her as she approached them, that as she spoke these terrible words to them she would laugh, her face had wanted to bend up into a spasmodical grin, her voice had trembled, she thought, with the effort not to snigger out loud.

"Except it wasn't laughter, not really. I went to the loo straight afterwards and burst into tears, and it felt just the same."

But that was long ago, of course, when she was new and hadn't had all that practice, it takes practice, obviously, to tell people gracefully that their death is upon them.

"I don't know," said the doctor at last. "It really depends on what they find at the splenectomy."

"Best case scenario?" I won't ask about the worst, Will told himself. I don't want to know, I don't need to after all.

She shrugged, to indicate how hidden from her eyes were the works of God and nature: "Ten years? Maybe more."

I'm not going to ask, Will reminded himself, and as the thought arose opened his mouth, and heard the words drop out of it all by themselves: "Worst case?"

She looked away. Poor bitch. What a job! "Months, I'm afraid, rather than years. But . . ." she looked at him again, "it's not helpful dwelling on such things. It's far too early days. Can you do this afternoon all right?"

Well, no, not really. Not the full armful of Valium and sleeping it off in a cozy sideward type of afternoon. Just the local anesthesia and a hellish quarter of an hour, though, he was up for that all right. And call-me-Julia. Who had, he noticed, recognized him. Not immediately, but pretty quickly.

"Sorry, I keep thinking I've met you somewhere before," she had said, as she opened the treatment room door and let him have his first look at the trolley where she was to torture him, at his own request.

Ah. That meant she was about thirty; plausible. Strange to think so few years had separated him from the main body of his admirers, though many of the letters he had spent so many hilarious afternoons wading through had clearly been written by girls much younger, barely into double digits.

"Ah, did you ever watch *Earth's Army*?"

Her face. Yes, clearly she had.

"Oh my God, you're Toby ffrench!"

"I hope you pronounced the two little f's" he said, as he usually did.

"Of course I did. *Earth's Army*, my God, how long ago was that? Fifteen years? Longer?"

"Longer. I'm afraid." She folded her arms, leaning back against the door. For a moment she'd forgotten, he saw. She was suddenly a woman meeting a man she used to be in love with; a nostalgic affection gleamed softly from her eyes. Sometimes they still said it, even after so long: Oh,

I was so in love with you! Sometimes, even now, he gets called Toby; going into a strange pub in London, for example, or collecting his dry cleaning. Not often, of course. Not now.

"But, how old were you, then?"

Ha. That bit still worked, usually. How much longer, he wondered, would he go on surprising old fans with his obvious youthfulness? And this one actually knew how old he was, of course.

He grinned at her. He was suddenly almost enjoying himself. Call me Julia. Nice bum.

"Nearly nineteen," he said, and she laughed. And remembered. He saw her blush. And that was it, for time out.

"Ah, got to ask you to lie down here, on your side, facing me, that's right. I'm going to numb the area as much as I can. But there's really nothing I can do to numb the bone. I'm going to have to sort of feel my way reaching the bone with the probe. The bone has no sensation but the lining of it does. You will feel it. It will be uncomfortable. I'm sorry. But I have to be sure you understand what's going to happen."

That was when he thought to himself that if she'd been ordinary looking or another man he could've changed his mind. Except that then he'd have the insoluble problem of his mother to deal with.

Of course I don't understand what's going to happen, he thought. I've never been tortured before. How do you know how you're going to manage pain until you feel it?

"I'll try to be quick," she said. Call her Julia.

And she had.

"One last try, then I'm going to have to go for more anesthesia, OK?"

"OK."

"Ready?"

"Yup."

Again pressure intensifies rapidly, through discomfort to pain to an agony he immediately bursts out sweating to. Again only numbers will come when he calls. He mutters them aloud.

One two three. Fourfive. Six. Seven eight

"OK, Will?" she asks.

"Don't interrupt me," he says lightly, "when I'm counting."

Taken so by surprise she can only utter the breathy little giggle he had, he realizes, exactly been aiming for.

"Done it," she says. "I'm in."

For a moment Will is flooded with something like bliss. The agony has vanished, turned back into the merest dull ache. And he has shown manly valor to a good-looking woman, and made her laugh. Audience response: better than Valium.

"Won't take a moment now."

Into my bones. She sounds triumphant. She could go on pushing, Will thinks, and skewer me right into the trolley, and go off and leave me nailed into place. He opens his eyes.

"Well done," she says, also lightly.

"I had the easy part."

"I think not," she says. "There. Finished." She holds up the test tube. So that's what bone marrow looks like. Darkish blood. Slightly surprising. Marrowbone jelly, so healthful for dogs, he thinks vaguely.

"Shall I get the nurse to bring you a cup of hospital tea?"

"Do I get a biscuit?"

"I'll see what I can do."

And he is left alone with his thoughts.

GEORGE RE-ADMITTED, 1954

H E DIDN'T MIND being back in hospital, not a bit. Pleased, in fact. Not
only because they were going to give him a new eye. But because he would
see Iris again.

The most important reason he was glad to be in hospital—that for a
while he would be away from his mother, who was so cross all the time
now—he did not acknowledge, since it was impossibly painful to look
at properly, like looking at the sun: blinding.

Iris. He longed to see her again, every night when he went to bed
he thought of her and the way she smelt and the way she had pressed
him to her lovely soft bosom. It was clear to him that, special and
beautiful as she was, she cared about him very much. Since he loved
her too, as soon as he got the chance he was going to ask her to
marry him.

It was funny they hadn't just given him the new eye straight away,
when he had hurt the first one. They'd spent ages trying to make
the hurt one work again. He had had to stay still for ages. They had
made him.

Iris had said it was a game. He had to pretend his head was a jugful
of water. When he moved he had to be careful not to spill a drop.

"That's it, head up, lovey, careful, slowly!"

When he was allowed to sit up he still wasn't allowed to look down.

"Not a drop, mind!" At mealtimes he wasn't allowed to feed himself.
He'd had to be fed like a baby. He hadn't liked that. It was silly. He wasn't
a baby at all.

And of course lots of the nurses weren't Iris. Some of them tried to be as nice as she was, some of them also loved him, he could tell. But his heart belonged to Iris.

Once he had cried. And then he had sat on Iris's lap. She had told him how they were going to go to the seaside together when his eye was better. They would go to a place she knew where there was nothing except the sand and the sea, she said, and a pub where you could stay and sleep upon feather beds like clouds. They would go by train and when they got there they would go straight to the beach. There were always lots of little boats on the beach, turned upside down, warming their stomachs in the sun, she said, waiting until it was time to go out on the water again. They would walk past the little sunbathing boats and they would walk along the beach beside the turning sea, all blue in soft stripes as far as the horizon. They would walk past the cliffs where the seagulls sat, and by a special little cave Iris knew about in the cliff they would unpack their picnic and spread their blanket and get changed into their costumes and go for a paddle before they made, no, not a sandcastle, they were going to make a sand dog, a soft sandy dog curled asleep in and on and of the sand, he would be lying with his nose tucked against his tail, Iris had made a sand dog, she had said, once before, long ago, when she was a little girl, and he was so looking forward to the trip that as soon as they were married they were really going to go.

He would have his new eye by then, of course. He hoped it wouldn't take very long to get it all done. And that he wouldn't have to do any more of that headful of water stuff. He was going to theatre this afternoon. So he hadn't long to wait. The only thing was, where was Iris? He'd been here since yesterday. It was the same room. And the sister was the same, so it was certainly the same ward. Of course there had always been times before when Iris had had days off and he hadn't seen her at all. She had always kissed him goodbye and told him how much she would miss him, and that she would be back soon to take care of him, but in the meantime he must mind what the other nurses said and be good. And he always had been. So if she had had yesterday off, and today—because sometimes she had been away for two whole days—she would definitely be here tomorrow, and how thrilled she would be to see him!

She'd be so happy. He was sure she had missed him as much as he had missed her. And what that other nurse had said this morning, that was a mistake. She was just a silly.

"Sorry, I don't know any Iris, dear."

"Iris is a nurse, she works here!"

"Is she a staff nurse?"

He hadn't known what that meant. He didn't know.

"What's her surname?"

And then he had felt a bit panicky, because he didn't know that either. Did it matter? Surely she was here, in the hospital, somewhere? She would come straight away when she knew he was back.

But suppose no one told her? Suppose she never found out he was here, and missed him?

No. Iris had always known everything. She was very clever. When she had done the bandage she had never ever hurt him. She knew all sorts of things. She knew how to drive a train, and she had been in a submarine once, and looked through the periscope and seen the white cliffs of Dover. She knew how to make sand dogs curled up on the beach. She was sure to be here soon. Then everything would be all right. He wasn't going to cry or anything, she might come in and find him crying like a baby and he didn't want that.

He did feel a bit like crying. It was lonely having to wait so long. But he wasn't going to. He was going to be a man.

And she was sure to get here soon anyway.

Very soon now.

SYLVIA AT HOME, 1995

———————

"Oh, hi!" Lulu, the Australian nanny, is actually standing in the hall, for Sylvia, of course, is late. "Everything OK?" Lulu asks. She has her coat on. It is the beginning of her weekend off, and she has complicated plans for it.

"Yes, sorry, anything I should know?"

If only Adam were here! But he is in New York, for business reasons Sylvia has forgotten the details of.

"Not really," says Lulu, swinging her enormous bag energetically over her shoulder. "I think she might be getting another cold? Bit sniffly? Temp's OK, though. I've settled her down, sorry, zit OK if I go now?"

"Of course it is, sorry I'm late, have a good weekend!"

"Thanks, bye!" The door clicks to behind her, and she is gone.

Sylvia is alone in the house, with the baby.

Very quietly Sylvia crosses the hall and puts the pile of notes down on the table. She is hungry, perhaps. She goes into the kitchen and opens the fridge. There is some ham in a packet from Waitrose. She peels off the top slice, rolls it into a sausage shape, and takes a bite. Lulu has left the dishwasher running, and the kitchen is full of quiet rhythmic sloshing noises.

Sylvia finishes the slice of ham and goes back to the notes. But before she can even open the first one there is a long rising wail from upstairs.

Clio.

Perhaps she will stop. Sylvia waits, tense in her chair, the notefile on her lap. Clio goes on wailing, at first rather sleepily; a brief silence; then abruptly the astonishingly loud screaming roars. Still Sylvia waits; perhaps, even now, the baby will just stop. The screams continue, racket up a few notches of intensity.

Sylvia pictures the baby's fat red face and thin dampened hair, the jutting lower lip. She hears rage and baffled command. She hears orders given.

I will not, Sylvia tells herself. I will not.

Upstairs, still bellowing, the baby begins to rattle the cot bars. She is trying to climb out, thinks Sylvia. She will be able to do so suddenly, she's growing so fast. She will be able to do it one day, when she couldn't do it the day before, and she will fall to the floor and be injured, and it will be my fault.

For a moment longer she goes on trying to sit still, trying to refuse the baby's furious demands, but the thought of the child falling untended is too frightening to ignore for long, and at last Sylvia puts the notefile down and goes up the stairs.

Clio looks exactly as Sylvia pictured her, standing upright in the middle of her cot, both fists round the bars, a miniature Winston Churchill barking with infantile rage. Her body is hot and stiff with it as Sylvia picks her up, and she goes on shrieking right in Sylvia's ear, while Sylvia shushes her and jigs her gently up and down.

"Are you hungry? Thirsty? What is it? There, there."

Clio goes on screaming.

Sylvia carries her down to the kitchen, where Lulu has left a bottle of milk ready to warm. She warms it, and tests it on the back of her hand, and Clio grabs the bottle with both hands, takes two big sucks—oh, the quality of the sweet silence then!—and then flings it away, backhanded, with such strength that it crashes into Sylvia's wooden mug stand, and knocks it over. The crash, as three mugs fall off and shatter on the flags, is so loud that for a moment Clio stops screaming again, in surprise, but not for long.

Sylvia is trembling now. A terrible sensation inside her, in her stomach, is to do with the fact that Clio does not want her. She is crying like this because she wants Lulu. Of course she wants Lulu. Lulu is her real mother, Lulu loves her. Clio's got it dead right. The feeling in Sylvia's stomach is very hard to bear, it feels like pain though it is much duller, a flat wide sensation that makes nothing matter very much at all somehow. No, nothing matters very much.

Clio goes on screaming.

Dimly Sylvia recalls her own mother telling her how much babies like not having any clothes on. She carries the howling baby back up the stairs again, and one-handedly drops the changing mat onto the floor, puts the baby down on it, on her back, and begins pulling off the Babygrow. The back is damp with the sweat of Clio's rage. Clio seems determined to fight her mother for every inch of Babygrow. She clenches herself together, she kicks hard with her fat little legs, she catches Sylvia quite a nasty blow to the stomach as she kneels beside her.

Face set Sylvia pulls each flailing arm free. Violently Clio kicks both legs, as if struggling with obstinate determination to stay inside her clothes.

Is the nappy uncomfortable? Too wet?

The baby keeps up her unremitting bellows while Sylvia picks at the tapes of the disposable. In defiance of the adverts the tapes refuse to budge, and then, as Sylvia tugs at the tag of one of them, it sheers off. A curious panic arises in Sylvia's breast. For a moment it seems to her that the baby is trapped inside a plastic nappy, and that she is powerless to do anything about it. She puts both her clever professional hands inside the waist of the nappy, and uselessly tears at it, while Clio's screams take on a new note of anguish and horror.

"Oh please," says Sylvia, unconsciously, "oh please."

At last she is able to throw the torn useless and bone dry nappy away. Clio, naked on the changing mat, goes on screaming. Sylvia leaves the room, and stands for a moment outside the door, trying to calm herself down.

It is only a baby crying. Babies do that. There are no neighbors to hear, and anyway it isn't that late. It is only a baby. Crying.

Armed with a new nappy she goes back. Clio is, of course, still screaming. She wants Lulu, of course. Well, sorry, Clio. You're stuck with me. And I, of course, am stuck with you.

Unfortunately, as even Lulu could testify, if there is one thing guaranteed to put Clio into a bad mood it is being dressed. While being undressed made Clio furious, being dressed again seems to drive her into a frenzy, a rapture of intemperate fury. She kicks hard, she waggles her arms, she bucks like a suffocating fish on the changing mat, she writhes and wriggles out of Sylvia's hands, all the while screaming as hard as she can right into Sylvia's face.

Sylvia slaps her.

She slaps her quite hard several times on her bare kicking tender little legs. Clio does not, of course, stop screaming. But the sound alters. The different note, of pain and fear, is slightly more bearable. She knows who's in charge now. She knows what she's up against. She's got to learn.

And the sound of the slaps, that sting her own hand, somehow calms Sylvia herself, though at the same time the dull pain in her stomach, which is to do with Clio really wanting someone else, is redoubled into a sense of hurtling unease, of momentum, as if the dull pain is going somewhere, reaching some point, some unguessable climax.

At last the baby is fully poppered back into the Babygrow. Picking her up, Sylvia rocks herself to and fro. She is unaware herself of the movements she makes. Still, strangely enough, they work. The baby, after a few minutes more of lower volume wailing, and then of smaller moans, at last falls silent. She snuffles against Sylvia's hair. Her body softens. She goes to sleep. Looking at the Mickey Mouse clock over the cot Sylvia sees that it is nearly eleven, that an entire hour of screaming has passed.

After a little wait just to make sure, Sylvia rises slowly and puts the baby back in her cot.

Done it again. Hit her again.

Only a slap. Only a few little slaps. Was that so terrible?

Sylvia simply doesn't know whether it is terrible or not. Perhaps it was only a bit terrible. Certainly there is no one she is going to consult.

Oh, hello, is that the Health Visitor? Would you mind telling me, please, how terrible it is if you hit your baby? No, just a few slaps. As yet.

Oh no.

Mum, you know when I was a baby, Clio's age, did you ever, you know, feel the need to slap me around at all?

No. Oh no. You know the answer to that one. Sylvia's mother, who over the years had hardly ever raised her voice to her child, let alone her gentle affectionate hand! Not to dogs, not to babies.

Adam?

Adam the stranger, who will want a fuck when he gets back from wherever he's gone. Well, that would stop him, at least:

Adam, listen, I don't love Clio at all, you know. I don't even like her. When she annoys me I hit her.

Yes. That would stop him dead in his tracks.

If I ever say the words, thinks Sylvia clearly, as she pours herself a glass of wine from the wine box in the kitchen, if I ever say the words I will seal them as true. While I keep quiet there is a chance that one day things will change, and then it will be as if it never happened. Because Clio won't remember. She doesn't. So it sort of hasn't really happened, has it? Surely?

Admit it and it will have happened. For good.

She drinks. The wine burns her throat. Presently she remembers the notes, thankfully, and goes back to their safety at last.

SLEEPLESS, 1954

IRIS COULDN'T SLEEP AT ALL. For one thing she was hungry. It had been impossible to eat much in the presence of Rob's parents, even though Rob had, she gratefully realized, tried to keep a conversation all the time, so that she had hardly had to say a word.

Though even that had its drawbacks. He spoke to his father about various doctors, free and easy about the Eye Ward surgeon Mr. Barr, for instance, and his dad chatted back as if on friendly terms with this great and god-like person, as if at any moment the awe-inspiring and terrible Mr. Barr might just pop in, and sit down next to Iris herself, and flare his nostrils at her, and expect her to talk back!

It was horrible. This, she saw, was Rob's world. A world in which you chatted in a careless friendly sort of way to the likes of Mr. Barr, as she, Iris, might pass the time of day with the woman on the fruit stall outside the hospital!

And Rob had never talked like that before; he had seemed to view Mr. Barr as if from Iris's own side of the fence, from a position of similar gulping servility, and all the time he'd been sort of pretending, because his dad had been at the same hospital for a while long ago, and called him by his first name, Oh, hello, Everard!

What else was Rob concealing, what else was she going to realize she knew nothing about? Did he still think she could simply hop into this world with him, and shake the likes of Mr. Barr by the hand as an equal?

I'm not a bit equal, thinks Iris now, sleepless in the beautiful little Victorian brass bedstead.

No one else is asleep either.

Far above, in her attic bedroom, Meadows is lying down cozily enough, but she is not even trying to sleep. She has a lot to consider, tonight. In both hands, just above the neatly folded top sheet, she is slowly drawing back and forth, as if to aid thought, a slender length of pale blue ribbon, which Mrs. Wilding would be quite vexed to see, since that lady spent twenty minutes looking for it the previous evening: it belongs, rightly speaking, threaded through the hem of one of Mrs. Wilding's own cotton broidery anglaise petticoats. Mrs. Wilding will come across it tomorrow morning, in a place she feels almost certain she has looked in already: these things happen.

Mrs. Wilding herself, of course, is also wide awake. I'm not a snob, she keeps telling herself, but really anyone would blanch a little at the thought of introducing Iris da Silva to the neighborhood. To Mrs. Danby, for example. Or Laura Cunningham. They'd be so kind to her. And the wedding, oh, the wedding! Iris da Silva would have family; it appeared she had an uncle, who was (here Mrs. Wilding flinched whilst lying down, rather a feat) a dustman. Who drove a dustcart slowly about the streets of Stepney and Bow, whilst his comrades cheerily rattled the bins across the pavements, and heaved the rubbish into the back!

Uncle George! Would Uncle George, and his doubtless Donald McGill-postcard-style fat termagant of a wife and their snot-nosed quarrel-some sniggering but dull-eyed brats sit on Iris's side at the village church, and afterwards say Blue Skies! or Cheerio! as they swigged at vintage prewar champagne?

I am not a snob, Mrs. Wilding told herself, in the teeth of a great deal of available evidence, I am not a snob; but there are some things which are clearly not going to work, and I just don't see how Rob and that girl can possibly be happy together, not for long, anyway; they are just too unalike in every way.

Had she known how similar Iris's own conclusions were at that very moment, she might, perhaps, have been able to relax enough to at least allow her husband to get some sleep, if not herself. As it was she poked him in the ribs every time his breathing grew noisier; she was convinced his snoring was keeping her awake.

Dr. Wilding himself, though he had risen too early that morning to stay fully awake about it, was also uneasy in his mind. He didn't like the boy prattling about Everard Barr like that. Didn't like Everard Barr. There wasn't any talk about the fellow; it wasn't like that. Nevertheless it was perfectly clear that Barr had what Dr. Wilding even thought of, in code, as serious faults: in his nature. Serious flaws; of character. Serious faults; dressed too well. One didn't want one's boy spending time in the fellow's company. Singling the boy out in the Mess, forsooth! Talking about his career, indeed!

The question was: whether to warn the child. Clearly Rob had some hero-worshiping feelings, and Barr was known to be brilliant, innovative, courageous. What a relief it was, that Rob had brought home such a very pretty girl! Lovely shy little thing.

A relief, but not, of course, an end to all such worries. For Dr. Wilding knew that sexual inversion, whilst in many ways scarcely credible to normal people, was also infectious. That was the sick mystery of it all. That once a normal young man had been coaxed, flattered—seduced, in a word, into inverted behavior, he was changed forever. He became one of them.

And could the wholesome appeal of an artless innocent like that poor little girl really measure up to . . .

Here Dr. Wilding's imagination, compressed over the years, like an ancient layer of soft organic matter, into adamantine rock, is too flattened and concrete to come up with anything specific. It supplies words only, terrifying in their vagueness, in their swooning implications: sensuality, debauchery, corruption.

Inversion, Dr. Wilding believes, offers a young man immediate gross pleasures unknown to natural intercourse. That is why, once tasted, they can never be forgotten, like the deadly transforming ravishments of the lotus flower. How wise the Mohammedans are, to arrange such early marriages! Dr. Wilding sighs loudly, causing his wife to click her tongue in frustration: Dr. Wilding takes no notice.

Of course Rob's always been perfectly manly: a fine naughty boyish little scamp, he was. But even Dr. Wilding can see that he has grown into a nice-looking young man. Charming, his wife says sometimes, breezily.

Beautiful, says Dr. Wilding, in his most secret heart, which was taught long ago to distrust beauty in all its forms, and fears it to this day.

"I prefer the simple things," he told his wife long ago, as they quarreled over Georgian silver, over delicate lusterware teacups. But he lied. *I fear the beautiful things* would have been nearer the truth. Beauty attracts admiration, but also excites evil: greed. Lust.

Better for Rob, to be less good-looking. It is dangerous, to be so beautiful, thinks Dr. Wilding fretfully, turning over and falling into a light doze, from which his wife instantly wakens him.

"Will you please stop that noise!" she hisses.

"Sorry," says Dr. Wilding, and immediately begins to snore.

Rob, hearing him, grins to himself in the darkness. He doesn't know if he has ever felt so happy before. All his favorite people under one roof! His dad's clearly nuts about Iris, as anyone would be, who had any sense, and Ma will of course come round. Sooner or later. Probably later, Rob has to admit. But it was very jolly talking man-to-man like that with Dad.

Impossible, of course, to sleep with Iris so near. Tomorrow, while Mum and Dad are at church, he is going to take Iris for a walk, through the little wood behind the house and out onto the cliff top. There's a place he knows, almost hidden in the gorse, where you can hear the sea crashing onto the rocks below but still be private and hidden: the vicar's hut.

Not the present vicar, of course, quavering away, "Eeow, Lee-amb of Gord, that takest away the sins of the wahld," not that tea-sipping addled old drip but a real old-fashioned early-Victorian muttonchop-whiskered nutcase, who had, it was said, once painted his pony in black and white stripes because he fancied riding about the parish on a zebra, and later constructed a sort of kite in which he was reputed to have soared like an eagle from the cliff top, hung for a moment suspended in the air, swooped heavily to and fro bellowing aloud in triumph, and dropped at last to the water a good mile out at sea, whence he had swum snorting back to shore with bits of broken harness and sailcloth trailing from his powerful shoulders.

They didn't make vicars like that any more, thought Rob, clutching at the sheet, laughing to himself in the darkness. But the hut. The flying vicar had built himself a lookout post on the cliff top, now hidden from all but the most knowledgeable local eyes by its thick covering of gorse. He had collected driftwood for years, the curving thick eternal oak planking of the sailing ships of that time, and fastened them all together using pegs of oak, and tar, and made a small neat curving house, right on the edge of the cliff, poised over the water. The eagle's nest.

They could take a picnic, perhaps. He would ask Meadows. And a rug. Just some lemonade and a bun or two. Iris would be enchanted.

Oh, Iris! And so will I, thinks Rob.

RUBY GETS ANOTHER LETTER, 1954

TED WOULD BE BACK from work soon, and then they would drive to London, to the hospital. Ruby wasn't looking forward to it. It had been quite a relief all round, not having the child at home all day, getting in the way, whining about boredom or saying that his eye hurt. Ruby especially could not bear him saying that.

Once or twice the thought of driving all that way to visit him had just been too much, and Ruby had talked her husband into staying at home.

"I mean, all that way just for an hour! By the time we get there it's nearly time to turn round and come back again. It just upsets him anyway, you know it does."

And this certainly seemed to be true; though the child seemed to greet them calmly enough, when they came to say goodbye he made no end of a fuss. He had made so much noise once that the Ward Sister had come and spoken quite sharply, to him for making such an exhibition of himself, and to Ruby for allowing her child to upset all the others, for by this time he had been transferred to the Children's Ward.

"It's kinder to leave him in peace, surely!"

Ted, who had been upset himself by the scene, agreed, and they had had a nice quiet evening at home, just the two of them, though he had given her, she thought, quite a strange look when she said how pleasant it had been, just like old times; and the following evening he hadn't listened to reason at all, and had gone off to the hospital all by himself. Ruby said she had one of her heads.

But the child was coming home today, so they wouldn't have to worry about that sort of thing any more.

Then she had come in from doing a few errands in the village, and there it was on the mat, waiting for her: another anonymous letter. But this time there was some small lumpy thing inside the envelope, some small thing padded in paper. She could feel the give of it, with something hard right inside.

She thought of chucking the whole thing straight into the bin. As she stood up holding it she saw herself going straight outside to the dustbin and throwing it in, and then emptying the dustpan of ashes from the boiler all over it, so that she wouldn't be tempted to try to fish it out again.

Then she imagined scrabbling about in the ashes after all. Could she really bear not to know what it was, ever?

Slowly Ruby went back to the kitchen, and sat down at the clean Formica table. She put the envelope down in front of her and looked at it.

She had told no one about the first letter. What was there, after all, to tell? She knew herself to be guilty as charged: she *should* have looked after him better. She *was* a cow. The letter had merely repeated what she knew to be true. It was just further proof, where none was needed.

She had torn it into strips and fed it to the fire, but she could see it plain as plain still. Was this the same hand?

Perhaps. Perhaps not.

Suppose there were two of them; suppose, in time, there were dozens? This was black ink. The other had been blue. But that needn't mean anything. Anyone could borrow a pen. Or have two.

Ruby took up the sharp knife she used to peel potatoes and slit open the envelope. She slipped the sharp knife back in the drawer, and looked. There was no letter. There was a tiny rectangular parcel of Christmas wrapping paper, green, with a pattern of little red Christmas trees on it. It was stuck together with sellotape.

Ruby unpicked it with her fingernails, and presently unrolled the paper to find a small pencil, a red coloring pencil. That was all there was.

She turned over the paper and looked again in the envelope, but there was nothing else to find.

She sat still for a few minutes, with her heart beating very hard and fast; then she stood up, gathered all the bits and pieces together, and scrunched them all together into a ball, which she set down again on the table.

It hadn't happened: that was Ruby's idea. What envelope, what pencil? Nothing like that here. She felt a powerful desire, however, to get out into the open.

For one thing she had the strangest pictures in her head. They were of herself, sitting at the kitchen table, opening the envelope, and finding the little pencil inside; Ruby saw all these things as they had happened, but from on high, as if from somewhere near the ceiling up by the boiler chimney pipe.

From this vantage point she could see the top of her own head, the set of her shoulders as she leaned her elbows on the table, the envelope with its neat slit, the little red Christmas trees so far away beside her hand; and at the same time the air in the kitchen seemed to have grown hot and thick and heavy, like smoke you could see through, though you couldn't breathe. You could hardly breathe at all.

It's really stuffy in here all of a sudden, thought Ruby, and she got herself to the kitchen door and nearly fell out of it as it swung open.

It was fresh outside, a chill sharp spring day. Presently Ruby's head cleared, and she felt better, and decided to do a bit of weeding before she went back inside. As she weeded she hummed quite loudly to herself. She knelt in her clean apron on the concrete of the driveway, pulling up everything she could see that looked small and as if it might be a weed. Her fingers were soon stained with brown.

Presently one of her neighbors went by, and Ruby said Good Morning, loudly, cheerfully.

It was Whatshername, that one who looked like a sheep, in her blue fitted coat and carrying her shopping basket. From across the road. She looked startled; anyone would think she'd never had a neighbor wish her Good Morning before. No reply, just a quick nod of the sheepy face.

Perhaps it had been her.

Ruby jumped up and peered over the fence as Whatshername crossed the road and walked up the path of her house and put her key in the side door and finally disappeared; she heard the tiny clunk as the door closed.

She went back to her weeding. Look at that, a whole big patch nicely cleared!

Neighbors. What was the point of them? They clocked what you were wearing. They knew what day you'd done your washing, and what you had to wash. They knew how often you changed the sheets. They knew how old your best dress was. They could hear it when you argued; they knew what time you went to bed and what time you got up in the morning. They knew all sorts of things. You couldn't guess how many things they really knew.

Ruby went on pulling things up, quite big plants now with bulbs on the end, and leaves like thick little spears, and other smaller skinnier ones, that broke sometimes as she wrenched them from the soil.

Presently she began to understand that she was rather wet. Her sleeves dragged on her arms, and the back of her blouse stuck to her, cold and clammy, as she leaned forward. It still did not occur to her that it was raining. Soon she was shivering with cold. The chill wet soil stuck to her hands, there was a great deal of mud on her apron, and her hair was dripping down her collar.

Finally, stiff from kneeling, she rose, shook off all the bits of leaf and stalk, and went back into the house. There was the ball of screwed up paper still sitting on the table. Her slippers were wet through, she noticed, and stained with mud, so she took them off on the mat and, humming again, leaving wet footprints of her stockinged feet, she took the ball up without quite looking at it, opened the kitchen boiler with the other hand, dropped it in on top of the glowing coke, and closed the lid. Then she took the rag from the sink and wiped the table.

"All done," said Ruby brightly, to no one at all, and then she went upstairs to get changed.

SYLVIA READS ON, 1995

———————

SYLVIA LIKED HOSPITAL NOTES; always had. Her public and professional view was that patients' notes were a rich resource; like court reports, they were a record of events, they were an important research tool, they were of incalculable human interest; they should thus be preserved, as they were, in perpetuity, easy to get hold of, portable, and, if possible, take-homeable.

Privately Sylvia had, perhaps, other more dubious reasons, connected with a personal fondness for fiction. Sylvia, in fact, was by nature a *reader*.

When she was a little child her mother, much harried by business concerns, found Sylvia's relentless bookworming dreadfully irritating.

"Will you put that book down and go and get some fresh air!"

And the small Sylvia had read so determinedly into the night that her mother had in exasperation finally taken away her bedside lamp, so that Sylvia was forced to read by the dim light coming in from the landing, and soon required spectacles to correct the resultant myopia. She had natural taste, bored by childish things before she was eight, plowing without effort, innocent as a gorging caterpillar, through works by every name she had ever heard of, Dickens, Dostoevsky, Lawrence, Wells, Austen, James, Eliot. It was like a task she had to get through, though what could lie on the other side of this immensity of print she had no idea, and no interest.

"Put that book down and come and help me with the dogs!"

For like most habitual readers, Sylvia had no idea how irritating reading can be, to nonreading friends and relations.

It looks so lazy, for one thing. There was Sylvia's mother, widowed early, earning a precarious living kenneling other people's dogs and cats, up early every morning, mucking out and feeding and otherwise tending all day a score of captive animals, all of them moping or frenzied or both at once, whilst Sylvia, home in perfectly good time to help out of an afternoon, simply sat as if in a daze at the kitchen table, taking forever over a cup of tea, a book always open on the table.

While Sylvia's mother sat struggling in the evenings with accounts and feed orders, Sylvia, homework over and done with, lay comfortably stretched out upon the sofa, merely turning pages, rapt, hardly present. If called, she would not hear her own name, not until the third or fourth repetition. Or yell. And it was her task to do the washing up every evening.

Why hadn't she done it yet, why couldn't she get it out of the way first? It was somehow always in the way, that pile of dirty plates and saucepans. It stopped Mrs. Henshaw's concentration, it peered over her shoulder at the messy VAT returns. She should get that sort of thing out of the way before she lies about reading, thought Mrs. Henshaw. Shouldn't she!

"Sylvie."

"Sylvia."

"SYLVIA!"

And how lonely Mrs. Henshaw often felt, during, say, a comedy program on television, when at a particularly good moment she would glance over at Sylvia to share the fun, only to discover that she had stealthily re-opened some book or another, and was only pretending to watch!

Sylvia did not, as A levels approached, consider literature as a possible study or career. When she fell off the wall behind the cricket pitch and broke her leg, a dashing and glamorous young woman house officer had treated her in Casualty; Sylvia had determined on medicine herself before the plaster was dry.

As a prize-winning medical student, Sylvia had often felt a little uncomfortable reading the glowing reports her various tutors wrote about her. So many of them mentioned approvingly her evident interest in the patients as people. Sylvia herself suspected, however, that she was in fact mainly interested in them as books. Especially as the exigencies of continual prize-winning meant that all fiction reading must henceforward of necessity be ferociously controlled, and rationed to very occasional weekend binges.

Was she not urged, however, to occupy spare moments on the wards in reading up case notes, those fine examples of narrative compression? All those bare biographical details lightly sketched in, and family history, and personal habits, and present difficulties and symptoms, were so very like those summaries her mother's weekly *Women's Realm* used to provide, outlining the plot so far before this week's installment: a literary aperitif.

Diligently, intelligently, Sylvia read the patients' notes, but with a secret sinful pleasure, and a vivid sense, as she closed each one, of those three magical words *Now Read On*. And whilst at some bedside taking a keen student interest, Sylvia was often at heart simply absorbing somebody's personal Chapter Three or Four: being told stories.

So it was with real pleasure and relief that Sylvia went back to the pile of notes, tomorrow's list, which she had left on the desk in her study. A refuge from all present dangers, in the complex medical details of other people's lives: stories.

Right. First one: very fat, thought Sylvia with anxious greed: would she have time to read it all? She would have to skim, but she was good at that.

Oh yes: him. Hadn't he mentioned St. Giles's, where Sylvia herself had trained? And aha, here they were, what luck that St. Giles's hadn't yet gone in for microfiche! Here beneath all the computer sheets were the actual old notes in their battered St. Giles's yellow, a good three inches thick over what had to be several decades, and all of it in varying handwriting and mismatched printed sheets from different hospitals, and fragile ancient furry-edged responses from this and that long-ago specialist!

Such letters often turned out to bear signatures Sylvia recognized from lecture halls or learned journals or her own bookshelves, now names of authority and distinction but here in, as it were, a certain state of youthful friendly medical undress. Dear Jim, thanks for sending me this pleasant young chap and signed Love to Irene and the boys, yours ever, Jerry: Sylvia's very favorite professional reading.

Starting at the back then: right at the beginning, the very first entry. All handwritten, faded gray-blue ink. September 9, 1953. Oh God, one of those accidents that make new parents groan and shudder. Admitted as an emergency . . . *foreign body deep penetration: globe disorganized with mass of uveal and retinal tissue protruding through wound, whole of inner eye occupied by hemorrhagic clots . . . straight to theatres . . .*

Rapt, Sylvia turned the crackling pages to the operation report. *Present in Theatre Two.*

Hey! Beaconsfield! Had to be Morry Beaconsfield, present all those years ago in some long-lost Theatre Two, Morry whom she had herself replaced, on his retirement from this very hospital five years ago. Sitting back in her chair, Sylvia did some quick mental arithmetic. Sixty-five in 1990, what did that make you in 1953?

Twenty-eight. Morry Beaconsfield! Nice old Morry Beaconsfield waving at her, from among these long gone strangers! Someone called Barr, never heard of him, a Pym, Sister Holt, Nurse Stoddard. All these faded gray-blue names. What had become of them all?

And then suddenly she understood the name at the very end of the list: the second medical student: *R. Wilding.*

Rob.

Surely not. Her heart had given a great twisting thump, just at the sight of the name. Could it be he?

Sylvia jumped out of her chair and paced up and down in the lamplight. Feverishly she did more sums, how old had he been, did it fit, oh, yes, of course it did. Rob, aged what, nineteen? Twenty? Watching Morry Beaconsfield, for heaven's sake!

Suddenly it was as if certain years had never passed. She remembered longing for him so vividly that for a moment it was as if she longed for him still. Her eyes filled. Everything in her life, she felt, was down to Rob Wilding.

Her job, with all its difficulties and deep pleasures.

Adam, for what was Adam but Rob's shadow?

Clio: the deserved punishment: what happened when you took the shadow and not the substance. Despair overcame her. For the space of several heartbeats Sylvia was lost.

Then, ashamedly, she forced herself to sit down again, to look again. Come on. Don't be so pathetic. Look: it's just a name. That's all there is.

Rob had been there, at the start. So it would be a shapely thing, thought Sylvia instantly, for me to finally sort out this poor man. Imagination immediately streaked ahead; it took photographs of the man all perfectly sorted out, and sent them on with a little graceful note. And an address.

Stop that, thought Sylvia, warningly to herself. A little graceful note to whom, to what? It was the Rob of fifteen years ago she wanted. And he, of course, no longer existed, any more than did the little injured boy in the notes before her. Forty years of hospitals ahead of *him*.

I could save you, thought Sylvia to the child in Theatre Two, I could save you from some of that life ahead. I can get in now, and alter the plot. Change the ending. If you'll let me. *Now* Read On.

And then abruptly she remembered Will. Later she worked out that she had thought of him because he was the only person she knew who would understand about seeing Rob's name, but at the time it seemed to leap out at her from nowhere, that he had so strangely called her in clinic, obviously urgent about something, and asked her to ring him back, and that she had said she would, was it only this morning? And she had forgotten him.

And it was already gone eleven; was it too late? It must have been something important, how could she have forgotten? Some friend she was!

Try him now then, his mobile first. She dialed the number, her face stiff with remorse. No reply: switched off.

His mother's number then. He might well be in bed by now. Is there an answerphone? Would Annie have one? Suppose I wake Annie up?

For a moment or two Sylvia hesitated. Wouldn't it be best to call to-morrow morning? She'd had such a long day herself. He might want to talk for hours. He might want to talk for hours about death and sickness and suffering and could she frankly stand a single minute, let alone say the sort of sympathetic things he presumably needed to hear in return?

On the other hand he had never called her at work before. Perhaps it was simply something medical. She could cope with that. She could manage being consulted. Good at that.

Ten past eleven, though!

Get it over with, she thought. It's always the things you don't do that you regret. It occurred to her as well that while Annie probably wouldn't have bothered to install an answerphone, Will would have: he would always need one for work anyway.

It'll kick in straight away if he's gone to bed. If it doesn't I'll just let it ring a couple of times, just so I can say I tried.

She dialed. And was immediately answered.

ROB AND IRIS VISIT THE VICAR'S HUT, 1954

IT WAS AN EXTRAORDINARILY beautiful morning. Larks rose from the field behind the house as they crossed it, and lifted singing into the air. The wood was full of bluebells, the dappled blue trimmed here and there with drifts of starry white anemones.

Neither of them was entirely happy. While getting Iris on her own in the middle of nowhere had seemed a delicious idea the night before, Rob couldn't help wondering, now he was actually putting it into practice, whether it wasn't a bit dangerous, a bit caddish, even. Suppose they got carried away? He had, it was true, remembered to bring the French letter with him, transferring it from his jacket to the pocket of his trousers. Though even that had made him feel a little ashamed of himself. Was it right, to do what he was planning to do, to plan it, at all? Wasn't he being rather cold-blooded about it, with his French letter?

Whereas Iris was simply uncomfortable. She had brought only high heels with her. She had not liked borrowing Mrs. Wilding's Wellington boots. They were too big for her anyway. She had had to pad them out with two pairs of Rob's old school rugby socks, and how could you possibly go for a romantic walk with your fiancé wearing two pairs of hard striped red and yellow woolly socks, and an enormous pair of ancient clumping rubber boots?

Also she had immediately pictured them wandering hand-in-hand through flowery meadows when Rob had suggested a walk, and the path through the wood was too narrow. Of course the bluebells were very nice

144

but she had to lumber along behind him, trying not to fall over knobbly bits of tree root, and her ankles were aching already.

"Rob, is it much further?"

"Oh come on, we've hardly started!"

Asked to comment on his sweetheart's appearance Rob would have replied, "What boots?" for he rarely noticed what Iris was wearing at all; generally she had to prompt him. Colors, textures, a perfect fit: they were vague details to Rob. It was Iris inside her clothes he was piercingly aware of.

"And it's not very far," he added.

Though once, when they were getting a little carried away in Iris's sister's flat, when Jo was out for the evening, he had been made aware of the color, texture, and perfect fit of that crepe de chine underwear, its sheen of palest blue, its trimming of tiny silken embroidered forget-me-nots.

Yes, sometimes under her nurse's uniform, why not?

Matching suspender belt, look!

And the camisole's got these little pearl buttons, see? D'you like it, Rob?

"Just along here, we're nearly there."

Out of the woods now, they cross a field, at last hand in hand. They can see the long low line of the sea ahead, the sunshine glittering on the water. The field gives way to a scrub of gorse bushes. The air is full of the sweet smell of gorse flowers, and the sound of bees.

"Here!" says Rob, after some time.

"Down there?" Bending Iris can just make out what looks like a rabbit track. The gorse on either side of it meets impenetrably, at waist level.

"I've come prepared," says Rob, shouldering off the rucksack. Beneath the thermos flask of coffee and the bag of buns, bent and squashed, with considerable effort, into manageable dimensions, lies his father's thorn-proof waxed cloth overcoat, of enormous weight and antiquity. It is lined with quilted tartan, and looks stiff and greasy enough to stand up all by itself. It once belonged to Dr. Wilding's own father; having sheltered the father, it has ever since shielded the son on his rounds, year in, year out. It has adapted itself to his huddled shape; empty, it still seems to shroud his thick strong shoulders and embonpoint, a wrinkled gabardine echo; it exhibits also a certain thin rustiness beneath the arms, and a plain manly odor of mingled sweat, canvas, and dog.

It is, in short, the most repellent garment Iris has ever seen. Rob holds it out with an inviting flourish.

"You want me to put that on?"

"Well, just to get through the gorse," says Rob. "It's completely thorn-proof, you see." Odd, he remembers, how unfussed his father had been about his borrowing this totemic family item. *The cliffs, oh aye, the vicar's wee hut: all right then.* If you didn't know him better, thought Rob, you'd almost suspect him of, well, giving you permission, practically encouraging immoral behavior. Which was enough in itself to keep you on the straight and narrow.

"The house is just down there," he adds. He gives the thorn-proof coat another waggle. "It's only for a minute."

First rugby socks, thinks Iris, then Wellington boots, and now this!

"Bloody hell, Rob!" she says angrily, and then suddenly bursts out laughing. She goes on laughing, helplessly, while he drapes the thing over her shoulders; by the time he has stuffed her arms inside each smelly gaping cavernous sleeve he too is in fits of giggles. They stand kissing for a moment, when he has buttoned her in.

"Nearly there!"

Crouching they squeeze through the gorse bushes. It is exhausting, and a particularly difficult trip in Wellington boots. Pausing now and then for a breather they navigate a series of twists and sudden bends, reach an open downhill curving slope, and at last arrive at a small stretch of grassy windblown cliff top. Far below them, but with a surging immediacy now, the waves crash against black and jagged rocks. It's a sheer drop. Iris, leaning over, feels a sudden queasy ache about her calves and shins, as if her legs have seen the danger, and want to hurry away, all by themselves if they must.

"Look!" says Rob proudly. Iris turns, moving away from the edge, and gives a little gasp of pleasure. For lying neatly, cozily, amongst the surrounding gorse, built right into the cliff which rises steeply behind it, its roof almost hidden beneath a green and pink-flowered weight of brambles, is the little house. The oak, just as Rob described it, has weathered to a silvery gray. Its sides curve outward, faintly suggesting the ships its boards once made. It has two small shuttered glassless windows, one on either side of the door, which is in two like a farmhouse door. Sea pinks nod their little heads before it in the warm breeze.

"Oh, Rob!"

"Come on, let's go inside." Rob turns the stout wooden peg that holds the door shut, and opens it, while Iris throws off the terrible thornproof coat, and the boots, and the socks, and prances barefoot on the wiry cliff top grass.

"Here." He picks her up, and carries her over the threshold.

Inside it is surprisingly dark and dry, and about the size of a railway compartment. Like the door the shutters are held by wooden pegs. The walls on either side of the door have long bench-like seats built into them, of the same smooth ancient timber, like the floor. It smells of earth and wood.

They open both windows, and prop the door open with a stone.

"Why did he build it?"

"Who, the flying vicar? Dunno. He liked sitting here looking out to sea, apparently. And fancied a bit of shelter. Look. That was me," says Rob, and he points out his initials, carved rather showily into the main trunk-like beam of the ceiling.

R. W. 1941

"I was ten," he adds. "Birthday penknife. Look there, too."

Others, Iris sees, have also left their mark. And their dates; *S. W.* had gone to a lot of copperplate trouble in 1848, and *T Mc C* must have worked for days in 1872, so deep and ornate was his first letter. Others, with less time to spare perhaps, had expressed the self-evident in ink or pencil.

Bill B was here 1915

Sam was here 1910

QP 06

"It was less overgrown then, I think," says Rob. "It's sort of got forgotten about."

"It's lovely," says Iris. "What's it like with the door closed?"

They close the shutters too. Twilight. One or two gaps in the shutters let in starry brilliant beams of light. Rob sits down. Sighing, Iris sits on his knees. They kiss for a long time, while outside the sea heaves and crashes far below, and the seagulls cry.

"Should we . . ." at last murmurs Rob. He meant to say, "Should we stop this, and have the picnic?" But can't be bothered somehow, as soon as he starts. He trails off, and Iris, who thinks he was asking about something quite different, slides round on his lap so that she is facing him, and bestride him.

"Yeah, let's," she whispers.

His heart stands still. His hands find their way to her naked thighs. Iris has undone his shirt buttons, and slipped her cool hand inside, the palm against his bare chest.

"Sure?" he manages, as his hands, of their own accord it seems, go on sliding upwards. She murmurs assent into his mouth. His fingers grope for the well-remembered, well-loved silk, grope, fumble, and at last stop altogether.

"Iris? Oh, Iris!"

She laughs softly, her lips parted, nodding; and he understands at last that he has taken a Sunday morning stroll, from his parents' house, and carrying a perfectly legitimate picnic, in the company of a girl who, whatever else she may have been wearing in the way of borrowed socks or boots or overcoats, has all the time, and by her own design, had no knickers on at all.

It is Iris's little surprise.

"Yes," says Iris. "Yes."

RUBY'S SURPRISE PRESENT, 1954

WHEN HE CAME BACK from the hospital he was different. He'd grown up a bit, Ruby thought. He was quiet. He was so little trouble that sometimes she almost forgot he was there, sitting in his room reading, or doing a jigsaw puzzle.

Once Ruby had offered to play cards with him. She had offered politely, with a certain sense of strain, as if he were someone else's child, on a visit. She had been relieved when he said no.

Every couple of weeks a new little parcel came through the post for Ruby. After the first red coloring pencil came a blue one; then a green; a lilac; then a stub of brown. Ruby opened the envelopes without inner comment, when she could be sure she was alone, and fed everything directly into the kitchen boiler.

Generally she tried not to look at the child directly, unless she had to. Not that there was anything to see, of course. She had to take him to the local hospital, seven miles each way on the bus, twice a week to have the dressing changed. The nurses there were very brisk, took him away into some inner room and told her sharply to stay in the waiting room, quite as if she had tried to go in with him. Sometimes Ruby pretended that she really did want to go in with him, now she knew it was safe to do so, and that it was expected of her.

"That's my brave boy!" said Ruby, as he was marched firmly away. She didn't like to think about what they were doing to him in there. And it was best, she felt, not to make any fuss about it afterwards.

"All done?" brightly, as he was brought back to her, in the new dressing, and then the long wait for the bus home. Once one of the nurses had said he was a little hero, and that he deserved an ice cream. Ruby had flushed with embarrassment and anger. It had never occurred to her to reward him. She felt reproached, and found out: a failure once more. On the next trip she had bought a tube of Smarties in the newsagent across the street from the hospital, and made sure a nurse saw her handing them over when the time came.

And he hadn't looked a bit pleased or surprised; just put them in his pocket without a word.

So I'm not going to bother again, thought Ruby. She thought she was angry with him, for not saying thank you. She did not notice that she felt like crying.

"Hold my hand," she hissed at him, as they walked toward the bus stop.

What of Ruby's husband all this time? Ted endured. He had been brought up to be strong, and silent; his personal code was that of his generation, which made no fuss, which gave away nothing, which put up and shut up. He knew his wife suffered, but she would not let him touch her; he knew his son was injured, but he thought of this as a physical injury only, one a healthy child would soon recover from. With his son he attempted jollity.

"Hello, old chap! How's the young Nelson?"

Truth was, Ted felt awkward; the kid had always been Ruby's job, not his. He just couldn't feel at ease with the boy at the moment somehow. Especially not with that ruddy great bandage all over his poor little clock. Perhaps things would be better when that part of things was all over. When it was all healed up perhaps they would take that trip to the seaside the kid had gone on about so much at first.

As if they could risk that raw empty socket on a sandy beach! Gritty sand, blown by the wind! It didn't bear thinking about. He couldn't bear thinking about it.

"I said no, all right?"

Too harsh, he had thought later, when the horror of the imagined grittiness had worn off a little and he was himself again.

"Be too cold right now, old chap. Perhaps in the summer, all right?"

He had nodded his cool little nod, and turned away, back to his book.

Quiet, thought Ruby's husband: the house was too quiet and tidy and all Ruby thought about was keeping everything just so; and it occurred to him that he should take her for a nice evening out. How long had it been, after all? Months and months. Not since . . .

No, not since the accident.

Would she agree, though? She didn't really like leaving the house, he knew, since it had happened; had some idea everyone was looking at her and blaming her. Well, that was crazy. He'd let her carry on like this for too long as it was. She was going to end up in hospital herself one day if she didn't look lively. She was a woman and women were often irrational; they let their feelings get the better of them; they needed a calm sensible man to look after them; he must let Ruby know that things had gone on like this long enough. He must assert himself.

At the zip factory Ted, as deputy dyehouse manager, was thus entitled to eat his lunch, using nicer cutlery, in a separate manager's lunchroom adjoining the works canteen, though the food was actually all the same. The factory as a whole, though, had a yearly party at Easter time, a dinner-dance which was to be held this year in the local town hall. Tickets for managers were not cheap, since they were subsidizing everyone else, but despite knowing what Ruby would say he bought two; then he did something he had never even thought of doing before. With tremendous discomfort, with shrinking embarrassment and general feelings of utter hopelessness, he caught the bus to town one Saturday afternoon when he had told Ruby he was going to watch a football match, and went to a dress shop he knew Ruby had once longingly mentioned.

Luckily there was a very nice woman inside who seemed to understand how he felt, and who held various frocks up against herself so that he could try to make some sort of decision.

Ruby had a better figure though, he thought. Wouldn't she look a peach in that sparkly blue one! But sparkling would not be Ruby's choice, he decided, finally. She wouldn't want to draw attention. This dark red one then?

"Discreet," said the shop woman, as she folded it into tissue paper. "But elegant."

Would Ruby go for discreet and elegant? He felt a certain confidence, holding the carrier bag as he waited at the bus stop, that discreet and elegant were the weapons of choice, as far as getting Ruby out of the house went. She would at least try it on, he was sure. Suppose it didn't fit!

If it fitted it would work, he thought. She would be pleased, she wouldn't be able to help it; that was what women were like. Irrational. Pleased by little things.

Oh please, God, let it fit!

He was expecting a few fireworks of course. Just at first. She'd be furious, she'd be scandalized at the idea of him going out and buying her a new dress just like that, she'd probably tell him to take it right back where it came from, and that she wouldn't dream of going out dancing with the child still in bandages, what did he take her for?

He heard all this so clearly that when in fact he handed the carrier bag over, and told her what it was for, he was all prepared. She was going to go off like a rocket, he thought.

The carrier bag had clean gray and white stripes on it, with a picture of a red rose in the middle.

"What's this?"

"Have a look."

Inside, of course, all you could see was the tissue paper, all nicely folded and tied with pink string.

"It's for you, Ruby. From that shop near the cinema. You know."

He couldn't understand it; she looked, if anything, frightened. She made no move to take the slender package out.

"What is it?"

"It's a new dress, Rube. Go on. Have a look."

"I don't want to."

"Please, Ruby. It's a present."

"I don't want no presents," said Ruby. She stood up and went to the sink, and started running the hot tap. He hadn't so much as sipped his tea yet, and she was trying to wash up; and she wouldn't even look at the dress. Panic seized him. It pushed him to his feet, made him reach out, grab Ruby's shoulder, and pull her round to face him.

"Just open it!" he shouted.

There was a long shocked panting silence. Both were aware of the child in the next room. Even he would have lifted his head from his book now.

Ruby turned the tap off, and dried her hands on her apron. With the stiff shoulders of deep offense she took up the carrier bag, and tipped the tissue-paper parcel out onto the table. Then she picked it up in one hand, and in a swift practiced movement opened the lid of the kitchen boiler with the other.

Ted gave an agonized shout, disbelieving; he could not move for astonishment; in stunned surprise he watched her tip the new dress, unworn, unseen, still in its nice little pink string, onto the red-hot coke, where it flared at once. Then she closed the lid.

"That's that," said Ruby, going back to the washing up.

WILL'S BAD EVENING, 1995

FOR LONG PERIODS OF TIME, on that first intolerable evening, getting his mother's supper ready, chatting to her, checking on her drugs, straightening out the room, he had been able to put the whole incredible shipwreck completely out of his mind.

It was only when Annie slept, and he went back into the living room and sat aghast in front of the television, that terror savaged him. For a few immeasurable minutes he had felt as if he might just die of this annihilating fear. His heart could not surely go on beating this fast for long without failing. He couldn't go on sweating this much, shaking this much, how could anyone feel this much sick horror whilst sitting quietly on a sofa watching *Friends*?

The breath of his own laughter had steadied him a little. He had straightened himself out from the clenched crouch, rubbed his face in his hands, and thought of the telephone. Obviously you didn't sit here on your own. You told people. You told your friends.

Hand out to take the receiver, he paused.

What did you tell them?

"Hey, Mark, mate, it's me. Got a moment?"

Perhaps he would have, and perhaps he wouldn't, he had the two little kids these days after all. And he'd be so upset, Will thought. How'd I feel, if it was the other way round?

I wish it was the other way round, came the instant craven thought.

Shut the *fuck* up, thought Will savagely to himself. Shut *up*. Now: are you going to call him or not? Think: he won't know what lymphoma is.

I'll have to explain. He won't know he's got a spleen. I'll have to tell him what it does. I'd have to talk and talk, areas of diffuse infiltration, bone marrow, laparoscopic splenectomy.

If I say any of it I'll have to say all of it.

Suppose I cry?

No suppose about it if I have to say that lot. Crying down the phone. Shaming. Impossible. And, Christ, to be alone here then!

I can't say it yet. I can't risk it.

Perhaps tomorrow.

Feeling better now anyway, he thought, realizing that this was so. It had come like a wave knocking him over. But then it had retreated. All by itself. For now, at least. For now, he just felt tired.

"Been a tiring day, Judy," said Will aloud to his mother's dog. She was peeping out at him from beneath the coffee table, her favorite spot if turfed off Annie's bed. She was unenthusiastic but he clipped on her lead and resolutely took her round the two loops of familiar infinity.

Not Mark at all, not tomorrow, anyway. Leave the poor sod alone. He had enough to contend with, new baby, Sue perhaps depressed again, toddler mayhem. Tell him when you know the results. Ten years, maybe, that wouldn't be so bad. Forty-five. Who wanted to grow old anyway? Tell him when they've done it. When the next bit's over.

Holly? In America. Too far away. And did he want Ozzie to know? No, Oz must not know until the last possible moment. Whenever that was. Brig perhaps. And Tim. Tim would be OK. Tim definitely. Tomorrow. Could he ask Tim to tell all the others? Would that be a bit much to ask? Or was there nothing now, that would be too much?

Sylvia of course. But then he'd tried her already. She'd been number one in fact, no contest. Some parlor game this is, he thought, standing for a while beside a lamppost, while Judy examined the base of it. Imagine you've got some mortal disease, who do you tell first, and why? And how?

Sylvia was of course the only one he wouldn't have had to explain things to. The only one, in fact, who might be able to explain things herself. It had been crazy, though, even imagining he could have told her then and there, in the daytime, fresh from Julia's surgical proceedings. He'd just felt impelled to talk to someone really.

Hey Sylvie, I just had a bone marrow sample, fucking painful isn't it, how are you?

And she was always so busy busy busy, saving sight and all. When, or really if, considering how distant she'd sounded at her clinic, if she called back he would say it was something to do with Annie, and all sorted out now, thanks Sylvie, thanks for calling back, how's things?

My leg hurts, he thought. Wonder what call-me-Julia's doing. Wish I was doing it with her. Whatever it is.

Apparently satisfied with the lamppost, Judy peed briefly upon it, and they passed on.

This is what you have a family for, thought Will. Brothers and sisters. A wife, of course. Children.

If Holly had married him when he had asked her to, would they be together still?

Perhaps he couldn't have children anyway. How would he know, until he tried? And he hadn't ever tried. Taken risks though. Clara that time, in that shop doorway in Barcelona! For instance.

All those other women. Once he had known how many. But he had got too drunk too often during a bad month or two in Los Angeles, and lost count, when he was twenty-five, just after his one and only film came out. Came out, and very properly went back in again, never to re-emerge. Warmth, attention, invitations to parties and openings and clubs, had also disappeared, as suddenly as Cinderella's midnight finery; bars, however, were still open to him, even welcoming, and cocaine was still to be had, whenever he wanted it, which was often.

And women, especially back home, still asked him in those days whether he wasn't Toby ffrench, with the two little f's, and asked him where his dizzying laser was, and told him how very much they had been in love with him when they were twelve, and what they were drinking, and what their telephone numbers were. So many of them.

And yet not once had he made anyone pregnant. And he'd always thought that was a good thing, until now. You had to have something really stable going on before you thought about babies. He had seen only the duties of stability and parenthood; he had never suspected that there might be rights involved, even privileges.

Because there was nothing like a death sentence, he thought, to make you see the point of marriage. Unlike any other family member, a wife was legal kin you had chosen. Who had chosen you. A wife and child were *chosen family*. Friends who were relations as well. When you got cancer that was who you told. No messing around worrying about their feelings, no choices, no pussy-footing. That was what they were for. It was family you told.

Why had he always assumed he had so much time? Maybe that had been his biggest mistake. Assuming things would carry on as they always had, until he changed them. What a stupid thing to do! Assuming something so enormous without even noticing you'd assumed it!

As it was the only next of kin he had was his mother. Who must not know at all. Who must be protected. Who must not suspect, or wonder, or even be worried.

I can't do it. Can I?

Will opened the kitchen door, and caught his own eye in the little mirror over the breadbin. I am an actor, after all. It will be a performance. I will be acting myself: myself in health. So I can't be doing with weeping friends, it occurred to him.

He raised one eyebrow at his reflection. We'll have to go out to weep, he thought, and grinned, suddenly pleased with himself. I'm being so fucking noble. Not a bad feeling, compared to some.

And perhaps this was partly what was so tiring, he thought: I keep being aware of all these feelings, and I keep having different ones. I have to keep on working out what they are. I sort of can't leave myself alone.

It was like having a constant mental debate going on; and his conscious mind, reluctant and powerless chairman, was completely unable to control this panicky internal shouting match, that leapt at crazed random from one viewpoint to another, and constantly demanded his full attention, his comments and interpretations. I just can't seem to shut myself up, thought Will helplessly, at intervals, over this yammering internal racket of anxiety.

Presently he remembered his mother's drinks cupboard in the little hall, where for years the same set of slightly sticky bottles, dating from various Christmases Past, sat unchangingly nearly full. Sherry, two of vodka, Tia Maria, Bailey's. Southern Comfort. Two tins of beer five years past their sell-by. And two unopened bottles of whisky, thank you God, a Bell's and a rather fancier purer kind with a picture of a stag on the label. The Bell's bottle chattered against the glass as he poured.

He gulped, his eyes watering as he coughed. God it was horrible! How did anyone drink this stuff? But almost immediately the present crushing wave of despair retreated. Whisky: Northern Comfort. He took another swig, then carried the bottle through to the sitting room and put the television on. Not comedy, he thought. Don't want laughter. Don't want tears. Don't want anything real. I want *Inspector Morse*. I want *Star Trek*. I want, oh God, I want *Earth's Army*.

What was in the video? Ah. Of course. *Pride and Prejudice*. So different, indeed, from the tatty touring version, something of a low point it had to be said, in which he had himself played Mr. Bingley. But then I always do, he thought cloudily. I always play Mr. Bingley: eager to please, easily led, talked into things and out of things, a bit on the dopey side. Even Toby ffrench, really: just an intergalactic space age Mr. Bingley. I'm a natural.

Slightly drunk now, he sat close to the screen, channel-hopping, looking for the impossible program, a story that could hold its own against his, make itself heard over the racket in his mind, but do so without involving any real feeling, since it was a surfeit of real feeling that was making all the terrible racket in the first place.

At half past ten, deciding that nothing short of a general anesthetic would make him sleep too deeply to hear his mother, if she called, he washed down Valium with a further generous shot of whisky.

For a while, as he lay in bed, the noise retreated. There was a short delicious spell of calm and quiet, and he slept. Presently the lovely Julia, in her white coat, came in and sat down on the end of his bed, and crossed her long slender legs.

"I've taken a good hard look at your notes," she said purringly, whilst demonstrating in some mysterious dreamland way that her breasts were very small and tender, and made to fit with swooning exactitude into the palms of his hands, "and it's all been a mistake. I'm so pleased. You haven't got anything wrong with you at all. You're absolutely fine!"

Will awoke aroused, and flooded with bliss. So it had all been a mistake! He'd always known it really. Of course there was nothing wrong with him. Christ, though, what a relief!

The consequent reversal, when he had finally understood that the nightmare was in fact reality, summoned another obliterating wave of despair. He could feel it coming. Sweating he flung aside the duvet, instinctively trying to run away from it. The next moment he was flung onto the carpet, his legs collapsed beneath him. The wave of fear crashed over him, a finality of terror, and took him into itself. A time followed.

He became aware that he was panting, and that his body had snapped itself automatically into a clenched fetal position, clamping his arms up round his head to hide his face.

Slowly he uncurled himself, and sat up, shivering in his soaked T-shirt. So the worst was over again, for a while. As he rose groggily onto his hands and knees, thinking proper thoughts by now, No more sodding Valium, never again—the telephone rang. He gave no thought to the answerphone, but simply picked up the receiver, so close to hand.

"Hello?" said a voice he knew but for a moment was too dizzy to recognize. "Will? I'm sorry it's so late. Are you all right?"

It was too much. The finest actor on earth, thought Will afterwards, could not have replied without tears to such a softly asked question at just such a time.

"Oh, Sylvie," said Will, and for a while could say no more.

ROB AND IRIS, 1954: LOVE

ONCE SHE CAME BACK from night duty—the month seemed to go on for ever—to find a bunch of flowers pinned to the door of her room. They were small dark blue irises.

"Saw these," read the note hidden between stems and wrapping, "and thought of you. Think about you all the time anyway. I love you very much. R."

Which was, without a shred of doubt, thought Iris and all her friends, the single most romantic thing that had ever taken place in the nurses' home since the day it was built.

The nurses' home at the time was set about with rules designed to protect its girlish inmates, their individual reputations, and thus that of the hospital itself. Visitors must be entertained in the sitting room, and must in any case leave the building no later than nine; off-duty nurses must be in by ten; anyone "sleeping out" on her days off was required to inform the home sister of her proposed whereabouts well beforehand, and to be back well in time afterwards.

Happy Iris, who could so easily circumvent these barriers with reference to so blameless a person as the elder sister who had brought her up! Perhaps, had any of the home sisters chanced to meet Iris's sister Jo on her way out of an evening, made-up and heavily perfumed, with her sleek black clutchbag beneath her arm and her mink stole slipping from one polished naked shoulder, they might have had an inkling that Iris's virtue was not in the safest of hands. But none of them ever did.

"Back about two, all right?" Jo might call, from the doorway, to the front room, where Iris and Rob might be having tea. Rob would stand up, politely, to bid her farewell; Iris would stand up too, the better to fling herself at him as soon as the door closed.

A great many things had stopped worrying Rob. Sometimes, hurrying down a corridor or along a pavement, happiness required him to leap up, arm outstretched, to touch the light-fitting or branch high overhead. He was always hungry. When alone he slept deeply, dreamlessly. He grew an inch.

He had the sensation sometimes of being right at the top of the roller coaster, poised dizzily, not climbing only because there was nowhere higher to go. The air was very clear up here, you could see your way to anywhere. Iris with him, of course. How astonishing, to have met with the love of his life! How lucky, to meet her so soon!

"It's you that's beautiful," said Iris to him one evening as they lay in front of Jo's gas fire. "Look at you!" She passed a hand down his shoulder, along his side to his buttocks, and beyond to his long legs. He was like a statue, she thought. Except not so muscley.

No, silly, she didn't like muscles, not all bulgy anyway.

The iris, said Rob, quoting a textbook, is the most beautiful muscle of the body.

His slender muscles, thought Iris, and his chest that was neat as a child's. His ribs showed when he took a deep breath. Her fingertips on the light ring of scar about his upper arm.

"A horse bit me."

"Pull the other one."

"True. At a point-to-point. I was giving a pony an apple. Its friend came up and bit me. Wouldn't let go. My Mum ran up and hit it over the head with her handbag."

Iris laughed too, but still the reference to his mother darkened the room. She would have to see the woman again eventually. Presumably.

"For Pete's sake," Jo had said. "No one gets on with their mother-in-law. She hates you, you hate her, it's a law of nature. It doesn't matter, OK?"

It does matter, Iris had thought. Once or twice she had felt Mrs. Wilding's eyes on her as if she were being ill-wished. Was there such a thing as the evil eye? Could someone do you harm, just by looking at you with hatred in their eyes? That woman Meadows, too; the pair of them were really a bit creepy when you thought about it. Best not to, then.

"Shall we go and have something to eat?"

Sometimes they went to a fish and chip shop on the corner; there was also a late-night coffee stall beneath a nearby railway bridge, where you could buy ham sandwiches, macaroons, and hot meat pies. The sweet cozy smell of nicely browned shortcrust pastry, the soft splurt of rich gravy at first bite, the voluptuous give of slow-cooked steak and kidney, all eaten outdoors on a warm summer night, whilst sitting on a park bench with Iris, were to haunt Rob for the rest of his life: nothing would ever taste quite as good as that again.

Once they went to Brighton for the day.

"It's all pebbles!" For a moment Iris was disappointed. She told him about the sand dog she had made once, when she was a little girl; they had gone on a coach ride from Coogan's Holiday Camp, and had egg and chips somewhere, and then walked along a cliff-top path to another beach where there had been miles of fine clean sand to play with; there had been a special little cave in the cliffs, big enough to go inside; there had been tea on a tray, in thick white china cups; then the coach had trundled up to take them all back again along the deep curving lanes to Coogan's.

Rob had listened enchanted. It was his own stretch of coast he was remembering; it seemed hardly short of miraculous that they had slivers of childhood in common. He had played himself on that very beach! Perhaps on that very day! Perhaps they had stood next to each other in the ice-cream queue.

"There's sand when the tide goes out. Come on. Let's go on the pier."

They paid Eva Petrulengro, Genuine Gypsy, to read their palms. Rob was promised a long life and three or four children; he was good with his hands. Was he in the rag trade, possibly? She could see him sewing, anyway. Curved needles. Upholstery, then? No?

Iris was promised a long life and three children too. She was good with flowers. There was a dark secret in her life. She should be careful

162

in fields; farmyard animals would bring her no luck, she should avoid them all if she could.

Entering the booth full of laughter, they had left it rather subdued. It had been a mistake, he saw. Iris was superstitious; if she forgot something and went back for it, she had to sit down and carefully cross her legs, pretending to some watching ill-fortune deity that she was back to stay, in order to avert the bad luck of just nipping in and out again. Single magpies must be politely greeted. It was important not to walk all the way round a church; one way was all right, the other terribly unlucky, and since Iris was incapable of remembering anything to do with left and right she insisted on doing neither, just in case.

It was the curved needles that had upset her, he thought. It had given him rather a thrill down his spine too.

"You going to tell me your dark secret?" he murmured into her hair, as they stood together at the end of the pier.

"You know it already."

"Do I?"

"I'm a bad girl."

"Iris!" For she was near tears, he saw. "What are you talking about?"

"You know."

"Oh, no. We're getting married, aren't we? I love you. You love me. How can that be wrong? She's just a silly cow. And you're supposed to avoid farmyard animals," he added. Iris gave her sudden snort of laughter, and everything was all right again.

Later they walked along the prom in the blue summery darkness.

"We're so lucky, living in England. You're always so close to the sea." The best thing about my parents' house, he thought, but he knew better than to say this aloud to her. "It's a sort of important sound, somehow."

Yes, thought Iris, remembering the flying vicar's little cliff-top hut, and the waves that crashed so thrillingly onto the rocks below. Yes: and it sounded so all night, and always had. That was something to hold on to.

"Oh, don't look sad! When we're rich we'll come and stay at the Grand, we'll have a room with a balcony and we'll leave the windows open and listen to the sea all night!"

They missed their train and spent the time waiting for the next one kissing on a bench at the far end of the platform.

It had been a perfect day. But then any day spent with Iris would be perfect, thought Rob.

RUBY'S BAD DAY, 1954

RUBY'S BAD DAY started like any other. She woke up very early, before five. She got up straight away, no point in just lying there. It was best to keep moving, Ruby thought. There was a kitchen floor to scrub, she could get it all done before breakfast if she got down to it now.

She put her crossover apron on over her usual old blue dress and went downstairs. She tied her hair up in a duster out of the way. When the lino was clean and dry she gave it a bit of a shine; you could eat your dinner off it, she thought, when she had finished. That moment of satisfaction was the best part of Ruby's day.

Firstly when she went to make herself a cup of tea she realized that the impossible had happened and that she had run clean out. Run out of tea! All yesterday afternoon she'd had this perfectly convincing picture in her mind of a spare packet in the cupboard in the hall.

"Caddy's empty," Ted had told her, as he brought her a cup the night before, and she'd thought, Oh, it doesn't matter, I've got a quarter pound in the hall cupboard. Ruby could almost hear herself thinking it, sitting there in the armchair being given the very last cup of tea in the house.

It was barely half past six. Her husband would be down at seven, and for the first time in his life very probably he was going to have to do without. How could she send him off to work without a cup of tea inside him? Could she borrow any? It wasn't as if the stuff was still rationed. For a moment of forgetfulness Ruby considered which of her neighbors would be up and about in time.

Then she remembered that she couldn't borrow anything from any of them, ever again. There was no telling which of them was sending her the envelopes with the pencils inside. There was no way of telling anyway how each of them really felt about her and what she had done to her child.

Not now. Not ever.

The loneliness of this brought tears to Ruby's eyes. Then she caught herself out feeling self-pity, and scornfully told herself to leave off. None of that crying. None of that. Sniffing, she got up. He'd have to do without, that was all. It wouldn't kill him, would it. Only she'd better tell him straight away, not let him come down all expectant and be disappointed. Arms folded, she went back upstairs.

Ruby enters the bedroom: the old blue dress has been old for a very long time. It was plain and bought for durability to start with, and years of being a dress to do housework in have not improved its cut or the hang of its skirt. The crossover apron is frankly dirty, particularly over Ruby's scant bosom. It too has the intimate sag of clothes worn far too long. Ruby's hair, graying especially in front, is partly hidden still in the duster, but some of the fringe, which usually hangs limp now Ruby has stopped putting it in curlers, is sticking out through the knot in the duster at various angles. Ruby's bare feet are in old felt slippers with holes worn almost completely through over each big toe.

Clad thus Ruby stands for a moment, skinny yellowish arms akimbo, until she catches her husband's barely wakeful eye.

"There's no tea," she says, and somehow instead of apologetic it comes out sniffily, as if she thought it was his fault. "We've run out," she adds, and this sounds sullen. Ruby decides to shut up. There is a pause.

Ted has woken with his usual morning erection. His full balls ache; he can't go on like this, he thinks. He looks at his wife over the length of his own body under the coverlet. I get to fuck that, are the words that fall into his mind. No. No, that's what I don't get to fuck any more. If I was to get a fuck at all, that's what I'd get. That.

Perhaps it is because this unaccustomed word is so painfully present in his mind, that when he speaks he somehow cannot avoid saying it.

He meant to say, Oh, go away and leave me alone. Or perhaps be sarcastic about it, Oh thanks Rube, thanks very much. But instead he sits up in bed with the sheet pulled close to his chin and spits the words out at her as viciously as he can:

"Tell you what, Ruby, why don't you just fuck off out of it!"

Pale as she is he sees her go paler. It's a first. It is, he understands, as if he has struck her. There is also no doubt that the child in the next room, always an early riser, will have heard him do it.

"Right," whispers Ruby, and turns, and goes quietly downstairs again.

SYLVIA ATTENDS A LECTURE, 1983

IT HAD BEEN a long time before Sylvia had realized why she looked forward so much to the ophthalmology lectures. It was not a specialty she was particularly drawn to. The whole thing was on such a, well, fiddly scale, it was surgery miniaturized. Doll's house surgery. At least there was no blood, as Philip Brownlow pointed out. Philip always tried to sit next to Sylvia whenever possible. He had problems with blood himself. So far, he explained to anyone willing to listen, he had fainted seventeen times during his surgical rotation. Seventeen times!

"Unfair female advantage," Philip told Sylvia. "Girls don't faint at the sight of blood, do they? They're used to it. That's why women ought to be doctors, and not men. Smaller hands too, I mean look!"

Here he had held his own knobbly immensity beside Sylvia's, had in fact taken her hand and held it palm to palm with his own. Even Sylvia, who at twenty-one regarded herself as something of a neuter, a determined chap among chaps, understood at this point that Philip was holding her hand because his feelings impelled him to do so. She looked at their two hands, hers a child's to his great hairy paw, and then, briefly at his face: a mistake. He blushed deeply. He had downy cheeks like a girl.

She felt the usual mixture of puzzlement and sympathy. He had no business having a crush on her. She had never given him, she knew, the slightest signal. She had been friendly and direct and entirely cool. A chap among chaps: not interested. Not until I'm finished, not until I'm where I want to be. Career first. All that other stuff a poor second. Didn't that show clearly enough?

"Better brain surgeons," he muttered.

"All that practice," said Sylvia, "doing our embroidery."

"Exactly," said Philip, recovering. "Clever little girly fingers. Dress making skills. It's obvious."

Behind them the auditorium was filling.

"You in clinic after?"

"No. Theatres."

"Free this evening?"

"No, sorry."

"Tomorrow?"

"No."

"Bum. Didn't think so. Just checking." He grinned, to demonstrate he didn't really mind, and Sylvia pretended to believe him.

"What clinic are you doing?" she asked.

"Dunno. Corneal, I think."

"Mr. Winter. He's very nice."

"They're all nice, to you," said Philip. Surgeons in general were not at all nice, he felt, to himself. They got narky, they made heavily sarcastic remarks when he had to sprint out of gore range. As if he was doing it on purpose.

"Whose theatre you in?"

In reply Sylvia tilted her head toward the lecturer, who had at last arrived. He stood for a moment shifting papers about on his desk. At the sight of him Sylvia's heart had given a sudden great leap inside her, and was now dancing, twirling lightly inside her with excitement. It had been a long time before she realized why she so looked forward to these lectures, but it was certainly clear enough now. Her hand as she picked up her pen to record his every word trembled. What luxury, to sit in the front row like this, to have so clear a mandate attentively to stare!

She did not in the least associate how she felt with, say, the way Philip, sitting beside her, felt about her. She knew the way she felt about the lecturer was girlish dream. It was exactly the sort of feeling she used to have aged thirteen for certain comfortably androgynous pop singers. It was safe, she thought. It didn't stop you studying or get you to waste time yearning beside telephones or messing about with

169

makeup and outfits or going on diets or hanging about in bars hoping the one you fancied would look at you. All that was reality, the real desperate mate-hunting chore. Whereas this was a useful mirage. This was willed fantasy.

While he sorted out his lecture notes she looked at him with conscious appreciation. Tall, very tall. Broad in the shoulder, though slender. The faintest suggestion of swagger in his walk. The thin face ascetic, troubled, almost suffering. The eyes dark, like the eyebrows; the hair white. And of course he was so distinguished. A leader in his field. Married of course; unhappily; a wife who drank; somehow this was generally known.

For Sylvia, Romance itself stood shuffling papers on the stand beside the overhead projector. She would feel a little awkward this afternoon, perhaps, watching him operate, a little tense and shaky, but she would manage. She was looking forward to it. No one would suspect her. Least of all the man himself.

At the stand Rob Wilding cleared his throat, and began.

"This morning I'm going to tell you about some aspects of reconstructive orbital surgery."

He turns on his slide carousel, and presently shows his students a large close-up of a pretty smiling blonde girl, with red lips and sparkling blue eyes.

"Danish beauty queen," he says. He's got them already. They all know an apparent non sequitur when they see one. They stare, rapt with misgiving, at the Danish beauty queen's innocent girlish smile.

"Why wear an artificial eye," Rob asks them, "what's the point? Lose a leg and even Long John Silver's wooden peg will keep you mobile. Captain Hook's hook has its uses. But a false eye doesn't see. What's the use of it?" He clicks the slide carousel again, changes the photograph, waits for the gasp.

The picture is clearly of the same blonde girl. Not smiling now. Nor pretty. This is not a portrait, but a medical record, as she looks steadily back at the camera with one eye of sparkling aquamarine and one dark empty socket lined with thin little pinkish tucks and folds of unnameable flesh. The upper eyelid droops over the cavity, dangling inward; the lower too has slipped backward into the void.

His audience obliges.

"Her boyfriend hit her," says Rob, "and now you don't see her at all, really, do you? All you see is what isn't there."

He clicks for the next slide. "Here she is before." The same girl, the same smile.

"And after," says Rob, and clicks again. The cavernous gape reappears. "Well, actually, I'm misleading you all a bit here. This one's really before her last operation. This one" (he clicks again, and the one-eyed monster is replaced by the pretty smiling blonde) "this one is After." He waits for the murmur.

"Yes," he says, over it, "this is what we can do nowadays. But I think it's clear what artificial eyes are for. They're not for the wearer; they're for the rest of us. They make us feel better, and that makes the poor sods who have to wear them feel better, and making people feel better is what we're in the business of, after all." He clicks again, and shows them the Egyptian glass.

"Made for a mummy case. Beautiful, isn't it. Nicely mascara'd. We think eyes like this would also have been worn outside an empty socket, on a head band, to make ancient Egyptians feel better; no one could try putting artificial eyes into the socket for several hundred years . . ."

Click

"when they began to try it with gold. Like this. Fifteenth century. Gold and colored enamel. The pupil is jet, and the white is mother of pearl. It is beautiful, isn't it, in its admittedly rather sinister way. Mimicking the jewels we all so unconcernedly wear in our faces, well unconcernedly of course before you start on the Eye Ward, and then concern is hardly the word . . ." He waits for the amused susurration.

Click.

"Now this is glass. Late sixteenth century Venetian glass. Solid. Bit like a marble, if any of you ever played with marbles. What would it feel like to wear? How would you keep it in place? It's heavy. It drops out into your dinner, it shatters. Dinner plate breaks as well. Everyone feels a lot worse. Venice kept its glass eye–making processes a secret. If you wanted a glass eye, you bought from the Venetians, or you didn't buy one at all. Then the Germans had better ideas . . ."

Click

"and started using blown glass. Shattered in your dinner, but didn't break the plate. But if you wanted a blown-glass eye you bought one from Germany or you didn't buy one at all. Until the war, when naturally enough supplies rather dwindled. And the Americans started experimenting with plastics."

Click.

"This is how we do things at the moment. After the eye is lost we straight away insert a plastic conformer, something like this, in order to maintain orbit volume. The holes in it are designed to let out any secretions that naturally arise behind it. There's often still a bit of a buildup of tears and secretions, which may suddenly release all at once, very alarming if you haven't been warned about it, but an entirely natural event. So: a conformer, silicon or plastic, in there straight away, to prevent scarring contractions, to maintain the fornices . . ."

Click

"though when I say lost, I mean salvaged, really. We don't scoop out eyes in entirety; we keep the good bits if we can."

Click.

"This is an evisceration; I've made a three hundred and sixty degree conjunctival incision, and recessed the conjunctiva and Tenon's capsule for a few millimeters from the limbus; I made a three hundred and sixty degree limbal incision to remove the cornea—I started with a scalpel blade, then it's generally easier to complete with scissors—then I took out all the ocular contents with an evisceration spoon. Come on Brownlow, chin up: there's really no blood to speak of."

Click.

"Here's the implant, pops straight into the scleral envelope; closed with 6/o absorbable sutures. What's the implant made of, anyone?"

Sweet little thing in the front row.

"Yes, good, Miss ah Henshaw, a very light acrylic. Now."

Click.

"This is another case. Following a complete enucleation; he's lost the entire eyeball altogether. After a gunshot wound, ladies and gentlemen. Here we have the empty socket. Obviously there's a huge loss of tissue there. In the old days we would have put in a big deep artificial eye; it wouldn't have looked that bad at first, but after a while the lower lid would start stretching beneath the weight. Also in the years following this sort of loss there's a slow redistribution of remaining orbital fat, giving rise to . . ."

Click

"post-enucleation socket syndrome. Like this poor chap here. Note the deep sulcus or hollow in the upper eyelid, along with the lid retraction and the downward displacement of the eye. Occasionally into his soup plate. And you wouldn't want to meet him in a dark alley at night, would you? So what do we do? We give him an implant too."

Click.

"We use something called a baseball implant. Using donor sclera, from a cadaver. Looking like a nice little bit of fresh pastry. Like this."

Click.

"We wrap our acrylic marble—we've been careful to choose the right size for the orbit, obviously, we wrap our nice little acrylic marble in our sclera, all smooth and fairly tight; and using 6/o sutures we sew it all up. It's supposed to look like a baseball, see, on account of the stitches, yes? I think it looks a bit more like a little fat Cornish pasty myself." His audience groans. None of them will fancy a Cornish pasty for a while.

Click.

"And then you open the Tenon's capsule with your scissors to expose the orbital fat, and in it goes; stitches to the back; then you're going to pass a double-armed 4/o chromic catgut through the tendons of the four rectus muscles, and attach them to your sclera."

Click.

"Obviously you've got to be careful that the Tenon's capsule and the conjunctiva can be closed over the implant without tension . . ."

Click

"and then when everything's healed up nicely the painted shell—the bit you see, that looks so real—is painted, hand-painted onto yet more acrylic, thin little piece, you can see why it's called a shell, job for the artist, see the blood vessels? and popped into place on top of the implant, like a big contact lens, when everything's healed up."

Click.

The smiling Danish beauty queen reappears.

"So. Movement. Limited, of course. But not a bad result: she looks left with both eyes."

Click.

"And she looks right. She looks up."

Click.

"She looks down. And she looks pretty well normal, doesn't she? We feel better, she feels better. Even Brownlow feels better, look."

Philip jumps to his feet and gives a small bow, acknowledging his applause.

Rob waits.

IRIS AND THE NETSUKE PIG, 1954

"You should go abroad," said Jo, emitting smoke. She sat as none of her admirers had ever seen her, in a gentleman's dressing gown, very old, with worn lapels of quilted silk, and similarly aged but comfortable slippers. She had removed with Pond's Cold Cream the sophisticated nighttime face she had come home in, and despite the cigarette and barely four hours' sleep now looked nearly as dewily fresh and eager as her sister Iris.

"I'm gonna make Andrew take me," she added. "The South of France. Or Rome. Norfolk bloody Broads."

"Did he bring all these? This one looks nice," said Iris, picking up one of the hotel leaflets.

"Bloody Cornwall," said Jo. She was intensely happy. Her eyes sparkled with enjoyable anger. She had done it; she had hooked Andrew St. John Mortimer, decent-looking kindly and tremendously well-off widowed stockbroker, after months of careful and highly calculated maneuvering; she had been so frightened, lately, more and more, that she had left it too late, and priced herself out of the advantageous marriage market. Twenty-seven: a perilous age for such as she. Time to settle. Andrew St. John Mortimer was pretty well as high as she could possibly aim for, higher than quite a few she'd already had a good go at; and with the careful expertise of much practice she had reeled him in gently and by slow respectable almost Victorian degrees, and lo! as of last week he was in the bag.

True, there were children in the picture, but fairly big ones. They were at school most of the time anyway.

"I know what it feels like, to lose your mother," she had said gently to Andrew St. John Mortimer quite early on in their friendship, and seen his eyes fill with tears. What a softie! It had been a sizable clue to his character, an immense help in landing him: he was nice.

She had scorned him for it at the time, privately, but now he had stammered out his honorable proposals she could see the advantages. He was a gent. There were all sorts of things he simply wouldn't want to bring himself to do. Or even be able to do. With any luck. Of course men were unaccountable. But looked at squarely, what were the odds of him getting pissed every Friday night, and knocking her about, or bellowing insults, or bringing home tarts?

You had to laugh just trying to imagine Andrew St. John Mortimer trying any of those. Of course he might be a bit dull. But she'd had enough adventures, thank you very much. From where she was sitting the prospect of that enormous comfortable house in Surrey, with some-one else paid to do the housework, and lots of money without having to work work work for it, and no more kowtowing to that old hag Morris, Yes Miss Morris, No, Miss Morris, I do apologize Miss Morris, it won't happen again, well, Ha! Miss Morris could just roll herself up in one of her own bolts of taffeta and chuck herself in the Thames for all Jo cared, or needed to now.

"At least a month in the South of France," she said, flicking ash into the saucer of her teacup.

"I'd settle for a night at the Brighton Grand," said Iris. Rob was away, visiting his grandmother, traveling in Scotland with his parents. She was a little anxious. A whole fortnight in his mother's company; what mischief might that woman make in two full weeks? "His dad wants to retire to Scotland," she added.

Jo grinned. "Outer Hebrides, I hope?"

"His mum won't let him."

"Pity." Jo rose, and stretched luxuriously, and wandered over to the window. She would have liked to open it, to take in a little of the warm summery morning, but the frame was rotten, the window held in with small nails Jo herself had gingerly knocked into place several years earlier, using the heel of one of her own shoes. Just a few more months in this crummy dump, she reminded herself.

Jo's flat was on the third floor of number twenty-two, Anstruther Walk, a once-imposing Victorian terrace. There was an aged and toothless old crone, Mrs. Bowen, who had lurked for years in the semi-basement, there was a newly married young couple on the first floor, and a scrawny buttoned-up bespectacled Miss Jarvis, who did something in an office somewhere, on the second, with the best windows.

The outside of number twenty-two, like the rest of the terrace, had not been cleaned or painted or subjected to any but the most urgent repairs since 1936. Deep cracks in the topmost parapet were partly concealed by the luxuriant foliage of the buddleia plants placidly growing in them, whereas number twenty next door was still standing only with the aid of large flying buttresses of timber. Number eighteen was a roofless ruin, and number sixteen, the direct hit, was the merest heap of blackened cindery rubble, fraught with broken glass, and hidden entirely from view for the moment beneath a fine show of willow-herb and bramble: mending Jo's rotten window frames was thus a good way down on the list of essentials, as far as Jo's ultimate landlord was concerned.

Not that Jo had ever met her ultimate landlord. Instead she had always dealt on a weekly basis with his agent, toothless Mrs. Bowen, paying a fairly heavy seventeen-and-six by now for the three top floor rooms, with use of the lavatory on the half landing. This meant occasionally running into Miss Jarvis, which was a chilly experience, for Miss Jarvis had encountered Jo racing upstairs of a morning in full seductive naked-shouldered evening wear once too often, just as she, Miss Jarvis, was coming down, respectably dressed for the City, sour-faced old cat.

Ha, there would be no sharing of lavvies in Surrey. No more trips down to the cheesy old basement, no more tripping over broken lino, no more mean little pimpled gas rings on landings. And above all farewell, goods trains: the line ran right at the end of the ruined gardens, shaking you awake at night now and then, whilst sometimes at home in the daytime you could hardly hear yourself think for whistles and shunting noises.

Jo drew on her cigarette as she stood by her window and looked out onto the sagging clotheslines and scrubby tarmac, and especially at the centerpiece of surface air-raid shelters, the flat concrete roofs of which were heaped with piles of junk exhausting merely to look upon—bicycle tires, saucepans, tins, bottles, cigarette cartons, bones, newspapers, chair legs, lamp shades—all tossed from the windows presumably, by neighboring tenants lucky enough to have windows that actually opened. Farewell to you too, rubbishy dereliction.

And the only fly in the ointment, thought Jo, jetting smoke out through her nostrils, was Iris. What would the poor kid do, without the flat so handy to run to? Pity she hadn't married her young man yet. She'd be all right when she'd married him. He'd look after her, wouldn't he?

He'd come in handy already, in fact, a doctor's son practically in the family. You'd never know whether a thing like that hadn't actually tipped the balance, when you'd been dealing with Andrew St. John Mortimer's early and of course perfectly well-founded suspicions about your reputation. On the other hand, well, on the other hand, he was marrying you partly because of your ever so slightly shop-soiled aura, wasn't he? A bit of excitement at long last, that's what I am, thought Jo: suits me.

There'll be a home for Iris in Surrey. As long as she wants one. A really nice room of her own. I'll have it done up for her. Everything just so. Fresh wallpaper and frilly curtains and one of those dressing tables with matching little skirts and three mirrors. And a proper new divan: in that room with the sloping ceiling looking out over the fields at the back. She'll like that. It'll be hers, I won't let anyone else use it but Iris. Not until she's married anyway.

"I've still got to look after Iris," she had told Andrew, knowing as she said it that it was the sort of thing he liked anyway. "She's my responsibility, you see. She's not . . . she can't really look after herself just yet. She's special. She's fragile."

"How much did you tell him about Mum?" she began now, turning back from the window.

"What, you mean Rob?"

"Yeah."

Iris shrugged. "Not very much."

"Only he was telling me all sorts of stuff about her last week. About her being in the rag trade and bringing home scraps of silk and velvet and making them into . . ."

"Don't," broke in Iris. "Don't, please."

"All right, all right. Any more tea in that pot? Look, I'm not saying anything. I don't mind you saying stuff. I know you don't mean anything by it, come on, look, I don't mind what you do. You know that."

The trouble was that while Iris was often inspired when it came to detail, like the patchwork velvet counterpanes she had so nicely conjured up from nowhere, she didn't always remember them clearly enough later on. Mainly, Jo had found, this didn't matter much, because generally the people she'd been talking to forgot most of them as well. People were like that: forgetful. Or not really listening in the first place. But you couldn't count on it. They might just be being tactful. That was what Iris never seemed to realize. Just because people didn't tell you to your face they thought you were telling whoppers, didn't mean to say they weren't thinking it.

But that was Iris all over. Childlike, really. Hadn't occurred to her that Rob might expect me, her own sister, to know about this sort of thing, and not look just the tiniest bit taken aback when he comes out with all that flogging-silk-to-fine-ladies stuff as well, as if Mum, poor cow, would have known a length of best shantung from a hole in the ground.

It's no good, Jo sees. Perhaps she should not have spoken: Iris's eyes are already full of tears. But what else can she do? She's got no choice.

"It's because I found this," she says at last, and reaches into the pocket of her dressing gown, and brings out the little carved figure. She hadn't worried about it at first. It looked like the sort of thing someone bought for you at the end of the pier: a knickknack. She had gone into Iris's tiny box room, just big enough for the bed and a chest of drawers, on the off chance that Iris, at the time incommunicado on Nights again, had left a usable pair of stockings behind. And she had, only they'd had this funny little pig-thing all wrapped up in them. Jo had pulled the roll of nylon out and it had dropped onto the lino with a light cracking sound and skittered beneath the bed.

Seemed all right though, when she had with some difficulty squeezed herself between the bed and the wall to retrieve it, and blown the fluff off. Some sort of weird stained brownish cream Bakelite, by the looks of it. A furry sleeping curled-up pig. With little tusks. It fitted rather nicely into your hand. But that was about the best you could say for it, Jo thought. Presumably Rob had his reasons for presenting his sweetheart with a small stained Bakelite pig; none of her business, whatever they were.

But she had pinched the nylons, needs must, and, late for work already, hadn't put the thing back in Iris's drawer, but on the mantelpiece, thus giving herself a tricky moment or two that evening when Andrew, kept waiting just a minute or two while she struggled with a recalcitrant earring, had gone prowling about and found it, and gone on and on about it, because it hadn't been a bit of old seaside souvenir Bakelite at all, but hand-carved ivory apparently, and something called netsuke, and what was more a very fine example of it, and possibly worth quite a bit, and she'd had to make up on the spot a convincing explanation as to why, if it had been in the family all those years as she had so lightly and thoughtlessly claimed, it hadn't been sitting there on her mantelpiece the week before.

"I said it was yours," said Jo flatly, when she had explained all this. "Well, it is, in a way, isn't it?"

"It's not a farmyard animal, is it," said Iris, in the tone of one hoping for reassurance. "It's a wild boar, wouldn't you say? Look at its tusks."

Jo gave her a look. Then picked the little figure up. Weren't wild boars meant to look fierce? This one's tusks curved about its snout in a way that somehow just made it look as if it were smiling in its sleep. Now she knew it was worth a bob or two she could see its charm; it had a dreamy peaceful look, she thought. Anyway: all those flowing lines delineated fur and farmyard pigs weren't furry, were they? And though at first she had thought it was supposed to be tied up ready for market, Andrew had shown her that the things wreathed about it weren't ropes at all but reeds. "It's leaning against this little rock, d'you see,"

Andrew had said, "and gone to sleep in a reed bed. Very jolly little thing. Quite delightful."

"Definitely a wild boar," she said, putting it down on the table again, and blessed if Iris didn't look relieved. God, she was a funny kid. Still couldn't meet Jo's eyes, so there was certainly something going on.

"His dad used to collect it apparently. Andrew's dad. Netsuke. Like this. He reckons this one's worth a fortune."

"Oh," said Iris.

Jo, watching her, sat down opposite and lit another cigarette.

"Who gave it to you, lovey? It wasn't Rob, was it?" She spoke very gently. She didn't want the poor kid going all peculiar on her. You had to watch your step, with Iris. That was another thing: she ought to have a word with Rob some time: he ought to know what was what.

Iris, of course, was shaking her head.

Oh God, thought Jo with a pang. She hasn't pinched it, has she? Be a bit of a departure if she has.

"That woman give it me," Iris said, very low.

"Who? What woman?"

"You know," said Iris sullenly. "That awful woman. Works for his mum."

Jo was baffled. "What, you mean the servant?"

Iris nodded, and caught Jo's eye. "She did," she wailed indignantly. "Honest she did. She come up to my room, and give it me."

"All right, all right. Keep your hair on." Jo left a little silence, and then went on, "But you can't blame me, can you? I mean it sounds a bit odd, that's all. What she want to do a thing like that for?"

Iris shrugged. "I dunno. I was leaving. I went up to pack my things and you know what? She'd already done it, done it all for me."

"What, gone through all your stuff?"

"Yeah."

"Gawd."

"Yeah. Folded it all up in tissue paper. You know, all me private bits and bobs. Everything."

"Gawd!" Jo was disgusted. The things toffs wanted doing for them! You'd think they'd have more pride.

"And I was just standing there looking at my suitcase, I was thinking of all the things she knew about me from, you know, fingering every-thing. And she comes in and I swear to you Jo she didn't make a sound. She was just there, all of a sudden! I nearly died. And she's just stand-ing there looking at me, really, you know, creepy. And she says, oh Jo! she says to me, *She don't like you*."

"What?"

"She does this," said Iris, giving a slow twist of her head sideways and downwards.

Jo hesitated, on the edge of laughter. "She did what?"

"She meant Mrs. Wilding. Rob's mum. Her downstairs, see?" Again Iris demonstrated the sinister twist of Meadows's short thick neck. "And she says it all quiet, *She don't like you*. She's got this sort of coun-try accent. And she says, *She ain't gonna let you take him*. That's what she said. And she called me 'young Missy.' *She ain't gonna let you take him, young Missy*. Look, it wasn't funny!" Iris shouted suddenly.

"Sorry," Jo tried to say, but it came out a splutter. "It just sounds a bit, well, you know, a bit Boris Karloff." Purest Hollywood in fact. Nasty old git, thought Jo. Wish I'd been there. Wish she'd tried that sort of lark on me, wouldn't I have sent her away with a flea in her ear! And a kick up the bum.

"She said she'd put the evil eye on me," said Iris, all on one anguished note, and began to cry.

Jo was instantly sober. "Oh for God's sake," she said angrily. "And you listened to her!"

"No, she meant . . ." Iris choked on her sobs . . . "She meant Rob's mum had. Put the evil eye on me."

"No one puts the sodding evil eye on anyone," said Jo. "Look at me, Iris. Come on. Look at me. No one puts the evil eye on anyone else, because all that stuff is all a load of old bollocks, see?"

Iris pressed her arm against her eyes. It was nice to hear this sort of thing, of course. And sitting here in Jo's sunny flat in the heart of the city you could believe it too. But Meadows never would. Meadows knew otherwise. And who could say who was right? Perhaps Jo was right here, and Meadows was right in the country. On her own ground.

"She said she was on my side," she went on, more composedly. "Meadows, I mean. The little pig-thing was hers. She had it in her apron pocket. It was her good luck charm. And I was to take it and not say a word about it to anyone and then it would keep me safe from the evil eye."

Jo was silent for a moment, considering her options. Perhaps the barmy old hag really believed what she was saying. And meant Iris well. Netsuke had been cheap, Andrew had said, ages ago. Before the Great War. It was perfectly possible that Meadows had been telling the truth when she said the thing was hers to give. Perhaps she had dozens of them. Perhaps she slipped one to all Mrs. Wilding's house guests.

On the other hand. Whatever the pig was worth before the Great War, it was worth a lot more now. Should it go back? Or should it, perhaps, find its way to a certain little antique-cum-junk shop Jo knew about on the Tottenham Court Road?

It certainly should, Jo recognized, had there been no fat jolly sapphire on her own left hand. She had to bear that in mind from now on: she didn't need to keep her wits about her in quite the same old way. Needed to look at things from quite a different perspective in fact. Was the fiancée of Andrew St. John Mortimer going to be the sort of person who flogged dodgy items up the Tottenham Court Road?

No. She wasn't. She was too fucking ladylike for one thing. And for another she didn't need to any more. She was on velvet, thanks to Andrew St. John Mortimer's well-hidden predilection for the ever so slightly shop-soiled.

Perhaps the person to consult, thought Jo, was Rob. If the netsuke pig actually had pride of place in his Mum's fancy glass-fronted cabinet or something he would presumably know about it. And it wasn't as if Iris had nicked it, after all. And another thing. If there was really something fishy going on the one who'd be most unhappy about it was Andrew St. John Mortimer. Shop-soiled was one thing, theft quite another.

She would talk to Rob. He was a sensible kid, and mad about Iris. She picked the little figure up, and put it back in the pocket of her old dressing gown.

"Come on, cheer up, my lamb," she said tenderly. "Let's not talk about it anymore. And don't you worry about it either, that potty old bag. Tell you what. Give us the paper. We'll go out on the town this afternoon, shall we? Up West? And see what's on at the Odeon?"

Iris sniffed, brightening up fast. "All right," she said.

RUBY'S BAD DAY CONTINUES, 1954

OF COURSE SHE WENT out as soon as she could and bought the tea. She left the boy reading *The Borrowers*, which she had got him the day before from the weekly traveling library in the church hall. He seemed happy enough with it.

"What's a wainscot?" he had asked. That was the only thing he'd said to her all morning. She hadn't known either.

She hurried along the three small streets of the village. A nice new loaf, still warm. Two packets of tea, one for the cupboard in the hall. A pound of apples. A big piece of haddock, do all three of them. A tin of peas to go with it.

Ruby kept her eyes lowered. One day she would look up and meet the knowing gaze of her persecutor. Often she thought she had.

Her, in the hat, flicked away, pretending to look in Cooper's window!

Her behind the counter, weighing cheese. Not looking at me.

Him. Why not a man. Why not him, the newsagent, read all the papers, knew everyone's address, why not him?

Often this morning Ruby remembered what her husband had said to her first thing and felt a little unpleasant fluttering round her heart. Not that she blamed him. What was she for, if not to do the shopping and keep the house? She had mutilated his only child, so it was no use saying she was a good mother. Being a good housewife was her only job now. And she'd run out of tea. You couldn't get more basic housewifery than tea.

"She couldn't make a pot of tea!" You heard that sometimes, jeeringly, about some young girl getting married without an atom of domestic know-how. Couldn't boil an egg. Couldn't make a pot of tea.

You're useless, Ruby told herself, as she hurried home with her shopping bag. You're no good to anyone. You're a waste of time. And everyone knows it.

She opened the kitchen door. He was there, the book open in front of him on the table.

"All right?" she said in greeting. She put the bag down on the clean lino, glancing sideways into the hall as she did so. Yes. Post. Another fattish little envelope.

Quickly, to get it over with, she opened this one standing in the hall, shielded by the half-open door. Wrapped in toilet paper this time, the hard shiny kind, with Izal Medicated printed in clean green capitals on every piece. She unraveled it, screwing it up in her other hand. But what fell out was not a pencil this time. It was a small metal thing, which dropped onto the hall floor with a little ching.

Ruby stooped to pick it up.

"Mummy," called the child from the kitchen.

"Just a minute." She turned the thing in her hands. It was a pencil sharpener. A little piece of new steel. Ruby began to tremble. What was she to do with it? She couldn't put this in the kitchen boiler. It wouldn't burn. It would drop through scorched to lie amongst the ashes tomorrow when she riddled the pan, and it would look at her unchanged. What was she to do with it?

"Mum," called the boy again. His voice was neutral, interested. Ruby thrust the pencil sharpener into the pocket of her old blue dress.

"What?" Without looking at him she came back into the kitchen and bent over her shopping bag, taking out the chilly damp package of fish in its outer wrapping of newspaper.

"Mum, am I crying?"

"What?" The cold wet package in her hand, she straightened up and finally looked at him. Leaking from beneath the bandage where his eye had been was a thin watery green runnel of what looked like snot.

"Am I? Mummy?"

Ruby did not speak. She dropped the fish and backed a few steps away from him into the doorway through to the hall.

"What is it? What is it?" His voice rose more shrilly. He put up a hand to the bandage, bending his head a little, and suddenly a great burst of white-flecked fluid gushed out, with more pus, with long elastic strings of brown old blood. Stuff dripped from his chin onto his clean white Aertex shirt, and splashed onto the book in front of him.

Ruby screamed.

"Mummy!" He made a move, rising, toward her, as if he would run to her, get that stuff all over her.

"Don't you touch me!" shrieked Ruby, and she turned and ran. Without thought she tore open the kitchen door and slammed it shut behind her. Where could she go, where could she hide? There was a place. Of course. She ran along the side of the house to the garage. It was dark and cool in there, and almost empty, a place to store things. Ruby wrenched open the door, and went inside. All sorts of things.

An old steamer trunk, a broken-legged sewing box, tins of leftover paint. Creosote.

Garden things, spades and flowerpots and so on.

A hammer. Nails. The stepladders.

Rope.

WILL AND ACTING, 1995

SUE ARRIVED EARLIER than usual next morning: she had put him and Annie first on her list, he understood, as he unlocked the front door to let her in.

"Oh I'm so sorry!" she cried in her warm cozy voice, and she stepped over the threshold and took him in her arms.

It felt extraordinarily nice, he thought, breathing in her perfumed soapy smell. And frightening, since it was a measure of her concern. Who had told her? Wasn't that against some rule or another?

But Sue's immense bosom had given him so many artless friendly signals over the last few weeks that he was instantly too taken up with it to mind: ah, much less squashy than you might expect, almost rubbery; lavish. He remembered his dream, and the tiny and no less lovely breasts he had given Julia.

Sue let go, her eyes wet. She would be so pissed off, he thought, if she knew how he'd been checking her out. Women could never see that you could appreciate kindness and affection and nice tits all at one and the same time.

"I couldn't hardly believe it," she said.

And breasts are so expressive, so full of personality, thought Will. As individual as faces, almost. It's such a shame women generally keep them packed away. Spoilsports.

"Helen told me," she added.

Helen? Ah yes, haggard woman doctor. They would all know by now, he thought. Within their small circle of nursing and medical concerns,

188

he had already been such a star: Doing such a Right Thing. Pity none of them was the right age to have known and loved Toby ffrench: remembered preteen lust being a great deal better than none at all. Maybe it was just too much admiring sisterly approval that had so unmanned him all these months. Unless, of course, having holes in your spleen made your cock drop off as well.

Diffuse areas of infiltration.

Though perhaps all the sisterly-type approval was now going to be laced with something stronger and more complicated. Now he was dying. Of course he was too young and good-looking to die. Still old to the young, of course. But extra young now, to the old.

"But if you hadn't found out now," Sue was saying anxiously, "you'd only have found out later, and this sort of thing, well, you catch it early, much better for you . . ."

"Yeah." Sorry: know you're right: still can't get up a lot of enthusiasm about it though.

Sue tilted her head toward his mother's room. "Does she know?"

"No. She's not going to, OK?" Alarm.

"No no. That's all your decision, OK? But. Well. You can't go on looking after her though, lovey, now can you?"

Will found himself suddenly unable to answer. It was her embrace, he thought, weakening him so. He wanted her to cuddle him again, he wanted her to pick him up and carry him away in her arms to somewhere dark and safe. I'm going potty, was a simultaneous idea.

"Sorry?" he asked, realizing that she had asked him something.

"I said, have you had anything to eat?"

He shook his head.

"I'm going to make you a bit of breakfast, and then I'm going to go in and see her, and then we'll sort out what we're going to do, all right?"

He nodded, thinking, Not long to go now. When would Sylvie come? She had said she would start early, that the baby always woke at dawn.

"Probably go back to London for a day or two," he said. His voice pleased him, it sounded almost normal, practically breezy.

"Good. Oh, I rang the hospice before I started out, on the off-chance," said Sue, busily cutting bread. "Anyway, there's a place going, I said I'd talk to you, and get back to them. Can I put a bit of sugar in this for you, my lovely?"

Another bad moment somehow, tenderly being called her lovely. Mum is awake, he reminded himself. In the next room. She mustn't hear anything.

"No, thanks. I'll need to talk to her first. I'm going to tell her it's work. It shouldn't be much more than a week. Well. A fortnight maybe."

It would be the greatest piece of acting of his whole career, he thought with a little tremor of preemptive stage fright. If he could bring it off at all. And no one there to see it, except his audience of one, who must not suspect any acting at all.

"I'm going to tell her a lot of lies."

"We all lie to our mothers, now, don't we. D'you want honey on that?"

"No thanks. God, oh God, the dog! I'd forgotten the dog, what am I going to . . ."

"Don't worry about it. Calm down. We'll sort everything out, OK? Now. Eat your breakfast, go on."

The toast, like all food he could even bring himself to imagine at the moment, was entirely inedible. He could see that it was warm toast, golden with melted butter, and it smelt nice, but it turned to something like cork tablemat in his hand: the Midas touch of fear.

Getting into such a flutter so fast about the dog. It was like being a fragile old lady, he thought. Panicking about pet care.

Now he could almost feel the wave coming. It was going to swamp him this time, it was going to hurl him rolling over and over helplessly to the very bottom. Mum in the next room, awake.

He stood up, and spoke. The voice he was trying for now was lively, eager, cheerfully ready for anything. Careful: you don't want *Blue Peter*.

"Tell you what," he said, and it was just right. "Ought to have taken the dog out first. I'll go now, while you're busy, OK? Judy, come on, dog!" called that resolute and daring young warrior, Toby ffrench.

Toby had always been good at escaping. Using wit and bravery and his famous dizzying laser and occasionally even his fists, one, two! he had escaped all sorts of horrors. Given the technological and cost constraints of British television at the time these had been largely represented by painted polystyrene in quarries, though he had also survived being ingested by the space amoeboid Zentor, the cling-film-like entity *Earth's Army* had encountered in episode seven; he had also spent an entire program hanging upside down in one of the skin-tight latex-like preserving tubes of the flesh-eating Arachnikons, with just one eloquent hand free to poke out at the bottom, and even the prospect of being therein minced and slowly sucked out as human puree like—well, thought Will now, like a dodgy spleen being laparoscopically splenectomized, had done nothing to daunt his reckless courage.

Good old Toby. An intergalactic Mr. Bingley, perhaps; even a bit of a pillock, if truth be told, but still always there when you really needed him. There to get into, protective, lifesaving, sealed up like a spacesuit. There to hide inside.

Good job, really, thought Will, that none of the nurses here knew and loved him. I might need Toby ffrench rather a lot in the next few weeks. Best if none of them suspect my fighting talk's all secondhand.

TED AND THE ANKLE CHARM, 1954

As soon as he got out of the house he was sorry. He'd regretted the words, of course, as soon as they were spoken. Saying them, and in such a vicious tone, broke some of his own deepest rules, and thus hurt him also.

Ted had been trained from childhood to treat women gently, because, as a corollary to their moral superiority, their physical weaknesses rendered them fragile. Men were robust, coarsely put together, tough as pewter plates; women were decorative, finely wrought bone china. You used them gently, the nice girls, or they broke.

He had left the house early without a word, breakfastless. He felt he would never want to eat again anyway. Pain of various kinds inhabited his insides already. He walked so fast up the lane that he saw he had a full fifteen minutes to wait before the works bus arrived. The thought of climbing on amid that half-respectful half-ironic chorus of *Mornings* from the factory women already on board turned his stomach still further.

Walk all the way, he thought. Why not? Only a mile or two. He kept walking, faster and faster. The road was very quiet. Birdsong rattled in his ears. The sun shone. He took off his jacket and loosened his tie. Then he wadded his good work jacket up in one hand and began to run.

He hadn't run for years, not since he left the army. He had run a great deal in France somewhere. He hadn't known where the hell he was and hadn't wanted to. Running along being shot at. Wish I was back there now, he thought.

Running toward the sea, then. Not Dunkirk as a matter of fact. No, Cherbourg. We were all along the coast at one point, yes. Straight onto a troopship, dumped ashore, packed onto a train, and then: then the strangest part, the part that popped up still from time to time in puzzling dreams: after a fortnight or so of running and hiding and starving and trying to snatch an hour's sleep in the rain, and all the time half out of his mind with fright, he and several hundred others had been put up for a night at this unbelievably swanky place, a college hall in Cambridge. In the evening of that same endless day he had been politely invited to sit amid a heady smell of steak-and-kidney pie at one of the several long dining tables in a place with all carving on the walls and a ceiling like a cathedral and candles and silver, and some old geezer with a teacloth folded over one arm had tapped him deferentially on the shoulder and murmured, *Beer or lemonade, sah?*

That jolt of displacement: horrible, despite, or because of, the comfort and ease, the staggering look of the place, the golden smell of pastry. All of a sudden he had felt as if he might have gone mad. As if anything he imagined might have happened, or the other way round.

Beer or lemonade, sah?

Felt like this, he realized. He slowed down to a limping jog.

Talking to Ruby like that. Like a brute. Like the sort of brutal man he most despised. What had come over him?

Ted stopped still. She doesn't love me any more, he thought. She's stopped. She used to like me well enough. And I used to like her. I used to like her a lot. I used to love her. But now she won't let me.

He walked on more slowly, his breath calming. His feet hurt, where the heels were blistering. He remembered how she used to look when they first went out of an evening. All dolled up. A right little cracker, she was. You felt proud, neat little woman like that on your arm. Such little feet she had, barely a size two shoe. Couldn't hardly find shoes to fit her, often. Her little dainty high heels. Like Cinderella. She liked high heels. Made her five foot three, her heels.

Once in the summer of 1949 she had worn a tiny gold chain round one ankle, like Barbara Stanwyck in *Double Indemnity*. And the same sort of shoes. She'd looked quite a lot like Barbara Stanwyck in fact, that was why he had bought the little golden chain for her.

"Isn't it a bit tarty?" she had said to him doubtfully, taking it out of the box.

But she had worn it just for him. He had liked her looking a bit tarty. Only in their own home, of course. Only in private. Only for him.

He had promised to cherish Ruby, and to stick by her no matter what. Sickness and health. That included children. Oh, poor little kid!

The thought of his son, and all that the child had suffered, suddenly acted upon him like a thrown switch. He had not shed a tear since his own childhood, not even in France, not even when the troopship pulled away from the harbor. But all of a sudden a huge painful sob came tearing up through his chest like sickness. A dim beady awareness of the approaching works bus got him safely over a handy five-bar gate and into a field, where his legs gave way. For an immeasurable length of time he knelt upon the tender grass, crying aloud. Traffic zipped past him, an occasional glittering noisy blur through the hedge.

Presently he recovered himself, and was ashamed. He sat up and pretended to himself that he was sitting in a field merely to enjoy the view, because it was such a lovely morning. Duly he looked around himself, at the three oak trees before him, with sheep already gathering beneath their shade. Insects hovered about. He saw some flowers, pink, white. Very nice, he told himself: the countryside.

He took out his handkerchief, boiled, washed, dried, ironed, folded and put away by Ruby. He wiped his face in its cleanly smell, put it squashed into a ball back in his trouser pocket, slipped on his jacket, arose a little stiffly, and began the walk back home. There was a telephone box beside the bus stop; he would call work, and tell them he would be late in today. Unavoidably detained. That was the phrase. He had not, he reflected, been late for work once, since the job began. Had hardly missed a day, despite everything.

He would go home, and maybe not go to work at all today. He would beg Ruby to forgive him. He would tell her how much he missed the real Ruby, the one he had married, the one who had worn the ankle chain and giggled when he nuzzled all around it with his lips. He would take her, his own Cinderella, the glass slipper of his love, that had so fitted her once. He saw himself kneeling before her, holding her little foot in his hand.

His own feet hurt him, but he hurried.

MAY WILDING'S LETTER, AUGUST 1954

SITTING AT HER eighteenth-century escritoire, Mrs. Wilding was writing a careful letter. It was the fourth she had written that morning, and the most important.

Already out of the way were, firstly, a longish note to her mother-in-law, thanking her again for her hospitality (unnecessarily spare, in Mrs. Wilding's opinion), and informing her of the speed and smoothness of their journey home, and of how pleasant it was to be in their own home once more, simple polite expressions, Mrs. Wilding knew, but all of them entirely alien to her husband's mother, who regarded all travel, particularly by private car, as a dangerous luxury, and whose reaction to normal social pleasantries like thank you letters was anyway one of puritanical and essentially (thought Mrs. Wilding) plebeian scorn: writing these to her was thus, then, one of those little tasks Mrs. Wilding generally undertook with a very light heart.

Secondly, with less enthusiasm, she had constructed an artful resumé of their Scottish trip for the benefit of Laura Cunningham, who must be led to believe, whilst not being told any actual untruth, that the Wildings had been traveling in the Trossachs without recourse to any elderly Presbyterian relatives in mean rural circumstances, whilst at the same time not given too much detail about what they had actually done, since any reference to any specific Scottish mountain, loch, river, stretch of moorland or romantic ruin of castle invariably prompted Laura to let Mrs. Wilding know which of her army of Scottish relatives owned it, which was not only sickening in itself but also created further irritations when, as sometimes happened, one of the army came to the village to stay with Laura, and over tea or cocktails Laura would tell Charlie, or Jean, that the Wildings, local sawbones, had visited Charlie's Loch This or Jean's Castle That, and Mrs. Wilding would have to pretend not to mind being held up in company as that epitome of the lower bourgeoisie, a *tripper*.

Stamping with some bitter satisfaction her inventively uninformative note to Laura Cunningham Mrs. Wilding had proceeded to deal with Mrs. Mace, who ran the dairy in the village, and who had unaccountably taken to sending round eggs barely fit for consumption, so elderly were they; Meadows had cracked one onto a dinner plate for her, so that she could see with her own eyes how it slackly spread itself flat like water, instead of sitting up proud and neat as a properly fresh egg should.

Mrs. Mace in her turn duly flattened, Mrs. Wilding had paused for thought. The final letter was to her dear son Rob. Who had so delightfully rung her up on the telephone a day or two after the end of their holiday, to thank his mother again for such a splendid healthful outdoor trip, everything so jolly; and then mentioned as he finished, just in passing, that he seemed to have come away somehow with one of his mother's little ornaments, the little netsuke piggy from the corner cupboard in the drawing room; he'd been taking a closer look at it, and somehow slipped it into his trouser pocket, and forgotten all about it, like a chump; so sorry; he'd look after it frightfully carefully, and bring it back next time he came home if that was all right, or should he send it, which did she prefer?

"Oh, no matter, keep it till next time, darling," she had answered blithely, but even then, with no time to think at all, she had known there was more to all this than he was pretending. And it was clearly something to do with that dreadful girl.

She had seen the netsuke figure was missing straight away. But she had known who had taken it all along.

When had the disappearances begun? Mrs. Wilding was not exactly sure. But a very long time ago. Before, even, she had had anything, from the antique-curio point of view, worth pinching. For several years, when Rob was a baby, small items of hers—a card of mother-of-pearl buttons, a set of safety pins, petticoat ribbons, a needle case—had one by one disappeared, stayed away for a month or so, and then mysteriously reappeared, generally only fairly near the spot they had originally vanished from, so that for a long time Mrs. Wilding had assumed that she had simply been looking in the wrong place all the time, and that motherhood and its attendant cares had made her more absent-minded than before.

The first important thing had been a cheap turquoise ring of her mother's. It had been the first disappearance she had minded about, for she had loved her mother, lately dead.

"Oh, Meadows, help me look for it, will you, oh dear!" and she had shed a few tears of distress and frustration at her own carelessness; and lo! Meadows had found the missing ring almost immediately, behind the curtain on the windowsill, where Mrs. Wilding had happened to have looked already, seconds before Meadows had entered the room.

"Oh, thank you, oh, Meadows, what would I do without you!" she had exclaimed joyfully, and not until Meadows had wordlessly stumped off downstairs again had she put two and two together and found that, try as she might, they kept on making four.

Meadows had found the ring because Meadows had taken it. She must have been carrying it on her. But why?

She had given it back quickly, when she saw that its loss was mourned. She had kept the other things for longer; their loss had merely irritated. Why would Meadows do such things? For a minute or two Mrs. Wilding tried to imagine herself summoning Meadows and simply asking her. Wouldn't say thieving, of course: borrowing, perhaps. Meadows, why have you been borrowing small items of mine, and then giving them back again?

Was she pawning them somehow? But none of the things had been worth more than a few shillings anyway. It was senseless. And if she was a senseless thief, what else was she? That stolid immobile face could hide anything.

A picture had suddenly formed itself in Mrs. Wilding's mind: she saw Meadows sitting quietly in the evenings in her armchair (superannuated from the parlor, but still perfectly comfortable) sitting quite still, face unmoving as ever, with the comb case, or the powder puff, or whatever it was, held gently in her cupped hands as if it were a little bird.

And as if it had some power or beneficence, like a talisman. Until whatever mysterious efficacy the object had was worn away. When she must replace it with another. It is not simply things she steals, Mrs. Wilding had realized. It is *my* things.

Oh, horrid! Oh, creepy!

She did not, of course, remember the gloves, all of five years old now, nor, naturally enough, had she any idea of the unspeakable happiness felt by Meadows on winter Sundays, on publicly wearing them to chapel.

(But then neither had anyone else; Meadows herself does not try to identify the emotion that fills her life with blessedness. It is just that sometimes, especially in the summer, the gloves are not quite enough. She does not fondle the items, as Mrs. Wilding so queasily imagined, or cup them in her hands. She carries them in her apron pocket, ready to be touched very briefly, lightly, with one careful finger-tip, ever so often during the day. The purloined powder puff was a little warm secret in her apron pocket, warm as a smile. Meadows stealth-ily petted it, softly, and every touch gave her a tiny revivifying jolt of happiness.

More than once, say, fingering the comb case in her apron pocket whilst simultaneously pretending to help Mrs. Wilding to look for it, Meadows had become aware of a certain sensation as of bafflement in-side her. It was uncomfortable. It was quite like the feeling she had when little master Rob kept getting into the coal shed and then wan-dering straight out of it into the drawing room, which was carpeted in palest green; her resignation had a painful edge to it. But the comb case had been very dear. It had smiled at her longer than anything else had. Mrs. Wilding's smile. By proxy.)

Guessing something of all this—oh horrid! Oh, creepy! impelled Mrs. Wilding up from her dressing table, where she had sat with her mother's turquoise ring still clenched in her hand, to pace the room near tears, wondering what to do for the best.

Her first immediate impulse, to sack Meadows out of hand, to get rid of her instantly, carried so many implications that she felt tired just enumerating them. How could she ever replace such a paragon among housemaids? No one she knew was looked after so well. The horrors of advertising, or of the Registry Office in London, of interviewing, of trial periods and training, presented themselves all at once to her anguished mind.

Laura Cunningham had had endless trouble with maidservants. Of course that might well be Laura's own fault, altogether both mean and high-handed, undoubtedly; but then poor dear Jane Vincent couldn't hold anyone either, and the wages these girls wanted these days! It was perfectly possible, Mrs. Wilding realized, that if she did not employ Meadows she would be unable to employ anyone at all. Who else would put up with the wages Mrs. Wilding was, currently, only just afford-ing? It was true that when her husband's partner retired their present money troubles should be over, but that was still three years away; how could she manage for three whole years without a parlor maid? And not just without any maid; without Meadows, beside whom any other maid would seem as nought!

But keeping Meadows on would mean employing someone unac-countable. A thief, in a word.

She gives everything back, Mrs. Wilding remembered.

If I sack her Laura Cunningham will get her. Hadn't that abandoned woman already privately intimated to Meadows that should she ever be at liberty she, Laura Cunningham, would be ready to consider her for a post at the Grange?

"Her offered me a job, madam." One evening not a year before, as they had been washing up together after one of Mrs. Wilding's bridge evenings.

"What do you mean, Meadows?"

"Offered me," said Meadows, sliding another delicate cup into the sink. "Mrs. Cunningham."

This, after stuffing her horse-face with more of Meadows's creamy egg mayonnaise and cress sandwiches than could possibly have been good for her! The treachery!

A pause to consider both betrayal and gluttony, to breathe them both in like a freezing draft of air, and then, measured, really quite success-fully calm and ladylike under the circumstances:

"And did you make her any reply, Meadows?"

Meadows handed over the cup, freshly rinsed, and took up another. "I told her I was settled well enough already."

Mrs. Wilding dried the cup. This was a long speech, for Meadows. Impossible, of course, to tell exactly what it meant. It had occurred to her that if Meadows were even slightly different she, Mrs. Wilding, would surely have grounds for suspicion. With anyone else, surely, this whole business might simply be a lie, a cunning ploy to extract a pay rise. But this was Meadows, who never, in four years, had told the smallest untruth, and whose strict adherence to the narrowest con-fines of Methodism was widely respected in the village.

"I should be very sorry to lose you, Meadows," she said at last. "Very sorry indeed."

"Thank you, madam."

Never guessing even now that her words were written still on Meadows's heart.

If she's so bloody honest, Mrs. Wilding had thought, pacing still, and suddenly angry as she reflected on this touching scene of servile loy-alty, how can she go on pinching things? How does that all square with the Brethren?

She gives it all back though, Mrs. Wilding remembered again. It's not really stealing at all. It's something else.

And really, what would I do without her? How could I man-age? Impossible.

And also: it had to be admitted that Meadows knew a thing or two. About herself, May Wilding; things which on the whole Mrs. Wilding would prefer to keep private, things which might, perhaps, leak out into village gossip should Meadows be summarily sacked from a job which, as she had said herself, she clearly felt settled in.

For Meadows knew how much Mrs. Wilding had not known. Mead-ows, for instance, knew how to correctly address the widow of a bar-onet, both in person and in writing; she knew who should sit where at dinner, and in what order the guests should arrive at table. True, Mrs. Wilding had been an exceptionally fast learner of such essential social detail, quick to pick up on the slightest sign or hint. But it had clearly been understood by both, in their early days, that Mrs. Wilding had often needed the tiniest shove in the right direction, and that such a shove, when given, would not be resented a bit, but gratefully accepted.

One might almost say, thought Mrs. Wilding, that she actually owed poor Meadows a certain amount of leeway, under the circumstances. And it would be so ungenerous to force so violent a change upon the poor woman, at her time of life. Perhaps, indeed, Meadows's time of life was entirely to blame for her unusual behavior; did not women approaching their climacteric often become quite unhinged, especially if unmarried and childless?

Would it not be outright cruel to sack someone in such a case? It might look so, thought Mrs. Wilding. Obviously one did not wish to be unkind. Ladies always dealt kindly with servants.

Would it, after all, be possible to pretend not to know? Suppose I hadn't just looked behind the curtain. If I hadn't just checked, I would never have realized. And who knows, this may have given her a fright. Perhaps she will stop anyway. Or at any rate not take anything important; clearly she didn't realize it was poor Ma's little ring. And it was risky, finding it so quickly, when she saw that I minded. Or is she just too stupid to understand that?

How stupid was Meadows? How anything? Well. Suppose, thought Mrs. Wilding, that I give keeping Meadows on just a try?

If knowing what she was privately up to turned out after all to be unendurable, well, she would let Laura Cunningham do her worst. And put up with the frightful consequences of maidlessness, which should be borne in mind when coming to any final decision.

And this, a task to be faced sooner or later, put off for another month, and then another, and never quite arrived at, had finally faded altogether from her mind. Meadows had gone on taking things; Mrs. Wilding had gone on pretending not to know she had. As the years passed, and Dr. Wilding grew richer, and Mrs. Wilding more practiced in spotting the well-turned, the classical, the antique, the particularly fine, Meadows too had raised her sights. An eighteenth-century silver brooch, shaped in a tiny bow and studded with paste; the lid of a tiny Georgian silver snuff box; an apostle spoon. Once, a little worryingly, the saucer of a Copenhagen teacup, her first breakable, returned, Mrs. Wilding noticed with relief, within days.

The netsuke boar, of course, was simply par for the course. Even as she had bought it she had known Meadows would covet it. Mrs. Wilding knew by now what size of thing Meadows generally preferred. But Meadows would not take it straight away. Like everything else it would have to be owned by Mrs. Wilding for at least a year or two before, somehow, it became worth taking. Worth borrowing.

The real question, thought Mrs. Wilding now, pausing after My Dear Rob, was why her dear Rob was lying about it. Of course he had not carried it away by mistake. The thing actually weighed a great deal more than it looked as if it would. No one could possibly walk off with it without being aware of the fact. Had Meadows done her stuff, and then somehow passed it on to Rob by mistake? That didn't seem very likely. Had Meadows dropped it, lost it? Or. Perhaps that unspeakably common girl poor Rob had got himself so entangled with, that Iris, seeing it perhaps in Meadows's room, possibly just left lying about—for she, Mrs. Wilding, had never stooped to prying, and for all she knew Meadows left each trophy on display on her chest of drawers or on her pillow or something—well, that dreary little trollop had come sneaking about up the stairs, seen piggy, and slyly helped herself, imagining that while she could not dare to steal from the lady, she might with impunity pilfer from the maid!

Dear Rob, of course, had no more idea than his father did of Meadows's little peculiarities. He would assume, of course, that she was above suspicion. Had she not been his mother's devoted servant since before he was born?

My dear Rob,
It was so lovely to hear from you, I'm glad you're settling down to work again, this is such an important year for you! I hope your cold is quite gone by now, and that dear little Iris is well. Do send her my best wishes.

As to the bit of ivory: rather a clever find of mine, in fact! Though
you know I have an eye for these things. I'd just happened to have
been reading up netsuke, though, and spotted piggy in Golding's little
emporium, absolutely fell in love with it at once—that place in Rope
Lane, do you remember? The rag and bone man. He had it in his shop
front window, surrounded, can you believe it, by a whole ghastly
menagerie of the most hideously vulgar glass and china animals all
the way from Margate, or Southend! Of course it is that sort of size; so
perhaps it is the sort of mistake anyone not in the business might be
expected to make. Joe simply had no idea, but of course he knows me,
and looked frightfully cunning as he named his price, no doubt four
times what he thought it was worth.

I haven't had it authenticated; it may be a fake; it's still
rather fine, though, don't you think? I won't burden you with its
possible price, if it really is Masatsugu. I know you'll take good
care of it, darling, if for no other reason than that it actually
belongs to

Your positively adoring,
Mummy XXX

Mrs. Wilding gave a small tremulous giggle as she stamped the envelope to this final letter. The whole thing was, perhaps, a little risky; one
was simply not in possession of all the facts; one knew, however, when
one's own dear boy was lying. One saw one's Machiavellian opportunity, and one took it.

Iris da Silva would be a disastrous wife for her son; it was her duty to
encourage him to realize for himself that a woman from such a poor
background would be a hopeless encumbrance to all his prospects in
life. Going to the bad was simply written all over her.

It happened that Mrs. Wilding was convinced the boar was genuine, an okinomo, or lucky charm: the dreamy serenity of the piece
marked it out for her as a work of highest art. The hieroglyphics on
its base, translated, would surely read Kaigyokusai Masatsugu, signa-
ture of the master.

Not that she cared one way or the other at that moment. For in her heart they now had another and more important meaning; like the storybook trophy designed by the gods of old to cause ill-feeling, the little netsuke boar had become in itself at once a cause and a warning; the message on its base must also now read *Discord*.

TED AND THE PENCIL SHARPENER, 1954

THE FIRST THING HE NOTICED was the fish. Nearly fell over the shopping: Ruby's old basket with the flowers, once red, now a faded purplish brown, worked in raffia on the side. Fish, obvious from the smell, on the kitchen table; basket on the floor beside the door. A chair pulled back from the table. A feeling in the air, that the house was empty. Emptied, scoured.

Ted picked the basket up, noting with a pang the two packets of Brook Bond, and put it on the table. He picked up the book that lay open there. The pages were dappled with droplets of something, stained and flecked, and still—he put out one careful fingertip—still damp. Strange.

"Hello?"

There was no reply.

"Ruby, it's me: I'm really sorry." The house was so small that standing here on the door mat, calling, he knew his voice would reach every corner of it.

"Ruby?"

He went into the living room. Empty. He turned to go upstairs when a tiny sound made him look down.

"Hello, what are you doing down there?"

He bent rather stiffly into a crouch, and pulled up a handful of the plush brown cloth that Ruby protected the table with during the day. The child lay there all curled up, his face turned away, close to the wall.

"Hello, son," he said. "What's going on? Where's your mum?"

At the sound of his voice it seemed to him that the child curled him-self up the tighter. His little shoulders were quivering, he saw. Dread began to work inside him.

"Turn round, now. There's a good boy," he said.

No move at all.

"I'm not angry with you, lovey. Come on, there's a good lad."

He reached out, and touched the child's back, stroking it, gently, awkwardly. He felt the little shoulder blades, the delicate miniature knobs of the spine, the little ribs, the smooth skin beneath the shirt.

"Come on, darling," he said. The child shifted himself backward, and turned round.

"Oh my Lord," he said, his voice immediately jocular. "Oh my Lord ain't you a mess! What happened? Is it hurting?" he added anxiously. And without further thought he reached under the table and pulled the boy out into his arms.

"There there." For a little while he sat on the carpet holding him, rocking both of them hard to and fro.

"There there. Daddy's here now. There there."

He hardly knew what he was saying. Dimly he remembered various warnings, of buildup behind the *God* the thing they had left in the child's head to keep the socket open, of sudden flushings, of normal consequences, of healing processes, and murmured some of them into the child's hair as he rocked.

"Just need to get you cleaned up a bit, don't we! Means it's all getting better! Means everything's all right!" But still the boy didn't cry, or speak. He hid his sticky face in his father's shirt, and said not a word.

"Best pop you back to hospital, I reckon," he said, now in conversa-tional tones. He stopped rocking and with some difficulty stood up so that he could sit down again on one of the dining table chairs, with the boy now on his lap. This felt more normal, and he could begin to try and think things out. If only he had a car, so that he could take the child there straight away! But where was Ruby?

"Get those nurses to sort you out," he went on. "Mum'd want to come too, though, d'you know where she's gone, lovey, did she go to a neigh-bor, go for help sort of thing?"

Should he call an ambulance? There was a call box at the end of the road. Of course, that was where Ruby had gone, he thought, with a flash of relief, and then remembered that he had walked past the call box just now, on his way home. No Ruby inside. No Ruby.

She must have gone to a neighbor, he could just about see her doing that in a panic, and she could well have panicked, but if she'd done that why hadn't she come back? Wouldn't any neighbor, all eager concern, have rushed back with her, straight away?

No: she'd just walked out and left him, poor little tyke. She'd walked out and left him all on his own. That's what it looked like. You'd have to be half crazy to go and do a thing like that. You'd really have to be mad. Oh, Ruby!

"You just stay here a few minutes," he said. "I'm just going to nip upstairs, make sure she's not . . ."

Not what? Not hiding up there under the bed, curled up like their abandoned son? She wouldn't—do anything would she? Try anything?

Why don't you fuck off out of it, he had said to her, so viciously, so cruelly. Had she done as he had told her? The doctor had given her sleeping pills, he remembered, and ran upstairs. The three little rooms were immaculate, as usual, and empty. He ran down again, and this time the child met his eyes.

"She ran away," he said.

"Where'd she run to, old chap? Eh?"

"Don't *you* go away, Daddy."

"I won't, I won't, I promise. Only I just got to find her, I need to tell her something, you see. Where did she go?"

"I don't know," said the child, but as he spoke he turned so that he was facing the window. Looking out straight at the closed double doors of the garage.

"Don't leave me, Daddy!"

"I won't be a minute—no! You stay here!" Ted yells, suddenly ferocious, and has time for a moment's relief, when the child sets up what sounds at least like a normal bit of wailing.

"I'm sorry, I'm sorry, honest I won't be a minute, then I'll come back, see? See? Just you sit there. I'll be back in no time, all right?"

Still babbling he runs out through the kitchen and hurls himself along the double concrete path toward the garage. The key is in the lock. He turns it, and pulls the door open.

Their eyes meet immediately, for a split second. Her eyes, hers still, are bulging in the stranger's puffed purple face, which then must turn with the swing of the rope. Her hands are tight at her throat, as if to pull at what is cutting into her there. She's sticking her tongue right out at him. Black and swollen, like a scream made thick solid flesh, jutting out of her mouth. The stepladders lie on their side beneath her. One pointing toe of hers is still making tiny jabbing movements toward a nearby edge, as if she would perch there if she could. She cannot reach it. The rope turns her back: her eyes plead.

Afterwards it seems to him that he proceeds with fabulous dispatch. An automaton built for speed seemed to take his place, taking one step to the right to snatch up the garden shears, and one step back to bend and pick up the stepladders, smacking them instantly upright and into place beside the strange turning thing that is Ruby. Then groans, carving at the rope, at the thick army kitbag hemp, sawing at it, he cannot save her the drop the fall against the stepladders, which he falls down himself as they slide sideways beneath her dead weight. Pull away her hands, tear with his fingers at the swollen dank skin of her throat, ah the thick mauve welt of it! pulling away the ligature, and all the while shouting her name, over and over again, though this he does not know or hear.

As she heaves and drags in the air, as she kicks convulsively and retches, he hears something metallic drop away from her and fall onto the garage's concrete floor. Lying beside her, sobbing for breath himself, unable for the moment to look at her for fear, he follows the sound with his eyes, and reaches out, and picks up its cause.

His fingers close round it: the small bright shiny new pencil sharpener.

SYLVIA AND CLIO ON THE ROAD, 1995

OF COURSE SHE'D HAD to bring Clio. That meant equipment: wipes nappies clothing socks nappy bags changing mat milk bottles teats dummies bottlebrush Milton travel cot pushchair banana (in protective Tupperware) plasticbib plasticspoon plasticmug plasticplate toybag sunscreen tapedeck tapes.

Clio.

"We're going to see Nanna!" Four hours at least, thought Sylvia, as she buckled the baby into her travel seat. She had never driven so far on her own with Clio before. The trapped-with-screaming-baby-on-motorway scenario played constantly in Sylvia's head as she stowed everything into the boot of her car. Baby on Board: Driver in Extremis. If only Adam was home! But then she remembered that of course Plan A rather depended on his being away in the first place.

Plan A had come to her as she paced her living room during the long and almost unbearable talk with Will.

"Look," she had said abruptly, cutting him off in the middle of a sentence as a solution had suddenly occurred to her, "d'you mind if I tell a few lies? I can be much more helpful if we're related. You need to name me as your next of kin. OK?"

She had realized as she spoke how isolated he was; did he actually have any family, really, other than his poor old mum? And he is the closest I've got to a brother, she thought, and her eyes immediately filled with tears at the thought of losing him. But don't you dare sound weepy, she told herself fiercely, blinking them away.

"OK, Will? Could I be a cousin or something?" There: cool and authoritative, as usual. Another pause, and then, plaintively:

"Couldn't you be an aunt?" he said. "I've always wanted aunties."

The laugh had made her cry. "Hang on a minute, will you?"

She had run into the kitchen for a glass, and poured herself a whisky.

"Sorry. Thought I heard the baby."

"How is she?"

"Oh, fine. She's fine. So. Cousin, OK?"

"OK. Thanks, Sylvie."

"Then I can really interfere. Well, that sounds awful, but you know what I mean. Soon as they know your next-of-kin's a consultant, well, it'll concentrate their minds."

"Make 'em nervous."

"Possibly. But the gains outweigh the snags, I think, on the whole. Anyway I can find out who's in charge and what they're like and whether you should go somewhere else and so on. And I'm coming to see you. Help get everything sorted out. It's my weekend off, and as you're my only cousin I'm going to get some compassionate leave." Or unpaid leave if I can't swing it. God knows I'm owed it.

"When? When can you come?"

"Well, tomorrow. I'll leave straight away," said Sylvia, "if that's all right. I can help deal with things, you see. It's something I know about."

"Oh Sylvie, that'll be nice, it'll be so nice to see you."

"Well, you're not that far from my mother, are you?" Sylvia had said brightly, again perilously near tears. "I'll drop in on her too, I expect."

Bribes, thought Sylvia, as she stopped the car to close the gates. What did Lulu always have to hand? Generally rather healthful treats: carrot sticks to gummily gnaw on, orange segments, plain wholemeal biscuits. Well, this is an emergency, thought Sylvia, and when she stopped at the garage to fill up with petrol went into the little shop attached and after some fast thought bought a large bag of chocolate buttons, a tube of the fruit pastilles she remembered liking herself once, and several small boxes of various-flavored fruit drinks, of the heavily sugared kind so rightly sneered at by Lulu.

Four hours worth, thought Sylvia, grimly. She caught Clio's eye in the rearview mirror, and smiled cautiously. "Going to see Nanna!" To her immense surprise the baby replied:

"Nanna! Doggies!" and gave a whole-body kick, arms and legs waving, as of pleased excitement. Sylvia had to glance back at her.

"Yes," she said. "Doggies." Clio's smile was rather charmingly lopsided, she saw. It occurred to her that the smile was entirely unselfconscious, and not meant by Clio to convey anything. It had just happened on her face, because she was happy at the prospect of Nanna and dogs. Or more probably, thought Sylvia, dogs and Nanna.

Still kicking, the baby embarked on a series of brief shrill howling noises, which Sylvia realized after some time were meant to be dogs barking. And the baby seemed to be trying to catch her eye, squirming about, bobbing her head. Listen to my virtuoso dog impressions, her round bright eyes seemed to be saying, aren't they funny, are they amazingly realistic!

She wants me to laugh. She wants me to be pleased. Why is she doing that?

"Woof," said Sylvia tentatively, her eyes on the road ahead.

"Woooaarrrgh! Wooaargh!" screamed back Clio excitedly.

"Woof woof!" said Sylvia.

ROB AND THE NETSUKE PIG, AUGUST 1954

SOMETIMES HE DIDN'T open his mother's letters for days at a time. They were so boring generally, merely a reminder of how chokingly dull a place his mum and dad lived in, how could they stand it year after year! Generally he answered them with a telephone call when he had the money, and not at all when he hadn't; once Mrs. Wilding had included with her chatty resume of absolutely nothing in particular a stamped addressed envelope, the nearest she had yet come to reproach.

This one was different, though. He hadn't wanted to open this one at all. He had quickly folded it over and stuffed it in his pocket and tried to forget about it. He wished powerfully that he had not called his mother in the first place. Why hadn't he stopped and thought things out!

He should have tackled Jo first. It was obvious now. The thing had been in her dressing gown pocket after all.

"I say, Jo, hope you don't mind but I borrowed your dressing gown the other night, and couldn't help noticing that . . ."

The trouble had been, of course, that he should never have taken the dressing gown in the first place. Admitting he had meant also admitting the fact that he had for reasons of the basest curiosity opened the door of Jo's room when she was out and taken a bit of a snoop round. Well, Jo was such a mystery to him. Iris's big sister. So like, so unalike. Once he had vividly dreamt about Jo, and felt quite unable to meet her eyes the following morning.

Anyway Iris had been doing something on the landing where the gas ring was, stirring a tin of soup or something, and he had without thinking about it at all opened the door of Jo's room and gone inside. Much bigger than Iris's room, of course. Sagging little bed, and Jo had gone out without making it; that had shocked him a little. His mother would never have done that.

There were clothes everywhere, hanging from several hooks on the back of the bedroom door and from others screwed directly into the walls, which had been papered in a pattern of small flowers so long before that the flowers were a soft sepia brown, and the background a mottled beige. Cracked brownish lino on the floor, and shoes everywhere, kicked about, most of them a bit scuffed and battered-looking. A glimpse of pale green enamel chamber pot beneath the bed: empty, thank God. A teetering pile of magazines and travel brochures. A chest of drawers standing in for a dressing table, its top stacked with feminine bits and pieces, a large roll of cotton wool, a box of face powder, a pattern for a long slinky-looking dress and a length of uncut material ("Midnight blue slipper satin" he had thought, touching it; the phrase had for some reason just jumped into his mind), several bottles of nail varnish in various pinks and scarlets, a little huddled heap of stockings, a pot of face cream, and a scattering of face powder surrounding a flattened and elderly powder puff.

In some ways the room reassured him. It seemed to show that Jo was just another girl. He did not think to ask himself in what way he had suspected her of being otherwise, because he was not fully aware of his suspicions in the first place. He could not, however, help being his parents' child. In his heart he knew that Jo was a bad woman. She was defiled. She was a bad influence on her sister. She was dangerous. It was well that as Iris's husband he would take Jo's place as Iris's protector; Jo's protection was in itself a hazard.

The ingenuous messiness of the room, its single bed, its clearly private and non-femme-fatale-like appurtenances, spoke reassuringly to these half-conscious concerns, reminded him how young Jo had been when she and her little sister were orphaned: no one to look after them all these years. Women never really grew up; they needed looking after;

so jolly good job for old pipe-smoking Andrew Thingummy-Jig, seemed very decent. And not before time.

There was that old dressing gown Jo sometimes wore, slung over the end of the bed; no screen siren Rob had ever admired from the stalls would have dreamt of keeping such a garment in her bedroom, let alone wearing it herself. If she is a bad woman, whispered Rob's deepest softest thoughts, if she is a bad woman she isn't very good at it.

So far no harm done. But in the night he had felt a bit sick. Something had disagreed with him. Twice he had visited the toilet on the half-landing, and on the third attempt had considerably startled Miss Jarvis from the flat below, who had been coming upstairs with her hair in two gray plaits and clad in respectable ankle-length wool tartan, as he had been on the way down, shivering, for it was a very damp chilly night for July, in what was, in retrospect, rather too small a towel, hardly more than a dishcloth.

So naturally he had remembered the dressing gown, and nipped back to Jo's empty room to fetch it. It had smelt nice, of Jo's perfume. He'd tied the belt and waited on the top landing by the gas ring, for the sounds of Miss Jarvis's descent. There. It wasn't until he was safely sitting down inside with the bolt drawn that he investigated whatever had been knocking into his thigh with every step. Hadn't even recognized it at first. Oh, my mother's got one just like this! was his first thought. And then he had shivered still, despite the dressing gown.

His mother's little netsuke pig-thing. This wasn't like it: this *was* it. How had Jo come by it? Or rather, how had Iris come by it? He turned the figure over and over in his hands, but he could come up with no explanation he liked.

Why hadn't he just asked Jo? Waited a day or so, and asked her? He should just have told her how cold it had been, sorry, I went in your room without asking, yes, so what frankly, this is far more important, isn't it, Jo, what's going on?

And instead he'd rushed off without a word about it in the morning and gone and bloody told his mother! As if pretending he'd somehow accidentally taken the thing himself was going to take her in for a moment! But he hadn't been able to stop himself hoping. After all, there must be hundreds of netsuke pigs knocking around. Thousands of them. That was what Orientals did, wasn't it? Reproduced things.

"Oh no, darling, mine's safe in the glass cabinet, what a funny mistake to make!"

But of course she hadn't said anything like that at all. Just chattered away as usual and all the time he could practically hear her brain whirring. She hadn't said, Oh, one moment, darling, I'll just go and check. Had she? She'd known already that it was gone. And hadn't mentioned it to him. Because already she had known. Suspected.

The letter folded in his pocket, waiting for the moment when he would have to stop arguing with himself and rip it open.

So what if Iris had pinched the nasty little thing. Didn't matter, did it?

I don't want you to have pinched it, Iris. Oh I don't. Because if you have, you're not who I thought you were. You can't be, can you? You're someone different. A stranger.

Rob puts his hand in his pocket, and touches the letter with his fingertips. Not yet, he thinks to himself. Not yet.

RUBY AND TED, 1954

A QUICK PANTING HIATUS; then again the thought-free speed-machine.
In a crouch beside her Ted rolls and pulls the limply heaving body of
his wife into his arms, staggers to his feet, shoulders his way *biff* through
the open garage door and lopes erratically up the crazy paving to the
kitchen, the door of which he slams shut behind him with his heel.

Not until he has belted gasping up the stairs and half-laid, half-
dropped her onto the yellow candlewick bedspread does he take a proper
look at her.

Colorful effects of strangulation: Ruby's face has gone purple, in thick
blotchy streaks. Her lips are navy blue. The rope has burnt a dark crimson welt right up beneath her chin, and the raw place torn by the cruel
knot, just under her right ear, is now listlessly bleeding.

But she is breathing, if still noisily. Dropped on her back she turns
sideways, and draws up her feet as she goes on spluttering.

"Hang on, Rube!"

He sprints to the bathroom, throws a towel in the sink and turns the
cold tap onto it, half fills the toothmug, and races back with both, to
mop splashily at the poor swollen face, at the blood.

"Come on, Ruby. There you go. There."

He speaks to her with an eager gentleness: she has, for once, done
something he can understand. There is clear cause and effect: he
has behaved with monstrous cruelty, and she has therefore wanted to
die. Somewhere deep within he is impressed and excited by Ruby's

217

resolution, and with his own astonishing power, for in one day he has not only prompted her death, but saved her from it.

"Little sip of water now. There you go. There's a girl."

What's Ruby thinking?

Her brain had suffered nearly two minutes' profound oxygen loss. When her husband cut the rope a sudden instant bounding flood of life suffused all through her. To mind and body alike this felt like joy. As she lay bruised and retching on the garage floor, though her throat burnt, though it hurt so much to breathe, though she could hardly move for weakness, deep within her mind and body were singing with a strange exultant happiness. Her renascent brain leapt with energy, with eager dispatch, sorting minor difficulties ahead, quantifying them, calmly arranging solutions.

Her throat was very swollen though.

"Police" was all she could at first get out, in a low mutter.

"What, Rube? What you say? Here, have another sip."

"Don't call the doctor: police."

"Oh Christ!" Ted sat back: floored. Of course; he must get a doctor, both for Ruby and of course for the child; and the doctor would take one look at Ruby and call the police, and the police would arrest her, and charge her with trying to kill herself, since this was at the time technically no less illegal than trying to kill anybody else, and there would be some sort of court case, and certain things would have to be aired, be discussed, be looked at from all sides; and all their neighbors, and everyone in the village, and everyone at work from his bosses to the women who swabbed the factory floor, would know everything about everything, for ever and ever.

"Oh, Ruby!"

But she waggles her fingers at him: don't fret, say the fingers. She beckons, now. Closer. Come closer.

He bends over her, his ear to her lips, nearly normal color now.

"Get the washing machine."

What? What did she say? Misheard, obviously. "What, Ruby? Sorry . . ."

She turns her head from side to side a little: yes, you heard. "Get the washing machine out," she murmurs again. Her hand plucks at her throat. "Scarf. Caught my scarf. In it." Her eyes close in exhaustion.

His widen. Of course! The detachable mangle that affixed onto the washing machine's hefty side. (For once, wearing rubber gloves to protect her hands from the soapy water, Ruby had caught the tip of her right glove between those heavyweight inexorable rumbling rollers, and had —she said afterwards that evening—screamed in terror as she fought to get the glove off before her flesh was drawn in and squeezed flat along with the tea towel; had somehow in her panic not remembered the emergency off-switch on top of the enamel housing, but gone on pulling and twisting at the rubber glove, which went on stretching until at last with a smack her hand came free and the glove shot through the rollers and plopped into the bucket on the other side with its middle finger torn right off.)

It would of course be astonishingly silly, to do your mangling whilst wearing a long floaty scarf. It was likely, he thought, that neither doctor nor police would actually believe the story at all. But then they didn't need to, did they? Surely the doctor wouldn't actually *want* to report her; surely the police wouldn't *want* to arrest her. They would merely need a reason not to. And now he could provide one. Clever Ruby.

He rises, hesitates, bends over her again.

"You know I wish to God I hadn't said it, don't you," he tells her closed swollen eyes. A tear runs out of one of them. He kisses it away and plunges back downstairs.

IRIS AND THE BLANKET BATH, AUGUST 1954

IRIS PUSHED HER TROLLEY from the sluice to the side room, knocked, and slowly opened the door.

On the top shelf of the trolley, neatly laid out, a credit to the Princess Louise School of Nursing and Midwifery, were two large enamel bowls of steaming hot water, an immense folded rectangle of soft white flannel called a bath blanket, three towels, two fresh flannels, one with a knot tied into one corner, a clean basin, a bottle of thymol mouthwash standing in a metal kidney dish, and a bar of hospital soap; on the lower, a fresh drawsheet, two sheets stiff with the vigor of clean new heavyweight cotton, with a pillowcase to match, and a hospital nightdress, patterned with meek blue flowers.

"Hello?"

It was a beautiful morning, and pushing all this splendor of equipage Iris generally arrived at a patient's bedside in the highest of spirits. Iris liked blanket baths. She liked almost everything about them. It was such an intimate almost loving thing to do for someone. You could hardly help actually loving the person a little bit, by the time you'd finished, thought Iris. And it was clever too, well thought out: you washed them all over and if you did it properly, the way you'd been taught, they never once felt exposed, or ashamed. And afterwards they felt so much better. You could see them sitting up in bed looking brighter, feeling fresher and better and happier all over because you'd looked after them properly.

But today, this morning, Iris hesitated. She left the trolley by the door and crept forward, trying to make no sound.

The poor thing was clearly asleep. Back out quietly, and come back later? She could easily do Mrs. Savage instead. But as she turned the patient opened her eyes.

"Hello. Hello, Silver."

"Hello," said Iris, turning back with a smile. "How are you feeling?"

"Not so bad."

"Fancy a bath?"

"Have I got a choice?"

"Well, no, not really . . . "

"Never mind. You go ahead."

"I'll be ever so gentle."

"I know. I'm glad it's you, Silver."

Iris at once grew very busy at her trolley, checking the things she had checked already, needlessly moving things about.

It was bad enough just to hear the things some of the nurses said about poor Helen Stoddard at report. The tone they said them in. And of course you could show her how you felt by all sorts of subtle unkind-nesses, firmly yanking her sheets straight, crashing bowls and basins about, leaving her on bedpans just a shade longer than you would any-one else. Staff Nurse Benson, for instance, did all those things. She and Iris had done the side room blanket baths together a day or so earlier: she had done nothing outright, but Iris had been ashamed.

It was that shame that made Iris scrabble now at her perfectly orderly trolley. For beneath Benson's obliquely jeering gaze she had not even dared risk a glance of sympathy.

"I'm glad it's you, Silver," said the patient; and Iris understood: don't think for a moment that I didn't notice.

She set herself now to convey by her every word and movement that from her at least Stoddard had nothing to fear. She went round the bed, gently loosening the coverlet and the topsheet, pulling very carefully at the foot of the bed so that Stoddard was not jarred.

Then she softly unfolded the bath blanket on top of the coverlet.

"Shall I hold it for you?"

"Yes, please," said Iris. Stoddard hooked her bony fingers on the bath blanket, holding it in place as Iris drew the back the top sheet and coverlet: Step One: opening the bed without exposing the patient.

Benson, strenuously busy, had flung back the sheets as if the bed were empty; several seconds had passed before Iris, taken by surprise on the other side of it, could race round for the bath blanket to hide Stoddard's scrawny yellowish legs, the rucked-up nightgown, the scruff of pubic hair, the dank indwelling catheter. And then Benson had shot Iris a carefully dirty look, an official dirty look, to make it clear that the patient had been unnecessarily exposed not because she, Benson, had been too quick, but because Iris had been too slow; taking herself in; perhaps.

"Face first," said Iris, tucking towels on either side of Stoddard's head. She took up one of the flannels, immersed it, squeezed it out, and handed it over.

Step Two, according to basic training: most people prefer doing their own faces. Men especially like to rub their faces much harder than you or I ever would, girls!

Stoddard raised her spectral hand, and pushed the flannel about half-heartedly. It was too much for her, Iris saw.

"Shall I?"

"Yeah, go on. Thanks."

"Here, lift your head up a bit. I'll do your neck."

"Thank you." Hair could do with a wash, thought Iris as she patted Stoddard's face dry. Maybe this afternoon.

"Now your hands." Carefully Iris took the soapy flannel round each finger. No rings, of course.

"Know what today is, Silver?"

"No, what?" Iris rinsed the flannel in her second bowl, and wiped the soap away.

"My E.D.D."

"Your what?"

"Expected. Delivery. Date."

Iris drew back. Her heart quickened. It was just this sort of conversation that she had hoped to avoid. She picked up the towel, and dried the slack fingers with it. It always felt a bit strange, actually, drying someone else's hands. Drying their arms and legs and so on, that was all right, but there was something a bit spooky about drying someone else's hands. You thought of it sometimes at home, drying your hands after the washing up, a tiny foolish dread that there might somehow be someone else's fingers lurking in the towel, waiting for yours.

"If I'd gone through with it. Maybe today. Though they're often late apparently. Babies."

Step Three: arms. Iris adjusted her towels, drew the bath blanket back from Stoddard's fleshless left arm, and took up the freshly soaped flannel.

"Are they?" she said gently. Avoiding Stoddard's eyes she lifted the arm just below the elbow joint and soaped it, paying particular firm and thus non-tickly attention to the deep hollow of the armpit. There was a little straggly tuft of dark blond hair in there.

"You seeing anyone, Silvie?"

"Might be."

"Means you are. Is he nice?"

"He's all right," said Iris warily. She wanted to cross her fingers. It felt like bad luck even mentioning the glory that was Rob. Especially here.

"I thought my boy was nice. He *was* nice."

Iris rinsed the arm, dried it. "Got any talcum powder?"

"In the locker."

Iris bent and opened the little cupboard door. Stoddard's possessions looked back at her. Two pink plastic curlers. A hairbrush with a comb wedged into it. A threepenny bit. A toothbrush. A little tin of talc.

"The finest that Woolworths can sell," said Stoddard. Iris tipped a little out onto her own fingers, and sniffed.

"Lovely." She patted it into place, and began the process on the other arm.

"I trained with Benson," said Stoddard. "Did you know that? Over in St. Mary's."

Iris shook her head, rinsing.

"She always was a cow," said Stoddard dreamily. "She on this morning?"

"Yes. And Sister Marshall." Meaning: so you're safe. For now.

"She's all right," agreed Stoddard.

Sister Marshall: in charge of Marshall Ward. Only underlings traditionally addressed one another by their surnames; on acceding to Sisterhood, one professionally gave up not just Christian names but one's surname as well. The present Sister Marshall, slight, dark, thirtyish, was known to sit with Stoddard sometimes at visiting time, and had once been surprised holding her hand. Stoddard never had visitors. Unless you counted the occasional policeman.

Powdering her other arm set her off again.

"He was nice right up until I told him. And then he just didn't want to know."

Oh, please, thought Iris, squeezing the flannel in the rinsing bowl, please don't say it all again, not today. Please. "Shall I do your front?" she asked aloud. "Then I'll get some fresh hot water, OK?"

Stoddard turned her head away.

Iris drew the bath blanket down to Stoddard's waist. You could see every bone, practically every notch, the dark brown nipples rather shockingly protuberant, studding each of the sad slacknesses that once had been her breasts. Iris folded the bath blanket carefully down to the flaring hip bones, tucked the towels into place on either side.

"Shall I?"

Stoddard gave a little nod. Iris drew the warm soapy flannel over the bones. You could see Stoddard's heart beat, she realized; the taut skin had a tiny pulse to it, a steady flutter just below the left nipple. Abdomen still almost covered with wound dressing, and the place where the drain had been taken out yesterday. All neatly in place.

"I tried those pills first," said Stoddard idly. "Worth a try, I thought. You know. Regularize your monthly flow. That's what I wanted."

"Didn't work." Iris rinsed her flannel and began again. Gently over the poor ribs.

"Nah. So you send away for the other lot. The stronger ones. Oh, you think, I should have gone for the stronger ones first. Pay twice. Oldest trick in the book. Apparently."

But the book was so very old too, thought Iris. Old and cruel and secret.

"*I* wouldn't have known," she said. She took a towel and pressed it over Stoddard's chest, pulled up the bath blanket, softly pulled the towel out from under. There.

"It was because he was so nasty as well," said Stoddard. "If he hadn't said . . . well, he said all sorts of things. See, I thought, well, I don't want his baby anyway! I forgot: I forgot it was mine too. That's a funny thing, isn't it? I forgot that bit. It was all his when I was getting rid of it. But really it was all mine all the time. My only, ever . . ." Her voice trailed off. You'd think she would have run out of tears by now, thought Iris unhappily, you'd think there'd just come a time when you couldn't cry another single one.

She remembered a little boy ages ago, a patient, crying, and how she had hugged him and made him stop. Georgie. But there was no doing that sort of thing here. There was nothing anyone could do at all: it had all been done. They had gone on cutting more and more out of Stoddard until there was hardly anything left. *Helen Stoddard, under the care of Mr. Cosgrove, total pelvic clearance following septic abortion*, read the staff nurses every shift-change at report. All Stoddard's own fault in the first place. That was Benson's line anyway.

"I mean, she's a *nurse*, for heaven's sake! She was in Theatres; actually worked upstairs in this hospital for years, you'd think she'd've known what can go wrong, she must've seen it often enough. You'd think she'd have a bit more self-respect in fact. Nice girls don't get into that sort of trouble in the first place."

Painful words for Iris. Suppose Benson was right, and nice girls always said no! Iris had said yes: was thus not nice.

Besides Marshall Ward as a whole was unnerving. Within days of arriving on it Iris had understood that everything she had ever heard whispered at school was true after all. In bearing children you stretched, and gave, and tore: down there. Sometimes *years afterwards* doctors had to try and sew you back together again. Infections sprouted there, discharging smelly purulence. Bladders eroded into vaginas, vaginas ripped into rectums, exposed varicosities pulsed with indigo blood.

While in the sluice room of Marshall, slopped into glass jars, labeled, waiting until it looked as if there were no more bits and pieces still to come, stood the bloody end results of still further specifically female disasters. Sometimes, as you tipped in the bedpan of fragments, something recognizably human would glisten in miniature amid the detritus.

Some of these particular disasters had occurred naturally. Some had not.

"Anything long and thin enough," Benson had said. "Knitting needles. Crochet hooks. But they don't know any anatomy, see. They're stupid. Don't realize the uterus bends right back on itself. So they go straight through the anterior fornix and out the other side."

Iris, checking pillowcases beside her in the linen room, had said nothing. It was just another cruel trick of anatomy, she had thought, to bend the uterus right back on itself. Because the only time you could actually feel and see a uterus properly was when it was full of well-grown baby. And then it all looked straightforward enough: anyone who'd had a baby would naturally assume that the vagina led neatly straight up into the womb, no sudden blind corners, no fleshy dead ends. How was anyone supposed to know that pregnancy began in a little curved pocket folded neatly back on itself? Well, perhaps you weren't supposed to know, thought Iris, perhaps you just weren't supposed to poke around in there with anything long and thin enough to reach. As if female anatomy itself had been designed to demonstrate the fact.

And perhaps it was something you should always bear in mind anyway, that nothing was as straightforward as it looked, that all sorts of things were secretly bent back on themselves, traps for the unwary, for those who assumed they could simply see what was what.

"I thought he was a doctor. The one who did it. He said he was. I believed him," said Stoddard now. The tears went on falling. She paid them no attention.

"Back in a minute," said Iris, and escaped for several blessed minutes into the safety of the sluice, where she shed a few tears herself. This was even worse than the poor mastectomy woman in bed two, who had inadvertently given Iris nightmares for days; the woman in bed two had been barely twenty-seven; it was not dressing the wound that had distressed Iris so much as the loneliness of the remaining little breast, which seemed to be forlornly trying still to look pert and cheerful all by itself; and the fact that it so closely resembled one of Iris's own.

Stoddard had brightened up a bit when she got back. She was like that: unaccountable.

"Tell me what you did on your days off," she said, as Iris maneuvered the trolley back in.

"Can you turn on your side?"

"Which way?"

"That way."

"Just a minute." Slowly Stoddard began preparing to make the effort, lifting her right arm, canting her top half slightly sideways. That was as far as she got; she was stuck.

"Can I . . ."

"Yeah, better . . ."

Iris bent and slipped one hand beneath Stoddard's knees under the blanket, and the other beneath her shoulders. It was like lifting a child over. She remembered the little boy again, and the pleasure of comforting him. But you couldn't lift Stoddard onto your lap.

"Best bit coming up," said Iris, tucking the towels round the long knobbly line of Stoddard's back. Her voice was muffled:

"Tell me about your days off," she said again. "Go on, Silvic. What's on at the pictures? Ooh, that's nice," she added, as she usually did when the hot soapy flannel was gently surged all over her poor thin back.

"Well," said Iris. "My sister's getting married. So we did some shopping, her and me."

"Oh, what did you get, where did you go, did you go to Bond Street?"

"Well, we didn't buy anything there. We looked in the windows. We went to Selfridges. And Lewis's to look at material. My sister knows about material. She's getting this woman she used to work with to make

227

her wedding dress. It's going to be ballerina style with a really full skirt, organza over satin."

"You bridesmaid, Silver?"

Iris rinsed. "That nice? Yeah. We looked at shoes in Selfridges. Satin shoes. Mine've got to be dyed to match my dress. Pale blue." Iris dried the poor small buttocks, and drifted a little talcum over them. "OK, legs, come back now, that's it, shall I . . ."

As she exposed the long skinny right leg Iris had a happy thought. "When my sister was still working, she was a buyer for Lewis's, on Oxford Street. And one day this really really pretty girl comes in, very chic, very little, all by herself: Audrey Hepburn."

"No!"

"And Jo's all of a tremble. Well, you do get stars and that, in Oxford Street, obviously. But she'd actually been to see her in that film with Gregory Peck a bit beforehand . . ."

"*Roman Holiday.*"

"Yeah. Anyway she wants to see . . . " For a moment invention failed. Had she told this story already? And was it quite this story anyway? Iris pretended to be absorbed in soaping Stoddard's sad yellowish foot and in between the toes. This little piggy, said Iris's mother in front of the fire, this little piggy went to market.

"What? What was she looking for?"

"Oh, evening dress stuff, you know, satin, taffeta. In dark blue. D'you know what they call the noise good silk makes, you know, that rustle? It's called scroop."

"What?" Laughingly. Ha: made Stoddard smile.

"Scroop," said Iris again in triumph. "Init funny?"

"It's what the material sounds like, I suppose," said Stoddard, and softly tried it: "Scroop scroop. Scroop scroop."

"Or frou frou," said Iris, powdering the dried toes. "That's the other word for it."

"Sounds French. It's the sound of French silk. Frou frou."

"Um, d'you wanna do down there?"

"OK."

Towel safely in place, Iris put the other flannel, the one with the knot in it, into Stoddard's hand, and let her wash her own private parts.

"Careful," she said, as the flannel caught on the catheter.

"I'd forgotten. There. Can I have the . . . thanks."

"Powder?"

"Yeah. Thanks. Did she buy anything?"

"Who?"

"Audrey Hepburn."

"Oh. Oh, well, that was the joke. I mean, just as Jo was working up to saying, Oh Miss Hepburn, you were so good in . . . well, that was the trouble, she couldn't remember the name of the film, see, this other woman comes rushing up, much older, very swanky, and Audrey says to her, Oh Dorothea, there you are, and the old lady drops a little curtsey! And off they go together. And Jo's thinking, honestly, curtseying to a film star, whatever next, and then her boss rushes up all pale and says, What did you say to her? Well, not much, says Jo, she wanted some midnight blue slipper satin and we hadn't got any dark enough. And her boss is all peculiar, why hadn't Jo come and fetched her soon as she'd seen who it was, why hadn't anyone fetched her a chair, why hadn't they got any midnight blue slipper satin anyway, you know, all in a right tizz. For Pete's sake, says Jo, I know she's pretty and all that but when it comes right down to it she's just a little actress. And her boss says, Are you mad? What are you talking about? Don't you know Princess Margaret when you see her?"

Oh, a real laugh this time. Iris too was enchanted. It was so plausible; perhaps it had really happened somewhere, to someone. *Roman Holiday* would put you in mind of a princess. And the other way round. They were both so dark and lovely and slim. Bit like you, Audrey Hepburn, so Rob had said more than once.

"I'm gonna get someone in now, help me change the bed; then I'll bring you a cuppa, shall I?"

"Thank you, Silver."

"Welcome."

"Silver?"

"What?"

"What's your real name? I mean your Christian name."

Iris hesitated. It was not done to tell patients your Christian name. It was not thought professional, which was partly why the nurses on the ward addressed one another generically as Nurse, or used one another's surnames, though so far no one somehow had ever bothered with the full Da Silva of Iris's, and she had grown used to answering to Silver and to its several variations, Silvery, Silvie, Silvia. Once, when she had been greeted thus by a passing workmate whilst in a cinema queue, Rob had wildly embarrassed her by loudly singing some song he said he had been forced to learn at school and never seen the point of until now,

"Who is Sylvia? What is she,

That all our swains commend her?"

And later that night back at Jo's he had gone on calling her Sylvia, as if he had liked her being two girls at once, especially in bed.

"I'm Iris," she said now.

"Thanks, Iris. I'm Helen."

I know, thought Iris, and then something seemed to turn very quietly in her mind, and a voice in her head said softly,

"Goodnight, Helen."

It was Miss Porter at school, dear old Miss Porter trying not to cry as she read the class *Jane Eyre* last thing on a Friday afternoon during needle-work. Helen Burns, Jane Eyre's dearest school friend, so ill; and Jane climbs into her bed one night, and after talking for a while they go to sleep, and Helen dies so softly that Jane does not wake, poor Jane, who now has no one left to love!

But Iris had thought, lucky Helen, having her friend so close beside her when she was dying, and dying so gently. Lucky Helen.

Iris smiled. "See you later," she said, and took everything back to the sluice room, dry-eyed this time, hot with varying uncomfortable emotions. As she stuffed the used towels, the damp bath blanket, into the dirty linen bag, she was counting in her head again. Dates, weeks, possibilities.

Surely everything had to be all right really? They'd always been so careful. Of course they had. No, it was absurd to worry, just because you felt a bit sick. Her thoughts went round and round.

For whatever anniversary the day was for poor Helen Stoddard, who might have had a child born on this very day, it was also something of an anniversary for Iris too. No matter how she worked it out, today she was exactly three weeks late.

ADAM GREY REGRETS, 1995

"Sylvia," said Adam, as they sat over tea in the tiny whitewashed kitchen of the Landmark Trust cottage in Cornwall where they had just spent such a pleasant weekend, "Sylvia, it's been wonderful, hasn't it, and I like you so much, and I think you like me, but we've got to be honest: this isn't a permanent arrangement, for either of us, is it? And I think it's time" and here he spoke so gently, and with such true affection and gratitude, that his eyes filled with tears, "that we ended it now, while it's still . . . isn't it? so wonderful, Sylvia, such a marvelous happy thing for us both."

And across the scrubbed wooden table Sylvia gave a quick little nod of understanding and assent, though her smile was perhaps just a shade too bright . . .

Abruptly finding himself back at his pavement table in his local San Francisco coffee shop Adam furiously blinked back the dream-Adam's tears, which had rather alarmingly seeped over from fantasyland, and took up his cardboard mug of ferociously strong black coffee with an already trembling hand.

That had been the obvious point, though, the weekend in Cornwall. When he'd first felt that smidgen, that first tiny pang of what had so clearly turned out to be boredom. Why had he ignored it? Why had he pretended, not just to Sylvia, but to himself? What had possessed him to carry on with an affair so ill-founded?

He sipped at his coffee, grimacing at its foreign bitterness. Oh, how homesick he was, and how little he cared to go home! For, lonely as he was after being away on his own for so long, and vexed as he was with today's latest round of executive obfuscation and delay, insomniac and dyspeptic and bored as he was, these things were as nothing compared to what he felt about going home again.

I'm not really homesick at all, thought Adam. I'm past-sick. I want my old life back.

He thought of his wife Margaret, whom he had met when they were both eighteen, and lived with almost ever since. He thought of her tempers and her wild hair going white in a broad streak at the front, he thought of her long legs and surprisingly big round bottom and impressive breasts, he thought of her running toward him down a hilly field one wintry afternoon, pushing the bouncing double buggy ahead of her, with the two little children strapped into it and all three of them shouting aloud with delight. Mother of his children, wife of his heart.

Wife-sick.

What had he been thinking of, how had it all happened? He'd been mad, he thought, with grief. It had been madness and vanity, because Sylvia was so delectably young and pretty, and yet wanted him.

He could remember the ferocity of his own desire; but it seemed to him now that this had had less to do with Sylvia's delectable youth and prettiness than he had at first supposed. He had assumed that desire was simply desire. When it had been (he thought now, taking another medicinal swig of coffee) about twenty percent simple desire, the rest of it a potently tumescent complex of bitterness, anger, and revenge.

With what fierce pleasure he had once imagined old friends all gossiping:

Did you know Adam's seeing someone?

Ooh saw Adam yesterday at the Brownlows', with his new girlfriend!

A lot younger than us. A doctor, well, a consultant, apparently . . .

It had been so luxurious a comfort, imagining the raised eyebrows and lowered voices; knowing that some version of such whisperings would soon meet the ears of his wife, and that no matter how happy she was madly pretending to be she would in truth be eaten alive with desolate jealousy. Maggie, you abandoned our house, so look! the door is slammed shut behind you! Your place is taken! Already!

It had never been love he felt for Sylvia, poor girl, what a swine he was, what a stupid selfish swine! Right from the beginning, he thought, it had merely been one long playground jeer.

She is a stranger to me.

And where this thought had once been almost unendurably exciting, it now provoked images not of fevered sex but of social embarrassment. As if he had woken up after a drunken binge to find himself stickily entwined with, oh, I don't know, thought Adam dismally, that nice Mrs. Hadlow from the post office.

For though the naked stranger in your bed was all very well, the neatly clad stranger in your home day after day was something else. The tidy stranger eating her somehow irritatingly small breakfast before clicking competently off to work; the cultured stranger playing depressing choral music at dinner, and of course never actually doing any cooking, being too important a professional to know one end of a garlic press from the other; the distant stranger with her head in a book, or sitting up late with her computer and her case notes; and altogether too often the maddeningly practical stranger with her undoubted gift for organization, for summoning nanny and daily and gardener and monthly window cleaner and arranging in one of the kitchen cupboards—how he had inwardly blanched at the sight! an entire shelf-full of little plastic bottles containing every single different stain remover in existence, explaining when asked that she liked to be prepared for every eventuality!

Sylvia, this shelf is a *symptom*, he had wanted to tell her. This is a shelf of anxiety, of misdirected fear. Can't you relax for a moment, Sylvia? Are you always like this? Or is it something to do with me, the used and tarnished man? One previous careless owner; splatted all over no doubt with the psychic rust marks and fingerprints and variously feculent accretions of twenty-five years with somebody else. Was there a little bottle on the shelf for a secondhand husband?

Oh, she was a stranger in his house. The stranger who was Clio's mother.

Clio altered everything. Clio had made what should so obviously have been a fling into something which must last for the rest of his life. Lose sight of Sylvia, lose sight of her child.

He'd been taken aback, of course, by the pregnancy, at first; had instantly suspected Sylvia of wanting not him, but a baby; reassured by her evident distress and surprise he had soon concluded that the child was purest accident, one that had happened to both of them but mainly, of course, to Sylvia; he had expected, since his own children, his real children, were grown up that for him this late new addition would rouse quite gentle and grandfatherly feelings, or even, he rather feared, none at all.

There was no limit, thought Adam now, to the ways in which he had got everything wrong. The way he felt about the infant Clio had served only to remind him of how he had once felt about the infant Gregory, the baby Oliver, and the delicate elfin Charlotte: a passionate consuming love, an aesthetic adoration, an absorbing interest in every unfolding detail of growth and blooming; and along with all that a panicky sensation as of iron doors clanging shut forever, and the deep-seated lurking fear that arises from being perpetually responsible for something at once most precious and most fragile.

From some of this burden his first children had in part released him, by growing into the three most interesting young adults on the planet, adults who could cheerfully look after themselves, and who, whilst naturally aghast, had nonetheless clearly supported one another through all the various recent misdeeds of their parents, and made astonishingly tactful visits to both parties, and touchingly careful telephone calls.

"How are you, Dad?" No longer a perfunctory bit of dutiful telephonic politeness, this, but meant. How *are* you, Dad? The balance of responsibility had already altered.

Witness Lottie this very week; one of his reasons for accepting this interminable trip had been the fact that she was over at Berkeley. He had driven the hired car carefully across the great bridge and through the strange dry scruffy brown hills to the dreamy green suburbia where she was renting a tiny apartment whilst conducting further research work into gummy plant substances.

Her line at parties, she told him, was Hi, I'm Lottie, I'm in mucilage. He had managed a smile, though he had felt like more crying at the sight of her, since he had not seen her for several months.

It had been a successful evening on the whole. She had invited several of her colleagues along, and talk was kind and friendly and general, if slightly more mucilaginous than anyone not in the business might have thought suitable. But when everyone else had gone and he too was putting his jacket on she had leant both her arms on the kitchen table where they had sat and suddenly said out of nowhere,

"Mum's split up with Les." Just like that.

No, not recently. Six months ago.

Well, because Mum had told her not to, that's why. Asked her not to.

No of course not, for heaven's sake, Dad, she was on her own. Fine though. Got this rather terrific job, actually. Organizing some Arts thing.

Any message, Dad?

He had shaken his head, feeling tired to death suddenly, jet-lag tired, desperate to close his eyes.

Message to Maggie, he thought now, as he looked round for the waiter to bring him the bill, what possible message could he send now to Margaret, wife of his heart?

You made my bed, Maggie, and now I've got to lie in it.

ROB AND JO, SEPTEMBER 1954

THE MORNING BEFORE she had vexed him by telephoning him at work. It was not done, to be rung up, particularly by girls, during working hours; a probationer nurse had been dispatched to summon him from the opposite ward—for Jo had not even managed to ask for the right one—and he'd been obliged to take the call not only at Sister Hardwick's desk, but beneath her basilisk eye.

"Hello, sweetie pie, guess who?"

"Erm, sorry, Jo, but this is a hospital phone, and . . ."

"Oops. I'll be quick, honest. I just need a word with you in private, it's about, you know, wedding plans, a little present for the bridesmaid sort of thing, could you drop by a bit early tomorrow?"

"Erm, well . . ."

"Say about four? I want it to be a secret, see, and Iris won't be back till six."

But he wasn't intending to meet Iris at Jo's; they had arranged to meet near Leicester Square, at their usual teashop. And he was going to have to ask her about the netsuke pig. An appointment he'd been dreading all week as it was.

"Well . . ."

Here Sister Hardwick made a tiny inhaling sound, menacingly indicative of rising temper.

"I'm afraid I really have to go."

"See you tomorrow then, bye-bye!"

"I'm so sorry, Sister!"

237

Sister Hardwick's answering smile flexed her mouth down instead of up; her lecture on the morality of making private use of hospital property had gone on much longer than the phone call.

In a way that visit had been the start of everything else. Impatiently clumping up the stairs to Jo's flat, feeling he'd been dragged halfway across London just to talk about plans for a wedding he couldn't care less about, frankly, he'd heard quite enough about finery and silly hats and honeymoons from Iris already, and he and she had more important things to talk about; he'd been even more fed up to find Jo clearly in no hurry, blithely insisting on tea and that she absolutely had to show him some bauble or another and then disappearing into her bedroom for ages. He could hear her rummaging around in there. He had got up and paced around unhappily, wondering if he should ask her about the pig before he tackled Iris.

It was quite hard to move in Jo's sitting room, because there were piles of moving-out stuff everywhere, cardboard boxes of crockery and saucepans, great wads of what looked like old velvet curtains, piles of magazines and newspapers, some trussed ready for the bin, some merely stacked; it was one of these he had accidentally knocked over on his way to the window. Cursing quietly he had crouched to pile the great slew of nonsense together again, and then subsided slowly to sit on the lino, the open holiday camp brochure in his hand, where Mum and Dad and the two children grinned from the seat of their family bicycle. Somewhere in Norfolk, he saw, from the text. The family bicycle Iris remembered riding so long ago at Coogan's, here set about with exclamation marks, New For This Year!

Different camp, he thought immediately. Different company. But he remembered Iris remembering bouncing this immensity along miles of clean sandy pine-scented paths, just like the paths mentioned in those very words in the brochure he held now in his hands.

Along miles of clean sandy pine-scented paths. Where are the great pinewoods, Iris, of Devon? And come to think of it what strapping family of athletes could pedal up and down those swooping clifftop hills?

And the notion that Iris had simply made the whole thing up at last fully occurred to him. No Coogan's at all. No coincidence of childhood.

No near-miss. As Jo opened her bedroom door at last and came out he looked up and managed, he thought, to sound perfectly casual under the circumstances:

"Oh, sorry I knocked these over, saw this one, what are they like, these holiday-camp places, d'you know? Ever been to one?"

Jo hardly seemed to be listening. "What?" she said, absently. She crossed the room and opened the door of Iris's room. "Oh, those places. No fear."

He jumped to his feet. "Oh my goodness!"

"What? Something wrong?"

Struggling back into his coat. "Gosh I'm really sorry, but I've got to go, I forgot . . . erm, I forgot something at work, oh my gosh, I've really just got to rush, sorry . . ."

Because he simply couldn't stand it a moment longer, what was he doing here in this scruffy airless little flat with this careless grasping painted tart? He had stuffed the rolled-up brochure into his pocket and made a run for it, hammering down the stairs and out into the blessedly windy street, where he had run all the way to the Tube station as if he had been telling Jo the truth. In his room he had ripped open the letter from his mother, and known Iris for what she was.

And gone straight out again and told her.

ROSEMARY HENSHAW AT HOME, 1995

Sylvia's mother, Mrs. Rosemary Henshaw, had been awake nearly all night. At fifty-eight this happened to her fairly frequently anyway, and she thought little of it. But there had been a reason this time.

It had all begun three months earlier, when, turning the pages of an unfamiliar glossy magazine at the dentist's, she had seen a small advertisement at the back: for dovecotes. At once her heart had given a little bang inside her. She had copied down the number, phoned as soon as her mouth felt normal (she had needed a filling replaced) and impatiently waited nearly a week for the promised brochure.

Which had been all she had hoped. Tearing open the envelope she had sat at the kitchen table and gasped aloud at almost every turn of the page. It had simply never occurred to her before, that you could acquire—actually buy—so potent a symbol of grace and tranquility.

Several great local houses had them, of course. Old inherited ones. The stable block at Old Soar had one, and so did the Barn at Woolsey Court; Mrs. Macy, possibly the kennels' very best client—for she never owned fewer than three Great Danes, and went away a lot—actually kept doves in hers, which stood in her garden on a high white pole, beneath the magnificent cedar tree.

What was most remarkable to Rosemary was that the brochure had pictures of all three of them: that, therefore, all these dovecotes were merely *types*, the small and wall-mounted, like Old Soar's, the immensity like Woolsey's, the high and beautiful little Gothic pagoda like Laura Macy's. All of them painted white, as pure and pretty as their occupants, with traditional pitched roofs and nice arched doorways; all of them rural romance itself, as far as Rosemary was concerned.

And available: if you had the money. Though every other purchase of Rosemary's life, especially since the early death of her husband, had been attended with all sorts of worries and caveats, this time her only point of anxiety was which one to go for.

Not that, these days, her usual worries were altogether rational. Bought for a song—for, in fact, less than two thousand pounds, in a state of some disrepair, but with its own woodland, six acres of arable, several outbuildings and a duck pond, Rosemary's house and business had turned over the decades from cottage to goldmine.

What had made the house almost unsaleable in 1961—its isolation at the end of a long bumpy and winding track, its grounds too extensive to be gardened but too small to be farmed, its low beams, drafty antique fireplaces, septic tank, steeply pitched roof of Kentish tile and cold flagged floors, made it worth more than a million by the early nineties; while the business, Rosemary's pin money during the brief years of her marriage, and almost sole means of support afterwards, had also changed, slowly at first, and then faster and faster, as fees rocketed.

In the sixties, Henshaw's Boarding Kennels had been (though no one, not even Sylvia, had ever formulated it thus) a working-class enterprise, run for the working classes and by them, Rosemary being a second-generation Londoner, fresh from the boring postwar settlements of Essex, a railwayman's daughter, a country girl devoid of country knowledge.

She liked dogs, and, finding herself immured once more in the countryside, having married Mr. Henshaw, noted the outbuildings, the woodland, the six arable acres mostly run to weed, and the isolation, and saw possibilities. Planning permission was a doddle; she designed and built almost everything herself, employing a workman only for the plumbing; and throughout Sylvia's littlegirlhood kept upwards of twenty dogs a night —generally Alsatians, Alsatian crosses, and every variety of poodle—for very reasonable rates, occasionally employing a local teenager in busy periods.

At that time Henshaw's Boarding Kennels smelt of disinfectant and creosote. Its bare concrete paths, laid by Rosemary herself, were decorated here and there with garden gnomes, based on Disney's seven dwarfs, and made by the small Sylvia out of plaster-of-Paris set in molds. Doc snarled beside the dustbins, Sneezy blew his nose among the french marigolds in the central flowerbed, and Bashful pointed the way to the outside lavatory.

Other garden ornaments included concrete woodland creatures, squirrels, hedgehogs, and toads, a set of enormous red-and-white mushrooms big enough for children to sit on, a bright yellow and pink secondhand plastic Wendy house (a mistake, acquired shortly after Sylvia had grown too old for such things, but kept for years, the difficulties of getting rid of the thing so far outweighing the advantages of doing so), and, outside Reception, an enormous concrete wheelbarrow planted with colorful begonias.

But that was then. Years have rolled by, and now Rosemary employs not only a full-time staff of two but an accountant. Forty pets may now reside in comfortable heated runs, each with separate sleeping area, and a further twenty strays, partly maintained by the Council, partly funded by Rosemary, bark in similar comfort in an adjoining complex, awaiting re-homing.

More than a decade of gardening programs has swept away all the concrete animals, carbooted them out, along with the yellow and pink plastic Wendy house and the wheelbarrow; the paths now are flagged, set with small-leaved thyme and camomile; Geoff Hamilton's climbing roses, Alan Titchmarsh's perennials perfume the air, wave lush graceful blossoms over rooftop and decorative wrought iron archway. The tarmac before Reception has been replaced with a gravel-pathed herb garden; Reception itself is decorated with hanging baskets full of geraniums and small white trailing violas.

This is a place Mrs. Macy, of Soar House, may safely recommend to her friends. And along with her home and business, Rosemary herself has also undergone some degree of gentrification, though without noticing it, since class as an idea has lately lost so much power and noticeability anyway. But the owner of a concrete wheelbarrowful of begonias would not have thought to call Mrs. Macy Laura. Nor would Laura Macy herself have noticed Rosemary Henshaw, proud owner of homemade hand-painted Sleepy, Bashful, and Doc.

Though during the same period Laura Macy's own inherent ability to refer out loud and without self-consciousness to little people, as in, "Marvelous little woman who looks after my dogs" has also died a natural death.

For nearly three months now Rosemary has forgotten even the last shreds of social unease in her eagerness to talk doves with Laura Macy. She has settled on a wall-mounted, three-tier pyramid beneath steeply pitched eaves, echoing the lines of her own house. She has signed and paid and taken delivery; she has climbed the ladder with her trusty Black and Decker and in triumph screwed the thing firmly into place amid the ivy; it looks exactly as she wanted it to; all she is waiting for now are the doves themselves, and they are coming this very morning, and she has not slept all night in glorious anticipation.

Rising as usual at seven Rosemary put on her usual jeans and soft wool shirt, and went downstairs in her socks. Today there were three dogs in the house with her: her own collie-cross Jimmy, and two boarders of a disposition too shy and anxious to stay out in the runs with the others.

Like most mornings this one began with Jimmy hurling himself toward her as she opened the kitchen door, trying to emit cries of joyous greeting whilst simultaneously not dropping his current favorite squeaky toy, a soft red thing shaped like a tomato. The timid greyhound beside the Aga sat quivering in its basket, eyes bulging, ears well back; while the spaniel was clearly hoping it was invisible, pressing itself flat in its bed with its eyes shut, though she could see from across the room how it trembled.

Sometimes Rosemary felt dreadfully bored by such carryings-on. Even now, after all these years, she was sometimes taken aback by what people were prepared to put up with, to love, in pet dogs; the bizarre canine neuroses involving only being able to pee on cardboard cut into certain shapes, for example, or spending all day hiding behind curtains, or obsessive soap-licking. But of course you never knew what you were getting, when you took on a dog, any more than you knew your own child beforehand. You had what you had, and if you were a normal person you loved it no matter how odd it turned out to be.

Today, however, Rosemary was not in the least tempted to tell any creature to for Pete's sake pull itself together, nor did she yell at Jimmy to sodding well leave her alone, which she often did, quite loudly. Today she idly told her dog he was clever, took the tomato in one dreamy hand, toast in the other, and threw it gently across the kitchen for Jimmy to pounce on.

Today she would get all her jobs done early, so as to devote herself to the doves when they arrived. Then she would phone Laura, who was going to drop everything and come over, and help her get them out of the carrier box and into the dovecote where, poor things, they must be imprisoned until they felt at home there; three weeks, Laura had said. Three weeks before she could let them play and flutter and call their coaxing warbles about the garden. But oh then! How ravishingly beautiful they would be!

Sighing with happiness Rosemary was putting her overalls on to make an early start on her multitude of morning tasks when the telephone rang. Was it the carrier? Was it the dove-breeding place? Had something gone wrong? Holding her overall trousers up with one hand Rosemary rushed to answer.

"Hello, Henshaw's."

"Oh, Mum—I didn't get you up, did I?"

"Course not. Hello, lovey, everything all right?"

"Well, yes, I am. And Clio, she's fine, but, erm . . ."

"But what, but what?"

Twenty minutes later Rosemary, with her old padded green nylon waistcoat on over her overalls, was mucking out Kennel One with all her usual energy, but when Christine Drew arrived at nine she didn't stop for their normal friendly cup of tea, but said she was too behindhand, and needed to get through Two first. Though in fact she had already done so, and was just avoiding talking to Christine, who was nice enough but hadn't worked at the kennels that long, only three and a half years, long enough to see immediately that Rosemary was upset, but not nearly long enough to be told why.

It would take too long for one thing.

Oh, Will, such a lovely boy! Scarcely older than Sylvia! Standing on her own in the orchard doing the chickens Rosemary, who was not at all prone to tears, was suddenly overcome.

Secretly Sylvia's mother had once had hopes of Will. First fears, then hopes. Sylvia in the lower sixth, doing so well, coming out of her shell a little, painting scenery for the school play, a co-production that year with the boys' school. Will acting in it, of course; Will at seventeen, a glitter of bright red stubble over his upper lip, starring in it: Romeo.

He'd come biking over at weekends once or twice, volunteering to help Sylvia walk the dogs. At the time Rosemary had lain awake at night worrying: he'd seemed a nice lad, gentle and sweet-tempered, but look at the mess Romeo had made of things!

Whatever it was though had fizzled out with no harm done. And then years afterwards, when he'd made all that money and Sylvie was renting a room in his London house, Rosemary had allowed herself a few small hopes. Will: a known nice young man. Doing well. Obviously it was a bit risky, being an actor. But he'd clearly made a wonderful start, not that that space thing had really been her cup of tea, she'd only watched it because of him.

Perhaps when he came back to England they'd start seeing a bit more of each other, and who knew what might happen?

More than once she had thought of Will's parents living not so far away, and how Asian parents managed these things, apparently, and imagined herself being able to just go ahead and give Mrs. Keane a call, arrange some honest practical discussions of their children's good and possibly less-good points, and how they tallied.

But instead, left to her own foolish heedless devices, Sylvia had gone on letting that man, married already and children and old enough to be her father, spoil her life for her, waste her time, make her so lonely and unhappy for so long!

Will had been the right path not taken, as far as Sylvia's mother was concerned. A possible right path anyway. Though this view had rather faded, since Clio. Clio made everything all right, as far as her grand-mother was concerned, even Adam.

But all the same, standing in the wet orchard, her doves forgotten, Rosemary wept.

IRIS GOES TO THE SEASIDE, SEPTEMBER 1954

––––––––––

SHE FELT QUITE HAPPY on the train. It was a lovely warm day of Indian summer. She sat looking out of the window at England thrumming past, at cows and sheep and haystacks, and orchardsful of apples and pears, and once a river that galloped along for a while beside the train and then swung away off on its own, and towns with traffic and people surging about and tiny glimpses in shop windows.

Once the woman opposite smiled at her, and offered her the newspaper she'd finished with. Iris smiled back, and took it, and even turned the pages as if she were reading it, to be polite, and because it had been kind of the woman, to notice she had nothing to read. She stopped when the woman got off at the next station, and went back to looking out of the window.

"Off on holiday?" This from the old lady who'd taken the seat two stops further on.

Yes, Iris had said, she was going to join her sister, for a few days by the sea, just the two of them; her sister was getting married soon, yes, she was going to be bridesmaid, in pale blue taffeta, her sister knew all about material from working as a buyer for Lewis's in Oxford Street, she knew about thread number, about varieties, about frou frou, about scroop; and then Iris talked about the time Princess Margaret herself had quietly appeared at the counter one afternoon, to inquire about some midnight blue slipper satin, and how her sister had made a beautiful deep curtsy before regretfully telling her they were fresh out of it, Your Highness, and Princess Margaret—so chic! so gracious! had thanked her ever so politely and gone away, and how her boss had then swanked up to her all scornful, and said, Well, of course she's very well known, dear, but when you come right down to it she's only a little film actress, what were you thinking of, you don't curtsy to Audrey Hepburn!

Iris wasn't sure this version worked quite so well; possibly, it occurred to her too late, the old lady hadn't actually heard of Audrey Hepburn anyway. She seemed quite posh and that probably meant she never went to the pictures.

Thinking this made her remember Rob's mother: bet she never went near the flicks either. Iris thought about Rob's mother not letting herself go to the pictures—denying herself its universal pleasures just because she wouldn't want any of her snobby friends catching her going in—for several enjoyable seconds before she remembered everything else. It felt like a great swinging crash inside her.

For a few minutes, talking to the old lady, she had stopped thinking about everything; the plunging overwhelming torrent of unhappiness with which she had lived now for days and days had been dammed up, and when a dam collapsed you got flooded. It would wear off a bit soon, Iris presently was able to tell herself above the tumult within.

"Are you all right, dear?"

"Yes . . . yes, thank you. Just come over a bit dizzy."

"Should I call the guard? Perhaps some water?"

"Ooh, no, I'm fine thanks."

And the old lady had felt about in her big black handbag and after a struggle with its lid handed Iris a small and frankly rather dirty-looking little squat green glass bottle, with crystals of white stuff in it.

"Take a good hard sniff, dear!"

Iris, by nature one to do as she was told, had done so, and the searing violence of the consequent burning pain in her nose made her eyes water; she had never met sal volatile before.

"Oh lumme!"

It had worked though. It was such a good distraction. One second she had been drowning in Rob's eyes; *you're a liar, a liar, and a thief!* and the next she was spluttering into her handkerchief, half-giggling with sheer surprise.

"It is a little strong," said the old lady anxiously, "if you're not used to it."

Bloody hell, Iris managed not to say aloud.

She was embarrassed afterwards. She had possibly gasped aloud, she thought, when she had remembered. Made an exhibition of herself. True one old lady wasn't much of an audience but it was the idea that you couldn't control yourself in public that was so frightening, not how many people got to stare at you for it. Thank heaven she was nearly there! Everything would be all right when she got where she was going. She was going to make everything right.

"Will your sister be there to meet you, dear?"

"Oh yes. She's expecting me."

She was sorry about Jo. The fact was some of the disaster was Jo's own fault. And Jo would see that soon. Why on earth had she left the little pig thing lying around? If she'd put it back where she'd found it no one would ever have been the wiser. And it wouldn't have mattered so much about Coogan's Holiday Camp. And that was Jo's fault too in a way. Leaving all those brochures lying around the flat.

"This, Iris. I saw this."

And he'd held up the Holiday Camp brochure for a place called Corton, near Lowestoft.

Of course that one hadn't been anything to do with Andrew St. John Mortimer, that had been the chap before him or tell a lie, the one before that, who hadn't had Andrew's class, not anything like it; he'd been the one who fancied a week away at a holiday camp, which had probably been one of the reasons Jo had given him the push in the first place.

"Seem familiar?" Iris had looked at the brochure photograph, the happy family on their funny family-size bicycle, the mother and father and two children all laughing and pedaling away together along the sandy woodland track, and seen at once what he was getting at.

"Coogan's don't do these. I checked. They never have."

Silence. What was there to say?

"You've never been there, have you?" His voice was very soft, but somehow not at all gentle. "Have you, Iris?"

249

Yes I have, she'd wanted to argue. Yes, I have, I saw you there, I saw everything. I made a sand dog. My sister bought me an ice cream. My mother wore a shady hat with a wide blue ribbon.

"You've told me so many lies, Iris. You've just told me lies all the time. I don't know if anything you've ever said to me is true."

It was all nice, Rob. I like things to be nice.

"And this is my mother's, isn't it?" His hand from his pocket, open now on the table between them: the little pig curled amongst the rushes, smiling in its sleep.

"You stole it."

"No I never! She gave it to me, that woman."

"What woman?"

"Her, you know, Meadows."

"Who's been with my mother more than twenty years. She stole this valuable piece of netsuke in order to give it to you. Is that what you're saying?"

Is this Rob, is this his voice?

"Stop. Lying. No: that won't work," he adds, as she raises her face all streaming with tears. "Just stop lying now. You liar. You liar. You thief." And then he had looked more like himself for a second, his face had gone all screwed up as if he was going to cry as well, but he just jumped up instead and walked out of the teashop where they had been sitting talking in such low voices that even as she got up too and ran after him she could see people not particularly looking round, not noticing that horrible wounds had been made in her body, that she could hardly hobble after him.

"Rob, stop, please!"

Dark outside, his hurrying shoulders down the street.

"Wait, please!"

And he had turned round and come back toward her so fast that she had been frightened and stopped short, there had been such violence in his face. He hadn't hit her though, not with his hand.

"Leave me alone. I never want to see you again. Got that?" And he had turned back, and disappeared and left her alone in the darkness, and then certain fears had taken their places beside her, had formed themselves soundlessly into something confining like walls all tightly round her, and her arms and legs hurt, and she heard whimpering noises from a long way away.

And I never got to tell him about the baby, she had thought later, on the way home. So that was one good thing. She'd been so worried about telling him, about how he'd react, whether he'd tell her to get rid of it like Helen Stoddard's horrible man friend had, whether he'd complain about how much it would cost him to get rid of it. Suppose he'd said that sort of thing?

That would've been very bad, thought Iris. That would've been worse. So that was one good thing.

"We're staying in a guest house," she said now, patting her eyes dry. "Not right on the sea, but very close."

"How nice," said the old lady.

"Yes," said Iris, and she smiled.

WILL AND SYLVIA, 1995

————————

AND THEN HE OPENED the door and it was Sylvia and he felt such relief, a great familiar flood of it all through him, that as he quickly hugged her, noticing all over again how small she was, how slender, he saw also that many of these constant deep surges of emotion seemed to stem from his childhood. Or at least vividly reminded him of it.

This happiness, for instance; as he pressed his cheek to the top of Sylvia's head he was in his heart turning a certain street corner in Bournemouth, aged six, and realizing that after carelessly losing sight of his window-shopping parents and enduring what had felt like hours of increasingly desolate wandering up and down he had by chance, and just before tears overwhelmed him, come across the small hotel they were all staying at.

The Rhylstone Hotel, he thought, and saw it vividly before him, the stunted palm by the front steps, Venetian blinds, clean cream paint-work, strip of well-polished brass at the threshold, oh, the safety, the relief!

While Sylvia collected her strength. It was scarcely six months since they had last met, she thought, but he looked ten years older. The skull beneath the skin, was it Auden or Isherwood or both of them? You could see poor Will's elegant skull beneath the pallor of his skin. And wasn't his hair thinning a little, at the front? Oh Will! Had he noticed her dismay? She was long schooled in hiding such things, but then he was long schooled in audience reaction.

"The nurse is here, with Mum. Let's go in the garden."

252

He led her through the house and out into the sunshine.

I'm pretty sure it's not leukemia, the oncologist had said. Gerry Waterlow, such a nice chap, trained with his wife, Oh hello, Sylvia, how are you, your cousin, oh really? Well, I'm sorry. I'm pretty sure it's not leukemia. Looking a lot like lymphoma though. Some of his blood tests are a bit peculiar. But it's often not a clear-cut picture at this stage. No, it's lymphoma. I'd say ninety percent. I'm ninety percent sure it's lymphoma. I'm so sorry. No, not at all, any time . . .

No need for Will to hear any of that.

"It's all arranged: I'm going in on Sunday evening," he said, as they reached the shade of the plum tree. "Tests all Monday, and operation next day. Was that down to you, it all being so quick? Thanks, I mean, best to get it over with."

Sylvia gave a tiny shrug: it was nothing, in order to hide the truth, which was that his case was too urgent for delay.

"You don't have to go in on Sunday," she said aloud. "Hospitals are such nasty places really, it's best to keep out of them as much as you can, so if you like you can sort of be admitted on the Monday morning, get your tests all done, and then go home again, be nil by mouth from midnight, go back in again first thing next day."

"Oh. That you again?"

"That's me. You have still got the flat, haven't you? In London? Oh and the dog. Mum's happy to take the dog. It'll be in her house, not in a run or anything, she said to tell your mother that. And for as long as you need, she said. No charge. Is that all right? Oh and I phoned the hospice, just to check on things, and they're expecting her and everything, and they're all clear about . . . well, what Annie knows, and what you've told her, and so on. And I said she was my aunt, and who I was. You know. Though actually people who work in hospices are generally above all worldly considerations, in fact. Is that OK? Will?"

Two or three days of stubble on his chin, she thought. It would be a gray beard.

Will was remembering something: the first time Sylvia had been here, at his mother's house.

"The train crash," he said aloud. "Remember?"

How old were we? I was thirteen. In the third year, Year Nine. And she'd just started at the Girls' Grammar, Sylvia Henshaw, first year, tiny and freckled, in ankle socks and plastic National Health glasses and tight plaits. And big bumpy forehead: a cartoon version of a brainy little schoolgirl. He remembered the care with which he had entirely failed to notice her.

But toward half term a goods train, inexplicably on the wrong track, had one morning run with a brisk shattering wallop into the back of the stationary passenger train he had just climbed onto, and Sylvia, who got on one stop before him, had happened to be sitting right at the very end of the end carriage.

Doors swinging open, passengers milling about all shocked and chatty and exclaiming, a bit of broken glass underfoot. Train bashed into an angle, biffed off track, Sylvia blinking on the platform, buttoned into her huge blazer, the only other child there. His own wild exultation:

"Hey, goods train went right into the back of us, fantastic!" It had been the first thing he had ever said to her. She had looked even frecklier than usual, somehow, as if she were wearing goggles as well as specs.

"You OK?"

"I left my bag on the train."

"Where?"

She pointed.

"Cor, you were right at the back!" He was impressed.

"Hang about," he had said, and he had nipped to the sticking-up end of the train where she had been. He had opened the door with some difficulty since it was on such a slope, pushed it right back, and climbed inside. He'd had to put one knee up to get in. Weird! The floor at a crazy angle! There was her rucksack, all new and stiff, still on the tipped up seat by the window. And this must be hers too.

"You rescued my library book," said Sylvia now.

"You didn't shed a tear," he said. "I was impressed."

"I was concussed," said Sylvia in return. "Can't remember much about it, actually."

This was untrue. In fact she had several very vivid memories of that day, nearly all of them unsettling: Will's mother making them both sugary tea, folding Sylvia into a nice soft blanket on the sofa while she tried to telephone Henshaw's; Will's house being so quiet and orderly, everything neat and new and clean; Will's father summoned from some-where, arriving with a car, wherein she lay shamedly on the back seat, also clean, while Will sat chattily in front, clearly trying to cheer her; and the desolating embarrassment of arriving home, to that sea of mud beset with canine howls, where Sylvia's own mother, wild-eyed in her spattered old overalls, was furiously shoveling aggregate into a con-crete mixer.

Aloud she said: "I was wondering if . . . well, I'd like it very much if you'd come and stay with me for the weekend. With me and Clio."

"What, at your house?"

She hadn't meant to get to this so soon. She gabbled a little: "Yes, well, Clio's dreadfully noisy of course but it's a very big house, and there's lots of lovely walks, you know it's by the sea."

"But, isn't it in Devon?"

She laughed. "It's not that far."

"What's Adam got to say about it?"

"Well, I told him you might be coming to stay. And why. He's in San Francisco again, actually. Back end of next week. So it's just me and Clio and Lulu. The nanny, well, she only lives in during the week."

"I don't know."

"Do come, Will. It's very nice, where I live. Cliff walks and every-thing. Or we could stay here if you want to. I don't mind. Whichever you prefer."

"Well, to be honest, I thought I'd just go home. You know, to the flat."

Up three flights of stairs, thought Sylvia. And when did he last live there? It would be all musty and untidy, he would climb all those stairs past two lots of other people carelessly noisily living their lives, two lots of thumping conflicting music, and he'd open the door and all the things he'd left lying around would be still lying there looking at him, and trains making the windows rattle all day long and there wouldn't be a single thing to eat, obviously, she would obviously go with him and get him sorted out beforehand but, oh imagine! Leaving him on his own, perhaps with his shopping in plastic bags all round him, oh Will!

"Please," she said. "Won't you let me look after you a bit?"

"I don't need looking after, not yet anyway."

"I'm sorry, I didn't mean it like that."

"Will, sorry, my love" came a voice from the house behind them, almost in tandem, "only I'm off now, if that's all right." Sylvia turned, and saw a fat woman in the doorway.

"Oh, just a minute, Sue, um, sorry, back in a minute." Will hurried off across the grass. Left standing on her own beneath the plum tree Sylvia found that she was trembling.

It had not occurred to her that Will might have plans of his own. She had pictured her favorite walk round Golden Point to the pub, where you could have crab sandwiches sitting outside on the cliff-top garden in the autumn sunshine. She had imagined the cliff-top path and the teashop just inland where they did that chocolate cake; she would divert him, engage him, comfort him, and protect him. Rescue him.

Surely if he gave it a moment's thought he would realize that he must not spend these few days alone?

Or was there someone, perhaps?

Of course. How silly she had been! Of course: he'd met someone. After all it was years, now, since Holly had left him and gone back to the States. Nearly two years. Holly and her little boy. And there was his old crowd, Tim, and Brig, or had he moved North? And of course others she had no knowledge of. She had been absurd to imagine Will needed her. Or was her responsibility in some way. She felt suddenly embarrassed: caught out making bossy and insulting assumptions about his life.

Will came back, leaving the door open behind him. "Well, they're coming this afternoon. For Mum. She'd like to see you actually, she's not too bad at the moment."

Hearing himself a wash of depression made him feel like keeling over where he stood and just lying there with his face in the grass. His mother and himself, what a dreary pair!

He tried to comfort himself with the thought of his house in London. Soon be back home, he told himself. His one wise move, buying property during what had after all turned out to be his only year or so of wealth. The number of people who'd told him not to bother! Suppose he'd listened to his dad! "Oh, you don't want to go saddling yourself with a house at your age, practically derelict, horrible area, what are you thinking of?"

On the other hand; triumph of foresight though the place had so quickly turned out to be he had to admit that he hadn't spent much on it for a long time. From being the only moderately done-up house in the street in 1981 it had gradually become the only tatty one. And the flat had been empty for weeks, it would smell funny. He would have to think about bed-making, and towels, he'd have to go to Sainsbury's, he would have to trawl round those familiar aisles as if everything inside him was normal. And ordinary small difficulties like getting stuck in the slower queue or someone accidentally standing on his foot wouldn't feel ordinary to him; he would burst out swearing or crying or thump someone or all three at once. And one of those terrible Moments might descend on him. The same old thoughts would race around and around in his head, he had no control over them.

Of course, Sylvia would know some of all this, he thought. Or at least she'd have more idea than most.

Baby though. Don't really know any babies. Ozzie had been nearly three. When first it was Holly and me. Nice little thing, Ozzie.

On the other hand it was so unexpectedly soothing to be with Sylvia. Soothing, perhaps, just to be with someone you had known nearly all your life. Dunno why, thought Will, it just is.

He sighed.

Oh, I don't want to go to sodding Devon though. I don't want to go anywhere with anyone.

But then I don't want to stay anywhere either.

"Aren't you too busy?" he said aloud at last. "I don't want to be, you know, a nuisance."

Don't want to go to hospital. Don't want an operation.

Don't want to die.

He interrupted the protest. "And Clio's gonna be OK with it? I mean, having a stranger around the place?"

And after that he just couldn't come up with any other reasons not to go. Sylvia was rattling on and on the way she always did. Of course this, of course that. She'd got it all organized and thought out. Perhaps he should just go ahead and please her, since he couldn't come up with any way to please himself? What else was he going to do?

"OK then," he muttered at last. He heard himself as graceless and mulish, but couldn't for the moment bring himself to care.

Sylvia heard fear and exhaustion.

"Oh good!" she said briskly, warmly, and was in fact so pleased to have got her own way that without thinking about it she reached forward and hugged him tight.

Instantly Will felt better. A pleasant thought struck him, and he spoke almost cheerfully into her hair, "Hey, d'you know, it's ages, it's *ages* since I last saw the sea!"

ROB REGRETS, SEPTEMBER 1954

HE'D REGRETTED EVERYTHING he'd said almost as soon as he'd said it; the way he'd said it; had hesitated at the mouth of the Tube and considered turning round and . . . but no. He couldn't take it back, could he? Everything he'd said had been true. She had senselessly lied and lied, about all sorts of things, right from the day they met: *I got a little brother just his age.*

And of course he'd cottoned on about that one almost straight away, because how could she have a little brother that age if as she claimed later on the only brother she'd ever had had died in the war?

He'd been puzzled, told himself he must have somehow got what she'd said all wrong, though really he knew that everything she'd said at that first meeting by the kid's bedside, every turn of her head, every sparkle of her eye, was written forever on his memory, so he'd worked it out that the poor kid with the eye must have just reminded her of the dead brother, fair enough; and later on when she'd told him the brother had been twelve when he died he had still somehow managed to discount it, to inwardly shrug his shoulders, five, twelve, was there so much difference, really? The stricken child, the lost little brother, you could see what she was getting at.

And then later still Jo goes and says Iris was the baby of the family! That the brother who died had been three years older than Iris!

Even then he had found it in himself to refuse the obvious explanation without once looking too hard at it. One ignored pointless claims. Weren't people everywhere making all sorts of small idle frothy pronouncements every day, the droll, the merely polite, the small talk, the chit chat? Wasn't Iris's funny little series of misstatements about her brother a similarly meaningless bit of nothingness one should lightly put aside?

Without any clear thought on the matter Rob had decided that it was. He had gone on looking firmly the other way whenever further discrepancies showed up; that her memories should occasionally contradict one another was hardly surprising anyway, he once came very close to consciously thinking, when you remembered what the war had done to her.

But strangely enough when he had at last inescapably discovered that she was a liar he told himself that he had known it all along.

What a weekend he'd had! He'd hardly slept or eaten. He had been too busy torturing himself: of course she had lied about loving him, too. She had lied about it being the first time she had ever done it with anyone, she'd probably done it with lots of men, and still was. Thought she was onto a good thing with him. Because look at her sister! Hardly more than a common prostitute.

He had gone on being miserably angry all Saturday, had that evening defiantly gone to the pub with some friends, and had woken with a staggering hangover late on Sunday, after another wretched night, and thought how if everything had been different they would be waking up together now in Jo's flat, since Jo and old Thingummy-Whatname were so neatly away for the weekend. He and Iris could have had a whole precious free weekend together. He imagined himself getting out of bed just about now to put the kettle on the ring on the landing, so he could take her a cup of tea, she so loved to be cosseted, poor thing, she'd had little enough of that; and longing swept through him.

There were some things she hadn't lied about. He knew that. She had not lied about anything important.

And even if she had; even if she's the best actress in the world and doesn't really love me at all; I still love her. No getting away from that. Oh, Iris!

"Nurse da Silva is still off duty. She has permission to stay out."

"Yes, yes I know, but . . ."

"You may leave a note for her, if you wish."

Running back to his lodgings he wrote two, one for the Home Sister to put into Iris's pigeonhole, one for him to slip beneath the door of Jo's flat.

Dearest Iris, I'm so sorry, I really didn't mean it, please meet me so we can talk about everything. I love you and want to be with you always, with all my love, R.

Buying the envelopes for these took nearly all the remaining change in his pocket; looking at this afterwards he realized that he had managed to spend an entire weekend-with-Iris-worth's the gloomily drunken night before, and then gone on spending, so that he was somehow going to have to survive for the whole of next week on less than two and thruppence.

For a while he hung around in the foyer of the hospital, hoping to bump into someone he could scrounge a few bob from, but no one turned up so as the afternoon wore on he had given the nursing home a final check and then decided to get to Jo's on foot. It took him nearly three-quarters of an hour's fast walking, and was in itself rather a triumph of navigation and memory, so that he was in higher spirits as he at last passed under the railway bridge, past the pie and coffee stall, closed, luckily, since he was beginning to feel well enough to be hungry, past the bench where he and Iris had sat so often in the summer evenings, and across the road to Jo's front door.

Third floor: three bangs on the knocker.

There was no reply. He tried again.

"'Ere!"

Looking down in the voice's direction he saw Mrs. Bowen, the basement crone, looking up at him, her tatty white head protruding sideways through the narrow aperture at the bottom of the basement sash window, the darting eyes just able to roll upwards high enough to spot him above her on the stone steps.

"They're aht," said Mrs. Bowen.

Once this same hag had been on her waddling way home as he and Iris set off for work early one morning; they had been laughing about something and without stopping their hurrying walk had turned to each other and quickly kissed, just lightly, on the lips, turning back to find squat Mrs. Bowen like a gnome in a headscarf not four feet away. Mrs. Bowen had smiled a surprisingly sweet smile, for all it was entirely gummy, and as they drew abreast she had spoken:

"Ain't love grand!"

For days afterwards he had made Iris laugh and squirm with his deft impersonations of Mrs. Bowen's pronouncement, her toothlessness a question of grinning whilst simultaneously folding the lips inward over the teeth, her extravagant practically Dickensian cockney a feat he could only aim at, though he came, he thought, pretty close:

"Ain't love *grend*!"

"They're aht," she said flatly now, and began immediately to withdraw.

"Wait, please! Mayn't I come in?"

The only reply was the brief grinding rattle of the sash closing. Should he just drop his note through the letterbox? No; the hallway was too communal; suppose it went astray, slipped behind Miss Jarvis's bicycle or beneath the balding ancient doormat? And there was always such a litter of papers and circulars left on the hall table; it might lie there unspotted for days.

Well, what else had he to do, why shouldn't he just wait for a while? Even if Jo had given up work her Andrew hadn't; he would presumably bring her home sooner or later before heading back to stockbrokerdom. Keeping his letter in his pocket he crossed the road to get a clear view of the front door and went back to the railway bridge, since it was be-ginning to rain a little, and leant against the sooty brickwork.

An hour passed, marked by quarterly bells, none of them in precise agreement. His stomach rumbled. Every so often a train roared clanking and snorting overhead, reassuringly, he thought, since otherwise the deserted Sunday afternoon street tended to put you in mind of the end of the world. Suppose Iris had gone back to the nurses' home? He could telephone, risking a few more coppers, but he couldn't see a telephone box. He could ask a passerby where the nearest one was, but there weren't any passersby. At the end of the second hour he was forced to squeeze himself behind a ramshackle sheet of corrugated iron at the far end of the railway bridge in order furtively to pee.

This, all this misery and waste, was due to that damned netsuke pig, he thought. Wish I'd never found it. Wish I'd kept quiet. Wish I'd thrown the bloody thing in the Thames.

If only he'd had a bit of delay. If only he'd given himself a day or two to think about things. Iris was still Iris, he could see that now, inside her strange carapace of lies. Why had she taken the netsuke? She must have had her reasons. There had to be a proper explanation. His arms ached to hold her.

I'll go at five, he told himself. And when all the bells in turn had reached five he decided to go at six. By then his legs ached with standing and his empty stomach hurt, while the hangover still throbbed behind his eyes; post the letter, said common sense, and go. Via the nurses' home.

But as he hesitated a large car turned into Anstruther Walk from the other end. A large car, a gleaming heavyweight, a Bentley. It could only be Jo and her Andrew St. John Mortimer. He leant back against the bridge while another train whistled and clanked above him. He watched Mortimer opening the passenger door and helping Jo out. He remembered the things he had thought about her and the names he had mentally called her and felt ashamed, more ashamed somehow, on seeing how Mortimer treated her: like a lady, of course, carefully taking her suitcase out of the boot, carrying it for her up the cracked path to her battered peeling front door.

Light glowed yellow through the fanlight, and then moments later, in Jo's top floor where the sitting room was. Would Andrew St. John hang around, was she making him an elaborate tea, cozily toasting crumpets and so on, or was she on a different tack altogether and mixing him a stockbrokery sort of drink, a whisky and soda perhaps, or a pink gin, whatever that was?

Ha! Neither. There he was again, cravat tucked into open shirt to signify debonair relaxedness, striding back down the path to what he undoubtedly referred to as his motor. For a second, watching him climb nimbly enough behind the driver's seat, Rob felt almost faint with envy, could almost feel that fine powerful wheel beneath his own longing fin-gers as the Bentley moved slowly away from the curb, backed, turned and magnificently sped away. Instantly he forgot all about it, counted to ten in case the old codger had forgotten something, and then ran across the street, and knocked three times.

"Oh, it's you, hello!" Jo looked very well, her cheeks pink, her hair glossy, neat in tailored blouse and skirt. "Come on up. Oh, did you get into trouble that time?"

For a few moments, tramping up the dark stairs behind her, he couldn't think what she meant.

"No," he said at last, as he followed Jo into the familiar little sitting room, bare of all junk now, he noticed. She'd been busy. "No, no trouble, everything was OK after all."

"Oh good," said Jo lightly. "Want a cup of tea?" Then, turning in the light, she saw his face properly.

"What's up? Is something wrong?" Her color changed; he saw her go pale. "Rob? Where's Iris?"

SYLVIA, FRIDAY EVENING, 1995

So FAR so GOOD, thought Sylvia.

And after all that worry yesterday about how difficult it was going to be with Clio in the car for the second long drive, back home, of the day; all that anxious picturing of hideous screaming and kicking, and poor sick Will, boxed in with all that furious emotion, that sheer energy of sound, and unused to it, and already in such mental distress! And of herself, helplessly apologetic at the wheel!

But in fact the only really bad moment had been at the kennels, when Mum had been clearly upset at seeing Will looking so rough, and Will had noticed. On the other hand they had made a very quick getaway, handed over the wretched little dog Judy without fuss, stuffed the baby and her accoutrements back into the car, and waved goodbye all inside ten minutes; and as the car swung up the drive she had been able to quickly divert him from the gloom her mother's reaction had clearly thrown him into.

"Actually I don't think she's afraid of you, I think the problem is you keep treating her as if she was human. When she's a dog. I mean: when you come into the house after you've been out, do you greet her? Go and pat her?"

"Well, yes, I suppose so."

"And what time do you feed her? Five, six? Then of course you eat later, right? That sort of thing. If you go to greet her, if you feed her first, you're telling her—in Dog, I mean—that you admire her and look up to her and expect her to look after you and find you nice things to eat, see?

And a poor little runt of a thing like Judy, well, obviously she's terrified, she can't cope with the responsibility. Well, that's the theory anyway. In the best doggy circles."

Secondhand dog lore had got them safely down the long familiar lanes, while Clio in the back had fallen fast asleep the whole way into London, through it, and out again onto the motorway, Will by then keeping up a bright cocktail party kind of chatting, bringing Sylvia up to date on the doings of friends of his she had met once or twice, and now pretended to remember, and about Holly, whose recent much-vaunted part in *The X-Files* had turned out to be screaming "Oh, no! No, please, not me, not me!" before having her head bitten off, which had caused certain difficulties with Ozzie, who had naturally wanted to watch his mother's latest role, and who had told all his friends about it beforehand.

Then, as if herself playing a part—pretending to be the sort of baby Sylvia had dispiritedly noticed once or twice in films or on television, equable babies, babies whose mothers were demonstrably the same people after birth as they had been before it, meekly portable babies whose arrival hadn't so much as given anyone stretch marks or piles, let alone obliterated anyone's sense of inner self—as if pretending for the moment to be this sort of baby, Clio had awoken and begun to whimper just as Sylvia passed a *Services 1 Mile* sign.

It had felt a little strange being in a public place with Will and Clio. Sylvia was conscious of how much like a family they looked. Whereas with Adam . . .

She snipped this thought off smartly before it could go any further, arranged to meet Will in the café, and bore Clio off to change her nappy. Clio seemed undeniably to be in a good mood. All those doggies at Nanna's, no doubt. At any rate she refrained from her usual irritable kicking, and chose instead to lie quietly gazing up past Sylvia's shoulder, with such intensity that Sylvia glanced up and back, but saw nothing in particular. Clio, however, seemed to have noticed the glance. The little kick she gave was one of delight, as if she were saying, You saw it too!

For a moment Sylvia forgot that she was dealing with a baby.

"What?" she asked. "What are you looking at?"

Again, it seemed the child looked raptly past her shoulder.

"Flower," she said, or rather exclaimed, and this time, turning back, Sylvia realized that she was looking at the light fitting, which hung down from the ceiling in a cluster of six pointed bulbs, a dusty flower of steel and glass.

"Flower!"

For a moment, Sylvia had a strange quivering feeling about her heart. Then she remembered Will outside, with no one to chat to, prey to terrors, and the feeling was replaced by a far more familiar tense awareness of the time all this was taking her, quick, Sylvia, hurry, hurry!

Outside he looked all right, though, standing with his hands in his pockets, hanging about with several other waiting fathers and husbands. Well, perhaps they all just looked the part too, thought Sylvia, and she smiled up at him.

"All set. Shall we have some tea, or something?"

"Yeah. Hello, Clio!"

And then he set himself, Sylvia saw, to charming the baby. In the queue he played hiding his face in one hand and letting her catch him peeping out at her. Later, at the table, he allowed her to hand him various objects—her bottle, her soft squeaky rubber thing shaped like a caterpillar, a teaspoon—and then shock and dismay him by implacably wresting them back again. Then he had gone through her animal picture book carefully supplying all the wrong noises, so that the pigs bleated, the lambs uttered ferocious snorts, the ducklings growled menacingly and the mother cow looked out at Clio and made the coughing roar of a revving motorbike.

He had somehow managed to turn playing with a baby into a performance. He always needs an audience, thought Sylvia, and remembered thinking this about him at intervals for as long as she had known him. It was reassuring, that despite everything that was happening to him he was still the same.

"I think she might be a bit young for motorbikes," she said, and of course he replied that no one could possibly be that young, and then while Clio demolished a sticky bun and played with the fragments they had talked about the several bikes Will had owned and loved and tinkered about with, and about Sylvia's own ancient-history Hondas, upon which she had so many times burnt up the Balls Pond Road at speeds very nearly in excess of fifteen miles an hour, and about the motorbike that still called to Will from time to time, rusted to a barnacle-encrusted shade, home to crabs and tiny fishes, from the bottom of the harbor at Cherbourg.

This reminded him of his father's surprise adoption certificate, and the impossibility of asking his mother about it, which kept them going until they were on their way back to the car.

"D'you think she'd let me hold her?" asked Will, as Sylvia set about stowing all the baby gear back in the car again. He had held out his arms and Clio had gone quietly into them, though she kept her eyes on Sylvia unhooking all the bags from the handle of the pushchair, folding the thing up, fitting it into the boot.

"She's not quite convinced," said Will. "Are you, Clio?" but Clio had turned upon him possibly the most coquettish smile ever seen, thought Sylvia, on a human face, and hidden her eyes against his shoulder.

She was flirting with him, Sylvia realized in surprise. This strange little thing, which had grown inside her like an organ, like a spleen, even, this internal organ which had grown inside her and been made free, to require feeding and clothes and swabbing and dandling, this mobile growth had *likings*. Liked a purple teddy bear, that had spoken to her from the pile of its fellows. Liked flowers, and saw them whenever she could. Liked Will.

Sylvia had sighed, and been glad that Clio had stayed resolutely awake for the rest of the journey, so that Will had stayed in the back with her almost the whole of the rest of the way.

Because there's really only so much of everything that I can deal with at once. Obviously it's best if Clio likes him, she told herself, with perfect truth, putting to one side her deeper shameful half-felt notion that Clio's natural response to Will's smile was further proof (and all of it was needed) that she was actually human.

Then she remembered the kittens again, the sewn-up eyelids, the . . .

"OK if I put some music on?" she asked brightly.

"Yeah, go ahead, we're fine. Aren't we, Clio?"

RUBY'S BAD DAY CLOSES, 1954

SOMEHOW, THOUGH, it all got out: the truth, some of the whole truth, and quite a few other things along with the truth.

Perhaps someone had kept an eagle eye out, when the doctor's Rover drew up outside the house. Perhaps one of the closer neighbors, the ones with views directly over Ruby's tiny back garden, had happened to look out of the kitchen window just as she opened the bedroom curtains. The marks about her throat took a long time to fade.

The doctor called it nervous prostration. Though he'd been quite shirty about the washing machine.

"D'you think I'm a fool?" he had asked coldly, the minute he'd come back down the stairs. "What really happened? And you'd better tell me the truth."

Ted had hesitated, but quickly agreed that he better had. So he had come clean about the boy's accident playing on Ruby's mind, and how it had all got too much for her, God help her, and how they'd had this terrible row that morning, doctor, he'd been unkind to her, God help him.

"'Yes yes yes," said the doctor, briskly cutting him off, scribbling already. Then he had handed over a prescription for sleeping pills, said Ruby was to take things easy on account of her nervous prostration, and taken the child away with him, in the Rover, to be sorted out and eventually escorted back home by the district nurse.

"Told you," Ruby croaked, when Ted brought her a cup of tea.

"He knew all along."

"'Course he did." She looked different, he thought. Her face all puffy still and bruised, but her eyes somehow lively again, interested again. As if she was looking out, instead of looking in. As if they were in this together.

He sat down on the bed beside her. "Did you tell him?" he asked.

"Didn't have to."

"I did. He made me."

"Trying to make sure you didn't string me up yourself, I expect," she said. Despite the croak her tone was light, almost playful.

"What!"

"Well. You wouldn't be the first bloke tried to do his wife in, would you? Far as he's concerned."

"You could of told me!" He was aghast; it had not occurred to him that concealing a suicide attempt might have had such potentially disastrous consequences.

"Keep your hair on," said Ruby. Carefully she took a sip of tea, swallowed. "Ow. He knows you didn't. He knows it was me. We just give him a story to stick in his notes, that's all."

"Oh, Ruby. I'm so sorry. What I said. I don't know what came over me."

"S'all right." Ruby carefully set the cup back in its saucer, her eyes averted.

Something was sticking into him, he realized; he was sitting on something hard. Without thinking he shifted his weight sideways, dug his hand into his pocket, pulled out whatever it was, and opening his hand found a bright shiny new metal pencil sharpener.

Odd. Where had that come from? He glanced back at Ruby who had frozen, gone all stiff and white apart from her purple bruises, her eyes fixed on what lay on his palm.

"Ruby?" At the sound of his voice she made a strange little whinnying noise. Baffled he held his hand out to give her a better look, and she flinched her whole body away from him, as if he was holding a snake.

What was happening?

"What is it, what's the matter?"

He remembered now. He had heard it fall. It was hers; it had somehow fallen from her as he caught her in his arms, as the terrible rope parted.

"Ruby, where did this come from?"

She turned away, closing her eyes tightly. She was trembling all over, he saw.

"Is it yours?"

The merest shake of her head: no.

"Well, I've never seen it before, it's not mine. Whose is it?"

She was crying, he saw. She shook her head.

"Whose is it?" he asked again, and this time she managed a whisper: "I don't know."

"Then what . . ."

Oh, God, here we go again, he thought, bleakly. Carrying on like a madwoman at the sight of a . . .

Oh.

"Oh, my God," said Ted softly, for light had dawned.

Though immediately he rejected the idea. Who would be so cruel, and why? Why would anyone bother? But then again, he remembered the parcel with the elegant yet discreet new dress inside. I don't want no presents, she had said, and tipped the whole thing unseen into the boiler. She had looked frightened, and he had seen it, and told himself her fear made no sense, discounted it. Ignored it.

"Ruby: did someone *send* you this?"

A pause; and then a tiny nod. Yes. Someone had.

Christ Jesus! He held his breath. The further obvious thought occurred to him. He leant forward, whispering too, as if his normal voice might hurt her further.

"Ruby, you got to tell me. Had it, had it happened before?"

She could not turn to him. The tiny nod once more: yes, it had.

He reached out a hand, and gently put aside a strand of her hair that had fallen forward over her face.

"Who's doing it?"

"I don't know," she whispered back, and at last turned to face him.

"What, you mean, anonymous?"

"Yeah." She looked timid, he thought. She looked meek. She had accepted it, he saw. Someone had set themselves deliberately to torture her, and she had accepted the punishment.

He took her hand in his.

"Someone sent you pencil sharpeners?"

"Pencils."

"And, what, often?"

There was a pause.

"Sorry," she whispered at last.

Ted's eyes filled. She was sorry, he thought, that she deserved everything that had happened to her. She was sorry that she was having to tell him all this awful stuff after all. She was sorry she had not been able to bear it all by herself. She was sorry she had made such a mess of bearing it. She was sorry.

"Oh, Ruby!" he said, on a sigh. Then he did something very strange, something he had never done before and would never do again. Where had the gesture come from, so foreign, so romantic? Some courtly Hollywood dream, perhaps? Some woman's magazine of Ruby's he had picked up and glanced idly through one dull evening some time?

He didn't know, himself. He didn't stop to think about it, he just took Ruby's worn hand, turned it palm upward, slowly carried it to his mouth, and tenderly kissed it. Then he laid it along his own hot cheek. For a minute or two he just sat there, rocking himself to and fro a fraction, holding Ruby's hand against his face, leaning into it. Then Ruby at last struggled upright, a little awkwardly, and put her other arm around him, and held him tight.

BUT PERHAPS THE one thing that made the most difference was the note from Lady Hardy, OBE, chatelaine of Woolsey Court and chairwoman of the local branch of the WI. As soon as the rumor of poison pen letters and attempted suicide reached her the Honorable Dinah, whose views were liberal, wrote Ruby a furiously sympathetic letter, and also sent her flowers from the Court's own gardens.

Ruby pretended to be amused by this letter. She read bits of it aloud to Ted, in Lady Hardy's own booming bray, but secretly she was thrilled and deeply proud. Such kind notice, from a real nob! She kept the letter in its envelope in her handbag for many years afterwards.

Though presently, it was clear to them both that they would all be the better for a new start. Besides, Ted had been promoted again. Further rumors had reached the ears of his immediate bosses; it was impressively evident that Ted's poor (and by now of course satisfactorily improving) home circumstances had not in any way affected his performance at work, which, bar just the odd day or so off sick, remained exemplary, innovative, inspiring; his new salary as Dyehouse Manager would enable them to buy a car and move house, to somewhere still fairly close to the zip factory of course, but not necessarily on the route of its works bus.

A new start in an even newer house, so new it isn't even built yet! Look, Rube, you can say what you want, d'you want a built-in soap dish beside the bath, we could have all pink bathroom stuff, a pink lavvy, a pink sink! Or leaf-green! Or coffee-colored! This size or that size? We could have a shower. D'you want a shower, Ruby? Built-in?

Georgie? What do you want, lovey? Hey, Georgie! No, put the book down, and come and have a look at this. Oh, go on!

No? Oh.

All right then.

Never mind. No, leave him, Rube.

Doesn't matter . . . he's all right. Leave him be.

AFTER THE LECTURE, 1983

Surely not; not again. Surely she'd simply forgotten where she'd parked it? But she knew all the time really. In any case as she neared the lamp-post where she had left it she saw the heavy length of chain discarded on the tarmac, still half-coiled, one link neatly sawn through.

"Bolt cutters," cried Sylvia aloud in disgust. Hell, hell, hell! And it was a busy road, and this was a lamppost; someone had sauntered up whistling with a pair of sodding bolt cutters over his shoulder and stolen her motorbike while a streetful of witnesses pretended not to see!

"Rotten sods," said Sylvia.

It was raining, too.

"Oh, bugger!"

And oh her bike, she had been fond of it! You could never swing yourself across it, rev up, and roar off down the street without a great surge of high spirits; no matter how cheerful you were feeling already jumping onto a motorbike always made you cheerfuller still, thought Sylvia. She gave the useless length of chain a little kick, bent down, sighing, to pick up books and files and heavy groceries, which would have all fitted so easily into the bootbox, and trudged off to find a bus stop with all the other forlorn and bikeless souls.

The pavement was packed, crowds at each bus stop. But surely this first one was the right one, since the numbers on it looked hearteningly familiar. She'd definitely got the motorbike stuck behind one of these buses practically all the way home, and more than once. With some difficulty she struggled through to the signpost itself to take a closer look

274

at the route map, which while relatively new-looking and fully in place and more or less legible seemed designed somehow actively to confuse the novice Londoner.

Apparently the bus, or these buses, beginning *over there* stopped at all sorts of unfamiliar places until it or they reached here, and then, continuing along broadly similar but essentially divergent pathways, visited further places Sylvia had never heard of, until they each arrived at one of three possible and entirely enigmatic final destinations, at which point they turned round and came variously all the way back again, but the most important and for Sylvia maddeningly unanswerable question was, were buses on this side of the road going the way she wanted, or were they coming back?

The bus stop sign simply wasn't letting on. Clearly she was here, almost centrally, at what even the bus stop sign grudgingly admitted was (hospital) but should she stay here or go to the zebra crossing, get across the road, and wait to catch a bus going in the opposite direction?

On the motorbike she would certainly start off this way, but look at all those completely unfamiliar stops on the route map! And of course she veered off to the right almost immediately, down that big road past the off-license; and it was all very well remembering following a bus with just this number several times, she told herself, but the more you thought about the more you knew you'd followed the sodding things both ways.

And while the buses themselves all had great big signs on their fronts, with their most important destinations in the biggest letters, this could only be helpful, thought Sylvia, if you happened to know where these important destinations actually were, relative to everything else, and particularly to where you actually wanted to go. But the much-thumbed A to Z was, of course, in the bootbox.

Clearly she should buy another, but there was no stationers in sight, and it was now raining so heavily that Sylvia gave up for the moment, put one of her bags down, and tried to turn up the collar of her jacket, to keep the water from racing down her neck. It occurred to her that the dye might well run; perhaps she'd take it off and be all covered in black when she got home.

275

She held up one hand, turning it over in the yellow lights from the lamps and the shops and the cars splashing by, trying to see if the drops falling from her fingertips were sinister with running dye, so she did not at first notice the car drawing up beside the curb, or its passenger window electronically gliding open.

"Hello, it's Miss Henshaw, isn't it?"

The voice was familiar, but even before she had fully identified it her heart had jumped to attention. Mr. Wilding! Oh wow!

"Can I give you a lift somewhere?" His face half hidden, half lit by the sliding golden bars of passing traffic. "Where are you headed?"

She named the general area.

"Hop in."

"Oh, thank you, um, that's very kind, I'm afraid I'm terribly wet, though."

It was quite some time since Sylvia had sat in a car, and anyway the last time had been in her mother's old blue van, which smelt irrevocably of dog. This was very different. This was luxury. Everything in the car had a sort of weighty smoothness, with some sort of quiet restrained Mozart-type piano music adding to the impression that this was a space quite cut off from the rain-soaked burdened scrabblers thronging the noisy street outside.

And there sat Mr. Wilding in his blue shirt sleeves, the cuffs rolled up, she could see the glint of blond hairs on his left forearm, so close by. She could smell his aftershave, and something else more delicious yet, more disturbing, surely she could, whenever he changed gear, just faintly smell him, a man at the end of a day's work, oh, my . . .

"I'm making your car all wet," she said, after some time. She had meant to sound apologetic. But she did not. She sounded quite different, so different that for a moment she was completely unable to say anything else. She lay back in the soft seat suddenly aware of her sensations, which were very like those she had last experienced whilst waiting outside the examination hall for her finals. Only this time instead of sick dread there was, added to the thumping terror, a tremendous sense of lightness and excitement.

I'm making your car all wet.

What had made it come out like that? Not apologetic, but complacent. What had given her voice that, well, that sort of purr?

"May I ask you something?" he said.

"Absolutely."

They drew up at a red light.

"Do you often wear leathers?"

She turned to look at him outright, in surprise. Their eyes met. It was all a bit much for Sylvia. She felt herself hotly blushing.

"Oh, well of course I do realize it looks a bit peculiar—"

"Not at all—" he said.

"But my bike got stolen. I mean I don't usually, well, it's to ride a motorbike in."

Helplessly she began to giggle. Somehow she had felt so angry at losing the bike again, with all the telephoning and police forms and messing about with insurance claims still so fresh in her mind from the first time only three months earlier, that she had not for a moment considered what she might have looked like standing at the bus stop in tight black leather trousers and matching figure-hugging zip-up jacket. And sleek wet hair, oh, gods of lucky chance, what more could a girl ask?

"I'm sorry to hear that," said Mr. Wilding, deadpan. "I thought it might be another side to your character."

So she had a character, thought Sylvia instantly. Yes, Miss Goody Gumdrops. Miss Butter-wouldn't-melt. Miss Good Sort. Miss Neuter.

"No, it's entirely practical," she said, briefly alarmed at her own mocking tone. What was going on? She liked it, though.

"So what was the bike?" He moved through the green light.

"Oh, it's just a little Honda, I'm afraid. Much as I'd like something with a bit more oomph. It had to be something I could lift up, you see. If it fell on me."

Sylvia had made variations of this perfectly truthful speech before, to her mother, for instance. It had sounded perfectly normal then, a sensible informative statement. But now, spoken with a smile in Mr. Wilding's sensationally beautiful car, and with a quick glance sideways at him, catching his eye, at the word *oomph*, well, she thought, you could practically write an essay on its implications.

I'm doing it, she told herself in gleeful surprise. I'm doing it, I'm being sexy! Mr. Wilding is flirting with me and I am flirting back!

How amazingly easy it was as well, what an easy almost jokey thing, a lively harmless game for two to play. And all the years in which she had consciously despised any girl who couldn't so much as say Good Morning to a man without trying to make him think about having sex with her fell away. What fun it was!

She crossed her legs in their tight damp black leather, and knew exactly how aware he was of every movement. Best, perhaps, to lower the temperature a little; she didn't want him to think she was actually seriously making a pass at him.

"So where do you stand on the great smoking controversy?"

"What controversy is that?"

"Clearly smaller than I thought it was. Minions only."

"Oh, the ban." He smiled: "Well. When I was your age the *patients* used to smoke. Especially male surgical, barely round from the anesthetic, they'd all be lighting up."

"What, you mean in bed?"

"Oh yes. Smoke-filled wards. Chap in the next bed choking with emphysema. It all seemed perfectly normal then."

"But, what when you needed oxygen?"

"Much more of a to-do in those days. You had to go and fetch a cylinder of it and get the key from Sister and so on. You didn't just flick a switch. So you had plenty of time to ask those nearest to stub out."

"D'you mean they had ashtrays? NHS ashtrays?"

"Well, I suppose they must have done."

Looking out of the window she realized how close she was to home.

"Ah, you could actually drop me about here. Thank you so much, Mr. Wilding."

"You're very welcome, Miss Henshaw."

"Sylvia."

A mistake somehow, she thought. He made no reply. She'd overstepped some mark; been too familiar. They drew up at another red light.

"Look, I could just get out here . . ."

"No, don't do that. Let me take you right home. Which street is it, actually?"

And she told him and that, she thought later, was when things really changed. Something in his manner. She should have insisted he drop her on the main road at the corner, she thought. Instead of letting him get a bit lost round the one-way system. Because he really seemed to get confused, especially when he'd tried to turn down that one-way street, and had to back up, and then obviously he'd got a bit tense because there really wasn't room enough to turn, and after that they got stuck behind a bus—ha! *that* bus, Sylvia had plenty of increasingly flustered time to notice—and by the time they finally arrived at Anstruther Walk all the fun had rather drained out of things and he would drive off, she thought, thinking only of how much he wished he'd never stopped in the first place, instead of what a surprisingly sexy young thing that brilliant Sylvia Henshaw was, which was what she thought she most wanted.

So it was a real surprise when, as she opened the passenger door, he got out too, on the driver's side. The rain had stopped. He just stood there looking all around him.

"Well, thank you so much, Mr. Wilding, I'm so sorry I took you so far out of your way."

For a second, as he looked at her across the bonnet, she had a distinct impression that her voice surprised him. That he had forgotten all about her already.

"Which number is it?"

She told him and he said, "Well, you see, I've been here before, I used to know someone who lived here years ago. But it's all so different. That wasn't there," he gestured with his head at the shopping arcade across the road, "and there was a gap. In the terrace."

Sylvia turned too, as if she might notice an entire house gone missing if she just looked hard enough.

"What number was it?"

"I can't remember." He shook his head. "It was a very long time ago."

And then the something within Sylvia that had spoken so thrillingly for her, that scorned the schoolgirlish infatuation she consciously entertained for him, that wanted action, that wanted the real thing and saw

279

its chance and took it, made her push the damp tendrils of her hair away from her eyes, and ask him if he would like to come inside, to her flat; he might see something that would jog his memory; perhaps he would like a cup of tea?

The long sigh he gave. Turning to her, seeming at last to see her properly, focus on her.

She lifted her head, smiled directly up at him.

I love him.

Another long look; one she could not begin to interpret.

"Well. All right then. Thank you, Sylvia," he said.

ROSEMARY HENSHAW AND JUDY, 1995

SHE KEPT UP the cheery waving until the car was out of sight.

I am getting old, thought Rosemary, noting her own sudden and unusual listlessness.

The late-afternoon sun was warm on the front step. She sat down, still holding Judy's lead. The dog herself did not move, but stood trembling with her back arched and her ears flat, back legs slightly bent and tail tucked in, a mime of canine misery.

"You and me both," said Rosemary, taking a small cube of cheddar cheese from the bag she always had ready in the top pocket of her shirt. "Here. How about that?"

Judy turned her head away.

Rosemary put the cheese on the ground in front of Judy's nose and waited. She stretched out her legs, and closed her eyes as she raised her face to the sun.

"He might not be looking that well," Sylvia had warned her over the phone, and she'd said, Sylvie, I haven't seen him for practically twenty years, I wouldn't recognize him in the street, would I!

But she had.

She'd remembered too the strapping boy with his dad, that time the train got shunted into; and Romeo on a bicycle, a few years later; and of course he'd been on telly in that space thing. Years ago. That was the point, presumably. He'd been so young. And now he must be what, thirty-five, thirty-six?

And aged, perhaps, by illness. Yes.

Or perhaps I'm just going potty, thought Rosemary, briskly sitting up. Judy, cringing as before, moved her head very slightly, in order to risk a tremulous glance at Rosemary's eyes. The cheese had gone.

"That's a girl," said Rosemary softly. Slowly she reached into the bag again, and took out another cube. "So you like cheese, do you? What a sensible dog you are. What a clever brave sensible dog." She put the second cube down and let Judy swallow it before reaching out slowly to fondle the fur beneath the small silky ears. Crooningly she went on telling the extravagant lies with which she so often regaled nervous animals.

"One of the most sensible of all the sensible dogs, yes you are, oh yes you are . . ."

Largely she was unconscious of saying anything at all; had been baffled and upset one evening long ago when the teenaged Sylvia had suddenly flung her book aside and positively screamed at her, at the top of her voice, not like Sylvie at all, to for God's sake, Mum, just stop doing that!

Doing what? Rosemary had asked, and for a little while afterwards had caught herself out telling molting Alsatians they were charming, or assuring yappy poodles they were serene, with an amusement which had gradually become an uncomfortable perplexity. How long had she thus been talking to visiting dogs? Always? Since poor Charlie's death? And if she was speaking unconsciously, why were her words so clearly selective? The whole business seemed to imply that there was a part of Rosemary's mind making playful and ironic connections, and getting her to say them out loud, while the conscious rest of her was somehow kept completely in the dark.

Perhaps it was some sort of self-preservation, she had eventually decided. If you spent a lot of time soothing animals you needed to take precautions against imagining yourself actually understood. Perhaps uttering teasing falsehoods was merely one of these precautions, undertaken by some watchful part of her unconscious merely doing its job as it should.

On the whole though this explanation was more creepy than consoling. It had implications Rosemary had no intention of looking at in any detail. But luckily she already knew that you could cure introspection with a nice fat tree trunk and a chain saw.

Later on it had occurred to her that, while she had always known that she was happier in the company of animals than in that of other people, she had never been altogether relaxed about this. In fact she had been, still was, a little ashamed.

That's what I'm doing, when I talk to them, she had thought. I'm making it clear that I may prefer animals but I'm not soppy about them. I'm not one of those women who coo over them. I'm saying, Look, I can see their faults! All those greedy dogs and lazy ones, all those jealous, nervous, vicious, stupid dogs: none of them hide their vices for long. When I tell fat basset hounds they are graceful, or craven mongrels they are bold and fearless, I'm sort of teasing them, as I calm them. I'm laughing at them, gently, behind their backs.

As if it was not really the animals she was talking to at all, but the human world; trusting it somehow to overhear.

A watchful unconscious is a very subtle thing, Rosemary had finally concluded, and then pulled on her gauntlets and goggles and gone out and taken a large sledgehammer to the obsolete concrete wheel-barrow, hidden behind an out-building by then, covered in brambles, and smashed it into gravel.

"Very sensible brave dog," said Rosemary now, and Judy carefully sat down and after a pause tilted her small head to one side to give the scratching fingers better access.

She would bring Judy's basket into her bedroom tonight, Rosemary decided. It was all she could do for that still un-met woman, Will's mother. And not such a small thing, really, not as far as Mrs. Keane herself would be concerned; this was clearly a much-pampered much-loved elderly beast, which had never been away from home on its own before.

"Tell her I'll treat her like my own dog," Rosemary had told Will firmly, knowing better than he did, she thought, how much that poor woman his mother would have invested in Judy, how much the animal had probably been standing in for, all these years. To comfort her dog would be to comfort her.

Rosemary's mind turned automatically to her own grandchild Clio. It had been nice having her all to herself for a while, Rosemary thought. Clio at the age she liked best in children, as it happened; mobile, underfoot, busily engaged in looking at things and dabbing at them, not saying much, and full of open joys or sorrows. Being a lot like a dog, really, Rosemary had to admit. No wonder Clio had liked Jimmy's basket so much. Plenty of room for two anyway.

And the doves, the longed-for doves, had arrived on time, and she had touched them, their whiteness and extraordinarily soft clean pinkish feet, and pushed them gently into their temporary prison; it had not been glorious, though. It had just been another thing to get over with before Sylvia got back again. There was white in Sylvia's hair. There is white in my baby's hair, thought Rosemary, and drew up her knees, to rest her forehead on them, one hand still on the soft fur of Judy's neck.

You don't think of that until it happens. You don't imagine your own child growing old.

Was it right, to stow Mrs. Keane in some hospital, pretending Will was busy?

"What else can he do, Mum?"

Rosemary thought of herself standing by the front door with Clio in her arms again, Clio's whole lovely little puppy-body waving, flexing and kicking with joy at the sight of her mother's car pulling up, Sylvia smiling within, jumping out:

"Hello again Mum, has she been all right? Hello my darling, how are *you*?" Passing the baby into her daughter's arms Rosemary had not noticed the passenger door opening, had turned and there he was, standing quite close to her, saying something, being grateful. She had been completely unable to frame any sort of reply.

"Oh God," said Rosemary now into her knees, considering this. How long had she stood there staring at him?

Because for a delirious moment she had not seen Will at all, but her own husband Charlie, Sylvia's father, dead nearly thirty years; Charlie young again, strangely wearing someone else's smile as he murmured hello.

"You remember Will, don't you, Mum?" Sylvia had said, and her tone had been clear enough, a warm bright everything-is-normal tone, the sort you simply couldn't argue with.

"Erm . . ." Dizzily, Rosemary, had seen all at once the strapping schoolboy, the cycling Romeo, Toby ffrench with his famous dizzying laser, the obvious ordinary continuum of change between them, and the lengthy jump from that to this.

"We've brought Judy," Sylvia had said, in the same bright tones, "an exchange of hostages! What shall we do with her?"

Then as soon as she could risk a proper look at him the likeness seemed instantly to drain away. Yes, the mouth was all wrong. And the shape of his chin, obviously. Really he was hardly like Charlie at all, what had she been thinking of?

Managing finally to speak to him: "I'm so sorry about everything. Your Mum. And everything."

"It's very kind of you to look after the dog for me," he'd said, and he'd put up a hand to push at his hair at the front, where it was thinning a little, and that had knocked her for six again, for her husband Charlie had pushed back his own hair at the front with just that same slender hand.

Rosemary, recollecting this, sighed aloud. "Tell you what," she said to Judy, "I couldn't half do with a cup of tea. What with one thing and another. Let's go in, shall we? Want a cup of tea? I bet you do. And sugar in it. That'll perk you up a bit, eh? Bold dog."

The small tail very faintly wagged.

ROB AND DR. WILDING, 1964

———————

"Ah, Rob, ma boy, good to see you! How's it going, how's the weans?"

"Weans are good," said Rob, taking his coat off. He was aware immediately of how different the place felt. "Teething: bloody noisy," he added. He followed his father through the hallway, crowded now with tea chests and other large boxes stacked in piles.

"How's the sales?" he asked.

"Steady," said Dr. Wilding. Their eyes met briefly. "Cup of tea?"

"Thanks." Rob looked round the kitchen. A good deal of grayish underwear had been draped over the bar of the Aga to dry; other crinkled personal items hung in festoons from the airer above. Everything was, he saw, just as clean and tidy as it needed to be, and no cleaner or tidier. How dark the kitchen was! He had never noticed it before. But then of course there was so little left, by now, to catch the light; all his mother's clever arrangements of gleaming silver, the dresserful of pink and gold lusterware, even the polished brass saucepans that had twinkled so brightly in other days were gone, picked over, valued, offered for, and sold.

"Did you *keep* a teapot?"

"I did. And you took as much as you wanted."

"All right, I know, I know. So, when are you moving?"

"Next week. They did me a wee party sort of thing. Retirement, you know. Low-key. Under the circumstances." Here Dr. Wilding's voice suddenly trembled, for even the most oblique reference to his wife's death still unmanned him.

"Oh, I brought you these," said Rob, remembering. He opened his briefcase and slid out the biscuit tin. "Homemade."

"She's a good girl," said Dr. Wilding huskily. He took a bag of sugar with a teaspoon sticking out of it from a cupboard, and set it on the table beside the opened bottle of milk. It was true that the teapot and the cups were undeniably Spode, but since Dr. Wilding had not bothered with saucers it was still, thought Rob, a rigorously manly tea that he and his father sat down to, with biscuits taken directly from the tin.

It was his father's only comfort, he suspected, this faintly school-boyish naughtiness, this glad seizing with both hands of the opportunity to give up side plates. It was the sort of behavior, he thought, that Dr. Wilding had gone in for whenever his wife had been away for a few days, the sort she would have exclaimed and tutted over when she came home: "Have you been putting a knife in this jam?" Half disgusted, half wryly pleased at this bluff masculine disregard for niceties.

He is sometimes still pretending, thought Rob. Will he be all right up there in Scotland all on his own? If only he was going to a town, even a village!

And then his mind took its usual turn, and he remembered how much his mother had loathed that damp cottage in the Highlands, and how, sometimes, it seemed almost indecent of his father to be shooting off there so fast. As if he was somehow getting back at Mum. Selling her stuff—well, he'd had to, there wouldn't be room for much of it in the cottage—pulling apart so briskly everything she had taken so long to build. Soon there would be no traces of her in this house, which was already on the market.

Oh, Mum.

"Thought I'd pop round later," said Rob, "and visit old Meadows. See how she's getting on."

"Right." Dr. Wilding looked vague. Meadows had caused him a certain amount of trouble in the months since his wife's death. At first she had been, as everyone said, a tower of strength, had simply carried on looking after the house and himself with all her usual remote thorough-ness. She had tactfully appeared not to notice those occasions when he had been unable to control tears. She had made no reproach when he sent back meals hardly touched to the kitchen. She had made no fusses, no pleas for special consideration, for any consideration at all.

It had therefore been next to impossible to tell her that he intended to sell the house and retire. Not without certain delicate preliminary inquiries: how much had she saved over the years? Her wages had been entirely May Wilding's affair.

He had approached the delicate eighteenth-century escritoire as a trespasser, though he knew his wife had never locked it. He had fumbled through the little glossy drawers, his great fingers too clumsy for their handles, finding clean new nibs, a new roll of lavender-colored blotting paper, paper clips, rubber bands, all sorts of small essentials neatly stowed, and felt the stupid tears running down his face again at the sight of all this familiar daintiness and order.

Her account books had been in the top drawer, with one or two wartime documents, ration books, her school certificate. Dr. Wilding sat down and opened the current one, his heart catching at the sight of her neat pretty handwriting, which spoke so poignantly to him from the lost world of four weeks earlier.

"What the . . ." Was this the right book?

He checked the date again, but there was no getting away from it. He turned back the pages to the first entry, then opened the drawer again, and found the book's predecessor, and then the one before that, which took him back to the war. And it was true: his wife had been paying Meadows almost exactly the same wages for the last twenty-five years.

What had she been thinking of? What had Meadows been thinking of? And why, of course, had he never asked, even idly, how much Meadows, the essential Meadows, had been earning, in his own house?

Of course she'd her board and lodging, he thought. And she certainly wasn't one for show. But then it occurred to him that perhaps the reason Meadows had seemed so attached to, for example, her prewar brown tweed overcoat was not so much an elderly person's faith in good quality, along with dislike of change, as an elderly person's absolute lack of funds. Pocket money: May had been paying the woman pocket money for years and years and years.

After the first shock he was inclined to blame Meadows for this. After all, it was more Meadows's business than anyone else's. Why hadn't the woman simply asked for a raise? May would certainly have given her one if she had. Had probably offered.

"Shouldn't I pay you just a little more these days, Meadows, the cost of living being what it is?"

"Why no, ma'am, I'm perfectly happy as I am, thank you, ma'am."

Perhaps that had been the way of it. She should have just insisted, though, thought Dr. Wilding. She should have just given her the money. Oh, May, what were you thinking of?

And what do I do now? I'm going to make the woman homeless. At her age. Whatever that is. Now there was a question. How *old* was Meadows? Surely she was well past retirement age anyway? She looked very little different from the way she had always looked. Just a bit more doddery, perhaps. There had been an incident just the week before when she had, for the first time ever as far as he knew, burnt the scones.

He looked through the drawer again, to see if there was anything in it about Meadows. But there was nothing. What on earth was he to do? He could hardly consult anyone. Some things were best kept private. And he must act quickly; he couldn't disappear to Scotland leaving the wretched woman destitute and homeless.

Obviously, he thought, I must give her an annuity; tell her May would have wished it. As no doubt she would have, if she'd known . . .

Or a cottage. Perhaps he should buy her somewhere to live. After so many years in his dear wife's service. There were plenty about. There were new bungalows going up at the end of the village. Perhaps she would like one of those. Peppercorn rent, of course. Clearly he should ask Meadows.

But he had addressed so few questions to Meadows over the years. Even now, in this last month, they had barely exchanged more than a few words. It had once occurred to him, with sad admiration, that Meadows was behaving exactly as if his wife was still alive, dusting and hoovering and polishing and shopping and cooking very nearly (bar those scones) as usual. Without thinking about it much he had assumed her to be doing so for his own comfort. What a good servant she was! Tireless, uncomplaining, dutiful, reticent, discreet. And, of course, as he now knew, dirt cheap.

"Have you visited her yet?" asked Rob, dunking a biscuit in his tea.

"Oh, ah, no, not yet, been so busy," said Dr. Wilding uncomfortably. He didn't like to think about Meadows's departure from his house. Of course he should feel sorry for the woman. But there was something about her that made this very difficult.

"But she's doing all right?"

Dr. Wilding shrugged, hoping his son would talk about something else. He could see why the boy felt the way he did; Meadows was clearly a family responsibility. But not, somehow, an affectionate one.

"To be honest," he said, "I don't think she has that much longer."

For Meadows, told of his plans, told further that she might consider bungalows and generous annuities, that she must fear for nothing, that he would look after her, or see that she was looked after, in comfort, for the rest of her days, Meadows, hearing all this, had made no expression or remark, merely stood up, brushed off her apron, uttered three words, "Thank you, sir," and toppled sideways onto the carpet at his feet.

It had been a profound stroke. She had recovered consciousness but her right side had deserted her. She could barely speak, other than a garbled quacking sound. For a while he had employed a nice local woman to take care of her, but like everything else in the house Meadows had had to go eventually. It was a perfectly adequate, even well-appointed nursing home that he had selected for her. Obviously it would be hard on her, leaving what had become her home for so long. But she would have had to go elsewhere anyway, he told himself, as he went upstairs that day with the ambulance men who were to transport her dead weight to the Home.

"Got everything, Meadows?" he had said, jovially, looking down at her. She had always been rather expressionless, of course; but now, he thought, the added inertia of paralysis had given her face a certain utterly still stony quality that was almost chilling to look upon, even for nerves as professionally hardened as his own.

"Not far to go!" he added, as the men slid the wooden poles into the stretcher canvas. Though it was a warm day he noticed that she was holding what looked like a pair of old leather gloves, squeezed tightly into her one good hand.

"Why . . ." And he remembered. Why, surely those were the very gloves he had bought all those years ago, in Jenner's department store in Edinburgh, before the war! He had thought to protect his lovely May from the cold, by buying her the brigand's daughter's fur-lined gauntlets. From "The Ice Queen," he remembered. He had the odd thought—the sort of thought he was subject to these days, strange silly almost girlish sorts of notions that came into his head, it seemed, from nowhere—that Meadows herself was a little like someone from the story of "The Ice Queen." Perhaps a fragment of ice had entered Meadows's heart long ago, and no one had tried to rescue her, no one had been able to see it or get it out, and now she was a helpless sick stone-faced old woman, being taken away from her home to be dealt with by paid strangers.

Yet here she was, holding onto his wife's old gloves as if for dear life. Perhaps after all someone had melted that fragment of ice; perhaps May had; perhaps that was why she had not thought to raise the poor old thing's wages; she had been family, perhaps, to May.

And had May been family, then, to Meadows? Why else would she be holding the gloves so tightly now, like a talisman to help her through this last sad journey?

He put out a hand, and touched the leather, worn soft with age. "I mind when I bought these," he said gently. "She couldna wear them; too big for her, weren't they." A sentence full of meanings he would never have come close to saying aloud: You loved, her, didn't you, Meadows? In your way. I applaud you for it. I loved her too. In mine.

One of the ambulance men coughed politely behind him, and he left the room as they got to work. She must be heavier than she looks, he thought, standing at the bottom of the stairs as they made their halting way down with her. Heavy as stone. As they passed down the hall, whose flags she had so often scrubbed, he stepped forward to bid her farewell.

"I'll come and see you very soon!" he said to her averted face, and made as if to pat the fist that still held the gloves so tightly.

To his surprise she instantly, energetically, flung her hand sideways out of his reach. The suddenness of the movement actually made him jump. There was a moment's shocked pause. He found himself flushing; both the ambulance men had seen her spurn him.

"Right," he said, weakly. He got out of the way, his heart pounding, and watched the men negotiate the front steps, swing their burden into the waiting ambulance, nod briefly and unsmilingly at him, and drive away.

He had gone into the drawing room and poured himself a drink with trembling hands. Obviously she hadn't wanted to go, but he could hardly be expected to tend her in her dotage, could he? It wasn't as if she were a relative; why, even if she were, the wretched woman needed proper twenty-four-hour nursing care, and heaven knew he was paying for the best, well, jolly nearly the best, anyway, certainly more than adequate. Really he had nothing to be ashamed of.

So why did he feel so ashamed?

"Funny thing," he said to Rob now, as he poured himself another cup of tea.

"What's a funny thing?"

"Meadows's old room. Got Mrs. Purdy to clear it for me, thought she'd packed everything up. Not that there was very much." He trailed off, remembering the threadbare prewar overcoat again, and Meadows's pocket-money wages. He need not trouble his son, he thought, with such matters. "But she missed a whole cupboard," he went on, "well, her eyes aren't what they were, and it's just that wee thing beside the fireplace, d'you know the one I mean?"

Rob nodded, though in fact he was not fully listening, and in any case had almost never penetrated the attic rooms where Meadows had lurked at night. He was thinking about visiting her, and how frightful it was going to be. Some grisly Home full of gaga old wrecks. Horrible. Himself pretending not to notice the smell, and making small talk to a woman who had almost never volunteered any remark of any kind. Who had always simply been there, in the background, all his life. He couldn't help but be fond of her, for old time's sake.

Though to be strictly honest it was a bit like losing the family car, he thought. Or the dog. You felt sorry, but you knew you could just go out and get another one. Not that there was any need for another Meadows. Not these days. Thank God.

"What?" he said aloud sharply. Something of what his dad was prosing on about had suddenly sounded like something he needed to know. "What did you say?" But in fact he had heard. The words had entered into him. He could look inside himself and read them off.

A cupboard, with two shelves. Full of little things: a pincushion shaped like a strawberry, a brooch of diamante and Bakelite, bought for a fancy dress party, a card of buttons, a china eggcup, a silk handkerchief, a dress clip . . .

There had been other things; Dr. Wilding decided to keep these to himself. Shocking things. *A used handkerchief. A pair of drawers. A tight coil of used sanitary towel, like a fat slice of Swiss roll. An old sanitary belt of pink and sagging elastic, one loop suggestively stained.*

That woman—Meadows—had clearly taken these things from his wife's dirty linen basket, or from the bathroom bin, and kept them, in secret, in a private collection of stolen items. It was at this point that Dr. Wilding would have preferred to let his imagination go no further. Though with the strange female persistence he had already noticed since his bereavement it sometimes seemed ready to carry on whether he wanted it to or not, and ever since Mrs. Purdy's discovery had presented him tirelessly with quite frequent pictures of Meadows, squat silent stone-faced Meadows, sitting foursquare in her armchair of an evening, and in her lap, clutched in those big strong fingers, was not mending or knitting, but a dirty pair of his own wife's knickers.

How much, too, had she heard, sitting up there in her attic room? How completely he had always forgotten her, at night! He had hardly given her another thought when she had said her cool Goodnight and stumped away. Suppose sitting up there with her collection she had been able, slightly deaf or no, to hear things?

And of course he had always been a passionate man.

"What, sorry?" he said aloud.

But what ailed the boy? What a face!

"I said, I *said*, are you sure Mum didn't give them to her, for Christ's sake!"

"What's the matter? What is it? No, I don't know, I don't think so, no, I mind her looking for the wee brooch, oh, years ago, and there were other things, she would never have given her, d'you know what I mean, oh, what is it, Rob?"

Weak tears of distress had sprung to Dr. Wilding's eyes. If only he could ask his wife, if only he could see her again, oh, May!

"I'm sorry. I'm sorry, Dad. I . . . I'm upset. We both are, of course."

And how tired the boy looked. His own grief, of course. And the new baby keeping him awake, perhaps. If only May had lived to see it! A wee girl, too.

"Have you, ah, have you said anything to her? To Meadows, I mean?"

Dr. Wilding shook his head. "Well, no. I mean, I havna been to see her at all. Yet. Perhaps you could ask her? If you think it's worth it, I think myself, erm, least said soonest mended, in fact."

"I don't think I will. Really. It's not as if any of the stuff was valuable. Was it?"

"Well . . ."

"Was it?"

Dr. Wilding pulled at his collar. He had meant to censor only the dis-gusting things, but given the extent of Rob's apparent distress at needle cases and eggcups it would, perhaps, be best not to mention the tiny seated glistening figurine of a shepherd boy which, after all these years with an expert, he was fairly sure was Meissen. And May's.

If Meadows had stolen the shepherd, why had May not called the police, or so much as mentioned to him that the thing had been taken? No use telling yourself Meadows might have bought it herself: not with those wages. Had May lent her parlor maid a Meissen figurine? It was the only possible explanation for such a valuable piece to be locked in-side a cupboard in a maid's attic bedroom, but again again, again, oh May, what were you thinking of?

Dr. Wilding hesitated, trying to work out how best to spare his son any further upset.

"I think Meadows may have, ah, helped herself from time to time."

"Right, right. And did Mum know? D'you think?"

"I just don't know. I don't know, son. Perhaps."

A silence. We have had a stranger living in our house, thought Dr. Wilding. A stranger who I think might well have hated me. Now there's a thing.

"Well," said Rob at last, and his father thought his smile made him look almost unfamiliar, a strange sneering smile, very unlike his usual sunny good-tempered grin. "Well," said this strange sneering Rob, "I don't think I will pop in on the old girl after all, somehow."

THOUGH IN FACT he did, the next morning. But the woman at the desk came back from Meadows's room with the tactful message that Meadows wasn't well enough at the moment for visitors: perhaps he could come back later.

"Do tell her I will," said Rob.

WHILE UPSTAIRS, STIFF in her untended bed, Meadows lay listening: perhaps they would let him in anyway. Let him come, then; or let him stay away. It was nothing to her what he did. Never had been.

She turned her head to the window. She could see nothing there but sky, a dull white today. At the movement a large tear slipped beneath the lid of her good right eye, and rolled down her cheek into her pillow.

Once it had been a long time since Meadows had cried; she had hardly shed a tear all her life, not since her arrival, aged five, at the orphanage, where, for a while, she had cried for whole days together.

But she was making up for all that now.

WILL AND SYLVIA, FRIDAY NIGHT, 1995

_____

"Who's got the birthday card?" asked Will, after a longish pause. "It's you, isn't it?"

Sylvia, startled, poured herself a little more scotch. They had never discussed the birthday card before; not mentioning it had been part of the joke. She hesitated; besides, she couldn't for the moment work out what month it was.

"Isn't it you?" she asked.

For on his nineteenth birthday Will had been so famous (at least to that female portion of the television-watching public aged between ten and about eighteen) that Sylvia had thought to tease him by sending him a secondhand birthday card. It had been Rosemary's own birthday a week or so earlier; it was the little pile waiting by the kitchen bin that had given her the idea in the first place. With half a dozen or so to choose from, clear winner was Aunt Monica's unusually dull photograph of a blobby purple flower. Silver lettering on the front read HAPPY BIRTH-DAY, TO A DEAREST SISTER, while inside more silvery discursive script read:

You're such a lovely sister,
The nicest one by far!
Here's hoping that your birthday
Is as lovely as you are!

Aunt Monica was the elder, and relations between the two, undeniably hectic in childhood, had been amicable for years, but still cool. Yet as if the card's interior had not gone quite far enough Aunt Mon had added, in splotchy pale blue biro,

Wishing you all the best love from Mon, Reggie and the boys XXX

It was perfect. In black biro Sylvia crossed out Sister on the front cover and after some thought wrote *geezer*, altering the inside to match, putting a hand-drawn line through Mon, Reggie and the boys and signing her own name underneath.

For days afterwards she'd had to laugh whenever she thought of it. Though as the weeks went by and Will made no reply at all, she had begun to wonder if there hadn't after all been some message in it, some half-meant warning against too much starry egotism, something a little churlish, perhaps, something a little resentful, from one of the provincials he had left so astonishingly far behind him. Perhaps he had seen the warning, and been hurt that she had seemed to think it necessary. Or perhaps stardom had changed him so much already that he hadn't been able to see the joke at all.

There hadn't been much time to brood about it, though, since this had been the summer of Sylvia's own A levels, and she wanted four grade A's.

Sylvia had moved her table into the attic, so that she could work without being tempted to stare out of windows; she bought earplugs to muffle the canine sound effects and her mother's newly acquired jackhammer, with which, at the time, Rosemary was enthusiastically cracking open the concrete paths she had herself laid a decade or so earlier.

By desk light all that spring Sylvia had filled postcard after postcard with tiny handwritten summaries, reducing two years' worth of Physics, Chemistry, Mathematics and English Literature into a fat wad of memorable palm-size outlines; she had composed and chanted acronyms, she had walked up and down the attic, ignoring the sunshine chinking through the eaves at her feet, reciting her postcards, learning her part, making herself word-perfect.

Doing all this involved the loss of half a stone and a sudden grasp of the importance of ritual. Every night before turning out the bedside light Sylvia allowed herself ten pages, and ten pages only, of *Middlemarch*, stopping at the end of the tenth page no matter how ferociously she longed to know what happened overleaf. It was also vital to mark each occasion when three further postcards had been completely mastered by leaving a small fleck of her own blood (pricked out from the middle finger of her left hand with a particular needle kept in a particular spot on her worktable) at head height on the top central beam of the attic; behavior that was to enable her, much later on, to be an unusually sympathetic student during her statutory psychiatric rotation.

Her birthday, in early July, had shone glitteringly ahead of her that year not only because it meant being eighteen and officially free to be adult, but because reaching it would mean that all possible exams had been taken and finished with. Often from the semidarkness of her attic she had pictured that birthday breakfast, the kitchen door open in the sunshine, the climbing roses looking in through the window where the curtains would stir a little in the perfumed breeze, all dogs for the moment quiescent after their morning walkies, only birdsong outside, and a just-right boiled egg neatly set out on the scrubbed kitchen table beside the plump little pile of envelopes.

In fact Sylvia very nearly missed her birthday altogether, having been out at a party the night before, where she had got so drunk that she was haunted for weeks afterwards by a vision of herself vomiting over a front wall into someone's garden, without any means of finding out whether she had merely dreaded this as a likely possibility or really gone ahead and done it. Arriving home at teatime, still sickish and crumpled from sleeping all day in her clothes, and miserably aware that Dorothea Casaubon would never have got drunk enough to contemplate throwing up in front gardens let alone kneeling down to let rip Sylvia had slunk into the chair beside the Aga while the kettle came to the boil, and, listlessly noticing it was her birthday, that this little pile of packets was her own, had fumbled open the top one, and found herself looking at Aunt Mon's dull photograph of a purple blobby flower.

Will had crossed out geezer, and in red felt-tip inserted *girlie*. Despite her condition Sylvia had uttered an instant crow of delighted laughter.

You're such a lovely girlie, said the card inside, *the nicest one by far! Here's hoping that your birthday is as lovely as you are!*

He had not only remembered; he had planned. Girlie; it was perfect, particularly for a woman determined on at least an Exhibition, every bit as gleefully slighting as being sent a secondhand birthday card in the first place. She had seen instantly that she must keep this precious document in a very safe place, and remember to take it with her to—well, one mustn't take things for granted—to wherever she eventually found herself next February.

For thirty-five birthdays since then Aunt Mon's card, increasingly furry as to edges, its cover and insides a mess of alternating indignities and deletions and signatures, had crossed the Atlantic, or England, or Finsbury Park. Once Will had disguised it, hiding it rolled into the inside pocket of the leather bike gear he had noticed in a childrenswear shop on Rodeo Drive; for his own next birthday Sylvia in return had shipped him out a present too, a picture, from the feel of the packaging, which he had with some difficulty removed to discover Aunt Mon's card, nicely framed.

Perhaps, Sylvia had since more than once thought, she and Will would really have lost touch altogether if it hadn't been for the unspoken necessity of sending one another the same battered birthday card year after year. All those changes of address, over all those years: easy to slip the barest note inside. Pleasant, too, even useful, more than once, to intrigue or tease a prospective new admirer.

"Oh, he saved my library book. In a train crash," Sylvia had told Rob Wilding, who had smiled over it, casually reading it one year beside the mantelpiece of the flat in Anstruther Walk.

"That one, oh that's from Sylvie. I don't think you've met her, have you? Very old friend."

"Isn't it you?" asked Sylvia now. It *was* May, wasn't it? She felt strung-out, tremulous with exhaustion, and at the same time wide awake, though it was long past midnight.

Will was sipping vodka, well-disguised with orange juice. "So it is. I've left it in London though."

Sylvia shrugged. "Plenty of time," she said. She thought briefly of having a birthday without getting the card back, of February coming round and no Will to post it off to; then wondered if this hadn't been Will's train of thought as well.

It wouldn't work now anyway, she saw; nothing like that would ever work again. He had been right to mention it, so flatly. All that was over.

"D'you remember when we went for that bike ride?" he said.

"Course I do. Linda Palmer had dumped you."

"So she had. God. Linda Palmer. I was so upset. I was moping. Just had to get on my bike in the end, wasn't really going anywhere."

"Ah, now it all comes out," said Sylvia teasingly. Within she felt a clear small pang of distress. So he had not, after all, been on his way to see her, when she had almost ridden into him at the turning of the lane! Supposing she'd left Henshaw's a minute or so earlier, or later; she would have missed him; he'd have gone off nowhere in particular on his own, and that whole strange special afternoon would never have taken place. And all sorts of things would have been different, she saw.

"It was hot," said Will, "it was really hot, d'you remember? We sat in a corn field, we had lemonade."

"I was doing brass rubbings."

"God, yes, you were so weird, Sylvie."

"It was just a hobby."

"Weird."

He remembered Linda Palmer, her long straight blond hair and sharp white face, and his own fevered awe at first sight of the shocking springiness of her breasts, and the breathtakingly delightful way the little pink noses of her nipples pointed akimbo at the sky when she sat up. But though he could remember being dumped, and certain private stifled tears at night, and saying no to several parties in case she was there, all memory of the actual grief itself had completely disappeared, wiped clean away by time.

"It was nice in the church, though. Really cool. Remember?"

Cool and almost dim, in the shade cast by the trees outside. He had sat in idle bafflement watching Sylvia's endless weird preparations, the delicate brushing and dusting, the measured lengths of tape, the thin white paper smoothed so carefully into position. Sylvia herself crouch-

300

ing or kneeling or astride the glittering brass knight she was working on: carefully putting no weight on him.

Sylvia in neat blue shorts, small slender legs like a child's, and a blue and white check shirt.

Ah, and he had been able to see all the way down the shirt sometimes, to what looked like a nice little white bra right enough, but whether the bra was actually doing anything in the way of holding anything up was anyone's guess. All the same he had looked at Sylvia, at her forearm golden with summer as it moved with such control over the great sheet of white paper, the fat coin of black wax in her hand tracing bit by bit the complexity of the knight's proud feathered helmet, and found himself remembering the posh house of one of his friends: Paul's house: where on a table in the enormous hallway had stood a special lamp, in the shape of a woman.

The lamp lady was very young. She was made of some sort of pale smooth ivory stuff, and stood very straight on tiptoe, leaning slightly back, her head thrown back too so that her bobbed hair fell clear of her face, which was looking straight up at the great round globe of light that she held as high as she could on one extended arm, the other delicately spread behind her as if for balance. She wore nothing at all, except a headband.

She was not like anything Will had ever seen before. There was certainly nothing like her at home in the bungalow, where light was firmly central, from ceilings, unless his mother was doing some sewing, in which case she switched on the squat brown china Timothy White's lamp on top of the nest of tables beside the armchair.

Several times, waiting for Paul, Will had dared to touch the lamp lady, to cup her lovely little bottom in his hand, to curve finger and thumb about her waist, to caress each hardly-there suggestion of a breast with the tip of his ring finger.

Sylvia's legs slender and delicate, her long golden forearm stroking wax over the smooth white paper—wasn't she rather like the beautiful little lamp lady, so slender all over, and lissom, and light?

Then the sunshine had caught Sylvia's spectacles and he had felt hot all over with shame. Having lascivious thoughts about weird brainy Sylvia Henshaw, of all people! What was wrong with him!

"You were bored," said Sylvia now, rather accusingly.

"You still got that brass rubbing?"

"Oh, yes, somewhere . . . I think. Want a top-up?"

But as she leant across the coffee table with the bottle the movement shifted Clio beside her on the sofa, so that she stirred in her sleep, and uttered a little preliminary cry.

"Oh, no, sorry, oh, shush, darling, there, there! Oh blast!"

After a few more hopeless attempts at pacification she hurried away, Clio bellowing red-faced over her shoulder, the row dwindling in stages as doors closed, but never quite fading out altogether.

Left to himself Will sniggered a little in the sudden comparative quiet. Christ, what a racket! He had forgotten how much noise babies could make. What would it feel like, to let go like that, and scream at full pitch? He closed the thought off abruptly: it was immediately clear to him that it would be a complete disintegration in the face of fear, and he knew exactly what that felt like, thank you very much.

He stood up and thought piercingly of a cigarette. But this was clearly the sort of place no one ever smoked in. Cream carpets, two white sofas! You felt grubby just looking at it. The thought of a bath made him re-member his mother, lying in her bed blissful at hearing his splashes. He hesitated; but they'd said any time, hadn't they? Someone would be awake. He found a telephone, white, very swish, one of those you could completely detach from its stand and walk off with, and dialed the number they had given him.

"Hello?" Absurd, the impulse to speak midnight-softly. Hello? Was that St. Joseph's? Could they tell him, please, if Mrs. Keane was all right, Annie Keane, admitted that afternoon? He was her son. Yes, of course. Ah. Good, good. Would they give her his love, then, when she woke, let her know he'd called? And he'd call again tomorrow. Thanks. Yes, thank you. Goodnight—

Will put the telephone back and stood looking at it for a moment. Despite everything he had told her, and himself, he had after all aban-doned her to paid strangers.

Suddenly the door biffed open behind him, and Clio's bellowing, which had not for a moment let up, instantly made it impossible to think about anything else. Sylvia, rather pale, he noticed, was trying to ask him something:

"Sorry, but do you think you could hold her for a bit? While I get her a bottle?" he gathered when she'd yelled this three or four times.

"Can I take her outside?" he shouted back. It wasn't clear that Sylvia had heard him. With Clio roaring and struggling in his arms he followed Sylvia into the kitchen, turned the handle on what looked like a back door, and went out into a moonlit garden.

It was fresh and cool out there, and velvety dark, heavily perfumed, practically vampish with springtime floweriness. From far away came the distant thrill of waves breaking; the grass felt tender underfoot. An elder tree held a hundred gleaming saucers of little white flowers in the light from the kitchen window. Clio immediately went slack in his arms, and presently fell silent, one tear like a dewdrop stilled on her cheek.

"Look," he said softly into the lovely quiet, "look, we're not going far. There's your mummy. See her? Getting you some milk. Perhaps we can see the moon. Eh? Can you see the moon, Clio?"

With a pang he remembered years ago reading Ozzie a story about a little boy who couldn't sleep for wanting to see the moon. Reading it over and over again, night after night, learning to watch Ozzie's face as they got to the end of the story, when the little boy's daddy finally gave up trying to divert him and took him outside into the garden, and the clouds moved just at the right time, and (turn the page)

There it is!

and Will's reward then was to catch Ozzie's smile of deep delight, just as if he were the little boy in the story, getting his innocent heart's desire.

"I couldn't take Ozzie out into the garden" said Will conversationally to Clio, who was sucking her fist on his shoulder, "because we hadn't got one. Not so much as a balcony. But you've got a lovely garden, haven't you, Clio?" He was tremendously pleased with himself for having quieted her, comforted her. And she felt really nice to hold, he thought, so small but so warm and so vibrantly alive; strength seemed to flow into him from her, though without taking anything from her, as if she were radiating energy, and he was simply being warmed in its glow.

Clio took her fist out of her mouth, and pointed behind him with her plump wet finger.

"What? What are you looking at, Clio?"

"Flower," said Clio, and smiled.

A KISS FAREWELL, NOVEMBER 1954

HE HAD TO SEE HER, to talk to her. There were questions he had to ask, even though he already knew most of the answers. But she did not answer his letter.

Rob made himself wait; wrote again. Another week went by. He wrote again. By now he could see her picking up the envelope and recognizing the handwriting and slipping it unopened onto the fire.

So one afternoon he looked up trains, and then walked from the station. Leaves rattled along the road ahead of him, swerving in the wind. After about twenty minutes he realized that he was walking the wrong way. Patient as any toiling beetle he turned himself round and walked back the way he had come, struggling against the wind this time, his hands deep in the pockets of his old raincoat.

She would perhaps be out. If she was out he would sit on the doorstep and wait. He would wait all day and all night if he had to.

Or perhaps he would go round the back and break in.

Suppose she had only been pretending to be out? She would be frightened, if he went round the back and broke in and all the time she was hiding behind a curtain or something. Well: too bad. She wouldn't be frightened for long, after all. Hello, he'd call. It's me, Rob, all right? I just had to see you. I'm sorry.

I'm sorry. I'm so sorry.

After a very long time, and he was very cold, he came to the right house, another red-brick whopper set well back from the road, with curly wrought iron gates and a yellowish varnished wooden sign with

Fairholme written on it in gothic script on one of the pillars, and a tall thick hedge of speckled laurel.

There were lights on in the house. A catch of movement in the front room. He rang the doorbell, which gave a surprising treble chime of three descending notes. He waited, ready to jam his foot in the door if she tried to close it in his face. But after a longish pause he heard Jo's voice calling something within, rather shrilly, and then the door opened, and without showing the least surprise or hesitation Jo walked straight out and closed the door behind her. She barely looked at him. She was wearing a black hat with a heavy lace veil that partially hid her eyes, a soft fur coat and high heels.

"Come on then," she said. "We can't stand about here all day." She set off fast down the drive, the heels clicking authoritatively on the neat bricks. She was carrying a small black suede clutch bag under one arm. On the pavement she slowed down enough for him to catch up, then shot off again, the coat swinging.

"So. Where've you been?"

She would not meet his eye, he saw. Well. Fair enough. He could hardly meet them himself these days.

He shrugged. "Nowhere really."

"Back at work?"

Her voice so sharp and bright; she sounded like someone else, someone pretending to be a duchess or something.

"Not really," he said at last.

"Daddy bailed you out, did he?"

"Yes," he said, as if there had been no bitterness in her tone.

There was another silence. They would come to the shops soon, he thought, the ones he'd passed already that afternoon, going the wrong way. Where were they going now, though? She doesn't want me in her house, he thought. Doesn't want there to be any chair in it that she can look at any time and think: he sat in that one. That Rob. There.

Jo's voice, a sudden furious cockney, broke in on these thoughts: "You could at least have come to her *fucking* funeral," she said. The energy with which she spoke these astonishing words so dazed and frightened him that he could not, for a moment, remember why it was that he had stayed away. His stomach turned over in an agony of regret.

Then he understood. "But . . ." he began, and stopped. He thought rapidly. He had no desire to land Andrew St. John Mortimer in it; but if he wanted Jo to talk to him he hadn't got much choice, had he?

"I was told you didn't want me to," he said huskily.

"Oh, was you," she said immediately, as if sneering, but he saw that she was at a loss. Yes: her stride slowed. She was thinking.

She sighed. "We cross here. Andy wrote to you. Didn't he."

"Yes."

I would like you to know that while my fiancée does not in the least hold you responsible for what happened, I think that she would nevertheless find your presence difficult to bear. I am sure you will understand how very painful it is for her to lose the very last remaining member of her family.

Like many other words these were written on Rob's heart by now, perhaps, he thought, for ever.

"In here. Come on."

It was a teashop, chintzy, with a steamy bow window full of fake dimpled glass and a smell of toast so warm and buttery that he was suddenly aware that he had eaten almost nothing all day, and that it must be past four in the afternoon, what with one thing and another.

"Good afternoon," said Jo to the waitress, very coolly, and in a completely different accent, the pretend-duchess again. "Tea for two, please. Hello, Joy," she added graciously, turning to the middle-aged woman pent up in the little wooden pay-kiosk near the door. "Busy today! Let's squeeze in here, shall we?" Now she was duchessing Rob; uncomfortably he sat down in one of the small booths, and she took her place opposite him, drawing off her gloves, luxuriously loosening the soft swathes of her furs, which fell back just far enough to reveal the black mourning band just above the elbow of her dark green jacket.

"Mink," she said, seeing his eyes. "You hungry?"

"I don't know. I think so."

"They do a nice toasted teacake here."

"All right then."

She put up both hands, and gently lifted the lacy veiling on her hat, folding it back over her bright hair. She looked at his face. He saw her lips part, and remembered how she had paled that last day when he had come to the flat, and she had realized that Iris was gone.

"You look terrible," she said, almost gently, as if in pity.

"Don't be sorry for me," he said.

She gave a slight shrug: "All right then. I won't. Oh, thank you," she added to the waitress, arriving with a tray. "And we'll have two toasted teacakes, please. I didn't tell him to write," she went on, dropping the duchess again when the waitress had gone. "Thinks he's looking after me, silly bleeder."

"You wouldn't have minded, then? If I'd come?"

"No," she said, with a sigh. "Not really. Not much."

He felt his eyes fill with tears, and willed them back.

"My dad," he began, but his voice quavered and he had to stop. After swallowing he went on: "My dad was at the inquest. You probably saw him."

Her eyes widened in horror. "It wasn't him that . . ."

"No, no," he said quickly. "He was there because he would normally have gone anyway, you see. He knows the coroner."

(Things not said between Dr. Wilding and his son: that it was sheer luck, Dr. Wilding had realized, that the poor lassie had been found just so, and not a few hundred yards further along the beach, and thus in his own patch. Or, called upon to perform the post mortem, he must either own up that the dead woman had been his son's mistress, or perforce open up that battered body to disclose the decaying frailty that would have been his own first grandchild. But the tides had been kind, Dr. Wilding had thought. Not said. Not sayable.)

"Kept you out of it anyway."

Rob looked down at the tablecloth.

"I'm going to the police," he had told his parents, his coat over his arm. "I'm going to tell them everything." And why, in that case, had he come downstairs, opened the drawing room door, and announced this to them in the first place? Hadn't he really been giving them every chance to talk him out if it?

His mother's little cry of horror; and his father's face! He had never seen his father look afraid before. His own resolve had crumpled on the instant, a feather in a flame. His father had spoken, with a strange unfamiliar gentle urgency, over the background of his mother's tears:

"Rob: they are policemen. They are not always very clever. They're not Sherlock Holmes. They're Lestrade. D'you see? If you go to them, in the sad state you're in, my poor boy, and tell them that you are responsible—they will listen. They will believe you. They will *agree* that you killed her. D'you see? Who is to tell them that you did not? There is a dead girl, carrying your child. You may say she hadn't told you about the baby, but why should they believe you? You'll have told them you had a row with her, finished with her. And she was found *here*: this is where we live. This is where you know the area, the whole coastline. This, they will say, is where you brought her. A pregnant girl, not of your own class, that you—I'm sorry, Rob, this is what they'll say—were tired of. Found dead. And they will charge you with murder. And you might hang. They might hang you, Robert. And your mother's heart would break and so would mine."

"They thought everyone would think I'd killed her," said Rob at last. He spoke with a certain irony. Their eyes met. She raised one elegant eyebrow.

"Fancy now," she said, and for a moment he could not understand her mild tone, until the battered silver salver appeared between them on the table. She lifted the lid, and there were the warm teacakes, golden-brown, oozing melting butter, sitting on a frilly doily in the dish.

"And even if they don't," Dr. Wilding had continued more briskly, after a pause, "even if they don't so much as charge you, Rob, what sort of effect do you think the case will have on you, for the rest of your life? On your career?" And then his voice had taken on all of its usual stridency. "D'you imagine the whiff of the unexplained death of a pregnant mistress is just going to disappear? Who would want to take you on, Rob? And in the eyes of some, don't forget, you are a rich man's child. You will be a rich man's child who got away with murder. For the rest of your life. And you will never know who is thinking it or saying it or making sure the rumors never quite go away. You've got to ask yourself, Rob, is it worth it? You can't bring her back, my poor lad. And . . . and perhaps you should ask yourself too whether she would have meant such things to happen to you; because" (suddenly very gently again, almost caressingly) "I don't think she did . . ."

"Go on," said Jo. "Take one."

He did as he was told, even took an experimental bite, but as he had expected, the thing had ceased to be edible the second he touched it. *The unexplained death of a pregnant mistress.* The words haunted him, he kept finding them running through his head like a fragment of catchy tune.

"Why'd you say all that stuff, at the inquest?" he said, laying the tea-cake down on the plate in front of him. She was pouring tea, having given the contents of the pot a good stir.

"Why'd you think? Use your loaf. I wanted an open verdict. I didn't want any silly cuss saying she'd taken the coward's way out or any of that other shite people talk when it's suicide. I didn't want any other silly cuss thinking for a second that I wouldn't have stood by her and helped her. I didn't want any silly cuss saying Andrew was ashamed of her, or that I was. We had it all worked out. And the funny thing is," her voice trembled a little, suddenly "he would have done it, too. He said so. If it's any comfort, Josie, he says, it's all true every word of it anyway, I'd have taken the baby on so help me God, he says."

She stirred her tea rather hard. Sighing he sugared his own, and tried a sip. A whole cupful; he wouldn't be able to manage it.

"And all that stuff about a sailor," she went on. "Well, I had to account for me not knowing him, the boyfriend. I had to make out she had all these secrets from me. But that was better than anyone thinking they knew her when they didn't. It was bad enough that gormless berk from the hospital shooting her mouth off—*was* it you in the cinema queue?"

Who is Sylvia, he had sung into her blushing giggling face, *what is she* . . .

"Yeah, course it was."

"I thought you were a goner there for a moment, to be honest. I thought, they'll look into this, and they'll find you out, matey. Not that it mattered to me one way or the other to be honest." Jo met his eyes, without heat. "But then no, she didn't really see the man properly, it was dark, she was running for a bus, and that was that; you were off, scot-free."

"Yeah."

"I can't understand how Iris managed to keep you two such a secret. I thought you were always hanging round the nurses' home."

"There's always medical students hanging round the nurses' home."

"And you all look the same, do you, like white mice?"

He nodded. "That's it. White mice."

"Well anyway. I said she'd taken my swimming costume, which was a lie because I didn't have one to take. And I told them how much she loved swimming and how she wasn't as good at it as she thought she was. And I said she was happy. Because whether Sailorboy turned up or not me and Andy were going to take care of her and the baby. See? Worked, didn't it, open verdict, that was really the best I could hope for."

"But why—why did she go—where she did? Jo? I thought it was because of me at first, of course I did. But it wasn't actually anywhere we'd ever been to, or talked about. She told me lots of stuff about Coogan's, you know the holiday camp—but she didn't go there. She was round the coast. They know from the tides where she, where she went in, and it wasn't near my parents' house, or Coogan's, so why did she go there, what was she doing?"

Jo cut her teacake into quarters, and arranged it into a star-shape on her plate. She drew a deep breath.

"I know what beach it was. Soon as they told me someone had been washed ashore there I knew it was her. We'd been there, her and me. That first summer after the war. My dad's brother had a win on the dogs. Give me some money to take Iris to the seaside. She ever talk about what happened to her during the war?"

"Not much," he said carefully.

Jo gave him a small smile. "She told you lots of lies, didn't she."

He nodded.

"Didn't steal, though."

He looked away. He couldn't go into all that again. There were inescapable facts:

311

"Oh, er, Meadows, the young lady who stayed here in May."

"Miss Iris, sir?"

"Yes: Iris. You, ah, didn't happen to give her anything, as some sort of keepsake, some little trifling ornament or something, did you, Meadows?"

"Me, sir? Why would I be doing a thing like that, sir?"

"Well, I don't know, obviously some sort of mistake, oh well, never mind, um, it's of no importance . . ."

Iris stole, or Meadows did. Try as he might he couldn't argue Iris out of that one. But almost certainly a one-off, though. Even her own sister knew she told lies, for heaven's sake, but no one had called her a thief. Except himself, of course.

"She just wanted things to be nicer than they were," said Jo now. "You know the Boy who cried Wolf? Well, Iris wasn't like that, was she? She wanted to make out things were nicer and more interesting than they were, that's all. She liked to cheer you up, or herself up, that's all. She didn't cry Wolf, she cried something else. Butterflies maybe. Something like that."

"So," he said, anxious to bring her back to the question he most wanted answered, "You don't think she wanted it to look as if I'd . . . well, as if I'd . . ."

"Murdered her? What, by doing it where she did?"

He nodded.

"No, I told you. We went there after the war. It wasn't anything to do with you. It was a coincidence, if you like, you being fairly nearby. And I didn't mind you thinking it was all on account of you. Felt like letting you stew in your own juice if you must know. I'd quite like it all to be your fault, you see."

Her voice quavered. She put up a trembling hand, pulled the veil down over her eyes, and sat in silence for a moment or two, clearly struggling to control herself.

"It *was* all my fault," he said.

She shook her head.

"No," she went on, after another pause. "I was too busy. I was too busy running after Andrew. I forgot what was most important, see? I'd got to thinking it was important that I got married, that that was the most important thing for me to do. But that was wrong. The most important thing for me to do was look after Iris. And I didn't. I didn't."

She rocked herself to and fro a little on her seat, tiny rocking motions.

He went to speak but she waved him into silence. "No, let me say it. That first summer after the war . . . did Iris tell you we got bombed? I was out. Nowhere special, just round a friend's house. And there was a raid, and it was a direct hit next door, and everyone was killed except Iris. Mum, and Dad, and our brother Mike, he was twelve. All dead. The dog, she was killed as well. Iris was the baby, she was only nine then. It was 1942. And she didn't speak afterwards. She was dumb. She tell you that?"

"No."

"No, well, she wouldn't. What did she say? She say Mum died before the war?"

"Yes: of a heart attack."

"In her sleep?"

He nodded.

"Well anyway," Jo went on, "she didn't speak. They thought there might be some injury somewhere at first, you know, that she'd been knocked deaf or silly or something. But she was all right that way. She could hear all right. She used to write things down. And she could read. I didn't know what I was doing, honest to God I didn't know what to do. I was only sixteen. I wanted my mum."

He took out his handkerchief and offered it to her. Clean and ironed and folded: Meadows's work.

"Thanks. Years this went on. She went back to school. She did all right. She just didn't talk. They said she was a Hysterical Mute. And then Uncle George had this win, and he give me the money, take Iris somewhere nice, he says, take her to the seaside somewhere quiet and peaceful, and I did. That's where we went. We stayed in this place, Uncle George knew the owner somehow, and it was posh! A nice pub, quiet, right next to the sea. With a sandy beach. We paddled. We played about in the sand. We didn't do much. I was bored to tears to be honest. She loved it though, I could tell. And toward the end of the week she turns to me and she says, "Can I have an ice cream, Josie?" Just like that.

As if nothing had happened! Not a squeak out of her for three years! Can I have an ice cream, Josie?"

"And after that . . ."

"She was OK. Talked like anyone else. Talked away nineteen to the dozen. Talked to me. Told me things." Jo's voice dropped to a whisper. Rob's heart knocked with distress. He glanced about, but no one seemed to be paying them any attention. He was aware occasionally of other people idling by, of chat and the comfortable rattle of china and cutlery. He sat hunched with his legs twisted together, as if constraining himself from getting up and running away.

"What things?" he asked, at last.

"Things," she said softly, and the hairs on the back of Rob's neck rose and prickled him with fear. "See. I think she forgot sometimes that her mum was my mum too." For an agonizing moment, she was overcome, her face squeezed shut with grief. Then she picked up her cup and managed a sip. He saw that he must ask again, though dread had seized him.

"Would it be better—I mean for you—if you were to tell me?"

"No. It'd just be worse for you."

"It can't be that."

"You don't know anything. Do you? And why should you, your age. Anyway it's not your fault. It's mine. I knew what she was like and I put off telling you. I didn't want to scare you off. I didn't want to spoil things for her. I should have told you earlier."

"Tell me what, for God's sake!"

"When the bomb hit," said Jo, not looking at him, her voice low, "the house collapsed. Everyone was killed straight away. I think. But it took a whole day to dig Iris out. She was under the kitchen table. Two legs held, I don't know why. She had just enough air. She could see Mum's hand but she couldn't move to reach her. She didn't know everyone was dead. Not at first. But it was hours, you see, all those hours going by, and no one spoke to her. No one answered. Mum didn't answer. A whole day."

She was rocking herself again, he saw.

"Go on," he said gently.

She touched her eyes with the handkerchief. "Well. Finally they get to dig Iris out. They'd heard her crying, you see. They'd been listening for her. And they start shifting things, see. A house. It's a lot of stuff. They moved things. Until they start to get close to Iris, and they move this great beam." Jo's voice sank; she was whispering now. "A roof-beam, it was, that'd come clean down, they shift one end of it and there's daylight, and as they pull the beam up, Mum moves, see? She moves. Sits right up. And Iris thinks she's alive. Just for a second, thinks she's alive. But it was the beam, see. It had crushed her face. It held her. So she sat up. And Iris saw. Mum alive, with no face. And she told me. And it was my mum. It was my mum too."

"Oh . . . oh God, Jo. Oh, God."

"Yeah. So. So now you know. She liked things to be nicer than they were. See? She didn't cry Wolf. The Wolf had already got her. Because she always thought she should've died too. She said that. Not often. Well, she did at first, when she first started talking again. And when she stopped I was still always afraid she was thinking it. I thought the nursing would help, I thought, well, she'll be doing awful things and seeing awful things, but none of them will be as bad as the things that have happened to her already, and she'll be helping people feel better, that will be good for her, that's what she likes. That's why I was all for it. Because still sometimes if things went wrong she'd start on about how she should've died too with everyone else. I'd say, What about me, Iris! And that's the other thing, isn't it; I was getting married. She must've thought I'd be all right now, you see. It was like: all this time I thought I was looking after her. Not very well, perhaps, but doing my best. And all the time perhaps she was just looking after me as well. Staying alive on account of me. Making the effort. And as soon I was getting married she was free. See? It might be: that she was always going to do it."

There was a pause.

"D'you really think that?"

Jo sighed. "Sometimes. And then I think, no, I'm just trying to make out there wasn't anything I could have done. Trying to make myself feel better."

It came to Rob that Jo had loved Iris, and also that this was something to which he had never before given a moment's thought. He had assumed it, of course, taken it for granted, in the manner of the

315

secure child; he had been taking love for granted all his life. He had felt it to be a sort of general rule, a more or less involuntary feature of being human, with parents, children, brothers, and sisters all qualifying for complete inclusion, and friends and pets and aunts and so on coming in for varying and lesser degrees of the same automatic simple bounty.

But now he understood for the first time how very particular love might be. Or, perhaps, always was. To generalize it was in a way to be-little it. Though at the same time, firm ground shifted queasily beneath his feet: if love was particular it followed that it could also be limited, on occasion; or conditional; or perverse.

She was gathering her furs together, getting ready to leave, he saw; there was nothing further to say.

"I wish . . ." he burst out, "I just wish it had all been different, I just wish I could go back."

"You weren't to know," she said, kindly. "I shoulda told you what she was like. I let you think she was normal, didn't I? And she wasn't. She couldn't be, not really. Look, I gotta be going, I gotta be going now. Or Andrew's mother will be worrying," she added, with a hard little laugh. "Making notes at any rate." She smiled across at him, suddenly look-ing like her old self again.

I have too much to think about, thought Rob, at the same time real-izing that he would almost certainly never see her again. Strange; one so seldom understood last meetings while they were happening, made so few final farewells.

Please don't go, he wanted to say. Please don't leave me. Not yet. But he could not bear to ask anything further of her.

She stood up, drawing on the fine black gloves; hastily he rose too. "Thank you so much for seeing me," he said, and put out his hand, not realizing, until she took it, how great a relief this would prove. "Goodbye, Jo."

She smiled. "The hell with it: one for my mother-in-law," she said, and she leant forward and gave his lips a quick kiss. "Good-bye, sweetie," she added, and then she was gone.

SYLVIA'S PLANS, SATURDAY, 1995

SYLVIA KNELT ASTRIDE the brass knight, on the cool smooth stone. He was a young man, with long flowing hair on either side of his boyish face, and hands folded piously over his chest. But he wore full armor, and spurs, and a great sheathed sword. The long end of his sword belt, Sylvia noticed, had been neatly folded back into itself, pliable leather clearly rendered in metal. Perhaps he had really worn it like that. Beneath his feet the beaked griffon flexed its eagle claws, and wagged its skimpy tail.

Hang on, thought Sylvia, in surprise. Why, it wasn't a griffon at all! It was a little dog! Where have I seen that dog before? Sylvia wondered, and as she sat back on her heels the knight beneath her turned himself a little, stretching out his long legs as if awakening from a deep sweet sleep, and then looked fully up at her, with living eyes in his glittering mask of brass.

Sylvia was not at all afraid. She was aware instead of an overwhelming feeling of having at last understood something: so that was it! At last, thought Sylvia, and full of joy and longing she lay down on the knight as his arms opened and reached up to enfold her. But before her lips could meet his she saw who he was, and woke up.

Christ, thought Sylvia feebly. For a moment she lay dazed, simply unable to work out where she was. She seemed to be lying face down fully dressed on the sofa in the front room; surely that couldn't be right? What time was it, what day was it? Every last fragment of the dream vanished as she sat up groggily and looked across the cluttered coffee table at the sofa's twin.

317

Will lay sleeping half-turned away from her, and tucked like a teddy bear beneath his arm against the back of the sofa, and also fast asleep, was Clio.

Nearly eight! And God, she felt rough. Sticky and rumpled and sick and desperate for a pee. Her head ached. No wonder, looking at the whisky bottle. Gingerly she rose. Was it safe to leave Clio with him like that? He must have been drunk too, though of course with his famous inability to like almost any alcohol whatever he had no doubt been less drunk than she.

I'll be quick, she told herself.

For a moment as she stood looking down at him she almost became aware of how exciting it was to have him with her, here, in her house, and for the whole day. But for various reasons this was too awkward a feeling to allow into full consciousness. Swiftly she stopped it bobbing any closer by pretending to meet it halfway: yes, she told herself austerely, she certainly was glad, to be able thus to help a friend in his hour of need. Very glad indeed, as anyone would be.

After that there was nothing for it except to stop staring down at him and start getting things done. Reviving in the shower, she reviewed possibilities. Janet would be here by ten, so that was Clio out of the way. If the weather held they could walk along the cliff to the Dolphin; they could even have lunch outside, perhaps, on one of those tables where the grass sloped down to the sand. And they could carry on toward the headland, if he was well enough, all the way over into St. Gabriel's, perhaps, where they could probably get a taxi home, or even a bus. She would take a rucksack, with coffee in the thermos and a snack, apples or something. And her flower book.

Unless of course he didn't want to do any of that. What he wanted to do most, she thought, was talk. Sometimes talk about what was of course never far from his mind. But mainly talk about anything else. Especially the past. And most especially the past they shared.

His condition gave both of them license, she thought, and she gave the shampoo bottle a hard squeeze.

"How old were you when he died, then?" he had asked. "So, how much of him do you remember?"

And she had found herself telling him what she had never told anyone else before, her one true (she was pretty sure) memory of her father, because there was remembering, and then there was remembering remembering, if that made any sense, except . . .

"Except one time; I suppose I must have been three, and he said to me, sounding all shocked, he said 'D'you know something? You haven't given me a cuddle all day!' And after that he just used to say, 'D'you know something,' and that was the signal for me to fling myself at him."

Crouching down to catch her, sweeping her up into his great arms.

"And a smell of a certain sort of tobacco, I think he used to roll his own, and there was one of my teachers at school when I was eleven, Chemistry, I remember him walking past me in the corridor and there was this fantastic powerful smell of my dad, I used to want to take hold of him, well, not him, his jacket, I just wanted to grab hold of his jacket and take great big sniff . . ."

School days were good. There were lots of laughs in school days.

"I know, I know, thank you, I know exactly what I looked like. It was the smallest size of skirt there was, they didn't come any smaller, not in the right color anyway, and Mum wasn't exactly expert with a needle—it sort of hung down in funny angles, didn't it?"

"Yeah, but you had your hair in these really tight plaits as well, and those enormous glasses, honestly, you looked like a cartoon version of a brainy little schoolgirl, you looked like something out of *The Beano*."

And how vivid it had all so suddenly become! For an instant she had been back on that long-ago train, ten long miles to the new and terrifying school, climbing into the train in her enormous blazer and cleanly new rucksack, and instantly aware of the big lone boy already in one corner, and of his studiedly averted eyes.

She had not expected the boy to see her, nor had she wished him to. Easy enough to carefully avert her own gaze in return. Though once or twice in that first term, when she had again happened to enter the carriage he was already sitting in, and inadvertently caught his eye, he had instantly winked at her, deadpan, not, of course, out of friendliness but merely to indicate that on a journey this tedious and repetitive he was prepared out of mingled kindness and boredom to bestow a little of his lordly attention even upon someone as entirely unworthy as herself.

"I was just being friendly!" Will had yelped, "for Pete's sake!"

Ah, but Sylvia had known exactly what he was up to.

"I mean I don't know what sort of primary school you went to but mine was pure *Lord of the Flies*." And she had told him about the great lumbering overgrown boy known to all, respectfully, as Buster, who happening upon Sylvia alone one day in a corner of the playground, had quickly picked her up in his arms, turned her completely upside down, given her a little playful shake, and let go.

The playground asphalt had been hard and gritty, and Sylvia's mother angry with her for breaking her spectacles, since Sylvia had merely reported falling over. For leaving aside the reprisals most certainly consequent on telling the truth she had suspected that Buster had not actually meant to drop her; that grabbing and inverting her had been his idea of a bit of boisterous friendly and possibly even admiring fun; he was the school fat boy, not the school bully. Nevertheless he had hurt her, and the sensation of powerlessness as she was swung through the air had been nightmarish.

"And that sort of thing happened to me all the time, you see. Being small and bespectacled, it was a sort of red rag to some people."

So she had pretended not to notice Will's overtures, limited as they were, and kept her eyes firmly on her book with no intention of letting her guard down. Other boys he knew got in at the next stop; if she returned even the slightest signal of friendliness he was sure to seize it and twist it and somehow use it against her with his friends. Boys were like that.

After several weeks, however, he had tried something else. As she sat already reading as the train pulled out of her station, he had come clumping up the carriage with his battered and much-doodled-on rucksack, and sighingly sat down again on the seat opposite.

"I was scared! You had such enormous feet! I knew you were up to something!"

She had seen those huge black school shoes beneath the lower edge of her book, and with pounding heart watched from behind it as he bent to his rucksack on the floor, wrenched it open, and pulled out a rolled-up magazine.

"*Sight and Sound*," Will had put in, grinning.

It had been impossible to carry on reading herself, so aware was she of his heavy breathing and fidgeting and crackly page-turning.

What was he reading anyway? She risked a glance to find out; and as she did so he had suddenly lowered the magazine to his lap and turned upon her a look of gentle inquiry, which had contrasted nicely with the fearsome blood-stained mouthful of plastic vampire teeth protruding from his lips.

"Made you laugh anyway," said Will. Laughing again.

And then unasked he had saved her library book. "Do you think we would ever have spoken, if it hadn't been for the train crash?" she had asked.

So then they had talked about that, too.

And he had said something new, that he had never mentioned before:

"All that space, Sylvie! You know, when me and Dad took you home. I could hardly believe it. All those fields and the woods, and the pond and the stream and piles of concrete and sand everywhere and all those dogs! And chickens, too, weren't there, and ducks? It made me feel really weird—I didn't understand why at first. But it was because I'd seen that not so long before that—well, it would have looked like paradise, absolute paradise, it was pure boys' playground, you know, full of potential camps and battlegrounds and earth-workings, and a concrete-mixer, for God's sake! And you could swim in the pond and dam the stream and there I was nearly fourteen, you see; so I could see all these possibilities and sort of dismiss them as babyish at the same time. It was like nostalgia, I think. My first taste of it."

Paradise indeed, Sylvia had snorted. And she had told him a few things: about the stickiness of clayey mud in winter, about helping to hose the runs down every morning before school, yeah, think about it! and about strange dogs in the house lurking inside cupboards snuffling or snarling as you passed, and having what her mother called accidents all over the kitchen floor, often runnily pizza-size on account of their nervous upsets, and about dogs sneaking up the stairs to pee on your bedside rug on purpose, about dog hairs all over your clothes all the time. Before you'd so much as got your new jumper out of its bag it would be covered in dog hairs, and there would be dog hairs in brindled tumbleweed formation rolling to and fro beneath the kitchen table and floating on the breeze and surfacing in your porridge; and finally about never, never, not until you'd actually left home for good, being able to sleep in because of the howling and screaming and yodeling . . ."

". . . yodeling?"

"And it was all right for Mum," she had shouted over his delighted laughter. "It was fine for her, because she was brought up in a shunting yard!" There was a second's startled pause while both of them grasped the clear implication that Mrs. Henshaw had not so much been running a business all these years as filling the void left by the roar and hoot of steam trains, and then for several minutes neither could breathe for laughing, Will had actually shed tears.

Well, it was so late, thought Sylvia now, grinning as she turned off the shower. And we were both pretty drunk.

And then of course they had gone out for the walk, two o'clock? No, nearer three. Surprising Clio into sudden entranced calm, trundling the pushchair over the cobbles in Silver Street and then all the way across Market Square and out again through the perfumed May darkness, without meeting another soul.

"That's my house," she had told him as they passed the cottage where, in another life, she had stood barefoot on the cool stone floor opening a bottle of wine. "That's my real house." And that had somehow lowered the mood. Or perhaps he had just remembered again.

"It's very grand, where you are."

None of it mine, she thought now, toweling her hair.

But she had thought then of what her life must look like from the outside, impressive useful work, good health, lovely baby, loving spouse, fine beautiful house beside the sea. How could Will not compare his own life to hers, and be given extra pain?

She had been pushing the buggy along Picton Street behind the Square, where the flagstones of the pavement made a rhythmic soothing *ker-dunk, ker-dunk* noise beneath the wheels. Clio, after a certain amount of good-humored shouting, had fallen silent again because Will had given her his key ring, which she was carefully examining and tasting bit by bit.

And Sylvia had begun to tremble inside, and her heart had knocked hard in her chest, because she was afraid she was going to (as she put it to herself at the time) *say something*, and she knew she must make the effort not to, because after all her secret was a shameful one and besides Will had more than enough on his plate already, didn't need anyone else's troubles, though of course you could argue that other people having troubles (especially herself) might sort of cheer him up in a way, and while she was still wrangling with herself along these lines her mouth opened and said all by itself:

"I don't love her, you know."

"What? Who?"

Heart hammering, she was silent, appalled. All the same she had made a tiny gesture, a shift of her head, toward the pushchair in front of her.

"What, you mean . . ."

Ker-dunk, ker-dunk, said the pavement cozily. *Ker-dunk, ker-dunk.*

"Not the way I should," she said. "I don't know why. I just don't."

"Could have fooled me," he said, after a pause. She could make no reply. There was such a burning pain inside her. It felt like fear.

"Didn't you—sorry Sylvie, I don't know much about these things—but didn't you have rather an awful time when she was born?"

She shrugged an assent; yes; so what?

"Well, you know Holly; it was one of the things she talked about. You know. She had all these books. And apparently," he said slowly, evidently feeling his way, Sylvia was touched by the effort he was clearly putting into sounding judicial, "apparently if you have a really awful time, and you don't get to hold the baby at the right time, and so on, your whole relationship with it can sort of get off on the wrong foot."

"Bonding," Sylvia supplied.

"Yeah, that's it. You have to bond. And you couldn't, could you?"

Sylvia made a small sound of impatience. "Oh, I know all about that stuff."

"Yes," he said quickly, surprising her, "I know you do. You know all that stuff. But that doesn't mean it doesn't still apply to you. Surely? Just because you understand the mechanism doesn't mean it won't all still work. I mean everyone knew all about you and That Bastard . . ."

"If you mean Rob . . ."

"I mean that bastard, yeah. That Bastard. I mean honestly, Sylvie. There you are, someone whose dad died when you were four, mad about someone—surprise surprise! old enough to be your father! It's the same thing: you think because you know about it and understand the theory behind it that it somehow doesn't apply to you any more, that you can see through it and discount it. But perhaps you can understand it all you like and it *still works*."

Ker-dunk, ker-dunk. At the corner, when she had turned the buggy onto the mere purr of tarmac, he said:

"You remember Ozzie, don't you? He was only two when I got together with Holly. And he was nice to look at but really he was so irritating, getting in the way all the time and taking up all her attention and always needing to be thought about first: irritating. And really slowly, took a year or so, I started to think that actually, he was pretty nice. And could be quite fun. And he started to treat me differently, he was all pleased to see me, wanted to sit on my lap, he wanted a story, that stuff, he wanted to play bears and there wasn't any dramatic moment or anything, I just slowly realized over months and years that I loved him, because he was lovable. No one could've helped it. And I've seen you with Clio. I've seen the way you talk to her and touch her: it *looks* as if you love her."

She had shaken her head, suddenly determined by then to tell him the worst. "Well if I have a bad day at work, and I get back late, and I'm really worn out, and Adam's away, because he often is, and there's always so much to do, you know, paperwork, I have to bring it home or I'll never get through it, and she doesn't want me, you see, Clio, she wants her nanny, and I can't comfort her, and I don't know what to do, and I get in such a state, and I—sometimes—I hit her. Smack her."

She had had to stop, outside the dark fish and chip shop on the next corner, to wipe her eyes. He had put an arm round her.

"Oh, Sylvie, come on."

"I'm so ashamed."

"Come on, everyone loses their rag occasionally. It can't be that bad. She looks OK. She looks absolutely fine. I've seen her in her bath, remember? I don't think the odd smack's going to do her any lasting damage. It's doing *you* the damage, isn't it? Don't you think you might be being a bit hard on yourself? It sounds as if you think you smack her because you don't love her, but you could just as easily smack her if you did; babies are hard work, they wear you out. And your job wears you out as well. Fact is anyone who's seen you with Clio can see you love her."

"It only looks as if I do."

"It will feel as if you do, to Clio."

"That won't be enough. She'll know when she gets older. She'll know somehow. She'll sense it. And besides . . ."

"Besides what?"

And she had told him about the kitten story, the terrible kitten story that had so haunted her, for months and months after Rob had told it to her, though of course he had told her about it as a medical triumph, a breakthrough, with no idea, obviously, how much it would upset her in itself nor how it would take up residence in her mind, insinuating itself into all sorts of other ideas.

"What kitten story?"

"Well. In the early sixties. There was this medical research. They took newborn kittens and sewed up their eyelids, one eyelid each kitten. So that when the time came for them to open their eyes, they could only open one."

Disgusted. "Oh, yuk."

"Yes. But the thing was—the thing that made the experiment a success—when they opened the eye they'd sewed up, later on, the kittens could still only see out of one eye. The eye that had been sewn up was stone blind. Permanently."

"So, why was that . . ."

"Showing, you see, that there is an optimum time when sight is developed. That these things don't work on a simple clock. The eye needs stimulus. It must receive light, images, to become a proper working eye. To make the right neural connections in the brain. If it doesn't get the right amount of light, the right amount of stimulus at the right time, it won't work. Ever."

"Ah, so you're saying that . . ."

"Yes! Suppose we are like that! Suppose we are all like the kittens' eyes, all over! Suppose we have to get the right amount of stimulus and light at the right time, and if we don't, the neural connections aren't made, and after that it's too late!"

"So you think that if you don't love Clio properly at the right time . . ."

"Yes! She won't recover, and she can't!"

"Oh, Sylvia!"

And they had walked along in silence, for a while, Sylvia trembling violently all over, trying to get the tug of the stitches in those tender little eyelids out of her mind. Of course it had been a great medical advance, a deeper understanding of the vast mysterious workings of the brain, and its two strange beautiful outposts, the eyes; evidence that such workings, once assumed to be so structured, so formally progressive and orderly, were in fact malleable as softened wax, plastic: for a while.

But in making this advance a human hand had turned the precious seeing jewels, the sapphires, the opals, the emeralds of living creatures, into sightless stone.

Will had shaken his head. "Bloody hell, Sylvie, you really like to make things difficult for yourself, don't you!" And then he had said, "This isn't science either."

"What?"

"This isn't science, not the way you're applying it. What happens to kittens' eyes has got nothing to do with you and Clio. You've just made a connection, and it's a crap one and it's making you miserable, so forget it, OK? Say: Clio doesn't need perfect love all the time, she just needs some, like, she doesn't really need a proper bath every day, just a quick wipe will do, sometimes. Sometimes a quick wipe is best. You can give her a quick wipe, can't you?"

She'd had to smile.

"Perhaps it's that you're sort of used to doing things really well. I mean, you've always been exceptional, haven't you; at school and so on. You've always been best. But for once you're just being ordinary at something, Sylvie, and it's hard for you to get used to, but ordinary is fine, it's enough; and anyway things might be completely different in six months' time. Or three months' time. God, or next week. Like me and Ozzie. Can't you just, well, not take it all quite so seriously? Just for a bit? Give yourself a break."

She had thought about that, as she turned the pushchair for home, since Clio had long since dropped off again. As they neared the Square again she spoke: "But I hit her. That is serious, isn't it?"

She had risked a glance at him, but in the darkness his face was unreadable.

"I don't know. You wouldn't want anyone to see you doing it, would you?"

"Is that how you judge things?"

"Well, sometimes. Why don't you just, you know, stop? Tell yourself you're never going to do it again no matter how maddening she is. Tell yourself you just don't have that weapon. Decommissioned. Put out of use. It's not a last resort, it's not something you can use as a threat, it's not the nuclear deterrent; it just doesn't exist at all. No matter what she does, you're just not going to do it. It's making you unhappy: so stop."

"It isn't that simple."

"Course it is. Who's in charge, after all? You, or a fourteen-month-old baby? Hey look: my keys."

And there they were in the middle of the pavement, where Clio had dropped them.

Tea, thought Sylvia now, looking zestfully into her wardrobe. Tea first. She pulled on her jeans and a neat shirt in her favorite blue and white, and ran downstairs, curiously light about the heart. Whatever happened, she thought, as she put the kettle on, whatever happened they were going to have the whole day together, and she was going to do everything in her power to make it absolutely perfect for him.

IRIS AND THE SAND DOG, SEPTEMBER 9, 1954

VERY LITTLE HAD CHANGED in eight years. Climbing down off the bus—and she was by then the only passenger, because after getting to the pub the bus had to turn round and go back the way it had come, having run out of road—she had sighed with pleasure: there was the pub, nearly at the very end of the low cliff, a shade less shabby-looking, perhaps, but with the same four stout tables set out on the seaward side, so that you could sit on the grass beside the sea, almost, at high tide.

There was the wall around the garden. And that window there, right under the eaves, that had been their room, where they had slept side by side on the two pretty matching wooden beds like a pair of princesses! The beds had had proper feather mattresses, that you had to give a great walloping to every morning, because if you didn't your bed felt like a stone, and if you did, and fluffed everything up as you should, you were taken into it as if into a feathery cloud, or a warm snowdrift, which billowed up and held you snug on either side.

Iris crossed the road, and hesitated at the foot of the slope of cobbles that led toward the pub's front door, which was standing invitingly open. When she and Jo had first arrived all those years ago, she remembered, she was still being very quiet. There had been a long time of being very quiet. Sometimes when doctors or teachers had asked her why she was quiet, and gone on and on at her until it was clear they weren't going to stop until she had at least tried, which was what they all said they wanted, Iris would write that it was best to be very quiet because if you spoke someone would hear you.

No one seemed to think much of this as an explanation but it was the best Iris could come up with. A voice was a signal. A voice would be heard. Attention would be drawn; so how then could you be safe?

She had thought such things, Iris remembered, but only in order to explain her dumbness to herself, rationalizing it, pretending to herself as well as to the doctors and teachers that somehow she had *decided* not to say anything. But really it hadn't felt like anything to do with her at all. It had felt natural not to speak. It had felt like obeying a natural law. It had felt reasonable.

Should she go in the pub and say Hello? The pub wasn't really so important. It was the beach that mattered. This beach, where she had been happy. It hadn't been exactly true, the happiness, of course. It had implied that all sorts of things were possible, when she could see now that they were not.

Still this was obviously the right place to come to.

She had forgotten how nice the pub had been. You could sleep and hear the sea all night long, and that was important.

As Rob had said.

It was important because it held off other sounds. It had held off other thoughts. It had been making just those same sounds since the world began. That was something to hold onto in the night.

And the pub landlady had Known, as presumably anyone who knew Uncle George would have Known, but she didn't say anything, she didn't try to get Iris to look at her or smile at her or anything. And Iris had been grateful. The landlady had talked to Jo about knitting patterns, quite cozily, and they had all sat listening to the radio sometimes, while she taught Jo to knit, and then she had taught Iris too, but without saying anything about That; just behaved in fact as if Iris was a normal girl, bit on the quiet side, perhaps, but perfectly normal, a girl anyone might teach to knit without comment. Jo's knitting had looked like a neat tight scarf quite quickly, Iris's had gone a very funny shape all curvy, but the landlady had just laughed and said the good thing about wool was that you could just unravel it and knit it up again into something different.

Peggy, remembered Iris, climbing the cobbles toward the front door, her name was Peggy; shall I go in? Will she remember me?

She wanted, she realized, to take another look inside the pub, where she and Jo had had bacon and egg every morning, and as much bread and butter as they wanted, because rationing was a bit different down there, Jo had explained. And then they had had whatever Peggy was having at night.

Suppose she went in and Peggy recognized her? She hadn't changed that much, not really, just got a lot taller. Of course Peggy might get in the way; she might delay things. Which meant more of feeling like this. Still it seemed wrong to just walk past, when Peggy had been so kind, just saying Hello Iris every morning and then not a word, not so much as a raised eyebrow, when Iris looked away; most people got shirty eventually. Teachers especially thought you were somehow doing it on purpose to annoy them. Mostly they ignored you, but if something else set them off, or they were in a bad mood about something, they would notice you sitting there not saying anything again and lay into you for a bit, being all sarcastic so all the other children would laugh, and go back to pulling your plaits again in playtime, or kicking your shins, to see if they could make you squeak. But of course they never could.

Iris reached the front door and looked inside. Immediately she could smell fresh paint. The wallpaper had gone, she saw, remembering posies faded to sepia with age. A fattish youngish man stood behind the bar, looking at a newspaper spread out on it. He gave her just a glance before he went back to it.

"We're closed," he said, and he protruded his lower lip, raised thumb and forefinger, wiped them lavishly around inside it, and turned a page.

Iris hesitated. She had never gone anywhere near a pub on her own before. Pubs were for men. You went to them with a man or not at all, unless of course you were a certain sort of girl and didn't mind people knowing it.

"Is Peggy here?" she risked, from the doorway.

The man spoke without looking up again.

"You're going back a long way, ent ya?"

Then he raised his head. "What d'you want her for, anyway?"

"Nothing," said Iris, "it doesn't matter." She went away, and the barman went back to his newspaper, and forgot all about her; for a while.

She felt much better on the beach. There were a few people about, sitting on the sand looking out to sea, or walking slowly along the shore line, because it was the first nice evening for ages, and the sea looked very clean and blue, and calm, with tiny little waves turning dreamily on the little pebbles at the very edge of the water. There were even one or two children with buckets and spades.

Iris took off her shoes, and, when she was far enough along the beach for privacy, slipped off her stockings as well, and stood for a moment digging her toes into the sand. It was tea time; soon the beach would be completely empty anyway, but if she just kept going round the headland she would soon be completely alone.

That was what she had been trying to do, she remembered, that time when she had been staying here with Jo. The beach near the pub had been a bit crowded. Not crowded by Margate or Southend standards, of course, but more crowded than it had been when they had first arrived. Better weather, probably. Anyway there were too many people there with their mothers and fathers. And dogs. They made Iris feel strange, empty and sad inside. She had left Jo dozing in a deck chair with her face hidden beneath a magazine called *Woman's Realm*, which she knew had a great deal of knitting in it, and gone for a walk all by herself to see if she could get away from all the families.

She had walked past the little boats lying sunbathing on the sand, and right round the curve of the cliffs until the crowds were out of sight. She had had no idea the beach went on so far. But then that was silly, wasn't it, if Britain was an island it had to have sea all round it. You could possibly walk all the way round it from top to bottom except it would take you years. Now the cliffs had big cracks in them sometimes. And caves. And ledges with seagulls sitting on them looking short-tempered.

Iris kept on walking, it seemed for miles, until there was absolutely no one in view in any direction. Then she walked down to the edge of the sea and walked along in it for a while. It was freezing. And then she had seen another lot of people after all.

Which was a bit upsetting for a moment, until she saw that the children were all three of them so big they were practically grown up, so their mother didn't count. They were having some sort of picnic, and the reason Iris had only just caught sight of them was that they were all crowded close together in front of a triangular cave in the cliff face, so big you could go right in. She had felt embarrassed, of course, having to walk past them while they were all sitting there, but there had been nothing else to do except turn round and walk back to all the mothers and fathers. So she tried to look as if she was actually going somewhere important, and strode along briskly as if someone was waiting for her impatiently at the other end of the beach, but as she drew fully abreast of the cave people she saw the dog, and had to stop.

It was a sand dog. It was curled right up tight, nose to feathery tail, fast asleep in the sand it was part of. Iris had never seen anything like it before in her life. She walked all round it, staring. Then she crouched down to take a closer look. The ears were right, too, you could tell how silky they would be to the touch. It was a little dog, small enough to take on your lap. It was Billie. It was Billie, her dog from home, Billie who slept curled up just like that on your bed if she could get away with it. From tip of tail to delicate little paws: Billie.

"Um, hello there." Iris had looked up and seen the mother from the cave people, a tall woman with her hair all done up in a scarf tied like a turban. She stood a few yards off, looking uncertain, and it came to Iris that this lady, or one of the children, had made this strange and lovely thing, quite as most people set themselves to make a sand castle. And why a castle, after all? Why not a little village, or a great big mermaid, or a dinosaur? You could do what you liked with sand, Iris thought. You didn't have to make a castle. And these people had known that and knelt down beside the water and made Billie, peacefully asleep on the sand.

"You . . . like our dog, little girl?"

Iris, of course, nodded. She could see all the children approaching now, two big boys and a girl as tall as Jo. But they were not at all frightening, with their smooth well-fed faces, there was even reassurance in their size, in their large-limbed complacency. They were posh, Iris concluded vaguely. And, she saw, they were wondering a bit whether she was going to hurt their dog.

She still had to touch it though. To reassure the mother and the big children who had made it she reached out her hand very slowly, to show

332

them she meant no harm, and gently laid it palm down on the dog's little head.

And it was sand, a marvelous game of a dog; and at the same time, it was a real warm living dog, it was Billie alive again under her hand.

But what would happen when the tide came in? How could they stand it? The water would lap and lick, and then nibble and gnaw, and finally melt away and destroy. It would be horrible to watch this dissolution. Perhaps Iris had glanced out to sea as this thought occurred to her, but at the time she had been startled by the big girl appearing to read her mind, for she had crouched down a little to speak to Iris, and she had said with a smile, "Yes: we always have to leave well before the tide comes in."

Always? So this was not a singular marvel? They knocked up something like this all the time?

"This is a particularly good one," said the lady.

Iris took her hand away. She felt very odd inside. She thought of the photograph album; not the special one with all the best photographs in, that had been bashed to bits along with everything else, but the other one, with odds and ends and extras in it, battered but intact and kept now in Jo's bedroom and full of images you could look at on special days: three of Mum and Dad at their wedding, and four or five pages of everybody since, all of them at Southend one time, except Mike had moved and made his head go blurry, one of Jo and Mike and herself all in their Sunday best, and one of a little girl Jo holding a bundle of baby, herself, on her lap, in a strange big chair with a potted palm beside it, and the really funny one of Jo herself as a baby, in a hat like a pie case, and cross-eyed, and so fat in the face that her lips seemed to be opening the wrong way like a beak on a baby bird.

But there had never been any photographs, of course, of Billie. Billie hadn't had any trips to the seaside. She had vanished as if she had never been. Sometimes Iris had seen other dogs that looked like her, but when you got up close, if you could, you could see that they weren't quite like her after all. This sand dog had been like having a special photograph of Billie to look at and touch. Or a visit to her, a visit to the past, when Billie had slept just like this on the rug in front of the fire, if there wasn't a lap to go to instead.

It was very strange. It was all so strange that when she had got up and nodded farewell and skipped away back to the other end of the beach where Jo was still asleep under her magazine she had wondered once or twice if she hadn't imagined it all or something like that.

That graceful lady and the three big harmless children, making a sand dog every day, that was all a bit strange, wasn't it? Unlikely? She would go back the next day, she thought, and see if they had made another dog and whether it would be another Billie or perhaps some other dog or even a cat. It occurred to her that while it had indeed been unlikely and strange it had also been very nice. It had been a nice surprise, a completely unpredictable pleasure. Suppose there were more of them to come? There might be all sorts of unforeseeable joys ahead. And you wouldn't ever guess what they were beforehand. You would just come across them and be pleased.

As she walked back through the mothers and fathers, not so many of them now because people were beginning to pack up for teatime, she saw the man in the little wooden kiosk outside the pub beginning to put things away for the night, taking his little stand of postcards in, and that reminded her of Southend again, where they had all had their picture taken, and then Dad had got everyone an ice cream, cornets for the children, and wafers for himself and Mum. Only grown-ups could manage a wafer.

Suddenly Iris had wanted an ice cream more than anything else in the world. She had run the rest of the way, in case the man shut the kiosk up before they could get there, she had run up to Jo and flung herself down on her knees in the sand beside the deck chair, and put her hand on Jo's arm, and without any thought whatever, without even needing to clear her throat, had simply spoken:

"Can I have an ice cream, Josie?"

So that had been two nice surprises in one day.

"I saw a dog like Billie," she had said also, later that evening, when Jo had finally calmed down a bit. "I saw a dog like Billie, and I stroked her, and so I was better." And Jo had been pleased. Jo had been fond of Billie too, of course.

The sun was just beginning to set as she reached the last curve of the beach and arrived at last beside the big triangular cave where the strange nice people had been. There was no one about at all. As she took off her clothes and folded them neatly Iris thought about the cave people and wondered what had happened to them, and what they would have thought if they had ever found out that seeing their game of a dog had let her speak. They would have been pleased. It would have been nice to let them know somehow. But when she had gone back the next day to the special place there was no sign of them, and Iris and Jo had had to go home the day after that.

Perhaps they had lived nearby, and so only came on the loveliest days. That would explain why they had known about the cave, too, and why they had been so good at sand dogs in the first place: all that practice.

She walked down to the water and felt it with her toes. Yes, it was pretty cold, it would hurt to get in. Luckily Iris knew how to get into cold water because Mike had told her long ago, at Margate. You jumped right in, and ran straight out again. Then you jumped in again, and ran straight out again. Then you went in again, and this time it wouldn't hurt. It would feel all tingly. You would feel as if your skin was the same as the water, and that was smashing. You couldn't stay in long, though, because you were right, you were getting to be the same temperature as the water and when the cold got all the way inside you, you would die.

She could just see him standing there grinning on the beach at Margate doing his best to frighten her: as if it was his duty. Strange he'd been so blond. But then Dad had been blond as a little boy, and with the same blue eyes. Mike hadn't lived long enough for his hair to darken, that was all. She thought of the little boy with the hurt eye, blond just like Mike: the one she had made feel better by cuddling him. She had talked to him about the seaside as well, the place where everyone was happy. She had even told him about the sand dog. He had liked it too.

Where had it been? She walked back toward the cave a few paces: yes, just about here, she thought, bending and pressing the sand with her fingertips. It felt silky but very cold to the touch: a little unfriendly even, strange nighttime sand. Still she heaped a little of it into a rounded pile,

335

then turned and went back to the edge of the water. The sun was very low now, just a thin orange crescent upon the horizon, sending out a long line of coppery brilliance upon the little waves of the surface, like a path that she could follow out to sea.

Right in quickly, and out again. It hurt, the first time. Like so many things, she thought. In again, and out, gasping. And then, shuddering, in again. And this time the cold sea burned her for an instant, and then cooled all around her, and became one with her, thrilling her all over with pleasure. She turned in it, making splashy movements with her arms, her eyes looking for the place where she had left the little heap of sand. She couldn't see it until she remembered to line it up with the mouth of the cave, and then suddenly she could. The sea would melt her away, she thought, as it had melted the sand dog; all her sorrows would cease and there would be nothing left where she had been but a smooth clean empty place, fresh as before she had lived.

For a moment more she stood on tiptoe on the bottom, her eyes on the place where the sand dog had been, her ears full of the sounds of the sea, and then she turned to the glowing path of light leading right out to the horizon, took a step toward it into the deep welcoming water, and let the current take her.

WILL AND SYLVIA VISIT THE VICAR'S HUT, SUNDAY, 1995

THOUGH IT HAD STARTED out fine enough, by the time they reached the cliff top the wind had gathered, and clouds were racing by. Presently the sun went in and the harder gusts of wind dashed rain in their faces.

But you could still look out to the horizon at all that empty space. You could still stand right at the wire and look down at the frantic crashing and foaming going on so far below, and at the rocks in their profligate variety, house-sized monster teeth, gravestone-flat slabs, stretches of tilted pavement you could see yourself teetering on, boulders as big as lorries and as small as half-bricks, all flung together at such satisfyingly stupendous random.

You could still take deep breaths of that special liberated air, and think as you always did about what it would feel like to be a bird and able launch yourself out into that invisible swing and pull and rush. You could let the clean salty wind stream into your face and pull at your hair and scour out your lungs.

"It's this way," shouted Sylvia into his ear. "Come on!"

For a moment he thought she wanted to turn back, but she was heading further into the wind, he saw. He followed her blue waterproof jacket along the cliff top, up a rise and down again. It was perfectly possible, he thought affectionately, that despite having lived here for years she would get them both lost; it occurred to him that he'd never met anyone like her for forgetting perfectly simple directions, or fretfully misreading maps: a real blind spot.

Presently though she stopped beside a noticeboard set into a heavy-weight iron box amongst the gorse bushes edging the fence.

"We can go in, shelter for a bit," Sylvia shouted; he looked, baffled, at the noticeboard, and read a polite request for upkeep money, from the National Trust.

"What?"

She beckoned, and they went on down a trim little path between the gorse bushes, edged with a low wooden fence. Presently they came to another sign, a big framed laminated thing with engravings reproduced on it, one of them a woodcut of what looked like an angel in breeches dangling in mid-air over a stormy sea.

It was raining too hard by then to stand about reading. He could feel dampness spreading quickly on his shoulders; Adam's waterproof not up to scratch, he thought, as he clambered carefully down a long zig-zagging stretch of neat National Trust gravel-stepped path. Where was Sylvie, anyway?

And then he was down, on a small flat apron of springy turf hanging right out, it seemed, over the crash and boom of the water.

"Will! Over here!"

For an instant, just as once he had gazed at Henshaw's Boarding Kennels and seen the boy's paradise lost, so now Will saw the cliff top Eagle's Nest of the Reverend Henry Foucault Hatchard, 1711–1799, antiquarian, naval historian, inventor and divine, and saw his own heart's most childish desire. A small wooden house right on the edge of the cliff! A hut almost in flight!

"Nice, isn't it!" said Sylvia happily, seeing his face. He ducked into the dark interior. "And it often gets a bit crowded at weekends so we're lucky in a way, having it all to ourselves."

Sitting on the wooden seat opposite, Will pulled the door to, and snibbed it shut, and sat down. It was almost dark, then, with just a star or two of light about the shutters. The wood beneath his fingers on the seat beside him was worn into smooth ridges. The sound of the waves outside was astonishingly muffled, perhaps by the banks of gorse on either hand. The hut smelt strongly, sweetly, of gorse flowers.

Sylvia was talking about the Reverend Hatchard, and how local legend had it that he had made himself a pair of painted wings and flown to and fro along the beach like a giant butterfly; that recent examination of his papers stored unregarded for generations in the vaults of the British Museum seemed to imply that long before any human understanding of the aeronautical power of thermals he had indeed designed something that looked intriguingly like a modern hang glider; though whether he had got as far as actually building a prototype was open to question, and his claims of actually taking a finished model out for a successful test flight were somewhat undermined by further notes, scattered throughout his writings, to the effect that he had conversed quite frequently with mermaids, and had sometimes been tempted to frolic with them in the shallows.

"You could sleep out here," said Will, still in small-boy mode. Be out here in a storm, fantastic! "It's completely dry!"

"If you didn't mind sleeping sitting up," said Sylvia. "Want some coffee?"

She opened the door, wedging it slightly ajar with the rock left there for the purpose, and took the thermos out of her rucksack. "You don't take sugar, do you?"

Perhaps looking at the sea was a bit like holding a baby, he thought; strength seemed to flow into you, though nothing was taken, or lessened. Or perhaps it was just being in this strange lovely unforeseeable place. But for the moment he knew himself to be piercingly happy, alive all over, soaring as if in reckless flight upon the wild sea wind outside.

He took the cup she held out to him. "Thanks. Thanks for this, too, all of it. I'm really glad I came."

"Good," said Sylvia, and smiled. It was a neat professional smile; she was aware of it on her face like clever makeup disguising a scar.

It had occurred to her that she had been getting him wrong for years, carelessly casting him as a bit part in her life. He had played the romantically raffish friend, counterpoint to her own orderly progressive career, and she had looked down on him, tutted over his professional doldrums, his lapses of judgment, his misuse of various illegal thises and thats, with

339

affection, because she had known him so long, and because he was charming as well as careless, an irresponsible lightweight.

But she had told him her secret; and he had listened. He had said useful things. He had given her sympathetic tentative advice, based on experience of his own: the most useful kind. He had talked about love without sounding self-conscious. And now he was looking at the sea with delight, from Death Row.

"Why did he build it, anyway? Get away from Mrs. Hatchard? I mean, is this a *shed*?"

"I don't know whether there was a Mrs. Hatchard. Not with all those mermaids about."

And, was it only yesterday? Yesterday, when he had opened the door of his poor mother's house, and embraced her, needing friendly comfort, she, Sylvia, vile perversity that she was, had flared all over with sexual feeling as instant as an electric shock. She hadn't willed it or expected it or enjoyed it much—it had felt more like suddenly feeling sick than anything else, really—and she had readily been able to ignore it. She had simply told herself that it hadn't happened, and believed herself straight away.

But she kept noticing things all the same. Ever since. She noticed the way his shirt fell, the clean male lines of it. She noticed the length of his legs and the angle of his hips. She kept on wanting to look at his mouth, because somehow she kept forgetting exactly how it curved, and needing to know again.

And as she had passed him the thermos cup his hand had brushed hers, the merest brush of his fingers on hers, and her whole body had once again leapt to sexual attention, so strong, so localized! How was it that she, an intelligent woman in her thirties, with a baby, could still be surprised by desire? The merest touch, and there it was again, hectically thumping away between your legs and radiating all over you, making you tremble, making even your lungs quake as you drew breath!

Could something so violent be completely hidden? She sipped her coffee, sitting very straight on the wooden seat.

Will pushed the window open. The wind had dropped; the rain was pelting down now, in heavy straight lines. Something about a mermaid, he thought gropingly, *Once I sat upon a promontory*, he remembered sud-denly, *and heard a mermaid on a dolphin's back uttering such dulcet and harmonious breath that the rude sea grew civil at her song, and certain stars shot madly from their spheres, to hear the sea-maid's music.*

"Are you all right, Will?"

He smiled at her. "In rep in Birmingham there, for a second. The Dream. Pitstop Theatre 1984. Bored school kids eating crisps."

"I remember that one! You were, whatshisname."

"Lysander."

"You did that thing with champagne at the end, you poured it over glasses all set up in a pyramid."

"That was all anybody ever could remember."

"No, it was lovely, it was set in the Twenties, wasn't it? You had a striped blazer on, and a boater. It was lovely. I came backstage."

She had gone backstage, she remembered, with Rob. It had been one of those times when he had said he had left his wife for good. She had been ablaze with happiness and triumph, she had seen herself in the mirrors of that crowded and communal dressing room, slender and brilliant-eyed in a white dress; there was Will laughing with pleasure at the sight of her, he had flung his arms round her and she had felt then, oh, of course, she had felt then too that instant arousal, but she had put that down to successful love, imagining that because she loved Rob, and was loved by him, that it was as if she was seeing or feeling everyone else, the whole world, through special sex-tinted glasses.

". . . with That Bastard," said Will.

Sylvia sat back. She asked lightly: "Do you have to call him that?"

Will appeared to consider. "Yep," he said after a pause. "Afraid so."

"Listen to that rain! Why? Why d'you have to?"

"I suppose . . . well, the older you get, the more you can see round things. You don't see round a love affair when you're young, do you? You're just in it, like in a sea, overwhelmed. But he'd have known right from the start, not a sea: just a lake. He would have seen all round it."

"He wasn't that calculating. He was unhappy."

"He messed you around for years."

"I wanted him to."

341

"Did you?"

"No, I suppose not." There was a pause.

"He an old-aged pensioner these days?"

"Retired early. Actually. He had arthritis. In his hands." She remembered him talking longingly of a place in Scotland where his father and grandparents had lived; he was always trying to make time to get up there. Was he walking the hills there now?

I don't really care what he's doing, thought Sylvia clearly to herself: I'm busy.

The rain was letting up, she saw. Perhaps it was time to go.

"Will?"

"*1852*! That the oldest?"

"No; there's one here, look, really small. Oh, the best one, actually, I meant to show you, look."

"Where?"

"In the ceiling. Oh, we need a bit more light, don't we, hang on." Sylvia opened one of the zipped pockets of the rucksack, and pulled out her keys.

Of course, he thought, with a little rush of affection. Of *course* Sylvia would have a tiny brilliant working torch on her key ring.

"There," said Sylvia, and she leant back with one hand on the seat behind her, the other holding the torch high above her head against the ceiling. "See it?"

He looked. *S.W. 1848*, he read again, in the harsh bluish light, and the smaller *T Mc C 1872*, and faintly *R.W. 1941*, and then, right at the top, he could make out another little carving, squat Gothic letters, two very complicated *H*'s interlocked, and *1790*.

"I think it's him, you see," she said, "H. H., Henry Hatchard, the Flying Vicar himself!"

She turned, and saw him looking at her.

"What?"

"You're wearing the same shirt. Well, you were wearing a shirt a lot like when we went on that bike ride."

She lowered her arm. "Was I?" What on earth did he mean, saying that? Why could he remember, anyway? Her heart gave a great thump inside her, and trying to ignore it she turned the torch onto the much-carved wall beside her. "Look," she said, "that's my other favorite. There's only one like that."

He leaned across. It was a heart, carefully gouged, with an R. and an I. inscribed within it, and a feathered arrow dissecting the whole. There was no date, but it had clearly been there a very long time.

"See it?"

"Yes."

She had looked so lovely, he thought, so strikingly lovely with the little light held above her; the same eager uplifted grace: the beautiful slender lamp lady, in a blue and white check shirt.

"Sylvia," he said. He laid the palm of one hand against her cheek. She was familiar, and she was mysterious; she was brave and clever, and capable of astonishing wrong-headedness, no, she was *crackers*. And she wasn't eight times nicer than he was after all, he thought: probably not much more than three or four times, really.

"What?" she whispered, at his half laugh, "what?"

"You're so lovely, Sylvia," he said, and kissed her.

It was the single most thrilling moment of Sylvia's life. Dazed consciousness even slipped a little, and showed her the glittering knight she had dreamt of, who had enfolded her in his brazen arms. At last, at last! She heard the sea crashing on the rocks, and the rain hammering onto the roof just above her head. She put one hand on the back of Will's neck, and felt the silkiness of his hair there.

A thought jumped into Will's mind so vividly that without thinking about it he drew back a little and said it aloud: "Sylvie, listen, all that stuff about Clio—last night . . ."

"What?" Terrified.

"No, don't worry, I just thought; you said you didn't love your baby, even though you behave all the time as if you do; but do you know, you haven't once mentioned, you know, Adam, not once! And Clio's his baby! And you haven't mentioned him, not a reference, not a memory, not one He always says this, or He won't eat that, you don't complain about him, you don't laugh about him, you just don't mention him at all—I just thought, if there's a real problem anywhere, I can't help thinking it's nothing to do with your baby, your *baby's* all right. It isn't your baby you don't love. It's your husband."

He said all this eagerly, with an unformed notion of simply helping her out; it was only when he'd come to the end of it that he realized quite how it sounded. She looked appalled. He began at once to backtrack.

"Oh, God, sorry, I don't know what I'm talking about, I had no business saying that, God . . ."

"It's OK," she said.

"Sorry."

"No. You are wrong, though."

"Of course, of course I am."

"No: I meant, you're wrong about Adam, well, you're absolutely right I don't love him. But we're not married, he's not my husband." Her voice quavered. "He's someone else's."

"Oh, Sylvie, don't cry."

"And I don't love him. I don't. I love you."

"I love you, too."

For a long intensely happy moment they embrace.

A certain small cool part of his mind is keeping out of this; it forms thought just below awareness. It requires him to ask himself: What am I getting into here?

It reminds him too that on the whole anything complex he gets himself into right now is of no import, since between his joyous galloping heart and his good old cock so suddenly, so exuberantly back in business, lies another far more secretive organ that may well soon put an end to all complications at once.

He is free, in a way, to do absolutely anything he chooses. Even more than free: obliged.

He caresses her hair with his cheek. "Shall we go home?" he asks her.

GEORGE AND ROSIE AND WILL
AND SYLVIA, SEPTEMBER 1996

HE RECOGNIZED THE MAN immediately, realized that he didn't just know the face, but that he had at some time drawn it. But where, and when? Then the door opened and some more people came crowding in out of the sudden rain and stood just in just the wrong place; George had to lean right back to get another glimpse.

No; it wasn't going to come. George reached into the pocket of his jacket, took out his diary-sketchbook, and stealthily opened it at the next empty page. Pencil in the other pocket. Stay still, please. Just like that, looking anxiously toward the bar as if afraid whoever was getting the drinks in wasn't going to come back at all.

Quickly, just one line, he caught the profile, the long delicate line of the jaw, the unusual slant of the eyebrow; nicely cut mouth like a girl's, hair just a little high on the forehead. A line too of shoulder, the shirt open at the neck, one arm across the top of the pushchair parked beside him. Dark smudges beneath the eyes. Good.

He looked up to see Rosie wildly signaling excitement at him from her place at the crowded bar. Look, she seemed to be saying, look who it is! shaking both hands at the small slight woman waiting beside her, who turned just as he looked at her, and cautiously smiled at him.

He knew her instantly, of course, with a tremendous jump at his heart. But for a second he simply couldn't place her, a small pretty woman in jeans and trainers, lilac top showing off her neat little curves, and then he understood that of course it was her, Miss Henshaw, Miss Henshaw in mufti, Miss Henshaw pretending to be a normal human being, and jumped to his feet, crossing the bar in two strides.

"Hello, hello, how are you!" He took the hand she held out in both of his own.

"Mr. Starling, hello, you look well," she said.

"George, please," he said. "It's really good to see you!" He felt like crying, he thought, at the sight of her. To think he'd been sure it wouldn't make that much difference! "Will you come and join us, please?"

Rosie was beside her, holding their drinks. "Go on, do, we've got a lovely big table, and it's just the two of us."

Miss Henshaw hesitated, looking past him, and he turned, and saw that she was looking at the mystery man, the one he'd drawn somewhere before.

"Oh, and you've brought Clio!" said Rosie, looking at the pushchair, and he remembered the story, hospital gossip of the sort she'd often passed on to him, only he'd actually listened to this one because it was about his darling Miss Henshaw, about her partner leaving her to go back to his wife; while she'd had someone else on the go all the time anyway, apparently. So was Mr. Mystery this new one, then? Where had he seen that bloke before?

"Well, if you're sure you don't mind. Just a minute, then."

There was nothing for it anyway, Sylvia thought, hoping her smile looked genuine. She had planned of course on sitting outside in the pub garden, on the low cliff top so close to the sea, since poor Will was having one of his bad days. In any case they couldn't stay where they were, so uncomfortably close to the door, with the pushchair in everyone's way; but would Will, presently so difficult, alternately doleful and apologetic, be able to cope with a little socializing?

On the other hand, it would be quite something, for him to meet George Starling. She could quickly tell him under her breath while they were gathering everything up to change tables: Will, it's Rosie's boyfriend, you remember Rosie, the theatre nurse, she's been going out with this man a year or so, told him I could help him, so he was a patient of mine, and guess what, he's the one! The one whose notes I was

346

reading that time, the notes with Rob in them from years ago, so I was upset, and thought of you, and rang you: that night. Remember?

He looked dreadful, she thought, with a little shiver of anxiety. It had been such a hard year for him. Best not to remind him of that particular night after all, perhaps. Best just to mention nice Rosie, and the better table.

"What d'you think? We could just go home, if you'd rather."

"Ooh good, look, they're coming!" Rosie hissed. "Hello, how are you, oh isn't she getting to be a big girl, look at her fast asleep in all this racket, oh and who's this, hello, hello Judy, hello, good dog."

"George," said George, holding out his hand.

"Will. Hello, Rosie."

Rosie looking into Will's face, putting two and two together.

"Oh, I'd forgotten—I mean Sylvia did tell me, but I've sort of only just realized—you were Toby ffrench, weren't you! With the two little f's!"

Will smiled, nodded. She was just the right age, he thought, as he sat down.

"I was so in love with you when I was twelve! *Earth's Army*," she went on, turning to George. "D'you remember it? On television."

"After my time, love."

"But—can I tell them, Will? There's going to be a new film, you know, a Hollywood version," said Sylvia.

"Oh wow!" said Rosie, "does that mean they'll put the real one out on video?"

"Well, probably," said Will. "Which is very good, of course . . ." Which had made him feel quite dizzy with violent emotions, when he'd first heard. But that had been before the next bit . . .

"But the main thing is, the new film, Will's going to be in it!" cried Sylvia, and he smiled across the table at her while this George, and Rosie—he could remember Sylvie mentioning her now, hadn't she been the one always getting off with unsuitable men? while anyway this Rosie and her George made all the right sort of congratulatory noises, and inside he wondered again how he was going to manage what could turn out to be three months away from home, from Sylvia, from Clio, from everything that at the moment seemed to be just about holding him together.

At first of course he'd hardly been able to believe his luck. The Hollywood version firming up just at the right time. A nice big part in *Casualty*, also just at the right time, just at the perfect time, in fact, on screen when just the right ex-pat British producer happened to be back in England, in a hotel, and in the mood for channel-hopping. Spotted, and nostalgically remembered.

He was wanted in order to add some sort of reference, it seemed, to the old television version. He was to add a certain gravitas. Not as Toby ffrench himself, of course, someone else would be Toby, which was peculiar after all these years, but he was going to be some sort of elder intergalactic statesman, someone whom British audiences would of course immediately recognize. Half-recognize anyway.

"It's your face, frankly, darling," his agent had said. "Right through the mill and out the other side. Beautiful, if a bit on the spectral side, if you don't mind me saying so."

As if I'd mind anything you said at all, Will had thought at the time, feeling as he did that he might at any moment pass out on the carpet with joy. But that had been before he had realized exactly what the film would mean in practical terms.

"D'you mind me asking where you're from?" This from George. Will looked cautiously at him. He was a big heavy man, about fifty, with a broad ruddy Slavonic face and hair drawn into a ponytail, rather crammed into the small pub chair, but clearly at his ease. He wore an earring. His mouth was wide and his teeth were uneven. He looked jolly and piratical, Will thought. What did he mean, where am I from?

"I seen you before somewhere. You from Kent?"

Will nodded, and named the village.

"Ah," said the pirate. "Now I know. Small world: my old mum lives next to your mum. Ruby Starling, at number 52. You . . . were you looking after your mother, she was ill, right?"

"Are you serious?" asked Rose, but George just looked at Will with a little lift of his face, clearly, delicately, asking him, further, how his mother was now.

"Yes; she died."

"Sorry to hear that."

"Thank you," said Will, picking up his beer. He remembered her now, her enormous old nostrils flaring at him, though he'd never managed to come up with *Ruby*, shriveled old Ruby talking refainement and antique Cockney over the fence, "And arz yer mum today? Iss lovely, what you're doin'," with her little old milky eyes filling with tears.

"How is she these days?" he asked politely.

"Oh her," said George fondly, "still going strong. Apart from stairs. That's why she had to move, not that she went very far. Tough as old boots otherwise. But sorry, I hope you don't mind, I was visiting, I saw you over the fence one time, here, I think it's this one." He had taken a small leather-bound book out of his jacket pocket. "See, these usually last me about a year or so, I think it's—yeah. Here it is." He flattened the book open, and passed it to Will. "There."

It was a small pencil sketch of himself, Will saw, sitting forlornly on the bench in his mother's garden, smoking a cigarette and looking very sorry for himself. The picture looked terribly real to him, made his heart beat faster. There was his mother's pond, where he'd sat moodily pulling carpets of algae out of the tepid water, there was the plum tree, a scribbly bit of shade.

That was a very bad time for me, he thought. That was the very bad time. This is the very good time. One day soon surely I will be able to feel that, not just keep having to tell myself about it?

He swallowed. "It's very good," he managed, and passed the book to Sylvia. Would she understand?

Yes. Of course she had, flashing him a glance of comprehension. "Oh, Rosie told me you were an artist," she said, as she looked at the drawing, "but I somehow thought—well, I didn't think of actual pictures. This is tremendously good."

"Well I'm mainly the pickled sheep," said George cheerfully, "this is just my hobby." He grinned, and Sylvia exchanged a tiny glance with Rosie. Sylvia's glance to Rosie meant: You've done all right with this one.

Rosie's glance to Sylvia said, You too.

Aloud Rosie said: "But isn't it an amazing coincidence, though! Next door like that!"

There was a general murmur of agreement, and then Sylvia said, "Though whenever I come across a coincidence like this I think, yes, but what about all the coincidences we never actually, you know, see? Perhaps they're happening all the time. And we just see the tip of the iceberg, and say, Oh how amazing! And miss all the others."

There was a little pause while all of them considered this rather unsettling possibility. Sylvia ended it:

"So, do you do actual portraits for a living?"

"That's right. Ten years or so now. Oils mostly."

"And you don't find your . . . sorry, perhaps I shouldn't get professional, but aren't you bothered at all by the lack of stereoscopic vision?"

"What?" said Will, and George shook his head.

"She's my doctor, your Miss Henshaw," he said to Will. "She made me beautiful." He laughed. "Honestly, I hadn't realized how much difference it would make."

"How much difference what would make?" said Will.

"You see?" said George to Sylvia. To Will he said, "Look at me, look at my eyes. Notice anything? Go on."

Will glanced at Sylvia, but her face said, Yes, go on. "What am I looking for?" George's eyes were a faded gray-blue, slightly protuberant, slightly bloodshot, wholly merry. There seemed absolutely nothing unusual about them at all.

"Nothing?" George moved his eyes to left and right, up and down, and then round and round in circles, so that Rosie giggled.

Will shook his head, faintly embarrassed.

"There you go," said George to Sylvia. "It's official; you're a genius."

Sylvia laughed. "Standard technique," she said, but she still looked pleased.

"What are we talking about?" Will was beginning to feel left out.

"My right eye," said George, turning, and giving Will a wink with it. "It's a fake."

"What?"

350

"Plastic."

Are you sure? Will managed not to say.

"Lost the real one when I was a kid; one of those stupid accidents, you know, it was wash day, see? And my poor old mum, never forgave herself, she'd dropped one of my dad's shirts on the kitchen floor, and I run in from the other room to show her my picture, it was a picture of her, my first ever portrait, I reckon, and I slip on the shirt on the lino and fall. Still had the pencil in my other hand."

"Oh, no . . ."

"Yeah, she'd just sharpened it for me."

"Oh, God!"

"One of those accidents," said George, lightly enough. It was such a long time ago. He can close a door upon all of it, without even trying. He suspects, when he thinks about it, that his life wouldn't have been that different if he'd had two good eyes; he would have been a depressive anyway, he thinks, but without the possibly useful focus. "One of those things," he said.

"But," cried Rosie, "I could see straight away when we first met he could get a better job done on it. Not that he believed me, did you?"

"Oh, I've had all sorts over the years, got fed up with the whole thing, just been wearing an eye patch for donkey's years, used to quite like it. Looked a bit Pirate Lego, mind."

"But—it moves, it looks exactly like a real eye," said Will.

He couldn't actually *see* with it, could he?

"It's a thin acrylic shell, painted," said Sylvia, "it sits on an implant that's wrapped in donated scleral tissue—a sort of special inner skin—and attached to all the main muscles that would have moved the real eye. The really clever bit is the implant. We used to use plastic, various kinds. But George's implant is made of something called hydroxyapatite. Oh, and you'll like this, Will, everyone does. Guess what hydroxyapatite starts out as? I mean, it's a naturally occurring substance."

Will looked round the table, George, Rosie, Sylvia, all looking at him intently, benevolently, all clearly in on this secret. He shook his head.

"It's coral," said George.

351

"It's a marine coral."

"With a micro-architecture almost identical to human bone."

"It's biocompatible—it's invisible to the human immune system."

"So George by now will have grown blood vessels and nerves actually into the implant. It's porous. The body accepts it as human, and vascularizes it. Well, makes it really human, in fact. It's brilliant, isn't it!"

Will was silent, turning something over in his mind. Coral becomes human? Who had said that wherever he went the artists had been there earlier, was it Freud? *Full fathom five your father lies / of his bones are coral made.* Ah, which way round had it been, though, had Shakespeare seen a precious exotic little chunk of this coral brought back from the other side of the world, and noticed how much like bone it looked? And who had first thought to check the likeness out at a cellular level, and what had that person expected to find?

It rather made up for the sewn-up kittens, he thought.

"So, this coral, and our bones, it's just a sort of coincidence, is it?" he said at last.

"One somebody noticed," said George.

"Yes," said Sylvia. She could remember him from his notes now: quite a few problems, once; but that had been a good while back. He seems perfectly all right now, she thinks. Recovered.

He raises his glass to her.

Many years have passed, much water flowed beneath bridges, many tears have been shed and dried away, since the unlikely accident that took the child George's living eye. Anyone reading that thick file of hospital notes might catch between the crackling brittle pages a faint whiff of the outpatient psychiatric hospital, of various legal and illegal drugs attempted, of relationships stymied, of courses abandoned and jobs lost and talent stifled, of unhappy marriage; an echo perhaps of much talking in semicircles with other sad types, of lying on couches addressing one paid to listen, of yoga, of transcendental meditation, of camping sternly alone in secluded woodland, of much cheap travel, of many paperbacks read and exchanged, of new prospects tentatively explored, of new paths followed, of truths uncovered, lines drawn, circles completed.

Quite a few mentions of Ruby, his mother, in those assorted aging papers.

By now Ruby, two decades widowed, has forgotten how completely she used to love her only child, and that this changed. For her George has shrunk to fit the love she bears him.

It seems to her that all maternal love degrades naturally, as the perfect baby becomes the imperfect adult; that such natural fading, from adoration to a gentle mutual fondness, is normal. It's certainly how all her three half-sisters (racketiness long subdued these days to various predilections for bingo, car boot sales, and line dancing) seem to feel about their own adult children. Perhaps she left the adoration off a little early; perhaps she didn't. It's all such a long time ago.

George raises his glass to Sylvia. "You know I almost didn't go through with it. But every time I look in a mirror and see it again, well, thank you."

His voice breaks slightly, and Rosie's eyes fill with tears. He smiles back at her.

It's all down to her, in a way. Anything Rosie thinks is a good idea is all right with him. Even trying for a baby, since it's so important to her. It's a bit daunting, trying to imagine going through all that again; he remembers early days as pretty hellish; but that, of course, was then, when he was younger and took things so hard. But he's pretty friendly with his own two now. What would they think of him giving them a little brother or sister? He ought to sound them out, perhaps, give them a bit of warning at least.

But if Rosie's so keen he's ready to try. He is still, sometimes, taken aback by the strength of his feelings for her. A *coup de foudre*, at his age! But it was true; he'd taken one look at her—she was in her blue nurse's dress and standing outside the hospital, shaking a collecting tin for something or other—and fallen desperately in love. Unbelievable, that such a lovely young woman should give an old wreck like him so much as a second glance! But he'd had such an overwhelming feeling of recognition with that first glance at her; as he fumbled for the coins in his pocket he had trembled all over, he could hardly trust himself to say a word to her. He felt straight away as if he'd been waiting for her, longing for her, all his life. Almost as if they'd met before, as if he was remembering her from some past life, not that he believed in that sort of thing.

It did not occur to him, how could it? that the sensation of recalling a long-lost passion might simply be real. There's no path back that far; he has no conscious memory of Iris at all, and it will remain a pleasant mystery to him that there was something about Rosie, her gentle face, her dark hair, the little mole just to the right of her mouth, that had instantly seemed to be his heart's oldest and deepest desire.

How he loves to draw that entirely special face!

Will is looking down at Judy lying as flat as she can beneath the table. So this is how Sylvia's patients see her, he thinks. This is what her work means, and the sort of thing she does every day. While he is all in a flutter about a bit-part in feeble Hollywood dross. He's a drone, he points out to himself. He's a waste of space. He should be down there with Judy, he's not good enough to sit at the same table with Sylvia. Let alone sneak into her bed at night.

"Will. OK?"

Sylvia's eyes say firmly: "Don't. Stop that right now."

Her hand on his arm says again:

Survivor's guilt, Will. You've had a terrible scare, you've had a death sentence. And it's well-known that a death sentence suddenly removed is somehow terribly hard to bear. You've looked so hard at death, you know it's real. And for a while, perhaps for the rest of your life, you go on knowing death is real; the rest of us, we can pretend otherwise most of the time, and that's best, really. We're happiest pretending. And all while your poor mum was dying—it's too much to handle. Too much for anyone, not just for you. You've got to give yourself time; it will get better. You will feel better. Soon.

"Sure," says Will.

And Rosie says, "Oh, you've been really ill, haven't you? You're looking very well now," clearly trying to be encouraging, since it is perfectly clear, Will thinks, that he looks like something out of a horror film; indeed, he has joked on the phone to Holly that he could get a decent part in *The X-Files* without needing any time at all in makeup. Ah, seeing Ozzie soon, too. His heart gives another little thump of anxiety and excitement at the thought.

And I will use all these feelings in my Art, some deeper hidden part of his mind suggests, complacently.

"Benign after all," he says to Rosie, and immediately is shot back to the consultant's office:

Consultant very bouncy:

"Benign after all, a littoral hemangioma in fact! Didn't think of that one, not for a moment! Never actually come across one before, jolly rare! Aren't even that many references in the literature. Completely benign, though."

"Benign? Does that mean—you could have just left it?"

"Well, possibly. You certainly didn't have a normal spleen. But then we're not altogether sure what being normal is, for spleens. It might have been perfectly normal for you."

"You mean there might have been nothing wrong with me at all?"

Hah, less bouncy now:

"Well, possibly; the fainting spells due to a coincidental viral illness, quite probably. Blood results not typical. But when we saw all those areas of what looked like infiltration on the ultrasound, well, we had no choice."

"So it was all due to ultrasound?"

"Um, well, we would still have thought you had lymphoma. Even without ultrasound. You had a palpable spleen, remember."

Only because you fucking palped it, Will had not shouted back, though afterwards he had wished that he had.

"Benign after all, something and nothing. Can I get another round? What's everyone want?"

"No, no, no. This is all on me. Please."

While George is away at the bar Clio stirs, awakens, takes a quick look round, and begins at once to whimper.

"Hey, hey, hey, what's all this!" Gratefully Will leans over to unfasten the straps that hold her into her pushchair. "Up you come."

It is such a relief to hold her. Strength flows into him.

He's so good with her, thinks Sylvia, also grateful. She likes the fact that her daughter seems to have two adoring fathers; it seems fair enough, when she herself hardly had one at all.

"Oh, I've got her bottle, hang on," she says, opening the rucksack. "Clio, want this? Want some juice?"

No; she wants to stand up; she wants to stand bouncily on Will's lap, the better to lunge over the table and make a wild greedy grab at the glasses just as George is putting the laden tray down.

"Whoops," says Rosie, but it is George who puts a fast hand up to hold her back, while Will hooks an arm round her middle, and Sylvia half rises too, and catches her daughter's small fat hand. For a moment all three of them are holding the child: all three of them, as it happens, related to her.

George son of Ruby, daughter of Mikhail Jasinski, who died of appendicitis in the opening months of the Great War; Will son of Joe, illegitimate son of Irena Jasinski, Mikhail's younger sister, who gave birth in secret, and who died of tuberculosis in 1921; Sylvia daughter of Charles, son of Maria Henshaw nee Jasinski, the second sister, whose photograph, together with other equally anonymous family connections, lie in a shoe box in the attic of the large house in Kent where Rosemary Henshaw, looking in despair at her husband's perplexing effects on his death, stowed them and forgot about them all as soon as she could.

While Rosie, looking with open adoration at the beaming toddler across the table, thinks how nice it is for Sylvia that her baby, with that coloring and that curly hair, might actually be Will's; and wonders whether, despite what Sylvia has privately told her, there is after all any truth in the rumor going round at work that in fact the resemblance is no coincidence at all.

"Nice catch," says Will.

"Any time," says George, setting out drinks, careful to put Will's out of Clio's reach. "Cheers!"

All of them raise their glasses.

ROB IN FLIGHT, OCTOBER 2006

EDDIE PHONED AT SEVEN, as the kettle boiled.

"What've we got?"

"Smack on and smooth," said Eddie, in gloating tones. "About eleven: so, Happy Birthday to you!"

"It's just what I've always wanted," said Rob dutifully.

"See you in about an hour?"

"I'll be there."

A golden morning, still a little pink round the edges. Rob switched the kettle back on again, and made himself a mug of tea. Happy Birthday to me; but not yet, please. Born at noon; still nearly five hours left yet of being seventy-four, and he was going to make the best possible use of them.

He'd loaded the car the night before, so there was no hurry. Rob sat down at the kitchen table. It had been his grandmother's; he had sat here, he thought, just here, when he was as little as his youngest grandchild Millie was now. Grandma at the range making drop scones. Giving him a hot brick, warmed in the bottom oven and wrapped in a knitted blanket, to warm his bed at night.

He sipped his tea, looking out of his window at the endlessly magnificent view, the mountains rising on either side, the slope before him, the long line of silver where the sky met the sea. Sometimes, on very still nights, he could still hear the sea turning. When first he had lived here, just after his father's death, he had heard it often, but the sea was not so noisy now as once it had been. Sometimes it lay quiet for weeks at a time.

357

Seventy-five at noon! Hard not to think about age, on your birthday. How many more returns, happy or otherwise? Fingers of one hand, perhaps. Though his father had at one point looked as if he was going to go on forever, still loping about the hills with his dogs into his vigorous nineties, fishing and playing golf and driving too fast and making a nuisance of himself complaining to the local council about salmon farms and street lighting and rogue caravanning, until the sudden massive stroke had felled him.

I'm glad he kept the range, thought Rob. For as old Dr. Wilding lay waiting for death, which had not been long in coming, he had it seemed time-traveled back to the beginning of his life, to stand beside the range as small as Millie was now: as Rob sat beside the bed, in what was now his own bedroom, his father had opened his eyes and spoken his last clear words, and they were a little child's, hopeful, plaintive: "Can I have a dippit piece, Mammy?"

A dippit piece. One of the few phrases that had survived Dr. Wilding's marriage. He had teased his wife, Rob's mother, with it sometimes, on a Sunday morning, wrapping mock-lascivious arms about her waist as she stood at the oven, frying pan in hand, asking him whether he wanted one egg or two.

His father good humored, strident: "Give me a dippit piece, woman!"

A dippit piece: a slice of bread, not fried, just lightly dipped on one side into the bacon fat. A treat of poverty; the fat would go further that way.

Can I have a dippit piece, Mammy?

Rob, frightened of doing the wrong thing, of sounding wrong and startling his father back to the present and the present's imminent close, had hesitated for some time before putting his lips to his father's ear, and whispering very softly, in as near as he could get to his grandmother's accent,

"Of course you can, of course you can." But his father had said no more.

Seventy-five at noon.

Jenny driving up with Millie from Ulverston around lunchtime; his younger son flying up from Bristol some time in the afternoon, cost a

fortune for all five of them. Anthony would no doubt call, from whatever time it was in Vancouver; he had sent another video of his foreign
family life; perhaps they would watch it at teatime.

He would enjoy all of it perfectly well, so long as the morning went
as he hoped.

Outside he climbed into the Land Rover and started up. It would be
better not to drive there, of course it would. Walked it easily ten years
ago. But not worth risking it now. Stopping to swing the gate to behind
him he bumped slowly along the track beside the cottage, left at the
cattle grid, and up and up over the familiar rocks and hollows. It had
been a drover's road, once, marked out by the passage of a millennium's
worth of sheep. His grandmother's land, then his father's, and now his.
More than a path to him now, though. It was a lifetime guarantee: access.
An essential.

Arriving he stood for a while gazing out and down, sniffing the air.
A little more than eleven, he thought. Rising. No further, please. That
was the trouble with this lark: you were so often disappointed. You
planned all week, sometimes you drove all day, you got everything ready
and: nothing doing. Too much wind. Just too little. Hardly ever just
right. Today, though: today was surely going to be perfect. He could feel
it. It could rise a little if it wanted. Autumn was always the best time.
There would be great slow thermals on a day like today, grand revolv-
ing whirlpools of moving air, that he would seek out, and ride upon. The
wind directly onto this very bluff, smack on and smooth, smooth.

The most difficult part for Rob was loading and unloading.

"Fine motor skills," he'd told Eddie, years ago now. "I've got no fine
motor skills, arthritis, it's why I had to retire."

"Won't matter," Eddie had told him. "Not once you're up."

Rob had hardly dared at first to believe him. How could you do something as extraordinary as learn to fly, if you couldn't decently waggle the
fingers of your own right hand?

The first time he had seen Eddie had been in 1980, well before old
Dr. Wilding's death. Rob was visiting; Eddie was trespassing. He'd
carried the kite all the way up from sea level, and Rob, out early one
morning with one of his father's dogs, had suddenly come upon him

behind a small rise, just set up and ready to go, a bearded heavyset six-foot Yorkshire dragonfly caught standing in a framework of singing wires; high above his head were taut shuddering wings of scarlet and brilliant yellow.

"How do," Eddie had said, nodding briskly, and then he had run forward, leapt into the air, and soared at once, like an angel, up into the sky.

In shock, in something he could identify as urgent delight only later, on the way back down, Rob had stood open-mouthed watching Eddie's strange bird shape until it was out of sight.

He had trembled, watching Eddie fly.

What might it feel like? he had asked himself. The flight had looked natural, organic, like that of a bird, yes, but would it actually feel like that, from within that metal frame and tensile banded cloth? Would it feel like the dream of flight it resembled, or would it feel mechanical? And how could the terror ever outweigh the bliss? And of course he was already far too old to find out.

Nearly a decade later, when on his father's death he had in turn come to live in his grandmother's house, he had merely let it be known that he did not object to flyers.

"You know what you've got here, don't you? You're on velvet here," Eddie told him. "You're the bee's knees."

Soon when the wind was in the right direction there were sometimes as many as thirty cars parked on his grandmother's meadow, or perched tipped sideways on the verges of the lane. Not all were hang gliders, though.

"Paragliders," said Eddie's pal Steve. "Single sail. Like a parachute, much easier all round."

That had been a warm day in May, with a mild smooth wind at eight miles an hour, and a whole shoal of paragliders were swinging from their curved single eyebrows of nylon, slowly rotating, almost static in the gentle lifting air.

Like the hang gliders they tended to go in for beards in a big way, Rob noticed. Like mountaineers. Perhaps it was something to do with altitude.

"It's the youngsters do paragliding," said Eddie, then in his mid-thirties. "Want it easy. You've not to carry a kite about, you see. It's the weight. And storage. Store a proper kite, you need a bit of space. But you're just hanging about, paragliding. You're not flying. You're floating. You're not so in charge. Hang gliding's flying. Proper flying. But it's all much harder. It's a skill. You watch: I'll be flashing through that lot like a mackerel through jellyfish."

An image so vividly, so playfully insinuating a curving flash of speed on the one hand and hopeless baggy drifting on the other that Rob laughed, though at the same time he felt weak with painful longing. And with a small sudden anxious dart of hope, because of Eddie's scornful use of the word youngsters. At any rate he finally took the risk:

"I'm too old," he said. "For any of it. Aren't I? Am I too old? Eddie?"

Sixteen years ago, forsooth. Sixteen years of flight.

Once he had tried to explain what he was doing to his daughter Jenny. It was to do with how he felt about this part of Scotland, he told her. This line of hills, this coast. That all his life he had made sure, whenever he was here, to be part of the scenery as much as he could, be part of the picture it made in his head. Join it somehow, by swimming or walking or climbing.

And that flying within this space, soaring above and through it, was being part of the view, the scene, in the most profound way he could imagine. Did that make any sense?

Yes, yes, of course it was a risk. Yes, he could misjudge something and drop from the sky to his death, but so what? He'd had his life anyway; and besides, couldn't she see that all his professional life had been risky? One risk after another, routine risk, the terror of cutting into another human being's eyes or face, taking it upon himself to manipulate, interfere, control, while that human lay passive, a life meekly handed over! He had taken these risks and mastered them over and over again. Could she not see that in flight he could get back something of that special pleasurable fear?

Because I miss it, Jenny. So much.

All of this true, of course. True, and not true. There's more to it than that.

HE'D BEEN BADLY frightened before his maiden flight, on a day in April 1990. He'd managed the course with flair, he'd been told. But he couldn't remember, waiting on the top that day, any other time in his life when he had felt so simply and so physically afraid, even in childhood.

Geoff his instructor, and Eddie and Steve and one or two other flyers in attendance, all of them buzzing around helping him rig, holding the nose until he's ready. His own dog Jago whimpering uneasily. It's all he can do not to whine and shiver himself, he thinks. Clipping in he is afraid someone will notice how violently his arms are trembling. No getting out of it now.

"All set?"

Yes, he's ready. He's one enormous heartbeat.

"Release!" And to his own surprise and relief, his voice sounds perfectly normal, at ease, just as it had while he scrubbed up before surgery all those years, while he bent to inspect one last time the numbed awaiting eye.

"Release!" They stand back, as, cool without, alive with fear within, he runs, jumps to a confused chorus behind him of shouting, and shrill cries from Jago, and then immediately the wind takes him, tosses him quite roughly into the air. Oh, terror!

The standing wave of movement arising from the ridge carries him higher, higher, he glances wildly about him at the ground flecked in fields and trees beneath him, at the vario, at the altimeter, wildly, and then less wildly. He's all right; he is in flight. He is in control. He knows what to do. He's doing it. Busily: there are adjustments to be made all the time, things to worry about and consider, there, no, there, is the field where he must land, no wires no trees no stock, keep it in view, turn, can I turn? Yes! Turning! Cheers sound very faintly below him, Jago's distant bark, and then suddenly he is hurled upwards, the wind roaring in his wings, flung higher and higher, Christ, a thermal! My first thermal, by Christ! A column of warm rising air, blundered into, and he is suddenly half a mile high! Blundered into, and then out of; he tries to turn, to find it again, but misses, carries on dropping, not too fast, gently, in quiet air.

Not until he has landed, perfectly, not until he has sat trembling with effort on the lovely grass as Eddie and the others and his dog run whooping exultantly from the gate, not until much later, alone at last, when he has stripped off the flying suit and collapsed dizzy with happiness and exhaustion on his own bed that afternoon, does he understand what has happened to him: that flight is joy transmuted into action; joy that makes him remember how he felt long ago, with Iris.

He sits up on the bed. He remembers the absurd local legends of his childhood, of the stalwart wildman vicar and his homemade wings; and Iris prances barefoot on the cliff top.

Ah.

For a long time, practically, seriously, he had thought himself recovered from the loss of Iris. True all through his twenties he would catch himself looking for her in the turn of someone else's cheek, in dark curls, in slenderness. For years any crowded place, a market or a concert hall, anywhere where many people gathered, would oppress him with the realization, yet again, that no matter how many faces he might see, no matter how diligently he might look into each one, none of them would ever again be hers.

Still he had taken it for granted that grief and shame would eventually dwindle, that he would at last be whole again; and presently he had found someone new, and married her, and made a family, and if that hadn't gone too well, if he had had affairs, and other affairs, and got divorced, and married someone else, and got sidetracked again, and divorced again, well, that was obviously unfortunate and messy but was it, really, that unusual, these days? Plenty of other people had made similar messes.

There were lots of people one might be happy with, he had taken that for granted too. Absurd to imagine there might be just the one. The One: that stuff was romantic fiction falsehood, from trashy novels of the sort his mother used to read. His lying mother. Her.

So it meant nothing if he'd always ended up mentally comparing whichever woman he was with to Iris, to a long-dead beautiful girl of twenty; he'd no doubt just been using her as an excuse for being shallow or heartless or selfish or wickedly bored or all of those things at once. Hadn't he?

Spending more and more time on his own as he grew older he had begun to feel less sure of everything, less scornful.

There was the simple unarguable fact, that despite all those restless years of looking, he still hadn't come across anyone to take her place; no one, in retrospect, had even come close. From this distance it was clear to him that his first wife had been perfectly right to divorce him for cruelty. It had been cruelty to marry her, merely liking and lusting as he had. He had been similarly cruel to every other woman he had ever been involved with; every other Other Woman: none of them had been Iris.

Sitting on his bed in 1990 after his maiden flight, weak with happiness, worn out with exertion and fright, he sees that while flying is joyful, and makes him powerfully part of this beloved landscape, and reminds him so marvelously of the creative exhilaration of his lost work, it is also the nearest he can get to Iris, the closest he has come in all these years to the man he was when she loved him.

What a gift, what a treasure! The years without her drop away.

SEVENTY-FIVE AT noon.

Opening the tailgate he catches himself waiting for Jago, poor old Jago, dead over a year now.

"Might you get another dog, Granddad, one day?"

"Get a puppy, get a puppy!"

He would have liked to oblige; of course the children had loved Jago, it had been Jago they had all spilled out of the car shouting to see. Which was good; meant that they would associate this wonderful place with happiness, as they should.

"Couldn't you get a rescue dog, Dad? Company?"

"No, Jago was my last dog," he had replied, without thinking. Poor Jenny! He hadn't meant to upset her. He had forgotten how young she was, still young enough to believe, deep down, that her daddy was immortal, or at any rate essential.

Far away a flash of windscreen turning into the sun: Eddie's battered Subaru had reached the bottom lane, with something yellow behind

him: good: Steve as well. Two of an increasingly grizzled band. Paragliding is still so much easier.

"We're a dying breed right enough," says Eddie, swigging his beer
with gloomy relish.

But I make them feel young, thinks Rob affectionately. He is aware
that he has a certain small and growing fame, amongst the company of
hang gliders, as veteran of veterans. Strangers rush to shake his hand
at competitions, or take his photograph.

Watching Eddie's car reach the garden gate far below, Rob begins as
usual to feel almost feverish with longing. He's hot in the flying suit,
the boots. Using his hands like bats he begins to unfold the tough nylon
wings. Soon, soon, he tells himself.

Once or twice, at this stage, he has lately found himself saying this
to her.

Soon, Iris, soon.

It's to do with that powerful feeling, which has not diminished with
the years, that in flight he can almost reach her.

Once or twice at night recently, with the house so very quiet all
around him, he has become aware of something; not a presence, exactly,
he wouldn't call it that, were he ever to speak of it to anyone. Not a presence, just a curious feeling of not being alone. It made him remember
a trip further north a few years ago, when he was joined during one
particularly thrilling flight by a kestrel.

He'd been wrestling hard with the air, fighting to stay within the
magic circle of a fairly narrow thermal and keep rising. The bird, close
enough for him to make out the neatly folded talons, had appeared
merely to drift, as if carelessly, wings spread wide. Clearly it had
seen him. But it had seemed quite unconcerned. For several minutes,
Rob and the kestrel rode the thermal together, swinging round and
round one another in the curving lifting air, almost within touching distance.

That was what it felt like, at night, alone and not alone in his empty
house, where on its own small shelf in his bedroom, alone of all his
mother's large collection, he has kept the netsuke pig. Proof there, thinks
Rob, of the significance of the material. The importance of things.

Things my life has depended on: a little carved lump of old ivory. A dressing gown; a man's dressing gown, because Jo, if it had been trimmed with feathers I wouldn't have borrowed it, d'you see? A brochure for a holiday camp. A certain photograph on the cover of the brochure, and not another one of people just jumping about in the sea or grinning from the sand.

Now and then he notices the little pig again and picks it up to note once again its mysterious weight and cool smoothness. It's beautiful, and so imbued with terrible luck that despite now being worth quite startling amounts of money (he has the letter from Sotheby's to prove it) he has willed it away from all of his children. It will be sold by his executor, and the money split between Eddie and Steve and Geoff. That's safest, Rob thinks. Buy the kites of your dreams.

And here's Eddie himself at last, cheerful and sweating, loud rock music beating through the open windows of his laden car.

"You know what you've got here, don't you," he'd asked all those years ago. "You're on velvet here; you're the bee's knees: you're *top drivable*."

Steve driving up behind him. The sky awaits all three.

"How do," says Eddie.

ACKNOWLEDGMENTS

Grateful thanks to Ok Thaller and Richard Harrad, for various complicated ophthalmological information and advice; and to Ian Ferguson, for his hang-gliding expertise, and for telling me all I am ever likely to understand about the joys of flight.